CROFT WAS ASKING QUESTIONS OF AN ALIEN ARTIFACT....

And Remson was beginning to wonder about his boss's sanity. The mystery surrounding the creation of that artifact should have told Croft that the Forat-Cummings girl—suddenly returned from Unity—couldn't be turned loose on Threshold. Because maybe she wasn't the Forat-Cummings girl at all, but some alien construct.

It was obvious to Remson, just as it was obvious that the intelligence problems surrounding this first contact with aliens capable of presenting a threat to humanity were manifold. And if those problems turned out to foreshadow real-time threats, there wasn't a weapon in the UNE arsenal capable of giving the Unity aliens a run for their money.

So why did Croft think they even had a choice? It seemed to Remson that if the Unity aliens wanted them to move their governmental center a few billion miles, the UNE could only say, "No problem." Because the alternative might be worse. Lots worse....

THE STALK

JANET AND CHRIS MORRIS

A ROC BOOK

To Ifrit, beloved companion:
Ifrity, Ifrity, Ifrity, life
is but a dream. . . .

ROC
Published by the Penguin Group
Penguin Books USA Inc., 375 Hudson Street,
New York, New York 10014, U.S.A.
Penguin Books Ltd, 27 Wrights Lane,
London W8 5TZ, England
Penguin Books Australia Ltd, Ringwood,
Victoria, Australia
Penguin Books Canada Ltd, 10 Alcorn Avenue,
Toronto, Ontario, Canada M4V 3B2
Penguin Books (N.Z.) Ltd, 182–190 Wairau Road,
Auckland 10, New Zealand

Penguin Books Ltd, Registered Offices:
Harmondsworth, Middlesex, England

First published by Roc, an imprint of Dutton Signet,
a division of Penguin Books USA Inc.

First Printing, January, 1994
10 9 8 7 6 5 4 3 2 1

 REGISTERED TRADEMARK—MARCA REGISTRADA

Printed in the United States of America

CHAPTER 1

▽

Be Careful What You Wish For

Humanity's two lost children were back on the space habitat called Threshold. Mickey Croft, Secretary General of the United Nations of Earth, once had wished for nothing so fervently as the return of the star-crossed young lovers.

But you had to be careful what you wished for, these days.

Ever since the aliens from the Council of the Unity had contacted mankind, materializing their uncanny teardrop-shaped ships in a polite parking orbit at Spacedock Seven, nothing could be taken for granted—not mankind's hegemony among the stars, not space, time, nor even physics. Not if you'd had direct contact with the Unity aliens. So you were very careful what you wished for, and what you thought, and what you dreamed if you had been contaminated by alien contact.

And Michael (Mickey) Croft, had been the first to be so contaminated. Or so he'd thought then. As Secretary General of the Trust Territory of Threshold, home to two hundred and fifty thousand souls in a stable orbit between Mars and Jupiter, it had been Croft's job to act as emissary and meet with the aliens aboard their incomprehensible flagship.

As a result of that meeting, Croft's world had turned upside down. The three hundred colonies of the United Nations of Earth (UNE) were no longer the boundaries of humanity's universe. Mankind was no longer master of all it surveyed. The UNE Secretariat no longer ruled creation from the Stalk, the administrative center at Threshold's axis.

Mickey Croft's office looked the same. Its soft blue walls obeyed a knowable geometry. Its staff still scurried busily. His mundane duties were no less pressing. Yet the phenomenal world as he'd known it could no longer be taken for granted.

The Unity aliens had come. And gone. Bringing gifts. Leaving confusion. Taking away with them a contact team handpicked by Croft (the beginning of a diplomatic mission) to their own cosmos. And leaving Croft to deal with the aftereffects of humanity's first contact with an arguably superior race.

In Mickey's office, with its trappings of power, everything looked the same. His panoramic window with its vista onto the stars showed them unchanged in their courses. Yet everything was altered. He was altered. Changed, like everything else in the universe, by contact with the aliens. All humanity's certainty had gone, disappearing into unknown reaches with the alien teardrop craft.

In their wake, nothing remained sure. No fact was certain. The power of the unseen was greater than the seen. The spacetime inhabited by Mickey Croft was no longer dependably proceeding from past to future. The comfortable "now" of human reality was no longer predictable. Everything humanity had thought it knew had been swept into a maelstrom of false assumptions and into that chaotic vacuum of uncertainty had come . . . the missing children.

The aliens had returned them. Perhaps found them. Possibly rescued them. Conceivably abducted them in the first place. But no one dared say that, or even think too much about the consequences of such a line of reasoning. The Unity aliens were too powerful to consider as enemies. And they were gone now, leaving behind the prodigal children and a mysterious sphere floating at Spacedock Seven.

Leaving behind a UNE Secretary General contaminated by the contact. Mickey Croft's mind, his soul, his personal spacetime, all were suspect, so far as his reasoning self was concerned. But he could convince no one of that. No medical workup showed a problem. No psych profile showed the damage. Mickey had tried to resign.

His resignation was not accepted. He had measured himself against a profile stored in his psychometric sampler-modeler and found no deviation. But that proved only that alien contamination was not measurable by contemporary standards.

At least, where Croft was concerned, the alteration was not outwardly noticeable. Yet.

Croft touched a control pad on his desk and the alien Ball appeared on the opposite wall: the artifact of the Unity sat quiescent, huge, silvery, spherical, silent, and smug, still surrounded by the scaffolding that supported the science station he'd had constructed to evaluate it. Were the aliens man's best hope or worst nightmare? Or both? The Ball had preceded the aliens, towed in as salvage by a white-hole scavenger named Keebler. At the aliens' request, Keebler had been part of the contact team who'd left for the Unity.

If Croft had known then what he knew now, he'd never have sent a contact team to Unity space. The team, a skeleton diplomatic mission, had not been heard from since. Three weeks, and no contact. If they were lost, or suffering, it was Croft's fault.

But at the time, he'd thought he'd been the first to contact the aliens. He hadn't fully realized that a pair of young lovers, lost in space, had preceded him. He hadn't known what the children would be like when they got back. The aliens had left as the children were returned, taking Croft's handpicked team with them: Director Riva Lowe, formerly of Customs, Commander Joe South, a Relic pilot relativistically delivered from Earth's distant past, and Mikah Keebler, the white-hole scavenger who'd salvaged the Ball and towed it to Threshold in the first place. Some said Croft had picked the team to get rid of troublemakers, but Croft had chosen those who'd been contaminated by alien contact, like himself, to make the journey into the unknown. It had seemed a rational decision, at the time.

It still seemed a rational choice, but whose? His? or the Unity Council's? Croft couldn't be certain whether he'd decided on his own or the decision had been made for him by the Unity aliens. His skin crawled whenever he tried to think about the events connected with the alien contact. He crossed his long, lanky arms and rubbed them with his palms.

He must get control of himself.

The Ball seemed to shiver slightly in Mickey's monitor. The real-time image took on a pinkish glow like sunrise along its eastward edge.

"No, you don't," Croft muttered aloud, and stabbed at the image control to wipe away the sight. The Ball obediently disappeared. Croft had too much to do to indulge in paranoia. Or to let the Ball mesmerize him. Whether or not the Ball had the power to twist spacetime and human minds, it was a fact of life now. It had sat there for months; it might sit there forever. The children were on this afternoon's agenda. And their parents.

The children; he should stop calling them that. They were teenagers, young adults who had caused immeasurable trouble with their secret marriage and headlong flight into alien arms and the pages of history.

But that wasn't why Croft dreaded the coming interview. It was the children themselves he feared to face. Or what they had become.

He had reports, from his executive officer, Vince Remson, on the pair. Remson's reports were cold, bloodless, factual, and deeply disturbing. The youngsters were changed, different, wise beyond their years and transformed by their flight to a youth hostelry at the edge of spacetime. But transformed into what? Aliens? They scanned to be as human as Croft.

So much for Remson's analysis of the children themselves.

The lovers' families, the entrepreneurial Cummings dynasty and the religious Forats, had become the Montagues and Capulets of the United Nations of Earth. Despite promises and endless negotiations, the feuding parents were refusing to let their children's marriage stand unchallenged.

And that was a blessing. Croft wasn't about to turn loose any alien-contaminated youngsters onto Threshold, let alone allow them to leave for their parents' vast holdings among the human extraterrestrial colonies.

So some subterfuge was in order to hold the children here until they could be evaluated thoroughly. Mickey Croft had once been a master of subterfuge. Now he was master of nothing, not even his own emotions. Holding the children in quarantine for their own safety was Vince Remson's idea.

Croft could think of little else but the Unity aliens, their sad eyes, the teardrop ships he still entered in his dreams, and the increasingly enervating task of holding body and mind together.

Concentration, once his strongest skill, was beyond him. Vince knew. Remson was taking up the slack masterfully. But that left Croft to manage the best he could alone, at times.

Unfortunately, this was one of those times. Mickey could have demanded that Remson make time to be present for the youngsters' interview, but he hadn't.

He needed to face them alone. They were only children, after all—teenagers. And he was the senior diplomat on Threshold. He had told himself sternly that if he couldn't manage this interview without support, he would resign a second time. And this time, he would let no one dissuade him.

And this time, he would let no one dissuade him.

So his career hung in the balance of this seemingly minor, if somewhat unusual, matter of the UNE Secretary General intervening in the case of a pair of wellborn children whose parents opposed their marriage.

If the children had not been explorers into alien space-times, the whole problem would have been so much simpler. Not even the UNE's Secretary General could grant the pair open-ended sanctuary on Threshold as if in a church, proclaimed the parents' attorneys. Croft could have let the parents deal with their offspring.

But the question of alien contamination raised the issue of the lovers' fate to the level of an interspatial security decision. If the children were noticeably changed, or represented any threat, they must not be allowed to move about Threshold or the colonized worlds, spreading their contamination or raising questions about the Unity aliens.

Croft knew the dangers of contamination personally. And as to questions, the less questions asked about the aliens—the first superior race ever to encounter humanity—the better. At least, until the Stalk bureaucracy had some answers.

Threat or salvation was out there, wrapped in a silvery Ball like a giant Christmas ornament at Spacedock Seven, and Mickey Croft hadn't the faintest idea which was the correct description. Even now, Croft couldn't articulate what had happened to him during his visit to the alien vessel. He couldn't remember, precisely, what had occurred. He remembered being invited aboard the alien flagship. He remembered meeting three aliens, including the Unity's Interstitial Interpreter. He remembered being returned to his own ship.

Sometimes Croft wondered if he had been truly returned safely by the aliens of the Unity to his native spacetime, or whether he was somewhere else, similar to but not precisely the same as the spacetime he'd left. A place where things were marginally out of whack, where time didn't flow as smoothly as he remembered it once had, where spaces were more malleable. Where the forward-moving arrow of Einsteinian physics meandered in its course, and bent, and wriggled, and sometimes fell spinning, out of control like a badly fletched crossbow bolt.

But Vince Remson was the same as always. Vince was Croft's touchstone, his assistant secretary, his executive officer. And Croft's office was the same—most times.

Mickey's office was dominated by a huge desk with a hematite top where schools of fossils were locked forever in black and silver profusion. Sometimes the fossils moved now. Sometimes, when he looked at them, he was sure they moved. He had taken to placing objects—a pen, a notebook, a paperweight—at strategically chosen angles to the fossilized schools to see if the borders he thus established would be violated when he looked again. Today, he was certain the school was at least six inches beyond its previous leftmost border.

But there was no way of telling whether the phenomenon was a function of disjointed spacetime, or whether the robot cleaner had disturbed things when it dusted during the night.

Croft rubbed his weary eyes and forsook his desk for the window. His observation window showed him a panoply of stars. The window was a symbol of his putative power over Threshold, displaying to all and sundry his perch at the "top" of Blue Mid, the Stalk's most "northerly" vista. His reflection, not the stars, stared back at him: a horse-jawed face collapsing in on itself from stress, pale eyes surrounded with so many circles that each seemed to be the center of a stone dropped into a pool, a mobile mouth that had finally taken a permanent downward turn, and thinning hair which had picked up a perennial static charge that made it unruly despite all cosmetic and antistatic measures.

Most of the things that were "wrong" in Croft's universe were much like the static in his hair: tiny, inconsequential, even laughable if their basic wrongness wasn't so disturbing. His entire life, since the arrival of the aliens, had taken on a wrongness alleviated only by an occasional sense of destiny, of power, of resonance, of harmony, that seemed even more wrong. Change itself was the most likely reason for the tumult of feelings within him. Change itself, unfortunately, did not explain the static charge in his hair or the cascade of wonder and terror in his heart.

He was different, since his return from ... what? A spaceship with vistas within, a teardrop portal into eternity? A journey undertaken only in his mind? He couldn't say. If just Mickey Croft were different, he would happily have declared himself mad and retired posthaste. But the universe was different, now that the aliens had come. Broader. Deeper. Mythic, almost. Mystical, certainly. And, for the first time in humanity's history, threatening.

Well, perhaps not for the first time. All ancient Earth cultures had feared the sky, the night, nature, the weather, and all things unseen and unknowable. Ancient man had peopled the universe with gods and devils, demons and dark forces, and enslaved one another for centuries using humanity's fear of the dark. Then had come Aristotle, Plato, Copernicus, Newton, Einstein, and the rest, lighting more lamps to chase back the dark of superstition and all mankind's demons with them. The lamplight of science had held back that dark night for millennia. Now, in the twenty-fifth century, the lamp of man's triumph over the dark was going out. Flickering. Sputtering. Croft didn't want to be the man who let it die completely, never to be rekindled.

The Unity aliens represented every fear of ancient man and every hope of ancient prophets, all rolled into one. They were gods and devils, the ultimate good and the penultimate evil. And when you were touched by them, you were never the same again.

Croft, who had been touched by them, knew he was changed. Proof was beside the point. So why was he afraid of similar changes in the children of NAMECorp's chief executive and the Mullah of Medina, Beni Forat? Croft had more in common with those two children now than with any of his staff.

That fact might be the most disturbing change of all. It disturbed Croft's aide, Vince Remson, and both of them knew it. Remson thought that Mickey was not objective where the children were concerned.

Children. . . . They were old enough to marry, old enough to thoughtlessly, selfishly become the center of this cyclone. At their age, Croft had been far more responsible than to reenact Shakespeare's most famous play with spaceships, hoping to write a different ending. Croft wished that he could turn back the clock, find the delinquent teenagers before they'd slipped out of his staff's grasp, and keep them from crossing the path of the Ball out at Spacedock Seven and being precipitated into the heart of this crisis.

Be careful what you wish for. In this undependable spacetime, thoughts could become reality.

Afraid, suddenly, that the past might reshape itself to suit his wishes, Mickey Croft counted up events on his long, thin, trembling fingers.

ONE: Before the NAMEcorp boy and Medinan girl sped off toward their destiny and an alien world, the scavenger had brought the Ball to Threshold.

TWO: Before that, intimations of an imminent first contact with a superior race had existed in a classified file of an experimental space mission nearly five hundred years old.

THREE: If the pilot of that mission, Joe South, hadn't turned up near Threshold, a Relic of the twenty-first century and an artifact of relativity, no one in the Stalk bureaucracy would have been at all prepared for contact with the alien Unity.

FOUR: The aliens had kept their distance for five millennia. Now they were here. Their housegift to Threshold had been the return of Richard Cummings III and Dini Forat, young lovers caught in a web of destiny.

Croft was out of fingers and nearly out of time. He went back to his desk and sat down, glaring at the fossils embedded in the hematite, willing them to be still.

Focus on the present. Romeo and Juliet were back, after more than a six-month absence. They had been places and seen things no humans before them had ever experienced. If Croft had the power, he would have made them wards of the state, but he did not have it. All he could do was try to maintain control of them temporarily by pretending to shelter them from their furious, vengeful, and powerful parents.

If the youngsters would cooperate.

Even that was not certain. Even that, which might be critical to mankind's survival, was not completely within Croft's control. Mickey Croft, Secretary General of the all-powerful United Nations of Earth Secretariat, was not accustomed to feeling helpless or inadequate.

The worst thing the alien encounter had done to him was thrust him into a nightmare where he was, continually, both.

A chime from his desktop sounded and he jumped as if he'd heard the sharp report of an emergency depressurization. "What?" he snapped.

Dodd, his secretary/receptionist, answered meekly, "Your two-o'clock is here, sir."

Not, "Romeo and Juliet are here," not, "The kids who found the Unity homeworld are here," not, "Rick Cummings III and Dini Forat are here." Sometimes, Dodd's dull wit seemed like heaven-sent implacability. The stolid youngster was hardly older than the Cummings boy, but Croft would have given his SecGen's prerogative as Commander-in-Chief of Consolidated Space Command in even trade for Dodd's equanimity.

In the face of it, Mickey stuffed his pocket handkerchief into his conservative suit, ran a palm over his wayward hair, and said, "Send them in, Dodd," as if they represented only another hour marked on his calendar to be inconsequentially spent. Croft leaned his elbows on his desktop for support. Under his hands, the fossils began to glide along agitated currents. Mickey Croft squeezed his eyes shut and willed the fossils to immobility once again.

When he opened them, in came the two youngsters who had upended humanity's future, arm in arm, pale of face, and glowing of eye.

Croft had heard from Remson that the kids' eyes glowed in certain light. Not a lot. Just a little. In reflected light, as if their eyes had become cats' eyes. Yellow lights gleamed and receded as the youngsters approached his desk.

He didn't stand to greet them. Young Rick Cummings had Dini Forat by the arm as he strode up to the desk, half-dragging the Medinan girl who, before coming to Threshold, had habitually worn a veil over a face that would have done Helen of Troy proud.

Then the children began to *slide*. They seemed to slip through the intervening space, rush up to his desk with their eyes preceding their faces.

Cummings extended his hand over Croft's desk and the desk disappeared entirely. All that existed in the universe was the boy's hand waiting for Croft to take it in his.

"Thank you for seeing us, sir. We really appreciate all you've done."

Arrogant. Proud. Knowledgeable. Perhaps smirking, or promising to share the secret of passing across space without traversing the intermittent ground.

Was this a display of power, or a figment of Croft's rattled psyche?

Mickey focused on the young man's face. Rick Cummings III was handsome enough to make a likely escort, a Paris to Dini's Helen of Troy, if these children were the Unity's version of the Trojan Horse.

Meeting the youngster's eyes, Croft suddenly couldn't believe there was any evil intent there, only an odd, slight glint of reflected light.

Time shifted under Croft. The fossils in his desk lived, and died, and became one with the rock that was their crypt.

The boy's hand was still outstretched to him, waiting.

Mickey half-rose to shake Cummings' determinedly outthrust hand before those glowing eyes could drop to his desktop and make the schooling fossils move again. Couldn't have that. Let go of the hand. Break contact with the eyes. Sit down yourself.

"Sit down, Mr. Cummings, Ms. Forat."

"Mrs. Cummings," Rick Cummings corrected sharply, reminding Croft that these two youngsters wanted him to solve their mundane problems, such as getting their parents to recognize their marriage.

"Sit, please," Croft said again. Dini Forat was already seated in one of the two chairs before his desk, her dark curls cascading down and across one breast. How had it happened? He hadn't seen her take a seat.

Never mind. Arresting woman. She'd left him nearly

speechless the first time he'd seen her. There was nothing supernormal about her extraordinary beauty.

Now, Croft couldn't afford to be mesmerized, not by her face, not by the way light came and went in her eyes or in the eyes of her young husband. Now he must gain their confidence, enlist them as allies, and somehow save both their lives from Medinan justice and Richard Cummings II's retribution, which would in all likelihood be worse than death.

Croft was mildly surprised that he hadn't realized how important it was to shield the children from their parents' misplaced fury. It might be the most important thing he ever did.

He must save them, of course. Fighting for control of his own thoughts, of his focus, Croft reminded himself that he must save these children not because he cared about their welfare, which he truly did not, but for his own reasons, for his own purposes, for his own needs and the security needs of three hundred colonies.

Mickey Croft seldom needed help. But he did, today, from these children. He smiled at them.

Two huge cheshire cat grins answered his, hanging in space above his desk.

Croft ignored the phenomena, but his eyes began to throb and he began to perspire at the collar.

"Well then," he said, and stopped. What should he say?

The two young people sat silently watching him with infrared eyes, their lips firmly attached to their faces now.

He hoped they would speak. They didn't, just stared at him uncannily.

Croft began again. "I'm sure we can find a way to solve this problem together." No reaction. "I expect," Croft continued, "that is, I suppose ... we may be able to work out something with your parents, but it will not be simple, and it will require great maturity and compromise on your parts."

"Just work something out that doesn't mean separating us," Cummings said brashly and craftily, "and we'll be as mature as you want."

The Forat girl shifted in her chair and said, "Rick means ... we must have our marriage upheld." And she caught him again with those eyes that had cat's glow in their depths. He was falling. He was melting through the floor. He was palming his way along a spherical surface that was flat to the touch and yet never intersected any other surface. . . . He was back on the alien ship.

And then he was free of her. But frightened. And sweating again. He was SecGen of the UNE, and he was sweating in front of these two kids. Remson had been right—Croft should have had this meeting with a one-star admiral and five aides in attendance, to take notes and generally support him.

But Croft had a running log of this meeting, as he did of all meetings—not that anyone would ever see him make such a display of himself, quail before children. . . . Croft said, "My dear, I know what you want. You and your . . . husband . . . must do exactly what I say to have any hopes of coming through this alive, well and together. You must realize that the diplomatic consequences of the incident you caused are substantial and not our only problems."

Croft didn't look at her again. If he didn't look at her, he would be all right.

Young Cummings said, "We're willing to work with you, Mr. Secretary. We said that. We have—" Cummings smiled a negotiating smile that was a chilling caricature of his father's "—something in common, don't we? And we've all got the same goals."

Croft wondered about that. What had he expected from these children? Some humility, perhaps. Contrition. Some fear. Some recognition of the depths of their danger. But not arrogance. Not glowing-eyed arrogance. Not wisdom beyond their years. They shouldn't have realized how much bargaining power they had, when Threshold was desperate for information about the aliens.

But they did. Clearly, they did.

Cummings had his father's predatory, blond, handsome, soulless confidence. Croft was suddenly angry beyond measure that the boy was so certain of his ground with the UNE Secretariat.

"I could have you both—" He stopped. What? Put into protective custody? Yes, that was it. He would rather have put them each in solitary forever and thrown away the key. But they would have demanded to be locked up together. "Put in protective custody of the Secretariat for the time being. But only if you will cooperate with my people and adhere to certain security conditions."

"What conditions?" Dini Forat-Cummings demanded.

"What kind of cooperation?" her husband added.

Maybe Croft was overreacting, attributing qualities and power to them because of their recent history that were greater than they deserved. Perhaps they were both just children, after all; teenagers facing terrible consequences from their forbidden love.

Croft said, "Place yourselves willingly in my hands. Give appropriate statements to be passed to your embassies. Vince Remson of my staff will help you. Undergo a thorough set of physical and psychological evaluations. And cooperate with my investigators completely, no matter what they ask of you." It was a tough offer, with no guarantees. Temporary safety in exchange for complete access to whatever they knew. But, children or not, they were in a tough situation.

"All right," Dini Forat-Cummings said softly, but it sounded to Croft like the tinkling of glass bells, not human words spoken from a human throat.

"You'll keep us safe," Richard Cummings III said, as if that were the agreement and the universe itself would mandate Croft's adherence to it. Or as if the aliens would.

Mickey Croft's body hair stood on end in a shower of personal static. He said, "Agreed," and once more offered his hand across his desk to the boy who had been six months in an alien spacetime.

When Cummings' flesh touched Croft's, the blue spark that jumped between their fingers was the size of a balled fist.

The snap and jolt of it numbed Croft up to the elbow. He cried out.

The youngster looked at him curiously, as if nothing untoward had occurred. "Is there anything else, sir?" said Cummings, ignoring the electrical discharge as if it hadn't happened.

"Ah, no," Croft said with utmost difficulty, managing to sound as if he were in control of this meeting. "Young Dodd out front will have Secretary Remson come and collect you. Stay in the outer office until he does."

"Thank you, sir," said the Forat girl in her chiming voice.

"Yes, thanks. I'm sure we'll all get along fine," said Cummings.

Croft wanted to throw a paperweight at the boy, or call

back his offer of aid, but did neither. He just watched them go without a word, out the obedient door that reacted to them as if they were human. From the rear, it was easier to think that they were.

Poor Vince. Assistant Secretary Vince Remson, fixer extraordinaire, was about to begin the most critical, and perhaps personally dangerous, mission of his life. There was nothing normal about those two youngsters. Croft, who had met them before their flight from Threshold, now knew that for certain.

But then, there was nothing normal about Mickey Croft anymore, not since his encounter on the alien ship.

At least his eyes didn't glow. Or did they?

Croft went again to his window on the stars, and then into his executive bathroom, where he stood for a long time, moving his head before a mirror, staring at his own eyes, trying to catch a glint of cat's glow in their depths.

CHAPTER 2

▽

Caution

Reice wished that somebody else had been given the job of escorting the Cummings and Forat brats to and from their various physical and mental evaluations.

The kids gave him the creeps. The girl was too beautiful and the NAMECorp heir needed a good punch in his well-bred jaw. But the Cummings boy was a third generation honcho in the making, and the girl was a Muslim from a fundamentalist sect which had nasty prohibitions about intermingling with infidels, let alone marrying one, so Reice was along to put muscle in the SecGen's decision to hold the kids in close quarantine until some diplomatic solution could be worked out by the likes of Croft and Remson.

Escorting the young couple around the Stalk was no harsh duty, up here where all the lifts worked only on security key cards and handprints and every meeting included a breakfast or a brunch or a lunch or a dinner of real food and good wine far beyond what Reice's salary could buy him.

He sat in the anteroom of Mickey Croft's private psycho-metric sampler-modeler installation and waited for the kids to come out. He could see them through the glass observation window.

They sat tamely enough, beyond the technicians and a second panel of glass, before a console where an audio-video display bank was taking readings from the helmets on their heads, the gloves on their hands, and whatever-all might be in the chairs they were sitting on.

Straightforward. Nothing to sweat. It was taking them

off-Stalk that bothered Reice. The kids had slipped Medinan and ConSec Security before, and ended up stealing a
ship and making a break for it.

Reice ought to know. He was the guy who chased them
and got a transcript of their ship disappearing in a
spongehole that opened up in front of that infernal Ball
that the scavenger had towed in.

Nothing like that could be allowed to happen again.
Reice was under strict orders to keep the kids in the Secretariat zone of the Stalk and not to let them roam Threshold,
whatever excuse they offered. He had two goons posted
outside every door the kids went through to make sure
those orders were followed.

So no sweat. It was safe. Watch the red and blue lights
playing over the modeler bay and relax a little. Keeping
the kids upStalk and out of Blue Mid, where they could
catch a nonsecure lift to anywhere on Threshold, was the
most important part of his job.

The youngsters seemed to know this was for their own
good. They were pretty reasonable, so far, even where this
psychometric modeling was concerned.

Reice wouldn't want his own privy person mapped and
modeled so that whatever the Secretariat wanted to do with
or to you, they could call up a walking, talking holographic
duplicate of you to question or depose at will.

The only reason these psychometric modelers weren't the
subject of massive complaints and legal actions was that
they were too technically sensitive and expensive to be
available to the rank and file policing agencies of Threshold. Reice wondered what it would be like to be able to
access modeled data in a normal ConSec investigation.

Consolidated Security Command was the agency that
ought to have a modeler like this, if anyone did. But rank
had its privileges, and this modeler was Mickey Croft's
private property, bought with his own inherited money,
and permitted only because Croft was the damned Sec-
Gen and could write himself any waivers he wanted from
rules and regulations meant to protect the Threshold population from invasions of their privacy or infringements of
their rights as citizens.

The kids had had to sign forms giving permission for the
modeling before the technicians would even let them in the
room. Reice had worried, then, that there'd be some scene,

but Cummings was uncharacteristically mellow—polite as you please.

Now both youngsters were in the modeler bay and the lightshow was revving up. Reice looked at his chronometer. Shouldn't be much longer. Next up on their schedule was a meeting with Assistant Secretary Remson and some legals from the Secretariat's pool, who were trying to set up a negotiation with the mullah about the marriage.

The mullah, Beni Forat, had this quaint notion that a death warrant issued by his religious court ought to hold on Threshold, and he'd put a price on the kids' heads—again—to add to the fun. Since the Medinans were not the most reasonable of races, the main threat that Reice saw was being set upon by a bunch of bioengineered Medinan "bodyguards," who were willing to die for the faith in the act of committing ritual murder.

Although it was unlikely that a bioengineered life-form—or a desperate human from the Loader Zone who wanted to collect the bounty—could reach this far into the Secretariat levels, Reice was armed to the teeth to prevent any surprises he couldn't handle.

And that was weird: walking around the Secretariat's wood-paneled and carpeted halls with a side arm. Especially carrying a side arm with more than tranquilizer darts in it. The SecGen was deadly serious about keeping these kids alive, well, and under UNE protection.

Reice pulled out his A-potential gun and checked its charge. Set to narrow beam, medium power, it could blow a four-inch hole in anything—flesh or metal or anything else on Threshold. Set on full power, wide beam, as it was now, it could port into another continuum the entire energy potential of any discrete system it encountered—vegetable, animal, or mineral—that was smaller than a six-foot cube. Reice put the gun back in its holster at his waist, a quick-draw unit low cut and secure on a wide belt in case he needed to get at it fast.

So Reice wasn't worried about Medinan assassins. Much.

A technician in a white coat got up from the control room and entered the modeler bay where the kids were. Reice got up, too, and rapped on the window between himself and the tech bay. When one of the techs turned around, Reice made a querying motion, and the tech gave him a thumbs up.

Inside the modeler bay, the first tech was removing the helmet and gloves from Dini Forat-Cummings.

The central console of the modeler was flaring colored lights across the visual spectrum. The lights started to form a cone.

Behind Reice, a door opened. He turned on his heel.

Vince Remson was standing in the doorway, arguing with someone Reice couldn't see.

Remson was saying, "There's no reason to be concerned, I assure you. We're proceeding through an evaluation standard for this situation—" Remson put his hand across the doorway, as if to block it.

Reice instinctively drew his weapon, moved fast to the far wall, and sidled along it. Maybe Remson needed help, maybe he didn't, but . . .

Reice could barely hear some muffled response from whoever was standing outside, past Remson, out of Reice's view.

Remson's stiff arm came down, no longer blocking the doorway. The Assistant Secretary said loudly, taking a backward step into the anteroom, "We're quite sure we're within our rights, Mr. Cummings. And if you don't agree, you are free to take it up with Secretary General Croft, himself, of course."

The loudness was, for Reice, a warning. He realized he'd better get the side arm out of sight just as Remson took a second backward step into the room.

Reice holstered his gun and moved smartly away from the wall, up behind Remson. "Is there anything you need, sir?" Reice asked in crisp professional tones.

"I think I can handle this, Reice. Let's just proceed as directed, shall we?"

"Yes, sir," said Reice. Remson didn't want to back off? Okay, Reice would hold his ground till hell froze over.

Now Reice could see Cummings, Jr., current Chief Executive Officer of North American Mining and Exploration Corporation (NAMECorp), and one of the richest and most powerful individuals in all the three hundred colonized worlds.

Cummings looked like an older, heavier, tired version of his son: blond and seamy-faced and substantial. There were three men behind him, and Reice maneuvered until he could see his own two ConSec guards flanking Cummings' men.

The ConSec guards looked grim and dangerous. Only Reice knew them well enough to see the uncertainty in their bearing. Remson must have waved them off. Now they were standing down, without moving back.

Nice mess, this.

Remson still blocked the doorway, just far enough inside to claim it as his personal turf. Remson was a big, athletic Slav with natural physical ability. Reice wouldn't have wanted to tangle with Remson. In fact, he'd go out of his way not to make the guy mad. One of the reasons Remson was Mickey Croft's XO was the combination of mental and physical skills that cut down the SecGen's need for personal staff.

Out of the side of his mouth, inclining his head just a little and never taking his eyes from Cummings' frustrated, flushed face, Remson muttered, "Hurry them up, can you?"

Reice hated to back off, what with the Cummings guys wanting to come in and Remson not wanting to let them.

But orders were orders. Reice turned to motion the techs to cut the session short and then stared in horror.

He heard the sound of another voice, which probably was Cummings, from the tone of injury and intimidation, but he couldn't make out what the voice said. He was too horrorstruck and fascinated by what he was seeing.

For some reason, the modeler was showing a full holographic image of a being. Not a person. An alien being. Something with a conical skull and funny body that didn't seem quite possible in its physiology. The model was rotating, and as it turned toward Reice, he was caught by its dark, sad, and then luminous eyes. It rotated away.

"Shit," Reice breathed, and nearly leapt to the first window to pound on it. Hurry up! he motioned urgently.

He'd thought the modeler was supposed to make a replica of the person being modeled, not show representations of what the person had stored in his or her memory banks.

Because that wasn't human, that was one of the Unity aliens, and Reice knew that for certain. He also knew that nobody like Cummings—a civilian, and a high-powered one—ought to be looking at highly classified data about Unity aliens.

Then Reice did pound on the glass with his fists and

turned around, leaning against the glass. No wonder all these security precautions. "Sir," he said in a parade-ground voice, "this is a classified session. I'm sorry, but I can't allow your visitors inside here. As a matter of fact, we've got to close that door right away. . . ."

And since Remson didn't tell him to stop, he hit the emergency override and the automated door started closing.

Cummings, Jr. threatened, "Remson, I'll have your ass for this. I want my son out of there and I want him—"

The door shut completely, cutting off exterior sounds. Reice waited tensely for an attack on the barrier or for Remson to tell him that he'd screwed up.

Neither happened. If there'd been pounding on the door, Reice would have heard it; if there'd been worse, Remson would have given him some direct order.

But there was nothing. No sound from outside. Vince Remson finally rubbed the back of his neck, turned toward the window into the modeling bay, and said, "Reice . . ."

Reice said, "Yes, sir?"

"Nice job, I think. Can you tell me why we're displaying aliens here? I thought we were modeling the lucky couple for posterity." Very calm. Very level, without a hint of accusation.

Well, then, Reice hadn't done the wrong thing, shutting off the confrontation with Cummings.

"Ah—no, sir. But I'll find out—"

"I'll find out. I just wanted to know if you knew." Remson moved by Reice in a rush of air and Reice smelled, unexpectedly, the smell of nervous body odor. So Remson wasn't as cool as all that.

Remson palmed the lock into the tech bay casually, as if he was in and out of there all the time. Reice had been instructed to stay outside, so he couldn't follow.

The door didn't shut on its own, though: he could still listen.

Remson's big head with its jagged profile dipped toward the white-coated tech, who stood hurriedly. "Why are we seeing that image, when you're supposed to be modeling persons for later study?" he said very quietly.

The technician was a woman. She straightened up, craned her neck, and said with vehemence, "Mr. Remson, you're seeing the result of the modeling of Dini Forat. Would you like to bring in another team to check our work? We'd be more than happy to—"

"What?" Remson took a step backward. So did Reice, in sympathy, and because maybe he'd just heard more than was healthy for a ConSec staffer.

"What do you mean?" Remson asked.

The woman technician had graying blond hair, and her fingers tugged at it nervously. "Whether what we have as a primary image is a function of some great trauma, or a malfunction of the system, what you are seeing is a psychometric modeling profile of Ms. Forat."

"But that's an alien," said Reice from the doorway, unable to help himself.

"So it is, Reice," Remson said, "and you never saw anything but a glitch resulting from command errors to the modeling system." He turned back to the technician. "I want absolutely squeaky clean and completely unremarkable human models of those two young people before you, or any of your associates, leave this bay. Is that clear?"

"Yes, Mr. Remson, but how can we—?"

"Reprogram your machines. Find an error. Make a whole new scan. I don't care what you do. I'm going to have to show these profiles to Cummings, you can bet. And they had better be as innocuous as we can make them."

"But the data," said the technician, turning white, "is absolutely cor—"

"—unacceptable. I told you, start over. From the top. and get me what I need. And before you do that, bracket the initial scans and I'll seal the files myself, while I'm here."

Reice sighed and backed away from the door, toward his chair by the wall. It was going to be a long, long session. He flipped out his communicator to cancel the kids' agenda for the rest of the day. If they *were* kids, and not aliens with conical skulls and physiologies that didn't quite fit into normal four-dimensional space.

CHAPTER 3

▽

For Your Own Good

In the soft, rainbow light of the modeler bay, Dini Forat-Cummings repeated implacably, "Assistant Secretary Remson, for your own good, heed what I say. In one hour's time, the Council of the Unity will provide a delegation out at the Ball to receive the UNE's answer to the Unity's message. The delegation will remain available for only a few of your hours. I suggest you end this session and concentrate on the matter at hand."

She tapped the message she was carrying from the Unity on one knee. Beyond Remson's imposing bulk, she could see her husband's beloved person, trying to assist the technicians whom Remson had instructed to perform the entire modeling procedure over again because Remson had not liked the results.

Results, Remson would find out, were not subject to change on a whim. Truth was not reinterpretable to suit convenience. Facts were not coinage, to be withheld and distributed for personal gain.

Remson had not adjusted to such new realities, that was certain. His large head with its craggy features inclined to her stiffly, an obligatory nod of respect, as he replied, "Once more, Ms. Forat-Cummings, I must remind you that what is happening here is of critical importance to your safety and that of your husband." His pale eyes flickered toward Rick, who had his hands up before his face to fend off the modeler helmet, then back to her. "I thought you two had agreed with Secretary General Croft to cooperate."

"We did. We are. We will." Time and tense was the problem, then. English was not her native tongue, and perhaps the confusion stemmed from that. But she knew better: UNE space was no longer her native spacetime. After so long away from this sequential reality, she was having difficulty separating things into their proper order. She must remember the teachings of her youth: forward, not back; noun to verb; past to present to future; from the beginning to the end. Humanity was still adamant about that, and about keeping its ever-present "now" central to its experience.

"Well, you're not cooperating. Not in my terms. If this message was so important, madam, why didn't you bring it up with Mickey—with the SecGen—during your meeting earlier?"

Remson's frustration, his uncertainty, hit her like swells of ocean surf carrying stones in their froth. The shock and subsequent abrasion was nearly physical. She shrank back, then calmed herself. She stood up.

Remson followed suit and towered over her.

She had made an error. *Earlier,* that was the problem. The big man did not believe her because she had not spoken earlier. Tense. Sequentiality. She was not convincing because she had not ordered her priorities in a human fashion. She wished she had her pets here to help her, to make everything behave: time, events, people. Mostly people.

But the pets could not come to Threshold. Dark furry faces and bright eyes gleamed in her inner sight. They were waiting at home in Unity space, and she would be home soon enough. The council had promised. She and her husband did not have to stay here. The council would protect them. No harm would come to them—not at the hands of their human parents. Not from the Secretariat. Not from the combined might of the United Nations of Earth.

"Answer me, Ms. Forat-Cummings. Your husband's father is determined to cause trouble. Don't underestimate him. With three psychologists, he can have Rick declared incompetent and remanded into his custody. I was told the two of you wanted to stay together. With less restrained measures, *your* father can have us knee-deep in assassins.

We need— and I demand—your full cooperation, or the Secretariat cannot be responsible for your welfare." He glared at her through those pale blue eyes surrounded with red-veined whites. "Now, answer my question: if this message is so important, why didn't you give it to Mickey when you saw him?"

"Why," she sighed, and the three-letter word tasted on her tongue like all of mankind's murderous obstinacy. This was her race, that was why. This was her price, paid for a new home and a new chance at happiness beyond the dreams of creatures such as Remson. "Let's go out of here, into the next room. We are disturbing your precious evaluation process."

"Gladly," snapped the big man, full of his own power.

She glanced back at Rick and saw for a moment her husband's distress and loneliness. On his lap, on his shoulders, with their little black hands wound in his hair, appeared the phantoms of their pets: the racoon-like Brows were as lonely as they, awaiting reunion.

If she had had her Brow in her arms, communication with beings like Remson would have been so much easier. But she did not have it. The Unity had decreed that this was a human matter, and that she and Rick were the best qualified to broach it.

In the outer chamber, the light was brighter, squeezed together into a soulless white that focused spacetime into a narrow band of sequentiality.

Remson slammed his hand against a palm-plate that shut the door between the two bays. He turned to the white-coated technicians, saying, "Out! Now!"

Two people in white scurried to obey. "If you'll take a seat," Remson ordered.

She did not.

Remson crossed his arms, spilling anger all over the room with his motion. The heat of it was a shockwave of red that sped toward her so fast she barely had time to deflect the effect.

"Let's have it," Remson said.

"Have what?" she asked, confused.

"An explanation. The message. I want to know why you're just getting around to telling us this now."

"Why," she sighed again, trying to understand the fury she felt emanating from the man, the urgency, and the clear hostility. She must make herself understood. "You're finally ready to listen, now. Secretary General Croft was not ready to listen, then. The message is for the Secretary General, from the Interstitial Interpreter of the Council of the Unity. Will you deliver it, or shall we? An answer must be soon forthcoming."

That should be clear enough. Even a child could understand such simple declarative sentences.

Remson held out his big hand, pushing it through his envelope of now into hers. It was all she could do not to shrink back yet again.

Remson said, "Give it to me. I'll take care of it. We need you here to finish the modeling, so we can placate Richard Cummings the Second before we have a lawsuit on our hands."

She held out the message disk in her own hand, praying he wouldn't touch her flesh when he took it. Touching was so difficult with uncontrolled beings. So much spilled over into you. . . . She'd been afraid she'd have to touch Croft, but Rick had shielded her.

Big, blunt fingers with ridged nails took the message media from her. Remson stepped back.

Released from her duty, so did Dini. She wanted to go home, back to the Unity. She'd been promised she wouldn't have to stay here. She was near tears and didn't know why. Rick was beyond a closed door, a thick wall, and she was all alone. . . .

"Can I go back in there now?" she asked. "I want to go back—"

"You'll be better off here with me until they're done with him." Remson was already sitting at a console, fitting the disk into a reader. He didn't look at her. His hunched-over frame spewed conflicting emotions.

And then she understood: the huge consular person was afraid of her. All the combative energy coming out of him was from fear, not annoyance. He was afraid of what he'd seen in the modeling bay. Afraid of the Unity. Afraid of . . .

She closed her eyes to avoid being distracted by the sight of him and his energies. Now she could only hear him, smell him, feel him. . . .

He was afraid of . . . contamination.

She opened her eyes and stared past Remson, through the double glass, at Rick. Her beloved's head was hidden by the modeling helmet. He had held back, to make sure he could save her if there were some awful trick of compulsion or mind control associated with the modeling bay. But the trick had been played on the modelers, not the subjects, when the results of her modeling were displayed.

Contamination with what? Happiness? Love? Peace? Life?

Were these people really living? She hadn't been, not on Medina, not even on Threshold. Not until she'd met Rick, and the furry, black-masked Brows that were his companions, and they'd fled for freedom among the stars.

She missed her new home, opalescent rings among crimson clouds in violet skies, and the peaceful green hills dotted with homes like temples.... She missed Rick. She missed rubbing against him, their combined nature. She missed the surety that came from being an extended entity, more than one circumscribed person.

She opened her eyes. Remson wasn't watching her. He was stabbing at his control panel as if his life depended on it. Perhaps it did. Perhaps all of these people's lives did.

She moved through the intervening space without displacing an atom. No need to cause alarm. No reason to disturb the fetid, recycled air. No benefit to alerting this prisoner of four dimensions. The UNE understood the fifth force, if rudimentarily: it had a crude form of gravity control; it collected antimatter molecules and stored them, one by one, in electromagnetic bottles; it tapped the A-potential force of the energy sea as if it understood the consequences. So why were these people so slow to understand their place in spacetime and change it? Why did they wish to change everything but themselves? Why did they go to such extremes to force the universe to allow them to remain as they had been when they climbed out onto some primal shore from the muck of creation?

She couldn't fathom Remson's fear of enlightenment, of metamorphosis, of evolution. Change was natural; only stasis was unnatural. People were creatures of evolution. Denying it was like denying the ordering principle itself—like denying God, her father would have said.

She found the wall with the palm-plate, although it was difficult to identify a particular chunk of matter when you were moving through it, rather than around it. She slid with just a shimmer and a shiver through the door it marked with its electromagnetic glow.

Then she reentered sequential spacetime with a shudder. She collapsed herself, petrified her every molecule, sucked up her being into arteries, capillaries, veins, organs, meat and bones.

For a moment, the compression was more than she could bear. But Rick was here, in this space, and she immediately felt better, sharing the moment with him.

His heart came into her. His emanations bathed her. His love surrounded her. His distress was . . . unexpected.

She looked through her human eyes and saw him, tense in the chair, his hands curled in black gloves with wires all over them; his head hidden in a black helmet with sensors deployed down to his jaw.

He couldn't see her, but surely he could feel her. She wondered if he could hear her. She said, "Rick . . ."

And people jumped up. White-coated figures moved quickly in incomprehensible patterns.

Then someone grabbed her from behind. The invasion of her personal space was nearly unendurable. The fingers on her arm seemed to sear her flesh with their heat.

"Let go of me," she demanded, and focused on the owner of the hand: Remson again.

"How did you do that?" Remson demanded.

"Do what?" she asked innocently.

"Get in here. Are you purposely trying to invalidate this evaluation? If you kids don't cooperate, we'll let your parents have you, and be damned."

"Be damned yourself," she retorted, wrenching her arm free from his unbearable touch.

Remson examined his hand, which had grabbed her, as if it belonged to someone else, or as if it had betrayed him. "End this session," he decreed, stone-faced.

Around them, the light of the modeling bay began turning white, bright, sterile. The modeler technicians were chattering agitatedly.

Her husband was letting the two white-coated people help him off with the helmet and the gloves.

"Let's go, young lady. You can wait for your hubby outside."

"I'll wait here," she said. "You promised not to separate us." She hoped her voice did not betray her.

Rick was moving toward them. She could see him concentrating on covering every step in between, one at a time. Arduous, unnecessary process.

Rick looked from her to Remson. "What's wrong now, Mr. Fixit? If you don't like what you see, maybe you'd better arrange to see what you like. These machines ought to be able to give you any fairy story you want." Rick motioned around the modeler bay.

"It's not that, Rick—it's the message—"

"Mr. Cummings, will you accompany us?" Remson interrupted.

Had Remson read the message? she wondered.

Beyond the bay doors, she realized that he must have. He took them straightaway to a secure lift, and up to the very top of the Stalk, without a word. The message disk was in his pocket. She could see it.

But Rick was with her, so she needn't worry. His energies mixed with hers, mingling together. Shoulder to shoulder, they could face anything. They were not two separate beings anymore, but something more. Was that so terrible? To become more than the sum of your parts?

It must be terrible to Remson. He stood opposite them in the lift and stared at them as though they were some travesty of nature. He clearly did not want to risk touching her again.

Good. Rick was all comfort and joy, willing to be together and not worry. Rick was not one for worry. But Rick had not confronted this obdurate person as she had.

The lift door opened onto a place she'd never been, where real marble and real wood supported and surrounded real paintings and real oriental rugs of great antiquity. The rugs were woven full with noble stories of man's ascent, of fables and history and promises between humanity and its gods.

When she hesitated over them, reading them as her own heritage had taught her to do, Remson whispered irritably at her to hurry.

This place was a museum, or should be.

In its depths, down three corridors, Remson stopped before a closed door and rapped with big knuckles upon the wood.

When the door opened, the Secretary General stood

there, a white towel around his neck and white foam striping his jaw and upper lip.

"Sorry to bother you, sir, but this is urgent."

Croft looked at her with tortured resignation and said, "Come in. Let me just close this door...."

Beyond, a barber stood, wiping a razor on his apron. Croft called softly to him, "I'll be a few moments," and a door slid shut between the rooms. Croft turned, wiping the foam from his face. "So? Let's hear it, Vince."

"They hand-carried a message in here, from the Council of the Unity. Don't ask me why they didn't give it to you before."

"Perhaps the time wasn't right," said Croft gently, and smiled a distant, wistful smile.

Remson gave Croft the disk. The Secretary General pocketed it. "So, Mr. Cummings, Mrs. Forat-Cummings, will you explain this for me, or must I go read it for myself?"

"Read it," Rick advised. "That's why we brought it."

"Do you know what's in it, Mr. Cummings?" Croft asked.

"Some. Not all," Rick admitted.

"And you, Ms. Forat-Cummings, what do you know about this message?"

Keen eyes met hers and slid aside. Croft remained with his back to the door, as if cornered, as if there was no room for him anywhere else in the large chamber full of beautiful antiques.

"We were asked to deliver it. You should respond to a Council of the Unity Delegation which will be available at the Ball for the next few hours."

"I should, should I?" Croft's eyes narrowed. "And how should I respond, Ms. Forat-Cummings?"

"I ... Rick?" She turned to her husband. She didn't want to say the wrong thing. Time. Tense. Past to future. They didn't know what was in the message, perhaps. Or they did, because Remson had read it and communicated the information to Croft, and Croft was seeking additional data. Or Remson alone knew....

Rick said, "The Council of the Unity requests an official response. We're not official emissaries." Rick shrugged. "We are here to show good faith, and to settle this matter with our parents, with your help. Not to negotiate or make conditions."

Croft sighed heavily. "Just stopped by to keep a promise, be special guests at a coming-out party hosted by your father, and then you're on your way, is that it? Back to Unity space. Is that what this is?" Croft slapped his pocket, where the message disk was.

"Those are the conditions under which we came here," Dini reminded the Secretary General, because she was afraid that Rick would not. Rick wanted more from this trip than she. Rick wanted peace with his father. Dini would have been content to stay out of harm's way, stay at home, and never see Threshold, or Medina, again. Despite the beauty of such rugs as she trod now. Despite the songs of history woven into them, which she had not realized she missed so deeply. She was here solely because the Unity had asked her and Rick to come. . . .

"We remember," Croft told her, and his large, mobile lips seemed unhappy with the form of the words. "We remember all our promises. You must remember yours."

He turned to Remson. "Vince, if its just a diplomatic message, and they were simply acting as couriers, why did you bring them with you?"

"Cummings Two made a visit to the modeler bay, complete with threats and a distinct degree of agitation. So I didn't want to leave them. And . . ."

"And?"

"Cummings The Second saw the Forat girl's scan."

"So?" Croft's limpid eyes flicked to her again but didn't come to rest.

"So, Cummings saw the modeler displaying a complete physioscan of a Unity being, not a human girl."

Croft closed his eyes and leaned heavily against the door. "I see," he said at last. "Well, couldn't be helped. Of course, this modeler data was the result of some error which we are rectifying?"

"Of course. Technical difficulties." Remson's white teeth flashed.

Dini Forat felt suddenly so heavy she thought she might drip down into a puddle, a casualty of unremitting gravity. Or fall through the floor entirely, and through every succeeding floor, until she had fallen all the way through the antenna-like expanse of the Stalk and out into free space. Free space . . .

Then she realized that it was Croft's heaviness she felt.

Remson was telling the Secretary General what the message said: ". . . the short of it is that the Unity wants the UNE to tow Threshold out to a new orbit beyond Pluto, if real contact, or commerce, between our civilizations is going to commence. The rest is technical detail. Except the time frame. They want an answer, sent back with the kids or personally delivered by you, by the end of the day."

A misery overswept Dini Forat that was so intense she leaned against her husband. She found herself fascinated by the face of the Secretary General.

"Can we do that, Vince? Give them an answer—technically, I mean. Have we the capability of doing it?"

"I think so. I'll get a team on it right away."

"Good," said the Secretary General of the United Nations of Earth.

"And you two, would you like to help Mr. Remson? I have rather a lot to do, some of which will surely include further negotiations with your parents. And we don't want you to be the subject of intimidation, whether verbal or more concrete. Do we?"

"That's right," said Rick flatly. "We don't. We'll be glad to assist Mr. Remson, if it'll help."

"And you'll be available to take a response to the Ball if and when we have one and decide that's the best course?"

"Delighted," said Dini's husband, and she was so glad she had married him. Rick understood people like Croft so much better than she ever would. Why was Secretary General Croft so agitated at the thought of going out to the Ball himself to meet with the Unity delegation?

There was nothing to be afraid of. Not out at the Ball there wasn't.

She straightened up proudly, taking strength from her husband. Soon they would be back where they belonged. Her father was not going to destroy her life. The United Nations of Earth would not try to keep them here against their will.

And there was a chance that the Unity would have its wish.

Although she still missed the feel of soft fur next to her face and small black hands tugging at her hair, the perfumed air and the kiss of sunset on the hilltops of her adopted home, she was no longer unhappy that she had come.

For all the Unity had given her and Rick, this one brief hardship was a small price to pay. After all, it was humanity's future that hung in the balance, not her own.

Mankind had a choice to make, and the hard decisions that would shape its future were just beginning.

She was glad she'd been here to see Mickey Croft's stooped shoulders straighten and his jaw firm with resolve.

It might be the right time for humanity. He might be the right man. For one crucial instant, all things might be in harmony and mankind might make the right choice.

Ahead lay salvation—or the loss of it, and a long slow slide toward the dark.

Between now and the moment of choice there was little enough that she and her husband could do. But there was something, and they would do it. They were a part of this moment, and all the decisions to come.

She could see her own reflection in the Secretary General's weary eyes.

CHAPTER 4

$$\triangledown$$

Feasibility Study

Reice met Remson at Spacedock Seven, double-quick as ordered, for a classified briefing to be followed by a technical evaluation of the task at hand.

Whatever that was. When Reice pulled the *BLUE TICK* into its parking slot among the strutwork of Spacedock Seven, he knew little more about the "task at hand" than he'd known when he'd left Threshold. He shut down his onboard systems, enabled his pressure locks to debarkation mode, and left the *TICK* carrying only a briefing bag with a notepad computer inside.

The lock station sighed, cycled to green, and opened onto a concourse with drink machines, escalators, and manned security stations across from a bank of pay comlinks. Reice didn't see anybody he recognized waiting beyond the security barrier or lined up to go through the security arch or at the octagonal desk that let you avoid standing in line to have your person and carry-throughs irradiated.

Funny, but not disturbing. Lots of people passed through Spacedock Seven every day. Lots of traffic into the facility beyond and out of it meant lots of minor gridlocks and traffic snarls and missed connections.

Reice stepped into the much shorter line before the octagonal desk, where you went if you were carrying sensitive materials you couldn't put through the scanner, side arms, or explosives, or had the clout to do so.

Distracted, he cut the line entirely, holding up his ConSec ID and walking unconcernedly between the human and automated system.

The ConSec guard closest at the desk nodded an OK at him, and that way Reice didn't have to check his A-POT gun or leave it on the *BLUE TICK*. Since he had it, he wasn't about to put such sensitive technology in any danger of being pilfered or misplaced.

On the other side of the guards, he passed through a wide space and looked both ways before he headed up a slope on foot. The Spacedock Seven facility was comprised of more than seventeen miles of corridors, labeled A-Z Ring, and you had to know where you were going to avoid either a long walk or hitching a ride on a cleaning robot.

Reice headed for the closest stairs and on through a door marked in red AUTHORIZED PERSONNEL ONLY, which he keyed with the card he'd shown the guard. All this fuss over ... what?

First, the kids are God's own priority; now, something unspecified knocks them out of the ballpark and they're somebody else's worry.

Nobody'd bothered to tell Reice even so much as what had happened to the young couple or who was watching them. Maybe they were under house arrest somewhere nice and comfy. Reice knew only one thing for certain: right now, they were somebody else's problem.

Almost nobody used the enclosed stairwell: you needed special access to get out of it on most of the Rings between B and Y. This was an old facility, once the biggest single construct in manned space. Now Threshold, growing daily, far outstripped it, and even the Stalk was bigger, with its multiple habitats, but Spacedock Seven was a ConSec facility, and Reice liked the feeling of being on his own turf.

If he knew why he was out here, he'd have liked the feeling even better. Except for the fact that the distribution list for the meeting included everybody who'd worked on the construction of the science station out at the Ball site, he'd learned nothing pertinent since he left Threshold.

But you knew something from the fact that the briefing was being held at Spacedock Seven in the first place. At least it had gotten him away from babysitting those spooky rich brats the Secretariat was sheltering.

Reice climbed onto a dirty white landing scarred by tens of thousands of highly polished black shoes pounding over it and ran his card through the lock before he pushed open a door with a large WARNING: RESTRICTED AREA. ALARM WILL SOUND notice on it.

No alarm sounded. Reice was cleared for every area in this building and glad to be on Y Ring, with its wide corridors faced with displays of ConSec triumphs in man's conquest of the stars.

He passed portraits of great ConSec officers, flags and doors of increasingly imposing size and decoration.

At the Joint Staff corridor he halted. He still hadn't seen a soul he knew, but down the hallway were two live ConSec honor guards, who indicated the door he wanted.

He strode across carpet, now, and past marble-clad lights. The officers at either side of the door stared straight ahead, unspeaking. Good men.

He keyed the lock and entered an anteroom, where he was greeted by a pretty woman and ushered—"Right this way, sir"—through three more doors.

When she opened a final portal for him, he realized why he hadn't seen anybody due for this meeting. People were standing around the long briefing table in knots, asking questions and looking at charts displayed on the wall grids.

Now you could find out what was going on in a heartbeat.

Reice put his briefing bag down at an empty place and headed for a group gathered around the mission-statement monitor.

My, my. Vince Remson, holding forth, right in their midst.

The blond Assistant Secretary stopped gesticulating and broke into a smile. "Mr. Reice, good to see you again so soon. Let's get this show rolling." The group parted for the Assistant Secretary as Remson headed purposefully toward Reice.

A warm glow of belonging came over Reice, even thought he'd had no prebrief whatsoever and had no idea what Remson might want him to do. But they shared a secret or two, and that was comradeship in these circles.

Remson handed Reice a sheaf of hard copy and said, "Follow my lead."

Hard copy. Stamped and red-bordered and classified out of all normal access channels. Reice skimmed the executive summary as he followed Remson toward the head of the table, sweeping up his briefing bag on the way, conscious in a pleasant way of the number of high-powered eyes tracking his progress.

Somebody good had written up this brief.

The executive summary said: "Determine Feasibility of Moving Threshold to Orbit Around Pluto in Response to Council of Unity Request."

That was why some of the people here had on striped suits and looked like they belonged in the Secretariat: they were from the Secretariat. Joint Staff meetings usually meant Consolidated Space Command (ConSpaceCom), Consolidated Security (ConSec) and whoever else was necessary for the mission in question, usually Space Marines, Army or Navy brass, Customs honchos, intel types, or Corps of Engineers.

There were lots of engineers here, with bells on. And Laboratory Command people, and technical intel types. Forty people in all.

Remson stood at the head of the table and Reice took a seat beside him. Remson held a remote for the briefing monitors in his hand and switched the lights off with it.

"Thank you for coming, ladies and gentlemen. Today we have a critical decision of technical feasibility to be made, and made fast."

Remson touched a monitor button, and to his left blossomed the insignia of the SecGen's office, with a string of security designators below in case anyone had missed the point and thought they could eat out on the results of this briefing.

Remson changed frames and the executive summary that Reice had just read was displayed in large type. "That's the problem. I need some solutions that will tell us whether this undertaking is technically possible. We'll let the security considerations rest until we find out whether we think we can do this job without imperiling either the structural integrity of Threshold or the safety of any of its inhabitants."

A three-star from the Corps of Engineers said, "You want to eat this elephant one bite at a time, boys, and be sure you got the right silverware with you. The physical stresses aren't so important to me as the level of commitment. We can deal with the stresses, if we've got the budget for scalar drivers and a whole lot of fuel to burn."

"You'll get it," Remson said, "but I need a cost estimate

from you, and an equipment list, and a time frame: how long to do the job?"

Somebody else said, before the engineer could answer, "Manpower's going to affect the timetable, here, both in feasibility studies and in operational phases. How many men do you want us to assign to this from the lab side?"

The engineer, smelling a funding channel, spoke right over the eager, fat honcho from Consolidated Laboratory Command: "When do you need that data, Mr. Secretary?"

Remson said, "I'm going to turn this meeting over to Mr. Reice, who's serving as my alternate. Mr. Reice is Logistics Coordinator for this program, gentlemen." Remson gave a horrified Reice the remote that controlled the briefing monitors, and as Reice stood up, whispered in his ear, "Try to keep the cost down. Don't let them turn this into a series of overstuffed, overmanned, overly expensive junkets. I haven't got time to wonder if they're playing me straight or jockeying for position. Get me an estimate by the end of the afternoon. I'll be in my office on Z Ring when you're done."

"By the end of the afternoon?" Reice was nearly dumbstruck. The words came out in a croak, his mouth was so dry.

"I'm afraid so. Remember, cost won't stop this initiative. But it takes time to spend money, and we don't have time. Keep this thing *small*, if you can. And don't let the labs use this project as an excuse to test prototypes. We want everything nice and dependable. Got it?"

"Got it." Reice wanted to say that he wasn't qualified for this, but nobody here was better qualified, that was for sure. Reice watched Remson head off into the darkened room and put both hands flat on the table, leaning forward toward the assembled group, now as hungry and attentive as sharks who'd had their first scent of blood in the water.

He waited in silence until Remson had left the room and the door had closed. Then he said, "I'm going to go around the table, left to right. Each of you is going to give me an estimate of what his service or agency can provide to this effort, at what cost, with what manpower, and in how short a time. Make the assumption that we *are* going to move Threshold to Pluto and we need to do it fast and safely."

He paused. Nobody said it was impossible, at least out

loud. Nobody grumbled about the abruptly instituted planning meeting.

"All right, the Threshold Relocation Planning Group is officially constituted and convened. Feed your data into your desktops before you give it to me verbally. We're going to hold you to it. We're coming out of this meeting with a lean, mean plan that we can begin executing today. There's no room for error and there'll be no second chances."

Somebody complained that there wasn't enough information on the table yet to do that.

Reice activated his monitor controller and, sure enough, a PROBLEM chart came up on the monitor behind his shoulder.

"That's what we have to work with. Maybe you'd like more time to check your files, but we haven't got time. Come on, fellas, we built the Stalk and everything on Threshold. We ought to be able to move it safely and cost effectively a few billion miles without wetting our pants. What's A-potential power for?" Reice keyed his remote again and, mercifully, a rotatable schematic of Threshold in three dimensions replaced the PROBLEM definition.

The fat honcho from the labs grumbled, "You're asking us to use scalar energy on a scale we've never attempted before. Where are we porting all the excess energy we're going to be generating if the job is to move the whole habitat without exerting stress on its structural integrity? It wasn't built to be moved. It's got a drag coefficient longer than your ID number, and it's not going to be moving through anything like pure vacuum. You've got a lot of serious problems here, unless you want to turn off the fifth-force generators altogether . . ."

"I don't care how you solve your technical problems, Doctor." He had no idea who the fat man was, but "Doctor" was a safe bet. "One thing we're not going to do is reinvent the wheel, or develop a new interstellar drive, or let you test some notional system you've had sitting on your desk for years. We're talking about a military transportation mission, a logistical priority, with nothing developmental or experimental about it. Remember, we don't need to move anything today, we just need to know what it's going to take to do the job and form into operational teams coordinated by Consolidated Logistics Agency and yours truly."

God, Reice hated grandstanders. And he knew damned well that if the only problems stopping the movement of Threshold to a new orbit beyond Pluto were power problems, or technical problems relating to reduced solar energy at the new site, then the Unity would help solve those technical problems if the Unity wanted the job done.

Finally, he understood what Mickey Croft and Remson were after: they needed to know the costs to the United Nations of Earth so that they could drive a bargain with the aliens. The Secretariat needed to know how many people, at what risk, would be involved in modifying what systems to get the desired result. And if there were any way to talk the Unity aliens into transferring some advanced power technology to the Stalk government to facilitate the efficient transportation of Threshold to a new location, then the Secretary General needed all the detail he could get to drive the best bargain for the United Nations of Earth.

You had to think fast in this man's Consolidated Security Command, these days. And you had to keep on your toes. Reice was almost euphoric as he faced the grindingly difficult task or getting these senior officers to work together for the common good without overmuch regard to budgets, turf battles, personal power enhancement, or interservice rivalries.

It was a tough job, but he'd do it. Remson had known that he, Reice, was the right man to get the job done. And if the result of this job was the acquisition by the UNE of advanced power technology of the sort that allowed the Unity aliens to pop into and out of complex gravity wells at will, without traversing much spacetime in the process, then Reice was going to be doing the most important job of his life. Maybe of anybody's life.

Finally, fate and Remson had given Reice a chance to prove he was good for more than babysitting asymptotic personalities and playing cops and robbers.

He wasn't going to let Remson—or himself—down. Not when so much hung in the balance and all he had to do was keep a bunch of propeller-heads with parochial interests in line.

By the end of this session, Secretary General Croft would have everything he needed to knowledgeably discuss the logistics involved in moving Threshold to an orbit beyond Pluto. If the session had to last all night, Reice would see to it that Mickey Croft had every advantage possible over the Unity aliens.

It was personal, now.

CHAPTER 5

▽

Children of Whom?

The Cummings boy and the Forat girl were really spooky. "The Forat-Cummings girl," Croft corrected himself, muttering it aloud for emphasis as the shuttle taking him to the Ball science station mated with the lock.

"What's that, sir?" came Remson's voice through the comlink in the helmet Croft wore for safety. Mickey Croft was not technically adroit. He destested all of the risk associated with checking his glove seals and his life support and the redundant command and control heads-up display that cluttered his visor with things he didn't want to think about, such as ambient pressure, external temperature, internal security status, and life-support monitoring.

"Nothing, Vince, just that our young marrieds are problematic, especially the woman."

"Yep," said Remson, distractedly, as with a slightly perceptible bump the shuttle came to a stop, gravity ceased, and Remson unbuckled his seatbelt to float toward Croft. "There's something I can't quite name here that rings false—beyond the obvious glitch of the modeler image, I mean." Remson was piloting Croft personally, now that the two of them had left the Secretariat flagship the *GEORGE WASHINGTON*.

The Assistant Secretary had met him on time, with a grin and a slap of a datapad in his hand. "All ready to face the unknowable, sir, with a risk assessment of the projected task and a task force hard at work on specifics."

"Good," Croft had replied, gruffly, hiding his surprise as best he could: Remson didn't like displays of emotion, and neither did Croft. But this time, Remson had outdone himself. Vince was as always a pleasant surprise—always competent, always giving better than any other man's hundred percent. But to have come up with a reasonable cost assessment of the aliens' request that Threshold be moved beyond Pluto in less than the time it took for Croft and his flagship to meet Vince at Spacedock Seven . . . Croft reminded himself to put a commendation in Remson's file.

In this crisis, Remson was a real and certain comfort, especially noticeable to Croft as Remson deftly guided him into the pressure lock, and beyond. . . .

As Croft faced the scant security of a paperlike access tube, which led through microgravity to the minimal facilities of Science Station Seven, he wondered how he could get along without Remson, and then told himself that, with any luck, he would never need to find out.

The tube was the equivalent of a red carpet, out here, present only because Croft was present. It was a godsend. Through its opaque exterior, he couldn't see the spidery scaffolding that secured the science station to the alien Ball.

Another manifestation of Remson's thoughtfulness. Croft muttered, "Declutter," and the telltale readouts of his pounding pulse and elevated blood pressure left the right upper quadrant of his visor. Croft didn't need to be reminded that he was tense. His head was throbbing. Damn those kids. And damn the minimal facilities at this station that meant one had to stay inside a space suit the whole time.

Recording the upcoming proceedings for posterity was not high on Croft's agenda. But the science station was minimal because it was posited so close to the alien Ball that no one had wanted to install fifth-force generators, initially, nor had the Secretariat been inclined to encourage a continuing presence.

The station was no more than a couple of spaceworthy modules interfaced with pressure seals that could sustain an atmosphere, had the proper life support been in place. It wasn't.

A dozen suited and helmeted staffers stood in close quarters, looking at monitors with their feet or arms thrust into anchor webbing.

Croft said to Remson, "Vince, find out if they've made contact with the Unity delegation yet."

He listened to the query, and the negative response, through the open comlink, but did not use it himself. He wanted to hear what was going on but not constrain conversation.

He heard: "Your boss sure there's some meeting scheduled out here?"

And: "We haven't scanned a sign of life. It's as dead in there as it's ever been."

And: "What happens if nobody shows? Does your boss get pissed when he's stood up?"

And, finally: "Let's have a little decorum, gentlemen." Remson's firm tone turned every other helmeted head toward his. "The Secretary General, I'm sure, would appreciate a look at what you've got for us."

Remson cleared the way and Mickey took a perch at the midpoint of the consoles, while around him people whispered on their allcomm: "Shit, I didn't know." "Don't worry, he couldn't hear us, I bet." "Probably still can't: they've got their own secure coms."

On the monitors that showed the Ball from every angle the scaffolding could provide, a silver sphere sat quiescent, as if waiting.

Waiting for what? Croft? He was here. The last time he'd been near the ball, a soap bubble had come to collect him right out of the *GEORGE WASHINGTON*'s airlock. The aliens had orchestrated everything. And now?

Croft suddenly had no idea what he was supposed to do. How did one signal that thing? What had the message from the Unity said? *"At the twentieth hour of this day, make your willingness known to us to move your Habitation beyond Pluto, where real commerce can commence between us."*

Everyone, including Croft and Remson, had assumed that the children had understood what the aliens meant.

Croft sat staring at the Ball. It tended to open up, occasionally. He didn't want it to open while he watched. He admitted, only to himself, and only now, that he was loathe to float up to it in a Manned Maneuvering Unit on a space tether and knock on its surface for admittance.

So he felt suddenly and completely embarrassed. He had scrambled every resource available and made a headlong dash to meet a Unity delegation that might not even be here. . . .

No one had seen it come. He could hear the staffers muttering in the comlink. And then the muttering stopped.

In the monitor, as Mickey watched, aghast and yet relieved, the Ball disappeared, to be replaced by a face.

And what a face. No human face had ever stared that stare. Sad eyes, deep and dark, regarded him. A harelip quivered and moved soundlessly. A skull or a crown or a coif of gold glimmered, surrounded by mist.

A voice sounded in Croft's helmet. He had no idea whether the others could hear it. It was coming through his helmet speakers. It said, "Mickeycroft, can we make an embassy here? We cannot. We are permitting great thanks, but this is incorrect. Come you to the outer reaches, beyond gravity's sway, and we will be together, yours and mine, under less troubles. Can you make this thing without help, or needing us, find another way?"

"I don't know, Your Excellency," Croft said, conscious that Remson could hear his response, and perhaps, if God was merciful, have heard the Interstitial Interpreter's remarks as well. "We will need longer to evaluate the situation. We're sorry you are finding this site unacceptable." He'd offered them the opportunity to build an embassy at the Ball site. After all, the Unity was already inhabiting those coordinates.

"Not sorry. Not correct. Humans young can guide, if Mickeycroft can protect. Protect, Mickeycroft?"

Protect what? Who? The aliens? The Cummings couple? He somehow didn't dare ask for a clarification. "Of course. The most important thing now is to determine whether we have the technical capability to do as you suggest. That will take some time."

Time was what he needed, sure enough. Time to find out if he was talking to anyone that the others could see, or hear—if this was really happening. He didn't dare look up or move, or perhaps he could not.

He couldn't get any closer to those aliens than this, that was certain. Not again.

"Time takes," said the sad-eyed alien face. "All beings it takes. Children grow. Safety promises. Return children to us soon, and with love."

Gibberish followed, and a shimmer in the transmission, a distortion that slid left, and right, and hardened into diagonal wavy lines that chased each other across the monitor from which Croft could not yet take his eyes.

He heard a last, faint voice saying, "Must trust, Mickey-croft. No needing fears, anxiety, and runnings back and forth. Use access we have given, please, for future."

He was just about to ask for a clarification when there was a spray of static that made him clap his hands to his helmet. The Ball reappeared in the monitors, leaving him confused, frustrated, and doubtful of what he'd accomplished here.

The chatter of the technicians, excited and inconclusive, tumbled into his helmet and jangled around inside it.

"Vince," he croaked on his private channel, "did you hear that? See that? Did the staff?"

"They saw the image, but they didn't get the audio. Neither did I. Meeting finished, sir, with good results, I assume."

Not a question, but Croft answered anyway: "Time, Vince. I think we bought some time." He was having trouble focusing. He wanted, desperately, to leave this place, now.

As if reading his mind, Remson came to help him from his seat. "Sir, you have a meeting with Mr. Cummings that we can't cancel. Time to go, I think. Unless there's something else?"

"No, Vince. Nothing else." Just get me out of here before I mess myself in front of strangers. Loose bowels and a heaving stomach weren't the worst of what Croft was feeling, but they were the most noticeable.

It took nearly the entire return shuttle ride to restore his equilibrium. Once they were back on the *WASHINGTON,* he had to prep for his Cummings meeting and look at the rest of the data that Remson's task force had assembled. There was no time for reflection, or for sick stomachs or pounding hearts.

So he managed, as he always did, to rise to the occasion. One day, he might not have the strength. But today he had had it. Just.

He sent Vince after the wayward lovers when the flagship docked at the Stalk and went alone to the meeting with Cummings. Not because he didn't want Remson with him, but because the children were becoming an ever increasing nexus of his concern.

He must stop thinking of them as children, he told himself as he climbed into his Secretariat limo on the spacedock apron, and it sped away into the tubeway and upStalk, drawing him inexorably closer to his meeting with Richard Cummings the Second.

He must remember to call them by their names, and to call Dini Forat-Cummings by her full name. From now on. They were becoming important players in this drama choreographed by an alien sensibility, and Croft could not afford to make a mistake in protocol.

If you said things aloud four times in succession, the recitation helped you memorize difficult material. It shouldn't matter whether the material that one was memorizing consisted of Hamlet's soliloquy from Shakespeare, Latin verbs, or married names of Muslim fundamentalist daughters turned interstellar corporate heiresses.

Shouldn't matter one whit. But it did. Mickey Croft was having trouble remembering to call Ms. Cummings, née Forat, by her married name. After all the modeler data he'd studied and transcripts he'd read that centered on the Medinan girl who was, to Mickey's sampler-modeler, identical in parameters to a Unity alien, he should be able to remember her name. . . .

Children of whom, were these star-crossed lovers? Or of *what*?

Croft sat bolt-upright in his padded seat, uncrossing his long legs so that he kicked the console across from him and its video terminal came to life, showing a ready screen and waiting for instructions.

Croft barely noticed. Why hadn't he thought of it before? Why hadn't he realized?

Nobody on Threshold—himself included—had ever had the opportunity to model a Unity alien. There was no comparable data, no baseline data, nothing to support any assumption that Dini Forat-Cummings was any more alien than was Croft himself.

Which, after repeated alien contamination, wasn't saying a lot.

But it was saying something. Croft pushed a button inset in the arm of the limo door and told the robot control system of the limo, "Back to my office. Now."

The roboticized system enquired in a simulated voice, "Coordinates, please."

Mickey usually used a consular car with a human driver. But not today. Today he had needed to be quite alone, before he confronted Richard Cummings the Second. Cummings was vocal and demanding of answers in response to what he'd seen in Mickey's modeling bay.

To placate the corporate magnate, and to throw his adversary off balance through a bit of mental Aikido, Croft had offered to go to Cummings for this bit of confrontation, which Croft hoped to turn to his advantage through adroit summitry. In Aikido, one used the opponent's weight and force against him, never exerting, only directing energy.

When Croft had agreed to the meeting, he hadn't realized that his staff's analysis of the Forat modeling data had been faulty. Must be faulty.

Croft gave the robotic driver his Secretariat office coordinates and sat back in the plush seat, weak with revelation.

Dini Forat had scanned as if she were a Unity alien. Cummings, Sr. had seen the scan in progress. But neither Cummings, nor Croft's staff, had been able to put the anomaly in context.

Therefore, reasoning from an insufficient base, they had preferred to come to faulty conclusions.

The blank video screen awaited his pleasure, humming softly to itself. The unit could be voice-controlled, which was a blessing. Croft felt as if he were at the bottom of a gravity well many times Earth-normal. He could hardly move. His entire body seemed far distant, a cavernous space on whose floor his paltry intelligence flickered. He told the vid system to put him through to Cummings, person-to-person, and the effort that speech took was prodigious.

Croft was feeling too old and too inflexible to guide his star-flung people through this crisis. What was needed was a younger man, a fresher intellect, one who could see the pieces of this puzzle in all its multidimensional complexity and not quail.

The design of humanity's future was at stake. Croft wondered how George Washington or Mikhail Gorbachev had felt, leading their flock into crisis because passing through the Valley of Death was the only route to freedom.

Dini Forat seemed to Mickey's sampler-modeler to be a Unity alien. More, to be an exact replica of a certain Interstitial Interpreter, emissary of the Council of the Unity to the human federation called the United Nations of Earth.

The Cummings boy had seen the model. The Forat-Cummings girl had seen it. Vince Remson and even the ConSec lieutenant, Reice, had seen the model, as had at least three technicians—and Richard Cummings, Sr.

But Croft had not seen it. Croft had not taken the time. He'd been satisfied with second-hand evaluations from his staff and a third-rate reaction from an irate father looking for trouble.

Cummings' face bloomed on the limo vid console, scowling. Richard the Second said, "Well, Croft, what now? Don't tell me you're going to cancel this meeting."

"Merely change the site, Richard. For your edification, and my own," Croft said as smoothly as ever he'd handled a man looking for trouble.

"And what if that's inconvenient?" Cummings demanded.

"We hope it won't be inconvenient." Invoke the Secretariat with the plural pronoun. Croft caught the father's angry little eyes in his. "We'll put a Secretariat car at your disposal. We need to evaluate what you saw in the modeler bay together, at the site of the manifestation." Be mysterious. Give Cummings a hint.

"I'm more interested in evaluating what Secretariat malfeasance has done to my son," Cummings' image retorted, but half-heartedly. Even over a secure comlink, digitized and miniaturized and thrice-filtered to avoid unauthorized audit, Cummings was clearly mollified and intrigued.

As well he should be. Mickey Croft was inviting the aggrieved parent into the modeler bay where so recently none of Cummings' massive clout could succeed in gaining more than a glimpse.

"Okay, Croft. But this better be worth it. Send your car for me. Right away. I'm a busy man."

"Certainly." Mickey Croft stretched out his foot and broke the comlink with a tap of his boot toe. A gesture made not in anger but in cold consideration of cause and effect.

He ordered the car for Cummings and then called the modeler bay to make sure things would be ready when he met Cummings there.

Dini Forat's psychometric model would be ready to display and question as Croft willed.

Why hadn't he put the pieces together earlier? The press of events? No excuse. All of his staff were more free of blame for this misreading of circumstances than he.

But only he and Remson had known at the time of the message hand-delivered from the Unity by young Cummings and his bride.

Time did not run smoothly, from past to future, when dealing with the Unity aliens. Croft had known it for a fact. Was tortured by the fact. In turmoil over the implications of the fact.

And yet the simple, flat, fact itself had been difficult to apply to events as they surrounded the Unity message, the Forat girl, or the crisis facing the UNE.

Croft rubbed his face with his hands as if he could wipe away all the confusion engendered by attempting to deal with beings whose home spacetime was different from that of human beings.

When the limo slowed and its door slid back, Croft was prepared as a man could be, when that man was facing multiple crises in eleven dimensions. Four dimensions had been difficult enough for humanity to manage during its ascent from the primal slime.

When Croft unwound himself from the confines of the limo, it sped quietly away down the Secretariat access tube, toward the private garage in Blue North. Mickey headed up a wide staircase meant to impress visitors attending diplomatic receptions who had special privileges and thus could use the Secretariat's private access tubes.

The facade of his residence was historically correct, with Doric columns and doors faced with real wood and brass. Inside, human security staff came to unobtrusive attention at desks on either side of the great reception hall. The UNE shield in marquetry on the floor proclaimed the heritage of the Secretariat. The needlepoint rugs beyond, and the seascapes on the corridor walls, reminded visitors of the provenance of democracy.

Of all the Secretariat's vast wealth, those paintings of historic America were Croft's favorites. But today was not the day to dawdle. He strode past staffers whose duty it was to make themselves invisible, as if this were a real house and not a working embassy.

Croft went through to the carefully marked lift and up into the heart of the Secretariat, where no attempt was made to evoke the past, only a workable future.

When he reached the blue-and-gray corridors that housed the modeler bay, he was winded. His blood thumped in his ears. Stress pushed his heartbeat against his chest so that he could see his body shiver with the pounding. Never mind. A little weakness, a little shortness of breath, were a small price to pay for enlightenment.

He could take control of this situation yet. He knew he could, thanks to the message of the children and the message sent via the children.

Into the modeler bay he went, and three white-coated technicians, plus three ConSec guards, came to attention.

"You three," he told the guards. "Outside. Mr. Cummings will be joining me. Alone. At my request."

He turned to the staffers. "Set up an interrogatory program and leave the room. Wait with the guards until Mr. Cummings has left."

The chief technician, a woman with graying hair, looked doubtful and opened her mouth to tell him that someone should stay to run the equipment.

"I designed this equipment, young lady," he told the aging technician. "I'm sure I can still manage to operate it. I'll call you if I need you."

She blushed and turned away to her control console.

Croft, for the first time in hours, checked his watch. The Unity still wanted its answer. Cummings had clouded the issue with his unexpected visit and the complications thereof. In order to control Cummings' loose-cannon behavior, Mickey was about to use an old but venerable trick, which had silenced many potential troublemakers in the past.

When Cummings arrived at the modeler bay, Mickey was sitting inside, soft lights playing around him, before the modeler itself.

He had left the door to the control room open. "Come in, Mr. Cummings, and let's get started," he called without rising.

Croft knew how he must look, underlit and haloed by the colored lights of the modeler apparatus: a wizard or a demigod could look no more imposing, sitting before an alchemist's workbench, or before a crystal ball.

Cummings was a man with an endangered son and a heart full of guilt. Despite everything the NAMECorp CEO might have planned or envisioned, the empty bay, cavernous with shadow, swept away all his righteous certainty.

Entering the bay, Cummings felt his way along. His voice was full of false bravado, but hushed, as he asked Croft, "What are you up to now?"

"Sit down, Richard, and we'll both learn a thing or two." Croft patted the seat beside him. Cummings must sit there, a willing participant in the action to come, not opposite as if the two were in conflict.

Cummings did, breathing noisily through his nose and demanding, "What's this all about, Croft?"

"You were so anxious to get in here, before, you forced my staff into an awkward position. As a result, you are now privy to classified information you don't understand." Croft went on carefully. "I am willing to put you completely in the picture, but only if you will agree to treat the information you are about to receive as highly sensitive."

How many other government officials before Croft had laid this trap and played this ploy on unsuspecting powermongers from the private sector? Many through the centuries. The mighty Kissinger had done it as a matter of course. An election had been won by a man named Bush through the same means. Nations had risen and fallen over the ability of people to restrict the dissemination of information by their enemies—by fully disclosing classified information to those enemies and invoking the law to keep that information under wraps.

Cummings, like so many before him, needed to know what Croft was about to show him. And like so many others, he said, "Fine. I'll accept your conditions. Just let's get on with it."

Croft handed a slate to Cummings to handprint and sign, the readout of which totally restricted discussion of what Cummings was about to see in any but a thoroughly controlled and secure environment.

Cummings palmed the slate and signed with a flourish of the lightpen, slapping the slate on the console when he was finished. "There. Now can we get on with it? What's going on? Why can't I see my son yet? And what the hell was that model of Dini—"

"The model you saw was an artifact of the difference

between our linear time stream and the aliens' multilinear one." Croft touched a control and the modeled psychometric profile of Dini Forat as a Unity alien sprang to life, towering over them, all clawed feet and flowing robes.

Cummings craned his neck to look up, toward the conical head, trying to catch sight of the sad, dark eyes. "That's not my daughter-in-law, then?" Confusion, disappointment, and relief mixed in Cummings' voice.

"That," Croft explained, "is a message carried by your daughter-in-law for the human race. A model can be interrogated. A lot of questions can be answered in the process of such an interrogation."

The Interstitial Interpreter had sent Croft a Rosetta Stone, carried by a child. Croft said to Cummings, "The Unity aliens want us to move Threshold out beyond Pluto. They are waiting for our answer, yes or no. We must respond to a delegation which will be at the Ball for another few hours. We're not sure whether we can, let alone should, answer in the affirmative. As the head of the most powerful corporate structure in the UNE, I assume you and your various companies will be a part of this massive undertaking, should we decide to go forward. So perhaps you'd care to ask a few questions of this model as to what technical capability might be necessary to accomplish the task at hand."

"I . . . I'm more interested in whether I've got a daughter-in-law or an alien posing as one," Cummings muttered half-heartedly.

"Then let us clear up that point before we get down to business," Croft said, and stabbed at his control panel like a striking snake.

"Who are you?" Croft asked the model which had been made of Dini Forat.

"I am your guide and your assistant, timely," said the model's voice.

Cummings sucked in an involuntary breath and leaned forward, composing his first question.

Simultaneously, Croft leaned back in his own chair. For the moment, he had won. He had put Cummings in a position so fully compromised that Cummings would not dare to act unilaterally in any capacity where his daughter-in-law or the Unity aliens were concerned.

As for the matter of moving Threshold to an orbit beyond Pluto, Croft still had grave doubts—not simply about the prodigious task, but about the kids who had brought the message.

And nothing this model of the Unity aliens' Interstitial Interpreter could say would allay those doubts. Unlike Cummings, Croft understood far too much about psychometric sampler-modelers to be convinced that the truth always could be found in one.

Nevertheless, for the moment, Croft was marginally in control. And time was, for once, on his side. Croft had no doubt that communicating with this model was the same as communicating directly with the actual Unity delegation that was waiting at the Ball site. If the Unity aliens could ever be said to *be* anywhere.

Croft looked up at the face of the model before him. As Cummings paused, trying to frame another question, Mickey Croft said, "May we assume that information exchanged in this mode is the same as information exchanged at the Ball site?"

The Interstitial Interpreter's form leaned forward slightly, as if to get a better look at Croft.

Or so it seemed to Mickey. Cummings was staring at him dumbfounded.

The model of the alien said, "Yesssss. All assumptions are one and the same. Time for discussions beginning."

Croft slapped a control that erased the model, and the air where the alien form had been was wiped blank, leaving only a swirl of colors and the potential of new images.

"Richard," Croft said, stretching his arms out before him and locking his fingers until the knuckles cracked, "I'm sure you realize that we cannot—do not intend—to hold your son and his wife from your custody indefinitely."

"I'm glad to hear that," said Cummings, who sounded not glad at all but confused, shaken, and uncertain.

"And I'm sure you'll agree that these complex circumstances demand that we proceed with all caution."

"Caution. Of course," Cummings replied, now a bit wary but still clearly off balance.

"One of your strongest claims has been that because of your son's initial contact with the Unity aliens, trading and commercial primacy should be yours. So I think we can come to an understanding that will allow your people to work with my people on this matter of moving the habitat—this theoretical matter of possibly moving the habitat—and do so while keeping under wraps all this classified information which you've received today, and making sure that our joint enterprise has the added benefit of your son and daughter-in-law's input. After all, those two children are our only resident experts on these aliens."

"Experts," Cummings repeated slowly.

"Experts," Croft said again, with a nod of his head and a slow-spreading smile.

CHAPTER 6

$\triangledown$

Questions of
Priorities

Vince Remson was chairing his sixth marathon seminar in so many days. Held at Spacedock Seven's secure facility, the purpose of the task force symposium was to define in detail the logistical problems involved in moving Threshold beyond Pluto. A feasibility study would be completed by the Secretariat staff using that input.

Vince couldn't get this group to realize that their job was not to debate the wisdom of moving Threshold. Remson wasn't accustomed to failure. The inability of this task force to focus on its purpose was maddening. The late addition of NAMECorp engineers—civilian contractors—to the mix, wasn't helpful.

Remson slammed his fist on the monitor controller and the embedding diagram of the spacetime route of Threshold from its current position, between Mars and Jupiter, to its projected new orbit, beyond Pluto, disappeared, taking with it all the controversial computations annotated in blue and the intersecting gravity wells and stress points plotted in red.

The blank screen that followed stopped an argument in full flower and silenced everyone in the room. Fifteen technical consultants stopped bickering, eyes front.

Finally.

Vince Remson strolled over to the blank screen and stood there, chasing a NAMECorp structural engineer back to his seat with a glare. NAMECorp had built Threshold on a government contract, awarded without a competitive bidding process because, at the time, NAMECorp had unique capabilities that made it the only shop in town that could do the job.

Now Cummings' staff was trying to assure similar primacy for the task of moving the habitat by complicating the issue beyond reasonable limits.

"Gentlemen," said Remson, "I hate to do this, but you give me no choice. Will all contractors please leave the room? In one hour, we'll reconvene with a decision as to what sort of task support is required for this mission."

The consultants and ConSec brass were spread around the long conference table at polarized distances from one another. Empty places marked hierarchal boundaries. NAMECorp functionaries rose from their places, pale-faced, and skulked away with not one word of protest.

You had to know how to play the game to win it. When the doors shut with a sigh behind them, Remson said to the government employees still present, "In one hour, I want a cost ceiling on this. I want a timetable in place that NAMECorp will be forced to meet. I want a worst case scenario with damage control measures. I want a damned evacuation scenario, if we need it—if Threshold breaks apart under the stress of moving it whole, how do we safeguard the lives of our people? And I want an alternate plan to reconfigure the habitat entirely: build a follow-on to the Stalk, and then tow the habitat modules out piecemeal. And I don't want any more arguments. Is that clear?"

Groans and sputters of protest answered him.

"Good," Remson said pleasantly. "Right now, I want our task force leader up here to thumbnail the problems, and the solutions, that we're considering. If we logically analyze the doubts you people are voicing, I think we'll find we've got a conceptual hurdle here, not an operational one."

The task force huddled, briefly, and a ConSec rear admiral waddled up to Remson and said, "We're ready to comply, Mr. Secretary."

Fine with Remson. He sat down without a word, glowering.

The navy briefer began: "As everybody knows, our technical consultants have doubts as to the viability of the move. Threshold will be far from Earth and the sun, although A-potential power sources, scalar drives, and zero-point energy can provide for the habitat's power needs with some minor reconfiguration and major retrofit that probably is overdue anyhow."

The admiral was an experienced briefer, a tall man with a shock of white hair and a cultured manner. He paused for a moment, then said: "Comments, gentlemen? Don't wait, just jump right in."

The fat lab rat wheezed and said, "I'll give you the benefit of the doubt that many of our objections are emotionally, not intellectually, based: people don't like changes. People really don't like major changes. But you're talking about punching holes in spacetime to get at the energy underneath its skin, and doing so on a day-to-day basis, not quick surgical in-and-outs. When we use A-potential energy to travel through spongeholes, we're not porting that energy around, we're porting ourselves around. Nobody knows what will happen if you open a leak, a rift, a hole in spacetime, and you won't allow it to seal itself up again. That's a simple way of putting it, but you're talking about siphoning a steady stream of energy out of a balloon on whose outer skin exists everything which we understand as reality. We build scalar drives, A-potential weapons, and use zero-point energy for communications across massive distances, but we don't really understand how the universe works. You're asking us to make up for the lack of available solar energy out beyond Pluto, and nobody in any of my physics departments is ready to swear that you can do that in a nonstressed, noncomplexified space where the interaction of solar gravity wells is minimal."

The fat man slapped his jellylike arms against blossoming thighs and his whole body rippled side to side in an exaggerated negative motion. Remson could hear him wheezing from the effort that the long speech—or standing upright so long—had cost him.

The admiral said, "Questions, anyone? Counters to the labs' positions?

A ConSpaceCom colonel said, "Seems to us that the real security problem here isn't a power problem. We're convinced from in-house discussions that we could tow the habitat intact, although the Secretariat might be happier with a new Stalk that incorporated new technology. The real problem lies in the fact that there's no advantage in this whole undertaking to anybody but the Unity aliens, who are asserting that their ships and members need basing facilities where spacetime is less warped by so many intersecting gravity wells. So we see a two-fold problem."

The seated colonel held up two fingers. "One, we've got an intel problem: our intelligence component isn't happy with doing anything radical unless there's a clear benefit to our side. We don't know nearly enough about these aliens to be inviting them into our solar system, despite the Secretariat's position to the contrary." The ConSpaceCom officer, who was in plainclothes and who hadn't bothered to hand out his card, ticked off his first point.

Then came his second objection: "And, two: security components want to have a clear understanding of what the downside might be if we make ourselves more accessible to these aliens. Do we want to make commerce easier for them? And does that mean we're making commerce harder for ourselves? Where's the upside? Does the Secretariat have information it's withholding? Can humans be comfortable for long periods of time where the gravity stresses we evolved in aren't present? Why should we go forward with any abrupt change in policy when we've had so little contact with these Unity aliens and know so little about them? What was wrong with them building an embassy out at the Ball site, the way we gave them permission to do? We—"

"That's enough," Remson interrupted sharply, usurping the briefer's prerogative before things got any worse. "What's your name, Colonel?"

"Martin, Mr. Secretary," said the ConSpaceCom colonel, looking at his hands with too-bright eyes.

"Don't sandbag these proceedings, Mister. Don't even think about it." Some damage was already done, but Remson was angry and determined to handle the grenade that ConSpaceCom had just thrown in his lap. At least he understood the problem now: he was facing concerted bureaucratic resistance, not contractor games from NAMECorp. "If you think you can stop this project by questioning policy in the name of security, think again. This session is classified, but we have the ability to take the whole matter public. It's to the benefit of humanity to establish relations with the Unity worlds: that's not yours to determine. It's a given in these meetings. Or should be. And if the military tries to obstruct the Secretariat, I assure you, everybody on

Threshold, from Blue North to the Loader Zone, will be informed through public media and declaratory language of the great opportunity awaiting the human race. If we need to, the Secretariat will convene a Security Council meeting. Got that, mister?"

The colonel didn't look up. His neck flushed red. The room was completely quiet. Into that silence, Remson threw his final challenge.

"Give me a finished report by the end of the week, with cogent operational recommendations. If you throw this up to the policy level and start an internal debate, you'll lose the ability to input even the operational planning. Policy responsibility for these matters, and the relevant decision making, are a Secretariat prerogative. This whole program is running out of the Secretariat Alien Affairs office. Period. Now stop squabbling and get me a logistical report I can use. Fast."

He turned on his heel and charged the door, which got out of his way with a hiss. He was going to make sure Martin realized that his career had taken a wrong turn and early retirement was his only option. It wouldn't solve the whole problem, but it would serve as an object lesson to the rest of them.

Remson had more to do than babysit these symposia. He had a model of an alien consular official—or the closest equivalent—in the Secretariat. His boss was asking questions of it as if it were a real person, not an artifact. The mystery surrounding the creation of that artifact should have told Mickey that the Forat-Cummings girl shouldn't be turned loose on Threshold.

Because maybe she wasn't the Forat-Cummings girl at all but some alien construct.

Intelligence problems. The only real intelligence problems in the room that Remson had just left was the sum of the IQs of the people inside. The real intelligence problems surrounding this first contact with aliens capable of presenting a threat to humanity were manifold.

And if those problems turned out to foreshadow real-time threats, there wasn't a weapon in the UNE arsenal capable of giving the Unity aliens a run for their money.

So when the Unity aliens wanted you to move your governmental center a few billion miles, you said, "No problem." Because the alternative might be worse. Lots worse.

CHAPTER 7

$\triangledown$

Stories From Beyond

"Ricky, you've got a great opportunity here," said Richard the Second to his son and heir. He put an arm around the shoulders of Richard Cummings III as they walked the parapet of the Cummings Blue North mansion. Ahead was a stairwell down which his son's new wife—she should rot in hell—waited with that dim, glassy-eyed stare. Above was a dome through which a man could see the stars.

"I know, Father." The boy exhaled in a long-suffering sigh. "But that's the trouble." Rick's tone was patronizing. "I'm not sure you understand the opportunity at all."

Richard stopped and took his arm from his son's shoulders. The boy turned to face him. It was all Cummings, Senior could do not to backhand his son across the face.

"Patronizing, arrogant, holier-than-thou . . . what did I do to deserve this from you, Rick? Just tell me? You smuggle contraband life-forms, drugs, and what have you. You get involved with a fundamentalist Muslim sect that likes to lop off the heads of their law-breakers in the Medinan town square. You elope and nearly get yourself killed in the process. You get rescued or captured and brainwashed by aliens nobody's ever encountered before, and you expect me to listen to a lecture on my opportunities? From you? From your Medinan whore? Or from your cone-headed alien buddies?"

"Dad—" The pain in the boy's voice would haunt Cummings forever. The look of shock and horror and hurt on Rick's face flared nakedly, to be replaced too soon with guarded, petulant wariness. "You don't understand. None of you do. We should never have come back. When we get home—"

Richard Cummings balled his fists at his sides to avoid striking his son. "Home? Somewhere in an alien stronghold? This is your home, son. What do you think I've spent my life building an empire for? You have responsibilities here, or have you forgotten? All of this—"

"Don't say it. Don't say, 'all of this can be yours someday,' because I don't want it."

Richard Cummings' temper flared. "Fine. Then you won't have it." He pulled out the memo pad from his breast pocket, actuated it, watching Rick's face, and said into its microphone grille: "This day and date. I, Richard Cummings, Junior, being of sound mind and body, et cetera, hereby fully and completely disinherit and remove Richard Cummings the Third from my will. Legal, execute, and annotate this order immediately, making sure that Junior benefits in no way from my estate, my death, or any NAMECorp holding or corporate entity now or in future. Effective immediately."

Cummings glared silently at his son for three heartbeats before he put the memo pad away. Then he gawked disbelievingly at the unresisting, unprotesting creature that had once been his son and heir, as if Rick had turned into a cone-headed alien with weird physiology, the way he kept expecting the Forat girl to do at any moment. "They *have* brainwashed you, haven't they?"

No son of his would have stood there and allowed the training and compromises, the endless preparation and arduous schooling of a lifetime, to be thrown away in one moment of family dispute.

But it had happened. It happened because the boy before him was no longer the son he'd raised.

Rick opened his mouth to speak, wet his dry lips with his tongue, and Richard's heart leapt. A hug, a kiss, a tearful apology, and all would be right between them once again. He'd void his order as quickly as he'd given it. . . .

Rick said defiantly, "You can bet your empire that the aliens have brainwashed me, in your terms. They've given me a chance to clean out my mind, to throw away all the filth you and your friends have filled me with. You bet I'm brainwashed. The Unity aliens washed me clean of all your greed and stupidity. They've shown me that there's more to life than cutting deals and making money, if that's what you mean by brainwashing. How much money do you need, Dad? How much power have you got, when you don't have a moment to call your own? When do you say enough? When you are going to have time for a life? You never had time for my life. Time is what's important. Time is the only irreproducible commodity. Time is all any of us have...."

"Sophomoric bullshit," said Cummings, his heart sinking down through his chest toward his feet. Before he showed weakness in front of his son, he turned away. Before he wept openly, he strode past Rick and toward the stairwell. Without turning around, he said, "I've never sanctioned this marriage of yours, you know. Neither has the Mullah Forat. Her father's on his way to Threshold. I'm sending word to him that, when he arrives, he and I are going to have a long and serious talk about you and your Muslim lady. Just remember, Mr. Cummings, oil and water don't mix."

Then he couldn't say any more, or his voice would betray him. The stairs were ahead. He had to blink the tears from his eyes or he'd fall over himself, trying to walk down them.

A stairwell to Hell could have been no harder to face for a father who had just lost his only son and heir to an alien power he did not understand.

CHAPTER 8

<svg> (decorative divider with downward triangle) </svg>

Out On The Town

"Come on, Dini, hurry," her husband called urgently. From the dark innards of a nondescript car that had pulled up to the Cummings mansion's front steps, his hand waved her on.

She knew this was wrong, but Rick had been insistent. Remson would be very angry at her—at them both—and Secretary Croft would be disappointed. They were on their honor to behave.

She knew that slinking off in a ground car pilfered from somewhere by Rick, to find some person in the Loader Zone, where only criminals and subhumans lived and worked, was not behaving, in the eyes of consular officials.

But Rick had had some terrible argument with his father, and her husband was inconsolable, full of anger and as wild as he'd been when they'd stolen a NAMECorp spaceship and run off to the stars together.

As soon as she was inside, Rick thumbed the door controller, the door shut, and he pulled the car away. Dini looked back longingly at the Cummings mansion. Such a place. Not even the Secretariat had its elegance, its exquisite appointments, its baronial splendor. The Cummings residence squatted atop Threshold as an eagle topped a standard. It should have been the capital of the UNE, to her way of thinking: the seat of power.

Inside had been every modern convenience that had been lacking on Medina: electrostatic showers and pure water bidets, foods from around the universe, human and automated servants of every sort. And antiques from Earth.

She had seen Earthish delights beyond price. She had walked an "atrium" and strolled a rose garden! A garden! Imagine, a personal garden of marvelous maturity and broad expanse.

Rick had picked a red rose for her and put it in her hair. She had never touched a rose, let alone smelled the real fragrance of one. It was heady to disregard such great wealth.

But Rick was adamant. Grim. Even proud, when he'd told her there was no place for them in the Cummings household anymore.

And she'd felt guilty, thinking of her pets at home and the green hills under lavender skies that were her true home now.

Rick wanted to leave Threshold. "While we still can," he'd said.

He was afraid of their parents, she knew. He drove hunched down, manually in control of the car although a red light complained from its control panel that he should cede control to the traffic center and sit back in his seat.

He did not. She tried three times to engage him in conversation, but he wouldn't talk; he was negotiating traffic she didn't understand, guiding the car into and out of tunnels striped with white guide lights and warning arrows that indicated turn-offs to adjoining tubes, lifts, and levels.

Once she thought she saw a sign that said LOADER ZONE, and cried out: "Rick! There! You've missed it!"

"Shut up!" he snapped at her, without looking away from the traffic that was all weaving lights ahead and beside them. "You don't know what you're talking about. We're nowhere near there. You'll get us into an accident."

So she sat back, hurt, and rode in silence, surprised at the vehemence of his reaction.

She was sure she had seen such a sign, but the truth of the matter, obviously, was beside the point.

Rick drove and drove and, finally, took a turn from the main tunnel into a side artery. By then, she had realized that only a Stalk dweller could have made sense of the spiderweb of passages that interlinked Threshold.

She wanted to say she was sorry, but one look at her husband's face told her she should not say anything. He was still radiating anger. He was full of frustration.

The car pulled to an abrupt stop, throwing her forward against her seat restraint.

Still he would not look at her. "Get out," he said.

The door on her side opened, taking her chest restraint with it. Outside she saw a public tubeway. Behind and before theirs, other private cars were stopped. On her side, traffic whizzed by. She nearly stepped into it and caused a whole raft of vehicles to veer to the right in deft synchronization.

"Get out of the damned traffic!" Rick shouted.

She ran around the car. "What about the car?"

"Screw the car. Let my father pay the violation!" Rick shoved her toward the public tubeway.

Here were more folk, more decisions, and finally a bank of lifts and a public tubeway.

Rick slapped a lift button and she stood meekly behind him. She knew now that she had been right: he'd been lost. She must pretend now that there had been no error. He was very like his father, was her husband. She hadn't known how much, until she'd been in the Cummings household these last few days. They could not abide errors in others and refused to be accountable for them in themselves.

When the lift opened, out came a camel-lipped, furry-cheeked Epsilonian woman with beads in the braided mane of her hump, her tail coiled around her arm. Beside her, a humanoid with desert waterpouches in his cheeks and semitransparent dual eyelids made way for her.

"This way to the Loader Zone," Rick said flippantly and with a superiority she did not understand. Rick brushed by the pair without waiting for them to exit.

This awkwardness reminded Dini that Rick had the prejudices of the privileged, and that subhumans and bioengineered humans were not treated as equally here as in the Secretariat.

When they disembarked from the lift, the Loader Zone was bustling with beings of questionable purpose and provenance. Bar signs blinked, and the exposed strutwork above sputtered and seemed to shiver as lights struggled for their share of inadequate power. She remembered this place, yes she did, from her first visit to Threshold.

But Rick did not want to have a good time here, tonight. He hustled her toward some secret destination unremittingly. They passed food stands offering exotic smells and restaurants spilling the music of mysterious worlds out onto streets, which were marked with color-coded bars along their centers, so dim and faint with age that Dini could make nothing of the information they contained.

Buildings loomed here. There was no image of a sky above, only the skeleton of Threshold. Sometimes she thought she saw people—or other beings—climbing among the strutwork above her head. Sometimes she thought she heard the music of her homeworld. Sometimes she saw small creatures scurrying in the dimness from one refuse pile to another. Always Rick propelled her forward. Her feet began to hurt. Her head was already swimming from the sensory assault of so many beings gathered in one place. Unhappy beings. Frightened beings. Oppressed beings.

There was no oppression at home in the Unity. Everything had its place and time and was friendly to biologically anchored beings. Not here. Time was the enemy. It was unflagging. It chased these folk, dogging their tired and hungry steps.

She longed to leave here. Rick had promised they could leave soon. Now he would hardly talk to her. It was her fault that he had been disinherited. Perhaps he was not as anxious as he claimed to leave Threshold, and all his family wealth, for her love and the Unity.

Perhaps he was having second thoughts. Perhaps . . . he didn't love her as much as he thought.

He wasn't acting as though he loved her. His grip on her hand was hard, sweaty, and far too tight. By it, he dragged her forward.

Panting, she caught up and said, "Rick, I love you." She said it very softly, in case the saying of the words would further anger him.

He said, without slowing, "I love you too, Dini," but it sounded like a rote formula, a prayer said too many times, a greeting without feeling.

She missed her pets. She missed her home on a green hill under lavender skies. For the first time since she had fled Medinan justice with her lover, she even missed her father. Just a little. Not as he was now, but as he had been, long ago, when life had been simple and she was a child of the desert on Medina.

Rick stopped and she nearly rushed by him. He jerked on her hand to bring her up short. "Here."

She looked where he meant, up crumbling steps, to a door recessed in darkness.

He went up to it and pounded. He pushed a plate, punched a button.

A grille crackled to life. A voice said, "Who?"

"Rick Cummings. You don't know me, but—"

"Then I don't want to know you. Go away."

The speaker grille grated to silence.

Rick pounded again. He released Dini's hand and she rubbed both her arms. It was dank here, chilly.

Eventually, the speaker grille responded to Rick's persistent demands. "Okay, okay, Sport. You and the lady can come in for a minute or two, stop making a scene."

The door slid open to reveal a human person with no shirt on. Dini nearly covered her eyes, then realized she must be brave and brought her hand away from her mouth where it had come to rest.

"This way," said the man with no shirt, an earring, and a long braid like a woman's down his back.

In they went, following the naked back and the braid.

"Watch your step."

She tried but tripped anyway over cables and pieces of metal strewn over the ill-lit floor.

"What was it you wanted, Sport?" said the half-naked man, lounging on a piece of derelict spacecraft, his navel undulating like a bellydancer's as he breathed.

"I heard you have a box that does funny things," said Rick in a voice she'd never heard him use.

"I got a bunch a boxes do a bunch o' things, Sport. Got some that don't do squat, that's why they're here—for repair. Somethin' I can fix fer you?"

"I heard you made a box that opened the Ball out at Spacedock Seven," said Rick.

"Yeah? Who told you that?" The half-naked man's navel stopped undulating. He stopped breathing, then began again, very shallowly. He crossed his arms over his chest.

"Let's just say we have it on good information," said Rick.

Dini said, "We know the fabricators—"

The half-naked man stared at her, leaning forward. "No shit?" he breathed.

"Shut up," Rick said, whirling on her with a glare, and then back to the half-naked man. "You made a box for someone named Joe South, a pilot. It opened the Ball. I'd like you to build me a similar box. Or rent me one you've got."

"If I had any such box, buying one would be way above your paygrade, Sport." The man took his braid in his fingers, put the end in his mouth, and twirled it with his tongue. His earring gleamed in the dim light, and as his eyes met hers, Dini felt a deep and penetrating curiosity and a predatory acquisitiveness behind it.

Her husband retorted, "Try me, *Sport*. Name a reasonable price, or maybe I'll decide I've got the wrong aftermarketeer."

What was Rick doing this for? They had a toolbox of their own, given them by the Unity aliens—to be used only if needed. She wasn't sure, until this moment, that Rick knew she'd brought it. Or perhaps he *didn't* know she'd brought it.

That was it. He didn't know. She'd assumed he'd known. There hadn't been time to discuss it, with all the preparations for coming here that were made so fast and simultaneously. Tense, again: past, present, future.

Future. Perhaps Rick truly was changed by contact with his father. Perhaps all of his Earthly riches, and his father's other wealth, were too much to give up for love. Perhaps he wanted his own toolbox because he was going to stay with his father's people.

Perhaps that was why Rick had brought her here; perhaps he did not love her and wanted his own toolbox to use for his own purposes. Perhaps this was his way of telling her that everything between them was over.

She nearly fled. But the two men were deep in discussions of price and purpose, technical talk. And all the while, the half-naked man kept staring.

She took a step backward, uncomfortable under the scrutiny of the half-naked man and the possibility of her husband's betrayal. Oh, why had they ever come back here?

"So, we have a deal. You take us where we want to go and bring your box. We'll pay for the rental of the ship, your time, and the box."

The half-naked man said, "As long as the little lady comes along, and the price is as we agreed, you got yourself a deal, Sport." He straightened up, strode past Rick, and held out a hand to her. "Name is Sling, Ma'am. Good to meetcha."

The smell of him was overwhelming. The intrusion of his flesh into her personal space made her retreat from the hand as if it were a desert snake ready to strike.

She couldn't touch the hand. Know the man. She wouldn't.

Rick understood. He interposed himself between her and the half-naked man called Sling. "My wife," said Rick, "is from Medina. Medinan women live sheltered lives."

Sling pulled back his hand and wiped it on his trousers. "Sorry, Ma'am." His jaw was stubbled. When he grinned, white teeth showed. "But you just relax, now. You're safe with me. I done more of this black box work than anybody else on Threshold. In fact, I done all of it. Want a beer?"

The beer was blue and she declined. Alcohol was not a Medinan drink. But Rick partook, and he and the man called Sling soon were laughing together.

She sat in a corner, listening, waiting, wondering, trying not to worry, until Sling left the room and returned with a shirt over his nakedness and a black box in his hand. "Okay, guys, we're cleared for departure on a good-as-gold vector. Have your tickets ready."

She didn't understand what was happening until Rick saw her consternated face and said, "Come on, Dini. We're leaving. Now. Mr. Sling is going to take us out to the Ball site. We can make it from there. No one will think to try stopping us. We're as good as home."

As good as home. He did love her.

She was nearly faint with relief. She didn't care whose toolkit they used to make the crossing, or whether Rick had first come here to do otherwise and then changed his mind when his temper cooled. She didn't even bother asking why he wished to leave by way of the Ball.

The sooner she was off Threshold, and back home in Unity space with her pets and her husband close by, the happier she would be.

Secretary Croft would be disappointed in her. She had given her word. But he had everything he needed, now, to make good decisions. She and Rick had made theirs. She was sure of that, at last.

CHAPTER 9

▽

Vanished

The children were gone. Disappeared. Vanished into nowhere. Or vanished into Unity space, which might be one and the same, for all Mickey knew for certain.

So said Remson over the comlink from Spacedock Seven that Mickey had ordered patched through to him in the modeler bay.

"It's not anything that could have been anticipated, Vince," said Croft kindly but briskly. Nothing was so demoralizing to a first-class trouble-shooter such as Remson as the unequivocal evidence of failure.

The tiny replica of Remson's face in the palm-sized monitor on the modeler console betrayed no sign of distress. "We should have been prepared for something like this, sir, and we weren't. I should have kept Reice with them. Somebody else could have handled the task force evaluation."

"And what would Reice have done, made a recording of unexplainable phenomena, as he did the last time? I'm coming out there, Vince. As soon as I do something about the uproar in the Cummings camp. Stay put. If you come across any phenomenological evidence that will show that the Secretariat in no way colluded, abetted, supported, or facilitated the Cummings couple's disappearance, it would be helpful."

"I'll come up with something, sir."

"No, Vince, I don't mean 'manufacture.' " Croft had to be sure that Remson understood. "It's not crucial to disprove accusations that haven't been made yet." But would be made, would be made soon—and at full voice. "Stay with your primary priority. I need you focused on the task force. Task the phenomenology of the children's—" He must stop calling them that! "—disappearance to ConSec here. Have the point of contact for that investigation report to my office for further instructions. And, Vince. . . ."

"Yes, sir?" said Mickey's executive officer.

"Have a good day."

The image shrank to a tiny dot, then that faded away altogether.

Croft sat back in his chair and stared up at the model of the Interstitial Interpreter, slowly pivoting before him, as the modeler refreshed itself in standby mode.

One way or another, fate was pulling Mickey Croft inexorably out into space, toward the Ball—and perhaps beyond.

He knew he should exit the modeler bay and face straight on the uproar caused by the disappearance of the Cummings boy and his wife. He was hiding in here, playing with his toys, some would say.

Putting off the moment of confrontation with Richard the Second. Staving off the necessity of getting into yet another spacecraft and personal life-support helmet and suit and confronting his fears at the Ball site. Why did custom dictate that the egregiously restrictive helmet and suit be called a Manned Maneuvering Unit? To Mickey Croft, the term seemed like an oxymoron. Wrapping oneself in an MMU was an experience most like therapy in a sensory deprivation tank. Maneuvering in one was confounding to one of Croft's limited technical ability.

But another junket to the Ball's accursed coordinates was in Croft's future as ineluctably as yet another confrontation with Richard Cummings the Second.

Croft reached out to touch a control on his com system and hesitated. Then he stabbed a button that forwarded his incoming calls to his Secretariat office.

Let Cummings wait. Let the task of finding fault and apportioning blame in the disappearance of Romeo Cummings and Juliet Forat-Cummings wait, as well. Mickey Croft was Secretary General of the United Nations of Earth and he had certain prerogatives.

He didn't feel like talking to Cummings now, therefore he would not talk to him. The uproar over the children's disappearance would be waiting for him whenever he left here. Which he was not going to do until he was ready.

When he was ready, he would plunge back into the tempest and let himself be drawn by life's currents out to the Ball and what awaited him there.

Now, he would stubbornly refuse to be hurried, or distracted from the task at hand, or allow his schedule to be made by events, no matter how critical. This was just another crisis in an unending stream of crises. What was the point of being SecGen if you couldn't control your own time?

The model of the Interstitial Interpreter spooled slowly around to face him, and Mickey Croft halted its progress with a touch. "Tell mē, Your Excellency, why the site of the Ball is not suitable for a Unity embassy, as we once agreed it was."

The model responded, "Mickeycroft, to be making a new link between worlds forever, there must be some reciprocal moving of things in time. Discontinuities affect possibilities, for humans and their universe shape. In clearer space, determinate time is possible."

"But, concretely, what purpose is served by this?" Mickey asked, still going carefully, still half-convinced that the model he spoke to in his private modeling bay was no less a representative of the Unity than the manifestation of Unity power he had spoken to aboard a teardrop ship in a dreamlike spacetime out by the Ball.

"Proof of commitment. Intent. Realization of possibility. Coming to meet," hissed the apparition that had come like a wraith in the wake of Dini Forat-Cummings and stayed behind like a ghost that had finally found the perfect castle to haunt.

The model was more than a model, this Mickey had already determined. But what was it? The children had been more than children, and where were they? Gone as they had come, Vince Remson thought, vanished without a trace to prove they'd ever been here, except a swathe of diplomatic wreckage left behind and this model, which was some incomprehensible channel to a race whose phenomenal now was nothing like the simple, four-dimensional domain of human beings.

The model of the Interstitial Interpreter regarded Croft with the same sad-eyed look that had mesmerized him aboard the teardrop flagship of the Unity, and the eyes left the head of the Unity being and seemed to float inches from his, the way the eyes of the actual Interpreter had then.

Mist seemed to fill the modeler bay as it had filled the teardrop ship, and unseen pots of smoking incense held by an invisible honor guard filled the air with a scent like gardenias and jasmine.

The smell brought back too many memories and broke too many natural laws. Croft was filled with fear, apprehension, foreboding. Perhaps "ghost" was the synonym for this model, but not the ghost of poor Yorick or any other spirit of departed humanity, real or fantastical. Rather, a ghost in the machine. A virus in the computer. A secret invasion underway that the Secretariat was not prepared to fight because he, Michael Croft, had refused to recognize the enemy when first confronted by it.

Was the Stalk's artificially intelligent memory core being infected by the model before him? Was it too late to do anything but follow the Unity's direction?

All of Threshold depended on computer power for survival. Without redundantly integrated and self-replicating, self-correcting systems, no habitation of space was possible, not on so grand a scale.

The model began rotating again, since Croft was no longer questioning it. To see what would happen, Croft posed a question while its back was to him.

"Where are the Cummings boy and the Forat-Cummings girl?"

If this manifestation was a real link to a Unity intelligence, not just a model of one, it could give him many answers to many plaguing questions.

He held his breath, conscious of the smell that filled his nostrils but couldn't be real: smells were artifacts of bits of matter entering the nose. Real smoke with real molecules of odor-producing pheromones could not be generated by a computer model.

The stately progress of the rotating model ceased as, abruptly, it faced him to answer his question.

That shouldn't happen, either.

The model responded, "Our children have come home to us."

Note the syntax, Croft: our children—possessive. Have come: a fait accompli. Home to us—

Croft couldn't deal with the implications.

"What will happen if I stop all work on moving Threshold, rescind permission for the creation of a Unity embassy, and recall my ambassadorial staff which I sent back with your first delegation?

"Nothing will happen," said the Interstitial Interpreter's model.

Threat or promise, Croft had had enough.

He cleared the modeler of the image abruptly and hesitated. He could bring up other models, to test the system: Riva Lowe, his ambassador to Unity space, perhaps, or Commander Joe South, whom Croft had sent with her. It had been too long since he heard from them.

But if he brought up their models and found that the models seemed to be communicating with him, not simply responding as a good psychometric model should, as an analog of the person in question, then what?

Before him now was a simple, light-swirled space full of holographic potential, not a mathematically impossible, direct communication to another spacetime or beyond the boundary conditions of the universe as man had always known it.

What possible benefit could there be to either race from commerce across such a gulf of different realities? What did the aliens have to gain from contact? Power beyond man's wildest dreams was clearly at the heart of Unity technologies, but the price . . .

And what did the aliens want from humanity in return?

These were questions that the model would answer only in riddles, if Croft were so foolish as to ask them.

He shut off the modeler entirely and brought up the lights in the modeler bay. Clear white light that simulated the daylight of Earth drove away the lingering smell in Croft's nostrils.

If the price to the human race was a loss of control such as Mickey had been experiencing since his first physical contact with the Unity aliens, perhaps the price was too dear by half.

Resolutely, he stood up. He forced himself to stand straight. He walked briskly to the bay door and beyond into the empty control room.

At the anteroom door, he hesitated, looking back through the two line of sight windows of glass beyond which were the modeler and the ghost which had come to haunt his castle.

Then he palmed the plate which opened the door that separated his sanctum from the everyday reality of Threshold, determined to do what needed to be done to restore order to his world, no matter how desperate the measures.

This uncertainty in the face of change could not be allowed to continue. Inaction ensured only a random result. Most likely the most undesirable one.

As he left the modeler bay's anteroom, Croft found himself in a small crowd: the modeler technicians, waiting for him to leave, were augmented by ConSec staffers and three Assistant Deputy Undersecretaries from the Secretariat with urgent messages for him.

Everyone started talking at once.

Croft held up his hand for silence. Among the gathered faces, there was only one he recognized sufficiently to put a name to it. Croft said, "Mr. Reice, Secretaries, walk with me."

The Assistant Deputy Undersecretaries jostled for position on Croft's right. Reice, on his left, was carrying an ominously full black bag.

"One at a time, gentlemen," Croft said, and pointed at random to one of the Assistant Deputies. There'd been a time when he'd have had their names on the tip of his tongue. He'd prided himself on it.

Never mind. The first, balding and wearing eyeglasses to demonstrate his Conservative bent and serious nature, which cared not at all for cosmetic augmentation, said, "Sir, Mr. Cummings of NAMECorp wishes to see you at your earliest convenience."

"I haven't one, not for him. I'll be in touch with him tomorrow. Pressing business, and all that."

The staffer raised one eyebrow above his mock-tortoise eyeglass frames and scurried away toward a bank of lifts.

"Next?"

The second said, "We have a communiqué from the Medinan embassy that the Mullah Forat will be docking this afternoon, and is requesting immediate access to his daughter. The Medinans are pulling every stunt from accusing us of holding her against her will despite diplomatic immunity to threatening to request an emergency Security Council session. They've also requested that we facilitate a meeting between the Medinan delegation and Cummings."

The second staffer represented the Medinan desk, then. Croft said, "Tell Beni Forat we don't have his daughter, or any information on her whereabouts. Remind him that he never asked us to monitor her activities. And tell him that we'll be glad to arrange meetings with any Threshold citizens as long as all protocols are observed and the Medinans behave themselves. Then talk to Cummings' private secretary and see if some sort of reception can be arranged. Make sure you're at any meeting you set up for the two of them. I'm officially out of pocket for the next forty-eight hours, so there can't be a Security Council session until I return. Our apologies for any inconvenience, and so forth. Got all that?"

The Assistant Deputy Undersecretary for Interstellar Affairs/Medinan Desk assured Croft that he indeed had every nuance and fell back.

The third staffer said, when Mickey eyed him, "Sir, we have an interim report from Mr. Remson's task force, and a request for permission to proceed—"

"Permission denied. I'm going out to the Ball site myself. No action is to be taken until I've reviewed all the details personally."

"Yes, sir," said the staffer doubtfully.

"And get with Mr. Cummings' office. Tell them that there'll be no further work for his firm on the Threshold logistical problem until I'm satisfied that everything is proceeding smoothly. Make the stop-work order retroactive to this morning. Make it clear that no hours are billable until further notice."

"Yes, sir," said the staffer, happier now that he could do some damage to someone.

Hitting Cummings hard, in the pocketbook where it would hurt, was Croft's way of reminding the NAMECorp magnate to be on his best behavior while Dini's father, the Mullah Beni Forat, was in town.

The staffer hurried away in a duck walk that testified to shoes too stylish to be comfortable and a new sense of importance too inflated not to give nightmares to the first luckless Cummings employee he contacted.

"And you, Mr. Reice?" Croft sighed, left with only the ConSec lieutenant accompanying him.

"Mr. Secretary, I've got some tracking information on those runaway kids, sir. Mr. Remson thought you would want it immediately."

And by courier. These halls were Mickey's private preserve. They turned a corner into a low-ceilinged secure corridor whose length was baffled with cloth constructs and tapestries and lit with fluorescents whose white noise defeated most recording equipment.

"What I'd like immediately is a summary, in one sentence. Or less, Mr. Reice."

"The kids are clearly no longer on Threshold, which means they're either being hidden on a ship somewhere nearby, or they've made a break for it. We're checking passenger manifests of outgoing traffic now."

"That's two sentences, Mr. Reice."

"Sorry, sir. I also brought a progress report from the Task Force. . . ."

"Give it to me now. I'll read it on my way out to the Ball site. I assume you're staying here to continue your investigation?"

Reice handed over the black bag, saying a bit wistfully, "I thought that was what you'd want, sir."

Croft sent the ConSec staffer off to make sure a fast cruiser was ready and waiting to take him out to the Ball.

The black bag in his hand was heavy. It represented thousands of man-hours squeezed into a very few days. If anyone, even Remson, could have been trusted with Croft's evaluation of the true nature of the modeler data taken from Dini Forat, much of this dithering could have been avoided.

But what did you say? Threshold has already been invaded, penetrated, and possibly compromised at its heart by the Unity aliens?

Croft wondered, all the long journey out to the Ball site in the sleek ConSec cruiser's VIP cabin, what use there was in pretending that he was in control when, clearly, he was not.

Although, he was trying his best to pretend. Space travel had never been his favorite pastime. Now, it excited all the phenomena he had been so stolidly trying to contain: time slipped back and forth for him, yawning endlessly, then compressing itself.

Reading the progress report Vince's task force had prepared was as arduous as reading the complete works of Henry James and as inconclusive as his own state of mind.

When the ConSec cruiser came up on the Ball site, the intercom in his little cabin crackled and a voice told him that if he wished to see the docking maneuver, he should come forward.

Forward he went, and there was the Ball. He sank into a copilot station and forced himself to look at it. Accursed thing, featureless and round. Was it a Stonehenge or a Rosetta Stone? Was it a place, or a portal?

He hadn't a single person on his staff who knew the answer to even those simple questions. And now the Ball would again be at the coordinates of controversy. Perhaps they should destroy the thing. Or find a way, as rumor said was possible, to get inside it. Joe South had gotten inside the Ball, so his records and some supporting evidence claimed, but Croft had sent South off to the Unity with the new ambassador.

Another error. Another piece of faulty judgment. Another decision whose provenance he now doubted was his own addled, aging brain.

The Ball didn't metamorphose under his scrutiny, as others had claimed to see it do. It didn't open a mouth to swallow him. It didn't change colors. It didn't disappear to reveal anything alien behind or within it.

It just sat there, looking like a Christmas ornament on a toothpick stand. And then, for just a moment, Mickey Croft thought he saw a leading edge of sunrise, a shimmer of color, lions holding open the doors of a portal, and dragons within the portal, weaving reality in great clawed hands.

He grasped the arms of his chair, and the phantasm obligingly disappeared. He had been reading too many reports. He had eyestrain. The pilot beside him was busy with docking maneuvers. Today had been a busy day.

Croft wanted only to leave the vessel, to walk over consistent ground. He wanted to greet Remson with no sliding of his person through collapsing spaces, no climbing of Escher-like stairs into peripheral dimensions, no treading of Penrose tiles into eternity as he tried to shake Vince's hand.

It was physical contact that kicked off the worst of Croft's symptoms, he knew. The interval in the modeler bay had almost made him forget the horrors of coming loose from Euclidian geometry.

Euclidian metaphysicis, now, that was another way to look at the phenomenal world. But Croft must look at the face of Remson, swimming before him, and make sense of the words coming out of Remson's mouth in backward streams of alphabet letters.

Somehow, the Secretary General of the UNE managed to make the long walk into Remson's ad hoc Spacedock Seven office without falling over himself, becoming a public spectacle, or saying anything to betray his sensory distress when faced with simple tasks such as climbing the stairless ramp that led into the bowels of the facility without sliding back down to the bottom and having to start all over again.

Remson was certain that the lovers had come as far as the Ball. "Mickey, I'm sure of it. They must have been smuggled out here by someone—or some*thing*. We logged an approach to the Ball that probably wasn't an error on the part of a freighter pilot. And maybe we had an unscheduled EVA. But the freighter was in heavy traffic, and it wasn't that far off course. There was no reason to think twice about it at Traffic Control. I wasn't even informed at the time. Only later, when we had a . . . disturbance here. You know the kind I mean."

"Lions and the portals and dragons all the way down," Croft said under his breath.

Vince Remson's head snapped up and he squinted at Croft as if Mickey had suddenly combusted before his eyes.

"You saw something on your approach vector?"

"I see lots of things, these days, Vince. Now what shall we do about children who travel in high circles in ways we don't understand?"

Remson got up and paced his Y Ring office until Croft saw a parade of Remsons following each other in close succession, a hundred Remsons, in single file, each with hands clasped behind a bent back, each with a bowed head.

Remson said, "Those kids didn't debark with the freighter, or with any other ship, onto Spacedock Seven. Either somebody's hiding them here for some reason or other, or they're gone. Okay. But how? Where? Here? In the Ball, if anybody can live in there? And why?"

"All work on the Threshold move has to stop, Vince, until we have some answers."

"I heard."

"Find me some answers, Vince. Or at least the right questions to ask the Unity."

Remson came toward Croft and a fan of Remsons followed, a conga line of individuals inhabiting every iota of space between Remson's starting point and Mickey Croft.

It was too crowded in here.

Croft said, "I'm staying out here with you until we know what we need to do next."

Next. The concept was central to man's survival in the universe: action, duration, event, and result.

Were the children here now? Did it matter? Was Remson, the most efficient of Croft's staff, aware of how contaminated his own reasoning was becoming?

Or was everything merely proceeding logically to an endpoint that Mickey Croft couldn't understand, but which, when reached, would give mankind gifts beyond measure.

Croft was too exhausted from the process of discovery to credit any speculation as to the quality of result.

The children had seemed happy. Now they were gone. Croft should be happy, too: he had avoided yet another confrontation with Richard the Second, and the beginning of a new round of difficulties with the Mullah Forat.

Work on moving Threshold anywhere was now stopped until Mickey was satisfied as to the risk involved. He should have done it long ago, perhaps. But time had less and less meaning, these days.

Outside, close by Spacedock Seven, the Ball awaited, with its leonine guards watchful and, within, seen dimly through his aging eyes, dragons upon dragons knitting spacetime unto eternity.

If the lions had greeted the vanished children, and remanded them into the hands of the dragons that Croft had seen, then he was worrying for no reason. Wasn't he? They had gone where they wished, of their own accord. Hadn't they?

To get the right answers, one had to ask the proper questions. If Croft had been asking the wrong questions of the Interstitial Interpreter all this time, and of himself, then whose fault was that? But what were the right questions?

All the Remsons before him closed up into one Remson.

The single Remson said, "I'm glad we're slowing this thing down, Mickey. Too much chance for an error this way."

And it made Croft feel much better, somehow, to know that Remson's judgment was in accord with his.

CHAPTER 10

$$\triangledown$$

Huddle

Down in the Loader Zone, at a bar Reice hadn't been in since he'd become so damned respectable, Reice poured blue beer from a pitcher and waited for his aftermarketeer contact to show.

The place was full of camel-lipped Epsilonians and worse, dank and smokey, styled like a twenty-first-century Earth bar, complete with a jukebox that played ancient music recorded with real analog instruments.

No chance of anything said in here being overheard, or recorded with any level of microwave directional technology, including lip-sync readers; it was too damned dark and noisy for that.

So Reice was relaxed as could be, and the blue beer further mellowed his mood. He was thinking about ordering some food at the bar, when a hand came down on his shoulder.

Reice was still carrying his A-POT pistol, mainly because he had the clout to do so, but at that moment he was comforted by its presence.

The hamlike hand that spun him around on his barstool belonged to a "bioengineered person" of test-tube descent who had a grayish pelt like a beaver's and musculature suitable for a vanadium miner on a two-gee world.

"Meester Reez, preeze cum dis vay," said the subhuman.

Reice delicately lifted the huge hand from his shoulder, loosening the numbing grip of its claw-ended fingers first with a light slap. "Sure thing. Wait till I get my beer."

He took the pitcher, told the bar servo to bring more

beer and clean glasses to his table, and followed the buck-toothed giant across the floor. It moved easily, despite its flat, spatulate tail, among the tables.

When it came to the wall of booths, it showed all of its sharp, white teeth. "Meester Reez bring beer, oh boy," it said.

Someone in the shadowy back of the booth said, "You take the beer, Barney, and go drink it with your girlfriend. On us."

The aftermarketeer's human hand beckoned from the shadows. "Siddown, Reice. Good to see you."

Reice slid into the booth, across from Sling, whose earring sparkled briefly in an errant beam of light. "I can't believe you're fond of this tourist trap, Sling. Why the theatrics?"

"Because nobody'd believe that I'd meet you here, or that you'd come here wearing that high-ticket hardware. Every macho fool in this place is trying to figure how to get it off you."

"I haven't had my exercise today, so let 'em try."

"Can it be you haven't arrested anyone for doing something wrong in a whole twenty-four hours?"

"That could change, any time. What's up, Sling? I got things to do and people to see."

"Important people, I hear."

"Sometimes I wonder whether that's an earring in your ear or a transponder."

Sling elaborately took off the earring and put it between them. Reice took an empty glass and put it over the earring. Sling said, "Okay?"

"Okay," Reice agreed, and said, "What's up?"

"Two kids, a black box, a joy-ride out to the Ball locus, a short spacewalk from which they never returned. . . . Who knows, might have the makings of a folk ballad."

"Might have the makings of a jail term," Reice disagreed.

"Come on. You know I came straight to you, soon as I could without arousing their suspicions. They didn't need my extraordinary technical skills: they had their own key to the highway with them."

"Alien manufacture?"

"You bet."

"Get a good look."

"Memorized it, for what good that's going to do. No obvious power source. Fiberoptics that terminated in n-space." Sling shrugged. "I'd draw it for you on the table in condensate, but the result might work and we'd end up in some other dimension—and me without my spacetime suit."

"So, what else?" Reice sat back and put up one knee as if Sling hadn't just given Reice the most valuable bit of information in the universe at this particular moment. "I don't suppose you ran a trip log?" Aftermarketeers ran close to the edge of legality. They usually had the brains not to leave incriminating evidence lying around in their electronics.

"I kept a running log of the trip on my little gray cells." Sling tapped his forehead, leaning forward. "What do I get? Paid, maybe? You have a slush fund for this? Or is it just blue beer for subhumans, and thank you very much, buddy."

"I'll go suggest a pension, a government contract, and a Secretariat medal. You never know what those UNE pukes will do."

"They ought to get Joe South and Riva Lowe back here, have you suggested that? Before any more weird modes of transportation crop up. Or before we're hip-deep in something we can't handle. Those kids were purely weird, and I know weird when I see it."

"I know you do, Sling." Reice felt nearly paternal to the aftermarketeer. "And don't worry, I'll take care of your missing persons report somehow that won't get you arrested for leaving the scene of an EVA without your passengers—some people would call that attempted murder." His voice was very low, now. "But we won't. And we'll keep the whole thing to ourselves. Assuming you'll help me make a good case to my bosses that we ought to do some damned thing to control that Ball access point to Unity space—especially considering what the runaway kids are like . . . were like."

Sling stood up. "Your place or mine?"

Reice stood, too. "Your place. I don't want anything official about this. I got my own channels, now."

At Sling's workshop, they could dummy up any kind of read-once-only deposition for Croft and his assistant secretary. And wouldn't that just make Remson's day.

The key to the puzzle might be staring at him out of the

only slightly drunk visage of Sling, the aftermarketeer, who'd been on the periphery of happenings at the Ball since it appeared out by Spacedock Seven.

Reice was whistling as he followed Sling out of the bar, into the anonymity of the Loader Zone. Some days, fate just gave you a break. Once Reice showed his new evidence to Remson and Croft, Reice was going to be the new fair-haired boy around the Secretariat.

Just leave it to the aftermarketeer to come up with the missing piece: he'd actually seen the kids do whatever they did when they got near the Ball. Seen them disappear, if that was what they did. Seen them use the conveyance mode that the Unity aliens used, if that was what they did.

An eyewitness. My, my, what a coup. All Reice had to do was keep Sling nice and safe now, out of the clutches of the Cummings dynasty or the Forat clan, and everything was going to be grand, just grand, from now on.

CHAPTER 11

▽

Cold Feet

The next time Croft visited the modeler bay, the simulation had replicated itself.

Self-replicating machines were nothing new to Croft, but self-replicating psychometric models? His fears of a virus penetrating the Stalk computer net nearly choked him. He could barely greet the Interstitial Interpreter model properly.

Now, in the light cone where the holographic image under scrutiny was customarily displayed, the simulation had company.

And what company! A bit behind the primary model of the Interstitial Interpreter were two more aliens—the honor guard, complete with their ceremonial smoking pots—that Croft had first encountered aboard the Unity flagship.

Three beings stared mournfully at him—or sympathetically. The odor he'd smelled in here earlier—of incense like woodmoss, jasmine, and copper—now had a real source.

Mickey was trembling as he said to the creatures in the light cone, "I can't keep on this way. I need real contact with you—contact that's creditable. And I need answers. Now!"

"Now we have not your questions," said the Interstitial Interpreter, if said was the right word; the movements of the II's harelipped mouth had no direct relationship to the words Croft heard.

He withstood the impulse to clap his hands over his ears. Instead, he sank down into a chair before the console and replied, "Then I will ask the questions and you will give me answers I can understand."

"Ask now questions comprehensible," said the II, "and answers will come forth to you."

Croft should bring someone with him whenever he was in the modeler. He shouldn't have these meetings alone. He couldn't trust his own impression of what was happening.

Too late to change it now. The honor guard were swinging their pots and the smoke was thickening. Around the three beings in the modeling cone, the colored swirls of holographic readiness changed to vistas of impossible geometry. Croft gripped the padded bumper of the console, hard. Now he must carefully phrase his interrogatory. So carefully . . .

Croft said, "Where are the Cummings boy and the Forat-Cummings girl?"

"Home with us, safely sound, and never fearing harm anymore," said the II. On his right and left, smoke billowed from pots swinging round and round in the honor guards' grasp. The smoke escaped the light cone entirely and began to roam the room. It touched Croft's face, his hands, brushing up against him like some animal trying to mark its territory. Wherever it touched him, his skin tingled.

He grasped the bumper harder and framed more words. "Why did you take them away now?"

"Not take, receive. Welcome. As promised. Safe haven requested, giving." The words rode the smoke into his mouth and they tasted true.

Croft took a deep breath and the smoke ran down into his lungs, filling every inch of him, spreading out, separating, meandering through his body.

He fought for control. Truth must be demonstrated, not tasted. He must reduce these exchanges to terms that humanity could evaluate. As much as he had dreaded, even avoided, what must come next, it was the only way.

He said to the three-fold image that was filling the confines of the light cone and overflowing it, "Will the Unity representatives meet with me in person again? Can we have a formal, corporeal—corporal—meeting out at the Ball site or near it? Your staff and mine?" It was the last thing he wanted, but he needed real-time corroboration.

"Yesssss, in due course of time, certain," replied the Interstitial Interpreter. Behind him, the honor guard began to hum—or sing—softly. "Embassy nearing finished reality. At Ball site soon manifesting. Okay meeting our embassy place, soontime now."

"Embassy nearing finished? At the Ball site?" What trick was this? "I have people at the Ball site. There's no construction going on, either inside the Ball or near it."

"Is very near reality," said the Interstitial Interpreter once more.

"But I thought you said you didn't want to construct your embassy at the Ball site. . . ." Croft reminded himself that he was assuming he was talking to something more real than a model.

The Unity alien craned its neck as if to peer down at him. In a distinctly tutorial manner, the Interstitial Interpreter said, "Constructing, with your permission, as agreed. Not manifesting now at site yet."

Croft's hackles rose. "I assumed—that is, I thought you wanted to put your embassy out near Pluto, and that's why you want us to move Threshold there."

"Will put, Mickeycroft. Will put when humans are going. Not staying longtime at Ball site, future. Pluto site much more better. As we agreeing, pasttime."

The smoke from their pots was wrapping itself around Croft like a shroud. He wanted to claw it away from his face, his eyes. He didn't move. He said grimly, "Until I understand completely what's going on here, all work on the creation of your embassy and the project to move Threshold beyond Pluto must be suspended."

"Not possible stopping. Not going on here, going on at Unity space. Putting at Ball site, soontime," said the II implacably. "Putting at Threshold's new place, when humans going, not beforetime."

"You're telling me that all this time you've been working away, constructing an embassy out at the Ball site, and we just can't see it yet? And that you won't stop now?"

The singing of the honor guard ceased. Their conical heads dipped low. The pots swung faster from their arms.

The Interstitial Interpreter said, "Constructing embassy, as agreed, Mickeycroft, for putting at Ball site. Not making at Ball site. Making in Unity spacetime. Not stopping, not be wasting worktime. Why would? Ball site no good longtime, fine good, soontime."

Croft didn't like what he was hearing one bit. But he

had to assume that he was talking to a real intelligence, and that he was understanding the conversation as it occurred. And he must respond, somehow. Regain control.

"I will send my emissary, Vince Remson, out to the sight of the Ball, to reevaluate the matter of what, if anything, is happening at the Ball site. With or without your cooperation. If something's being built there, we'd better see it *soontime*. Until that evaluation is finished, everything stops, including the development of plans to move Threshold."

"Nothing stops," said the Interstitial Interpreter. "All things continue." And, more softly: "Humanity wants continuing, safely, with Unity, yes?"

"Ah—yes. I think, anyhow. Safely, definitely. We can't keep meeting like this," Croft said. "It's impairing my ability to function." The words came out of him very slowly, leadenly. It seemed as if he were reciting a rote speech he'd forgotten that he'd prepared.

"Not impairing, Mickeycroft. Improving. All spacetimers growing up now."

"Maybe, and maybe not," Croft said. "You must now show my emissary, Mr. Remson, your progress at the Ball site. He will report to me. And I'd like to see my ambassador to Unity space there, too, and her companions, to compare status reports. I can't credit these unofficial meetings with any diplomatic significance, because you're not here in person. If you want to meet with United Nations of Earth representatives, then you'd better manifest your damned embassy and yourselves out there—and quick."

"Quick now becoming easier," said the Interstitial Interpreter. "Soontime greetings, your person."

"First Mr. Remson's person," Croft said dryly, and pried one aching hand loose from the bumper long enough to end the simulation.

The Unity aliens disappeared too slowly, as if reluctantly, and the smokey smell of incense remained in Croft's nostrils too long.

Spacetimers growing up now.

The luckless spacetimer named Croft had grown up fast, in one horrific meeting. He was limp from it.

So there was something happening at the Ball site, despite what he'd thought.

Had he just misinterpreted the aliens? Or had they changed their minds?

There was no possibility of proving the truth, one way or the other, by checking the log of the modeling sessions. What had been said didn't matter, because it had been said by models.

It was going to matter one hell of a lot if a finished alien embassy appeared from nowhere, out near the Ball. Especially after all the Unity doubletalk about moving Threshold to an orbit beyond Pluto's.

Perhaps the Unity aliens were not as beneficient as they claimed. Perhaps Croft was only paranoid, and they were still mankind's greatest opportunity.

Perhaps both statements were true, not mutually exclusive.

Whatever the truth of it, Croft now had to face Dini Forat's father, the Mullah Beni Forat, and Richard Cummings the Second, and tell them that their children had left for Unity space of their own volition.

Without a word of goodbye. By unknown conveyance. Without a trace left behind.

Croft called Vince Remson from the modeler bay, on a secure audio-only channel. "Vince, get out to the Ball site. Shut down the task force evaluation team. Close up Science Station Seven. Stand off at a safe distance. I have reason to believe that a finished—or nearly finished—Unity embassy may pop into spacetime near the Ball site at any minute." Just because the UNE's paltry technology couldn't dream such a feat, didn't mean the Unity aliens couldn't do it with one smoking pot tied behind their collective back.

Remson's small voice said, "Understood, sir."

"Reroute traffic to make sure none of our ships are too near the Ball site when and if this manifestation occurs. And . . . oh, yes, Vince: Wait for a communication from the Unity aliens that they're ready for a face-to-face meeting with you, my designated representative and ad hoc emissary. When you have made contact with them, find me. I'll be with the Mullah Forat and Richard Cummings, trying to explain how those kids got away from us."

"Yes, sir," said the attenuated voice of Remson, crisp, unquestioning, and uncomplaining.

Croft hated to put Remson in danger of contamination by the Unity aliens, but someone else had to deal with this new chapter in UNE/Unity relations. Mickey Croft had reached the end of his ability to endure, persevere, or even trust his own judgment.

Vince, at least, could be counted upon to follow through in a predictable fashion. To report dependably what occurred. To make sure that all possible precautions were taken against accident or error.

Very little of Mickey Croft's world—of his personal spacetime—had even that much to recommend it anymore.

CHAPTER 12

$$\triangledown$$

Passing Strange

The Unity Embassy—or something—manifested less than a hundred nautical miles off the Ball site, at the juncture of Ball Latitude 42 degrees and Ball Longitude 60 degrees, in a stationary parking orbit perfectly synchronized not only to the Ball but to Spacedock Seven.

And there it sat, silent and virtually motionless, while every asset available to Vince Remson, the Secretariat, Consolidated Security, and Consolidated Space Command scanned, measured, probed, and evaluated with every technique known to humanity.

Fourteen hours after Mickey's message, and six and two-fifths hours after the manifestation of the Unidentified Stationary Object itself, the USO sent Remson a message, just as Mickey had predicted.

When the message came, Remson was in a situation room in the bowels of Spacedock Seven, up to his armpits in microwave radar scans and LIDAR scans and every other sort of scan which hadn't been able to penetrate the exterior surface of the USO sufficiently to determine even if it was hollow.

Nor had more pedestrian methods been able to identify the alloy of the USO, which was shaped roughly like a hangover-induced seven-dimensional nightmare of a Moebius strip with lots of little energy ports that Remson's radar reconnaissance and electro-optical and black-body detection specialists were calling thermionic thrusters, for lack of a better definition.

The message was delivered by hand—sort of. The sixth

nonlinear surface from the southern axis of the USO opened up and out came a completely transparent soap-bubble thing with a bona fide Unity person inside.

Remson had the whole adventure on tape in six frequency modes and 3-D video. The soap bubble meandered up to Spacedock Seven's cargo lock, oozed inside, and fused to an open pressure lock.

Then the Unity representative walked through the lock—without waiting for it to cycle—and began wandering through Spacedock Seven's vast honeycomb of corridors without regard to security or priority.

Wandering *through,* not *along,* the corridors. Neither doors nor walls nor floors seemed to mean a thing to it. But every time it encountered a human being, it stopped and politely asked for directions to "Emissary Remson's place of being."

So Vince had to go out to meet the damned thing, which had on a long skirt that partially concealed either a tail or a pair of extra legs with no feet on the end of them.

If there was contamination involved with meeting the Unity aliens, that contamination was no longer restricted to the Secretary General of the UNE Secretariat. The alien had encountered cooks, noncoms, field-grade officers, shopkeepers, and sentries before Vince caught up with it.

He'd gone as fast as he could, but the damned thing moved in all directions, so you couldn't catch it unless you could anticipate its movements: a human walked along a floor until it got to stairs or a connecting hallway; a human didn't drop through the floor or rise through the ceiling or slide through walls instead of taking the stairs.

Near the situation room, Remson caught up with the damned thing. Here was Vince's alien, just as Mickey had promised, calm as you please, although alarm bells were ringing at earsplitting volume, announcing the penetration of an unauthorized person into a secure area.

Vince signaled a stand-down to a couple of sentries who hadn't gotten the word not to shoot and were slinking along the corridor, low and flat to the wall, as if they were in commando training school. "Go shut off those damned alarms," Vince yelled in their faces. "And make sure nobody else perceives this as an unauthorized penetration. This person is an invited guest who's unfamiliar with our customs. Harm it, and you're history."

The men scurried away.

But now there was the alien.

Vince walked up to it, arms away from his sides, and smiling broadly. You couldn't yell at it, and the bells were still ringing.

When Vince was maybe ten feet from the alien, the bells stopped ringing, and in the shocking silence, Remson gathered his courage. "I am Vince Remson, United Nations of Earth representative. Greetings from Secretary General Croft."

The alien said, "Meeting being now, on our embassy place, and you are coming."

Vince didn't want to look in its dark eyes. He focused on its conical skull. "Ah—not so fast, okay? We must contact Mr. Croft. There's some concern about whether this is the right time to ... manifest ... your embassy here."

"No concerning, having meeting now. Our place. Your convenience, yes?"

"Yes, but—"

Vince was too late.

The alien started sinking through the floor, about to leave the way it had come.

"Stop!"

"No stopping, now. Convincing all humans no reason not moving habitat to better spacetime, now. Coming soon, please. Your ambassador happy to see all humans again. Bring Mickeycroft. He is missed, still."

All the while the alien was babbling, it was sinking further and further through the floor.

By the time it had finished speaking, its head was disappearing.

Remson stood over the conical skull as it sank through the floor as if through quicksand.

Well, Mickey wasn't going to be thrilled that the aliens wouldn't hear of removing their embassy, or even of putting a hold on things, but you could only do your best, in any situation.

Remson's best would be required in reporting this to Croft without seeming to have failed, or taken too much liberty with his instructions.

The floor was solid now, marred and gray and unremarkable. Remson stepped on the spot tentatively. It was as solid as could be. Time to go call the boss and tell the whole story to higher authority.

Vince Remson turned on his heel and headed straight for the situation room, hoping against hope that the multidimensional Unity embassy would have disappeared by the time he got there.

But it didn't disappear. It sat there, with lights blinking on its eye-teasing expanse, waiting for humanity's representatives to come on over and take a look.

CHAPTER 13

▽

Compromise

"Dead in the water," was the expression normally used for diplomatic initiatives in as much trouble as the UNE's attempt to normalize relations with the Unity aliens. So Croft said it aloud once, and then again, in the privacy of his space suit's helmet as he waited his turn to be ferried over to the Unity Embassy by soapbubble.

In the *GEORGE WASHINGTON*'s airlock, waiting for Unity transport, water metaphors occurred to Croft by the dozen. Humanity was storm-tossed, lost in a sea of misplaced expectation, perhaps already shipwrecked on the shore of an alien continuum.

The tempest was upon the arrogant children of some fated primate, upon the *spacetimers.*

Croft had sworn he would not come out here again, therefore the Unity representatives had all but demanded it. So here he was, waiting for one more cotton-candy day at the carnival from another dimension.

Remson was already over there, conveyed in his own private bubblestuff ship of transparent design and scintillant hue. How might they look to some observer, each of the humans, caught in a soapbubble that had a mind of its own and negotiated microgravity environments without any visible means of power but as unerringly as if traveling some infrared roadway.

The wind and the rain of destiny was driving humanity toward that Escher-designed embassy over there, and Croft was reading the white instead of the black of every line that fate wrote for him to read.

The bubble that would take him to the meeting he couldn't, somehow, avoid, grew out of one of the rings on the embassy's lower midsection as if, somewhere behind the scenes, a giant child was blowing through a ring held to its lips.

The colors reflected in the bubble as it sought Croft were all the colors of his own childhood, lavender and sunrise, cerulean and peach blossom, sunflower and daisy on a summer's afternoon in grass so green that it promised to last forever.

The bubblestuff colors of the Unity conveyance were mirrored in the Ball, which was giving off a light show that the Spacedock Seven optics specialists couldn't characterize, let alone explain.

All Mickey's cats were out of all the Secretariat's bags, now. You could pretend you were in control, stop work on this or that to try to stave off panic and save face, but the technical types knew from the urgency of the evaluations underway that no one in the Secretariat had the faintest idea what the United Nations of Earth ought to be doing about this invasion.

For that was what it was, an invasion in waltz time. Cummings knew Croft had lost the reins. The Mullah Forat, complete with tribal headgear and disdainful frown punctuating his waist-long beard, knew the humans were out of their depth.

Croft had almost invited the parents of the twice-missing children to come out to the carnival site with him. Croft would have done, if he'd been sure he could get Richard the Second and Beni Forat soapbubbles of their very own.

A ride into another dimension was humbling, and Mickey's twin albatrosses could use a dose of that.

But Croft, if nothing else, was a good bureaucrat. He would remain so to the end. Even when being a good bureaucrat meant answering the summons of an alien race at great personal cost.

The bubble was so close now that he could see a funhouse-mirror image of himself in it: stretched, distorted, a faceless man in a spacesuit holding onto the lock webbing for dear life, with a wriggly waist and curvilinear bones and a helmet that drew up into a conical crown.

The bubble nudged its way into the airlock. This time, Mickey didn't retreat. He held his ground, hands locked tight in the safety webbing, trying to feel a pop or sense a shift as the thing enveloped him without ever losing the internal buoyancy which allowed it to keep its spherical shape and its shiny skin.

He felt nothing. But his fingers found themselves wrapped in nothingness, and under his feet, an invisible surface nudged up to support him. This time he didn't palm his way around the inside of the sphere, which from his perspective was not spherical at all, but flat-floored and many sided. He simply clasped his hands behind his back, stood up straight, and arranged his body so that it would telegraph self-assurance, calm under pressure, and all the other diplomatic graces.

He had no trouble keeping his feet. The ride was as smooth as that of a moving walkway. Let the log equipment from the *George Washington* and Spacedock Seven record that Secretary General of the United Nations of Earth, Michael Croft, went to his first official meeting at the insystem embassy of the Unity with aplomb.

Only the physio-metering of his helmet's heads-up display knew better. And those readouts could be classified as internal and personal.

Closer and closer he drew in his iridescent bubble to the hole out of which it had come. Croft's guts churned. The hole seemed too small for a human being, at first. But as the bubble neared its destination, Croft realized that his concern was born of an optical illusion and a misapprehension of scale.

The Unity Embassy was huge, now that he was nearly within it and could judge it against a human referent. Why hadn't the briefing he'd had bothered to mention its size? Or was the highly specialized, extremely expensive, and infinitely complicated sensoring capability of the UNE as thwarted as Mickey's eyes by the multidimensional character of the Unity construct?

It stuck out into human spacetime, into the Einstein-Friedman spacetime manifold called home, as the tip of an iceberg floated above the surface of an arctic sea.

As he was cast against its side and sucked into its hole, Mickey realized that he ought to have been taking verbal notes for the benefit of those monitoring his progress. But he was speechless with the enormity of the thing into which he was being swept without protest.

Then he was inside what seemed to be a coiled tube and dizziness overcame him. Despite his resolve, he sank down on the "floor" of the bubble to fend off vertigo. He closed his eyes. His stomach spun. His ears emitted high tones, popped, and began to thunder with his own pulse. He grasped his knees and kept himself from collapsing to the floor entirely by locking his elbows and bracing himself on stiff arms.

The whirling sensation stopped and his ears cleared. He opened his eyes and saw a flat surface, close at hand, on which Remson stood with his helmet under one arm. Beyond Remson, there were others, standing on less discernable surfaces. Some of those seemed, to Croft's assaulted senses, vaguely human. Others were clearly alien, but only a few had the conical heads, the long skirts, and the auras of smoke that Croft had come to associate with the Unity.

He got to his feet with as much dignity as he could muster.

The bubble around him disappeared.

Beside Remson, who seemed to be smiling slightly, a trio of aliens appeared, trailing their smoking pots.

Why did Remson have his helmet off? Mickey couldn't communicate with him on the comlink.

Croft said tentatively, "AD Six to SD Seven, do you read?"

Spacedock Seven did not read.

The Interstitial Interpreter and his honor guard were approaching.

Inside his helmet, a soft voice said, "Take off headpiece, Mickeycroft, for real greeting and breathing human air nowtime."

He might as well.

He could see better without the helmet. It probably wasn't able to record in here anyway. The heads-up display superimposed on the inside of his helmet wasn't telling him anything he didn't know. In fact, it wasn't telling him anything at all. It wasn't even giving him current data on his heart rate, pulse, or the state of his nerves.

Glove seals, first. Then helmet seals. His hands moved without difficulty in an atmosphere that didn't fry his skin or rot his bones or freeze his fingers to brittle clubs.

Off came the helmet, with a twist and a pull, and the Unity embassy was all around him. Closest was the Interstitial Interpreter, all eyes and friendly smells and smoke trails. Remson was a bit back, behind the honor guard, still watching Mickey as if something very pleasant was about to happen.

The Interstitial Interpreter said, "Time being now is at hand, Mickeycroft. Have brought emissaries, yours, to meeting. Riva Lowe, Ambassador is manifesting soontime, with Pilot South and Valued Friend, Keebler. All reuniting with humans, any moment you say."

"Let's say a few things first, Mr. Ambassador." Might as well set up some protocols, before all was lost without them. "If all of my people are unharmed, and their reports and recommendations are satisfactory, then perhaps we can continue as we began—working toward real cooperation, creating a permanent Unity Mission here, and discussing moving human habitats to suit alien convenience."

It was difficult to concentrate on his prepared speech, with the alien smoke in his nostrils and so many strange sights teasing his vision and pulling his attention toward roller coaster images he somehow couldn't resist.

But he was ready for them, this time. He wasn't about to let his intellect be swamped by their sensory overload methodology. He didn't want this huge, clearly threatening construct sitting in the middle of humanity's home solar system without so much as an official by-your-leave. He didn't want to provide easy access to UNE space to all the beings he saw in the crowd who didn't have conical heads or seem familiar, until they *were* familiar, until the UNE had been formally introduced to each and every one.

He wasn't about to open diplomatic relations with this crowd of creatures as if formal relations weren't something that must be earned.

But none of the things he thought came out of his mouth. None of what he'd intended to add would formulate itself into cogent sentences.

The Interstitial Interpreter was speaking, not to him, but to the crowd, in a language that had great gaps of soundlessness interspersed in it, as far as Croft's ears were concerned.

Then the Interstitial Interpreter zoomed its eyes close to his. "We are saying greetings, nowtime, from your persons to ours. We are not saying fears or pasttime limits." The Interstitial Interpreter waved an arm about and vistas opened before Croft, as if they'd been hidden by the smoke that the II brushed away with his spread hand. "All accesses, now, being possible. No babytime contest of strength, here. Just opportunity for learning new things for spacetimers with minds open."

"Tell that to the parents of the Cummings boy and the Forat-Cummings girl, then. Tell them there's nothing to worry about. They miss their children—their spacetimers who are not grown up yet, and who need their parents."

The II's black-in-black eyes were so close to Croft's he could see only twin pools of deep space. "Not? Are. Growner up more better than old thinkers. Old thinkers stopping everything. Why do? Can't work. Time moving."

"Until I'm satisfied," Croft crossed his arms, "that you'll abide by our rules in interactions with us, nothing more in the way of cooperation will be forthcoming from the UNE side."

"Side? Side, how many? Four? Six? Seven? Eleven? Mickeycroft, the universe begins, maintains itself, makes spacetimes, all times, from same stuff. Universe is creating itself from discontinuities. In that, all secrets. In that, all power. In that, all life begins. Nothing more. Nothing less. Come see, nowtime, with your people, or stay in little box of human four dimensions. Your choice. But some of you ready are, more better than others."

Mickey wished he had a physicist with him. The universe was created from discontinuities? Which one? Or was there really only one universe? Was this all really happening? And was he, in truth, too old to steer humanity's course through its sea change?

He felt inestimably sad. The black eyes of the II receded from his, and Remson's took their place.

Remson spoke next, confidentially close without having moved nearer, on breath that smelled of peppermint. "Everything's well in hand, Sir. They want to have a diplomatic reception in your honor. A little party. They've brought our people back. I've spoken with Riva Lowe, Joe South, and Keebler. They've convinced me we should try to develop a working relationship."

Croft searched Remson's face for hidden meanings. Did

Vince mean that the UNE had no choice? Or that all choices led to the same result?

No answer was forthcoming.

Remson moved back from him, or rather sped back faster than human legs could carry him.

Croft, still smarting from the Interstitial Interpreter's lecture, given in front of Remson and a crowd, said, "We'll see. I need to be convinced of their goodwill and their ability to understand—and comply with—the conditions necessary to establish full diplomatic relations." Which might include taking this damned oversized staging area back where it had come from, if Croft had his way.

The ground under him started to slide, gently at first, then faster. He was moving without taking a step. Remson, ahead, was moving at the same rate and in the same direction. Mickey looked over his shoulder and saw nothing resembling the hole through which the soapbubble had brought him to this place.

No way out. Not for any of them, not now.

Ahead, beings were flowing together, merging on a track, moving in a stream toward a glorious collection of spires that resembled a Monet cathedral: no lines, just lights.

Their progress increased. People and aliens merged together, reminding Croft of an ancient child's tale in which different creatures spun and spun and spun so fast that they all merged together.

Croft saw a whirlpool of intelligence, all fusing. He saw interstices of data creating self-organizing streams. And he saw the face of his female Ambassador, sent so long ago— or was it only recently?—to this place, swimming before him.

She was a pert, pretty woman with dark hair and gamin eyes. The human face was something he could fix upon, a safe refuge for his eyes, until she turned into Dini Forat.

Croft blinked, and the face of Riva Lowe, his first ambassador of Unity space, was once again before him.

She had a drink in her hand in a perfectly normal Earth-type champagne flute. Behind her was a wall that reminded him of a perfectly normal Secretariat wall. Near her was Remson, surrounded by the honor guard with their smoking pots.

Croft said, "Riva, is that you?"

A laugh which tickled his memory reached his ears. A

soft, husky voice said, "I was about to ask you the same thing, Mr. Secretary."

"Is it ... that is ..." Croft searched for words. "Is your mission staff with you, and are you all satisfied that continuing this contact is wise?"

The Riva Lowe image seemed to consider that. Her face fell in on itself and kaleidoscoped in a shower of colors, then reformed. "Better than a poke in the eye with a sharp stick," she said gravely.

Relief flooded Croft from head to toe. If nothing else, he was now sure that he was talking to the real Riva Lowe, former Customs Director, now first Ambassador to Unity Space.

He reached through the fog of color, the mist of time, and the smoke from the honor guard's pots to take Lowe gently by the elbow. "Madam Ambassador, I have so many questions to ask you, I don't know where we'll find the time. . . ."

"Not a problem," said the gamin woman with the whirlpool eyes. "We have all the nowtime we need, Mr. Secretary. And more chance to win soontime than you might think."

The eyes of the woman were the size of the entire chamber, and galaxies sparkled in their depths.

Then she winked at him, and Mickey Croft felt time and space come into focus once again. He had sent this woman, and her two companions, into unimaginable peril, because he needed to make a judgment about whether contact with the Unity aliens should be encouraged or discouraged.

Now she was back with her compatriots, and more answers than he had questions.

CHAPTER 14

▽

Doability

Reice couldn't believe that the Secretariat had allowed the SecGen to go aboard the alien construct with only Remson to protect him. What the hell did they scramble half of ConSec and most of ConSpaceCom for, anyhow, if they were going to go do that?

Reice took his own cruiser, the *BLUE TICK*, out to keep watch over the Soapbubbles From Hell that picked up the Secretariat's most prized person and his executive officer. Then he sat there, growling orders through his allcom back to Spacedock Seven, until two more soapbubbles emerged, one at a time, to bring the men back home.

Damned waste of time, except that no other UNE ship had the clout or the balls to go where Reice had gone: right up to the entry port of that stomach-churning leviathan and sit on station there.

Reice would have sat on station until he ran out of life support, ready, willing, and able to chuck a couple kinetic kill torpedoes into that alien space habitat, and follow up with an A-potential missile or two, if Remson and Croft weren't returned on schedule to the *GEORGE WASHINGTON*.

But they were, and seemingly unharmed.

Disappointed, Reice brought his ship back to Spacedock Seven, parked her, and went loping up the ramp toward the situation room to see what the scans on the nature of the Unity construct were like and get his people together for a final sanity check.

By the time he got there, the team had had a priority

message from Remson to go forward immediately with the feasibility study for the Threshold move, finish it ASAP, and in general go from full-stop to full-bore with no warning whatsoever.

Reice was going to tell Remson, the next time he saw the SecGen's XO, what it could do to the morale of a team to turn them on and off and then on again.

But by the time the report was finished, Reice wasn't thinking about anything but his work. And his people. And what this much effort ought to be worth in the way of perks to the people who'd sweated blood so the Secretariat could look its best at its damned diplomatic receptions, or whatever was going on between the UNE dips on the *GEORGE WASHINGTON* and the aliens on the Unity construct, which people were beginning to call the "Embassy."

Reice wasn't calling it no embassy until somebody goddamned declared that full diplomatic relations had been opened between the two societies. Not after he'd seen the SecGen sitting on his butt in a soapbubble.

You learned not to take things for granted, when you had Reice's experience.

Reice was about to experience the joys of whipping a feasibility study into shape that should have been ongoing for the last ten days and hadn't been, due to a Secretariat-mandated shutdown that meant personnel had been reassigned to other duties, contractors issued stop-work orders, and everybody generally had gotten cold on the project.

Great.

Brilliant planning on the part of the United Nations of Earth Secretariat. Reice wondered aloud, when he called his alternate to tell her the good news, whether the Secretariat had ever heard the adage that "a lack of proper planning on your part does not constitute an emergency on my part."

But the adage wasn't true in this case, and they both knew it: a request for finished product immediately did constitute an emergency on their part, when that request came from the Secretariat.

The ensuing time was one long, sleepless, thankless interval full of damage-control and disintegrating team cohesion as hours got longer and tempers got shorter.

But nobody ever said they couldn't do the job. Nobody went off shift sick. Nobody faltered. Nobody failed.

When it was over, Reice's body felt like it had been turned into a headache with sore feet. But he was in good shape, compared to his staff, after two-hundred and eighty sleepless hours.

You never saw a sorrier lot than the fifteen men and women who had worked around the clock on the "Final Recommendations of ConSec/ConSpaceCom to the Secretariat on the Threshold Relocation."

Dandruff-speckled uniforms, red eyes, sunken cheeks, and cracked, dry lips attested to how much sleep had been lost over this one. But they had a report. Remson thanked everybody and even patted the fat lab rat on his gelatinous shoulder.

"Go do good for yourselves, folks," Reice told them. "We've got a little stand-down celebration in the executive dining room. I'll be along as soon as I deliver this."

None of these people could go right to sleep. They needed to talk off their tension, argue out their positions, and generally decompress in a secure environment. Disbanding them without some food, drink, and time to exult over having done the impossible was cruel and unusual punishment.

And they deserved a little something for their efforts.

As Reice was carrying the final draft up to the carpet-and-marble hallowed halls of Y Ring, a two-star came from that direction.

Reice saluted and thought to go on by.

The two-star stopped him. "We heard you finished your report, Mr. Reice. Congratulations." The general shook hands with him gravely and squeezed his shoulder for good measure. "We're all very proud of you. Only thing that could have been better was if a ConSpaceCom officer was with you, wearing a navy uniform, when you put this mission together. Maybe next time, we can do that, too."

"Yessir," said Reice. "Thank you, sir." And that was the first moment that Reice felt that *he* had done anything. For an instant, the clouds of imperatives, timetables, future crises, and operational problem-solving parted. He had accomplished something. A discrete success. He'd made ConSpaceCom sit up and take notice. A feeling he'd seldom had, of warmth and belonging, spread over him. He was being treated like one of the armed services' own, not like a cop, an outsider, an anomaly.

Well, fancy that. Having won in real terms, he was at a loss for a moment. Then he remembered that real terms weren't necessarily his terms.

He still had to deliver the evaluation to the boss and get Croft's okay.

You did that by putting one foot in front of the other until you got where you were going. When Reice got into Remson's Y Ring office, the Assistant Secretary was still on the *GEORGE WASHINGTON*.

Remson didn't want to have that report delivered, even in summary, over any comlink, so Reice had to cool his heels until Remson could come over to Spacedock Seven.

The party for his team was going on without him. For the first time in his life, Reice, an inveterate loner, actually wanted to go to a party, to be sociable, to share his feelings.

Oh, well. Maybe there'd be another time.

But there'd never be another first time to be accepted by the military. Reice sipped overcooked coffee from one disposable cup after another, and waited for Remson because that was his job.

When Remson showed up, the Secretariat XO seemed pale and wide-eyed. Reice wanted to ask how it had gone over on the alien habitat, but it wasn't his place.

He said: "Sir, here's your report, in good order, on time."

Remson looked like somebody who'd had too much lyposuction, too fast. The skeletal Secretariat Assistant Secretary said, "Thank you, Mr. Reice. Can you give me a quick summary?"

"Yes, sir." No wonder at the feat accomplished. Just a demand for a good reason not to have to read the product of all those hours. But Reice was ready for Remson. "There's a one-paragraph executive summary on the first page, sir." He paused to let Remson know that he, Reice, could tell Remson to go read the goddamned summary, like he was supposed to do.

Remson looked at him mildly, waiting, if not patiently, then distractedly, until Reice was forced to speak again. "In summary, sir, we've got final specs. Cost breakdown. Capability matches. Operational tasking. We can move Threshold anywhere you want beyond Pluto. It's going to take a tremendous effort and require a redeployment of force of massive proportions, but it can be done."

"Thank you, Mr. Reice. I'll tell the SecGen what you've said." Remson took a desultory note on his deskpad.

Reice got out of there as quickly as he could. Still time to catch the tail end of the stand-down party.

Maybe he'd been a fool to expect more than a cold thank you from Remson, but Reice's task force had just done the impossible, double-time. Maybe they didn't understand that at the Secretariat level. Or maybe some things never changed.

Whichever, Reice couldn't wait to get back among the people who'd sweated blood with him to get this program up and running. Maybe if he got there soon enough, he could stop feeling like such a chump.

CHAPTER 15

Turnabout

"Dad! Dad. Dad? Dadaddaddaddad. . . ."

Richard Cummings II sat bolt upright in bed, staring into the dark.

"Dad! Dad. *Dad! Dad?*" he heard.

The sound reverberated in his ears, in his skull, in his heart. His fists balled up wads of sheet and blanket. He felt as if his heart would break.

Was this it? The end? Was this the way Death would come to him, calling in the voice of his lost and wayward son? Was he having a heart attack? Would he be found in the morning, sprawled across his ancient Tudor bed, his mouth full of blood and his eyes staring at a horror no one else would ever see?

"Dad? Dad. *Dad?* Daddaddaddaddad. . . ."

Cummings had brought the Tudor bed at great cost and effort from Earth to Threshold. The curse attached to all things Tudor had never frightened him. Surrounding himself with antiquities from Earth's misty past was a privilege he savored.

The ghost called again. Cummings' hackles rose. His son was missing, not dead. *Not* dead.

Perspiration broke out on Cummings' brow, under his pajamas. The dark into which he was staring became grainy as his eyes strove to find a source for the sound. He fancied he could feel the impact of distant light sources on his eyeballs, stimuli tickling his retina. For there were light sources.

His bedroom had a churchlike stained-glass window

which angled toward the stars. Through it, starlight and the Stalk's nightglow streamed in colored rays that toned the darkness.

If there was something to be seen, some presence in the room, be it a ghost or a holograph or the spirit of a lost child, Cummings should have been able to see it.

He saw nothing but the half-visible, half-memory shapes of armoire and desk, touched by the colored window light. Around him, the thick, rope-carved posts of the oak Tudor bed were boundaries of pure blackness. Around them, the darkness was alive with errant light.

But no son moved there. No ghost sought him across the lightyears. No apparition moved, nor phenomena materialized.

Only the sound came to him: *Dad. Dad? Dad? Daddaddad.*"

Cummings pulled his covers up around his throat. He wanted to say, "Hello, son." He couldn't speak. He couldn't take the chance of encouraging irrationality in himself.

The noise might not be real. The sounds might be only in his mind, not in the air. Cummings didn't run a log in his bedroom. A man had to have somewhere to speak his mind, have his privacy, keep his own counsel. He had gone to great lengths to assure himself that no one else could record what transpired in this room, either. No covert surveillance was acceptable, here. No corporate enemy or Secretariat bureaucrat could be allowed to penetrate this sanctum. The bedroom was snooped for bugs on a daily basis.

But someone had penetrated this hallowed space, created a sad and sorry seance for him. Or he was losing his mind.

Moving as little as possible, Cummings reached for the notepad computer he kept by the beside and engaged its voice-command mode.

He held the notepad in his lap and waited.

When next the voice spoke ("Dad. Dad! Dad? Daddaddaddad."), the words appeared on the notepad's tiny screen, just as Cummings had heard them.

Unless he was muttering them himself, and thus was already hopelessly mad, he was not imagining the sounds.

That was something, anyhow.

The voice faded to nothing—or almost. Now Cummings

fancied he heard breathing, a shallower, quicker pulse than his own.

A presence in this room, uninvited, unannounced, and unseen, was impossible. Logic would not support the thought. Reason would not give credence to the possibility. Every security measure that NAMECorp could command was dedicated to assuring that incidents of intrusion such as uninvited guests in the CEO's bedroom were purely impossible.

And yet ...

"Dad. Dad? Dad! Daddaddaddad. ..."

"What?" Cummings snapped, nearly shouted. Then whispered, "What, what, what. ..." And finally dared: "Ricky, is that you?"

And the whisper from the brownish darkness beyond his canopy bed and before the stained-glass window said, "Yes. Yes! It's me!"

"Thank God," breathed Richard Cummings, though he did not know why.

"Dad. Dad! Dad? *Dad?* Daddaddaddad. ..." Again, the voice of his son resounded in the darkened room.

Cummings looked down at the computer notepad again. The notepad had recorded every spoken word of the disembodied source, interspersed with his own responses.

Something real was happening here, then. At least, something was saying the things he heard.

The next time the interrogatory began, he covered his own mouth with his hand, to make sure he was not speaking. The words continued to resound in his ears, and his notepad continued to transcribe them.

Cummings erased the dialogue glowing on the notepad's screen and set the device back down on his bedside table. He wanted no record of this encounter, however it might turn out.

"Dad. Dad! Dad? Daddaddaddad. ..."

Softer, now, and wispy. Sad. As if it were losing hope. Giving up. Drifting away.

"Son? Son, don't go. Talk to me." Cummings knew he sounded like an idiot, talking to the dark. Talking to his own guilt, an empty room, or worse, to his own imagination. But talk he must, or face an agony of regret, of answerable questions, of self-doubt and even self-loathing.

No one was here to laugh at him. No one was here to

find Richard Algernon Cummings, Jr. guilty of gullibility, or worse.

No one was here at all. Just himself, and a voice from another time and place. "Talk to me, Ricky," he said again, afraid he'd waited too long, done too little, been too skeptical, expected too much, once again, from his son. "Tell me you're safe."

The maddening voice whispered, "Dad. Dad? Dad! Dad, Dad, Dad. . . . Safe and sound. Come and see."

The new words were heaven-sent, gifts of riches beyond price, a balm to his anguished heart.

They'd never gotten along together, in truth. Never found a way to be comfortable. Richard was too competitive, too judgmental, too—busy—for a child. And now, what had he left?

A voice in the dark. A dream son. A phantasm of his misery. The boy had fled him, with his accursed Medinan girl. Fled him not once, but twice. Now Cummings was dreaming—must be dreaming—what he could not face in daylight.

The boy was lost to him forever, by intent or accident. No more would there be time for reconciliation, for learning lessons and setting examples. This could still be a dream, up to and including the dialogue entered in a dream version of his notepad computer. Must be a dream. In a dream, Richard could admit that he missed his son more than he'd imagined possible.

He'd never imagined that he'd lose Ricky. It was incomprehensible to him that a man could suffer as he was suffering and still survive. Richard Cummings would destroy every enemy and idiot government bureaucrat who had abetted the crimes of commission and omission leading to the disappearance of Richard Cummings III, but only because he must to save face.

His heart could not heal with this hole in it. His soul could not escape from the ice encasing it. Death and loss were his sole companions, and he could never forgive himself for letting young Rick slip away.

And thus, this dream so real that he could swear he lived in it, moved in it, thought in it, and talked in it. When he awoke, there would be his notepad computer beside his bed. A simulated morning would be dawning, another day yawning, and in that day would be no Rick Cummings to make his father's life a nightmare.

The trouble with dreams this real was that they contained all the stuff of life except reality.

Ricky Cummings had always been an innovator. Stubborn. Determined. Combative. Proud. It was so like Rick to find a haven that NAMECorp wealth couldn't reach, that NAMECorp strength couldn't corrupt, that NAMECorp control couldn't compromise, that Richard was proud of his son's determination, his creativity.

Proud, and mourning what was lost.

When Cummings awoke, he promised himself, he would sit down with Dini Forat's father and make peace. Peace for the children's sake, in case they still lived. This dream was telling Richard that much. No more time for posturing. Time now only to salvage what was not lost forever.

If he had believed he was awake, he would have dictated a memo on his notepad. But he did not believe it.

If he was asleep, he could talk to the disembodied voice of his son and be none the worse for it. He could believe, in his dream, that Ricky really was trying to contact him. He could. He would.

"Ricky," he said, "are you still there? Rick?"

"Dad! Dad? Dad."

"Ricky, where are you?"

"Here, Dad. Over here."

"Where? I can't see you."

"Here," said the darkness in the middle of the room. "Come here, Dad."

"Ricky, I've missed you so. I'm sorry we quarreled." Cummings cleared his throat. "I ... forgive me, son. I ... was wrong."

"Dad? Dad! Come with me. Come now. There's nothing to be sorry about. Come now. Come see."

Richard Cummings threw off his covers and got out of his bed. The floor under his feet felt solid, cool, and then warm and yielding as he stepped onto a Heriz rug and moved toward the sound.

"Okay, Ricky, here I come," he said very low. He could have turned on the light, in this dream that had so very much detail, like cool floors and warm rugs, but he did not. In case it was not a dream, he did not. In case, somehow, there was a disembodied force in this room which was his son, he did not wish to do anything to disturb it, to break the spell, to ruin the chance.

He walked toward the sound, in the dark.

A dream had never felt so real. He had never felt so foolish, or so desperate. He said, "I'm coming, Ricky. I'm coming, son."

And the darkness said, "Here, Dad! Dad! Dad? Dad."

Cummings moved softly over the rug, toward the sound. The closer he got to it, the louder it seemed. As if a person were standing there, before the stained-glass window, in the dark.

His eyes ached as he tried to penetrate the gradations of darkness. If a youth stood there, would Cummings be able to see some sign? Would there be the soft spill of lighter darkness over a young cheek, a shoulder, a thigh? Would there be something? Anything?

Richard Cummings said, "Ricky, I don't want you to be afraid." If there was no person there, or if this manifestation were something from beyond death's door, he must not squander his only chance. "Don't be afraid, here I come."

"Here, Dad! Dad? Dad! Here I am."

Cummings would save his son, if he could, as he had saved everyone he loved from all of life's threats ever since he'd been old enough to realize his destiny. He would talk to a ghost, if he must, to give it comfort. He was nearly sure he wasn't dreaming, now: the tears streaking down his face and into his mouth were too salty to be dream tears.

Whether they were from the strain on his eyes of trying to discern a wraith in darkness, or from grief, he could not have said did his life depend upon it. He was lost, and found, and lost again a thousand times in hope and despair as he put one foot in front of the other on a journey toward reconciliation with . . . something.

The dark was purer, in this part of the room. The stained-glass window was red, yellow, and blue, pure and backlit, a mandala from some ancient time. He'd found it in what once had been Cambridge and brought it here. Carefully. Patiently. Without so much as adding a scratch to its surface.

The window was like a wheel with ornate spokes. Colored light was trapped between the spokes. The spokes began to move, at first slowly, then faster, clockwise.

Beneath the spinning mandala of light, a dark place

ahead of him was shimmering. "Come on, Dad. Take my hand."

Cummings almost faltered then. He almost ran back to his bed, jumped in, and pulled the covers up over his head. This couldn't be happening. But it was.

He saw the dark before him as a shape, and that shape was the shape of his son. A hand of thick black substance came out of shadow and lesser dark to envelop his. He felt substance there, human bone and human flesh. He clasped the fingers hard in his own.

"Ricky," he said. "Ricky, it's really you!"

And then the dark all around him exploded in a kaleidoscope of light, and he was falling. The hand in his clutched him tight. "Don't be afraid, Dad! I've got you. Don't be afraid. Dad! Dad? Dad. Daddaddaddad. . . ."

Down they tumbled, in an impenetrable night of blackness, limbs entwining and separating, always together, always apart. Just as they had lived, they fell forever through blackness without form or stars, skydivers through eternity executing some random ballet.

Cummings' tearing eyes were whipped by the wind of their fall and dried when their falling stopped. A hand was still grasped tightly in his. He couldn't see a thing, but under him was a surface that was solid and welcome.

A voice close by said, "Dad! Dad? You made it. You did it."

But what had he done? Where was he? For he was somewhere. The boy's hand in his held tight. He knew his son's grip. He'd felt it over too many years not to know it. The hand of a baby, the hand of a toddler, the hand of a youngster, the hand of an adolescent: the hand in his was all of these hands, and more.

Richard Cummings held the hand of a guide and felt his way forward toward the light.

Cummings thought the light must always have been there, a pinprick, a glimmer, a star, a nebula, a universe, waiting. It was beautiful, and he moved toward it without fear that he might fall again, his son's hand in his own, content now to follow along wherever fate might lead.

What was happening to him was beyond his experience—perhaps beyond anyone's experience. Anyone except his son, he corrected himself.

Rick's hand in his was his touchstone, his connection with

reality. Nothing mattered so much as keeping direct contact with the flesh of his flesh. He had thought he might never again have the opportunity to take that hand in his.

They climbed a hill together, his feet told him. They climbed down the hill into a valley, and the star before them never wavered. This valley was filled with a lighter darkness, as sunrise on Earth lightens the dark when day is still an hour or two away.

He would take Rick out of this place, home to Earth, to the Cummings' ancestral places. Rick could bring his new wife as well. All the carping and the bickering and the foolish attempts of old men to force their preconceptions on the young would stop. He would grab old Beni Forat by the straggly beard and make the Muslim cleric see reason.

Reason was all about him. It wafted on a cool breeze moist with forming dew. It sang a distant song of morning's chorus from the throats of waking wildlife. It glowed from the dark sky above, turning purple in the light of a sun yet unrisen.

Let the morning star guide them. Let the boy beside him say his name like a mantra: Dad! Dad? Dad. Daddaddad-dad. Fathers give up all other names when they hold a newborn.

He should have remembered. How had he forgotten? How long had it been since Richard Cummings had shouldered the responsibilities of a man, lived the life of a man, known the joys of a man, cried the tears of a man?

He had become a force of unnatural progress, a field effect, a magnate of the expansion of humanity of among the stars.

And he had nearly lost everything he truly cared about. Walking with his son toward the morning star, up a soft hill of good ground springy with turf and fragrant with grasses, he said, "Thank you for coming to get me, Rick."

"Dad, I had to," said the voice of his son.

Cummings risked a look away from the morning star in its purple heavens, toward the dark shape beside him. He could almost see a shape now, almost recognize the beloved form of his son.

He could almost dare to hope that this was truly real, really real, and not a phantasm of his tortured soul.

It smelled real. It felt real. His skin, which was privileged skin that on occasion knew the touch of an Earthly breeze, knew what a real breeze felt like, what treasures of nature it carried, what promises it made when it was salty from a sea nearby, fruited from the berries growing on the shore, piney from the woods that broke the seawind's force and tamed it, and perfumed from the flowers in the meadows sheltered from the storm.

Only as he looked back again, ahead, and to the morning star, did he finally realize that this place, this fine and welcoming place, was not his own beloved Earth, but some other world as natural to man as breathing.

The sky above was glowing with promises of day, and the morning star was fading. As it faded, rings appeared, golden, glowing rings with clouds among them. The vault above turned violet, then lilac, and finally lavender as day came rolling in like thunder.

Rick squeezed his hand. "Dad! Dad, isn't it beautiful? Isn't it grand?"

"It is that, son." It wasn't Earth. It wasn't a place that Cummings had ever heard discussed among all the colonies of man.

The hill before them stretched gently up, its green grass full of flowers. Atop the hill, as the sun arose in earnest, Cummings could see a white portico, columns, and wide stairs on which a small, human figure stood and waved.

"It's Dini," said his son, and Cummings let go of Ricky's hand.

"I see it is," he meant to say, but nearly growled. "What is this place?"

"Our home," said Rick, all the glorious light running down his cheek as if he were in a shower of it.

The words hit the elder Cummings like a slap. "Where is this place?" said Richard, determined now to know what was happening.

"Far from harm. Close at hand." The boy shrugged. "Home. Don't you recognize it?"

"Son, your home is with . . ." Cummings wanted to shake Rick by the shoulders, but as he turned, scowling, the sky above his son's head was filled with darting, glowing spheres that soared and dipped and floated along, then stopped stock-still in the middle of the air.

"Dini's waiting, Dad." Daddaddaddaddad.

Rick's face was happy, proud, and eager to share all this

with a father who was not too much a fool to know what he was saying.

Richard Cummings had allowed himself to become many things, but never a fool. The spheres above their heads were nearly magical: no bird or plane could move that way, among the clouds, down low to the ground, then up until they disappeared among the ringed heavens' arch.

Cummings walked up the hill with his son, to meet his daughter-in-law, wondering how the boy had brought him here and what the future would hold for humankind if lives could be lived in such idyllic harmony.

The girl ran down the hill to meet them, and the radiance of her face nearly shook Cummings' faith in his own senses.

Had his son found the Garden of Eden? The Promised Land? Or had Rick simply come home, the way he'd said?

It didn't matter. The girl was running toward them, nearly floating down the hill. In the shadow of the gleaming columns, up the stairs, figures darted—not quite human, strangely dressed.

But Cummings was not afraid. He knew the future when he saw it. Nothing he could offer could rival what Rick and his wife had here. Nothing any man could offer another could be weighed against these scales and win.

His son had come home. A Cummings had found a world more beautiful than words could say, a mode of travel beyond price, and a deep contentment that Richard envied.

He was old. His son was young. The girl flinging herself into the dale to meet them was full of life and health and promise. And on the hill above, among the columns of a temple or a house, unearthly beings shyly waited.

High above his head, glowing spheres did arabesques in fleecy clouds, and their shadows touched his son's face, so proud, so calm, so happy here.

He'd tried to keep Rick from this. He'd used every power at his command to trap the boy, the girl, to make them as unhappy as everyone else he knew. He was infinitely sorry he had done so.

When Dini reached them, he took her hands and said gravely, "Your home is very lovely."

She smiled. "It's your home, too. Can't you feel it? We're so glad that you could come."

How had he come here? He asked, but Dini tugged him onward, up the hill, and Rick was saying, "Wait until you see the house, meet our friends. Then you'll understand it."

On the steps, Cummings saw furry mammals, like raccoons, that purred and hopped up into the arms of the young couple.

The pets pulled at their hair and climbed on their shoulders, as Dini said, "This way," and led him through the portal.

Richard Cummings knew the pets were called Brows, telempathic creatures, rare and strange. His son had named them, found the species, brought them with him. They weren't local animals. But they were clearly at home here, and a part of this place in a way that Cummings didn't understand.

Nor did the aliens he met inside, sad-eyed, soft-spoken beings of infinite patience, belong here any more than he. They welcomed him gravely home and walked with him around the hill's crest, their heads bowed, their crowns gleaming.

When it was time for him to leave, Cummings knew it as much by the sadness in his heart as by the setting of the sun. His son said, "Dad, you must return, nowtime. Home is always here, when you want it."

Strange turn of phrase, doubtless picked up from talking with the aliens. Cummings was overcome with love for his son and sadness at parting, but there was much to do, now that he had met the aliens and begun to understand the Unity.

His son walked him down the hill, into the dale, and over the crest of the hill beyond, alone. "Dad, we can go back whenever you need us. But we don't want to."

"I see why." Cummings felt, with every step away from the hilltop where Dini watched them go, as if he were losing something. A connection. A chance. A lifetime. A soul. His son. Again. "Come back with me, just for a little while, Rick." He hadn't meant to say it. It slipped out somehow.

"A later time, I'll come. Spacetimers need to talk to you, not me. And you'll stay longer, nexttime. With us, at home. See the sunset?" The youth raised a pointing finger on a straight arm.

Cummings sighted along it, into the ring-lit sky. Flaring clouds rayed the light into a prism of pink and gold and green. The plasma spheres danced and swooped, spinning out the end of day.

No place such as this existed but in man's memory. Cummings was about to say that to Rick, to make one more clear entreaty, when he blinked. An instant of total darkness enveloped him. His lids would not open for a heartbeat. And when they did, his feet were on his Heriz rug and his bedroom all around him.

He rubbed his eyes. He'd gone on a long journey, wearing pajamas, barefoot, with his son as his guide and his soul on his sleeve. It had happened. It was no artifact of stress, no dream, no hallucination.

There was grass between his toes, green grass stains on the bare soles of his feet, and even a small bug that had ridden from somewhere else to here on the big toenail of his left foot. He leaned down and coaxed it onto his thumbnail.

He stood and brought his thumb up to eye level. The bug was red, with tiny black spots and a hooded head. It resembled an Earthly ladybug. He must get a plant for it to live on. It was his proof that he'd gone somewhere, done something—in case Threshold drained his certainty away.

He would not forget. He would not convince himself that he'd been mad for an evening. He would not succumb to fear. He would not fail his son. Or his daughter-in-law. Or the human race.

He would not.

And that day, he did not. After finding the ladybug a fern, a rose, some daisies, and a vase, he began his work.

He called the Secretariat and told an astonished Mickey Croft that he, Richard Cummings, was implacably in favor of open trade with the Unity aliens, and he expected the Secretariat to do its job—facilitating the welfare of its citizens—by supporting the opening of complete diplomatic relations with the Unity worlds as soon as possible.

The tiny Croft in Cummings' monitor wanted to know, "What's up, Richard? Why are you taking such a hard line all of a sudden?"

"I've heard from my son. He's safe and well. That's all I needed to know. Now, you do your job, Croft, and I'll do mine—in lockstep. Or I'll find somebody else to work with, somebody who can handle a transition of this magnitude."

"Mr. Cummings," Croft began, but Cummings ended the

transmission with a deep feeling of satisfaction. Croft had once ended a discussion between the two of them as abruptly. *What goes around, comes around, Mickey.* The old saying was as true today as it had been centuries ago. And many other century-old truths might be proven before the UNE and the Unity had developed a working relationship. That was fine with Cummings. He had seen the future in his son's eyes.

Next on Cummings' list was Beni Forat, father of Dini, and mullah of the Medinan colony. Cummings intended to make sure that Forat knew that he, Richard Cummings, was no longer opposed to his son's marriage to the Medinan girl, and that all manner of benefits would accrue to Medinan citizens if Forat could find a like sentiment in his heart.

That thought reminded him to reinstate his son in his will, which he did immediately. There was no reason to delay. He had seen something so mysterious, so full of promise, and so undeniably appealing that no human could resist it. His son had found a world on which NAMECorp could build a new empire, far greater than before. Or so he told himself as he ordered his priorities.

After the mullah, he would start private negotiations with the Unity aliens on acquiring the transportation system that Rick had used. The aliens had a construct near the Ball site. They must have representatives there.

Lobbying was something that Richard Cummings did better than any man living. Getting what he wanted was never difficult. Determining what he should want was always the problem.

First he would convince Beni Forat that the imam of Medinan culture should want an infidel for a son-in-law. Then he would convince the Unity aliens that NAMECorp was its best hope of controlling the access of humanity to its vast resources. That would not be difficult for a man of Cummings' stature, especially since Richard's son and heir was already inhabiting a Unity world and sharing Unity secrets.

Cummings had never had a better day, or a harder one. When he came into his sanctum after five meetings in a row, he was whistling. The gay mood stayed with him until he saw the vase of flowers he'd ordered for the Unity ladybug.

The flowers were dead, shrivelled, their petals strewn on the carpet. The ladybug was nowhere to be found.

CHAPTER 16

$$\triangledown$$

Politics

"... so we just give 'er a little push, Secretary Remson, and off we go," the two-star general from ConSpaceCom Logistics Agency said dryly. ConSpaceCom's General Granrud was short, stocky, with faded red hair thinly sprinkled atop a pear-shaped face. He looked older than he was, perhaps because of his pale and hooded eyes, and a thin skin that showed every vein around his nose and in his high forehead—or perhaps because of the responsibility loaded onto his rounded, heavy shoulders. Everyone in the Secretariat had begun calling him The General, spoken as if there were no other. He had taken control of this mission early on because of his Logistical Agency's primary responsibility for organizational redeployment of forces and had maintained a complete stranglehold on the operational side ever since. "If the stresses caused by the initial acceleration of an asymmetric mass like Threshold don't set up so much vibration that the Stalk shakes apart," the general continued, "then we don't have any problems we can't handle—until deceleration, when we find out how badly we've fatigued the superstructure."

Remson rubbed his jaw and stared at the rotating display, which hovered in midair between them, holographically projected from a deskpad unit that the Logistics general had brought to Remson's Y Ring office. The miniature Threshold could be rotated 360 degrees, viewed from any angle, and put through a simulation of the stresses involved in accelerating a basically cross-shaped object with unevenly distributed concentrations of mass to a good fraction of the speed of light across a complexified spacetime.

The miniature Threshold seemed suspended in a conical tube of distorted ellipses, some of which traveled with it, some of which did not, as it "moved" across the topologically-mapped graphic which represented the intervening spacetime, with its interacting gravity wells, toward Pluto, whose solar orbit varied from 2.8 billion miles at perihelion to 4.6 billion miles at aphelion.

The ConSpaceCom Logistics Agency staff had spent a lot of time and money creating the projection which hovered over Remson's desk. The least he could do was sit through the entire program and appear impressed when it had run its course.

The tiny Stalk, with its adjoining and cross-beamed habitats and modules, reminded Remson of a piece of ancient Chinese calligraphy, and the embedding graphic seemed like the warp and woof of the rug into which some unseen hand was weaving an indecipherable message. Threshold had never been meant to move.

The Stalk had fifth-force generators, which had provided artificial gravity for three hundred years, precluding the necessity of axial spin as a consideration when expansion modules were designed.

If the local solar spacetime were truly empty, the vacuum that ancients had imagined, moving Threshold up to speed would have presented no real-time problem. But the local spacetime was not empty. It was filled with bits and grit, plasma, gases, particulate matter, human-made space junk, meteoroids, meteorites, and the occasional eccentrically orbiting asteroid.

Many of these catalogued objects were represented in the holographic scenario. Obstacles popped into view with ever-increasing frequency as the model moved along its projected flight path. Collisions, near-collisions, vector-clearing explosions, occurred at irregular intervals. Course correction requiring complex realignment of axes was represented in patterned plumes of light coming from a multitude of attitude adjustments from banks of plasma thrusters. Grosser changes were accomplished using ConSpaceCom heavy cruisers, fast ships, and freighters retrofitted to provide each major module with its own integrated life support, propulsion and navigation capability, in case of unintended separation.

The whole uniquely roboticized mass of ships, drivers, thrusters, and cargo—Threshold—was synchronized through an artificially intelligent network of command and control stations that showed on the holograph as a great spiderweb whenever it was called upon to take action to protect the security or structural integrity of the Stalk and the two-hundred fifty thousand souls who lived on its periphery in Threshold's habitats. Seventy-three color-coded areas newly designated as "fracture zones" on the holographic image must be made completely impervious to stress and redundantly self-sustaining in case of accident, poor planning, or the failure of reality to behave as tamely as it did when simulated.

Catastrophic failure was a real possibility, but Remson didn't see it characterized in the simulation. The externally propelled unit of Threshold and its auxiliary guidance and propulsion spacecraft managed to avoid radiation sinkholes, multi-spectral magnetic and planetary turbulences, infrared and radio storms and sources, and wandering matter vortexes. In the actual operation, any or all of these dangers could fragment the Stalk, shake Threshold apart, separate her from critical portions of her external command and control suite, or leave whole habitat modules behind in her wake.

Somehow, the combined and redeployed forces of ConSec and ConSpaceCom must move the Stalk and its connecting modules safely past all of the calculable—and incalculable—dangers awaiting. Propelled by auxiliary thruster power modules, space tugs, and primary scalar drive assemblies designed to pull and push and guide Threshold through an increasingly crowded obstacle course toward a rendezvous with destiny, the model looked too unlikely, too fragile, too ad hoc to survive.

Remson waited until the model popped safely into a custom-drilled hole in spacetime made by crossing two A-potential beams from escort destroyers directly in the model's path. Then he couldn't hold back a comment any longer. "Isn't this just a little too pat, General? A little too perfect, too easy?"

The general said, "We'll run the disaster simulations after we finish with the operational scenario, Mr. Remson—

if you don't mind. It's a lot easier to contemplate what could go wrong with a plan once you *have* a plan."

Remson looked away from the holograph purposely, to make the general pause the scenario long enough to take up one or two discussion points.

The general froze the action and glowered at him, trying every tactic of body-language intimidation short of actually getting up and walking out. The two-star crossed his arms over his chest. He kicked back his chair onto its rear legs and balanced it. He fixed Remson with an unwavering, glittery, and openly pugnacious stare that dared Remson to critique his plan before it had played out in full. His chin doubled as his shoulders rose to protect his neck. His complexion reddened and his nostrils flared as he took deep, rhythmic breaths.

"I can't imagine," Remson said levelly, "that you expect us to take this sort of risk on faith, without a proof-of-concept demonstration of some sort."

"There's no alternative to this plan, if you want to move the habitat," the general said through a mouth so dry that Remson could hear the other man's tongue move. "Every technological asset we have is utilized in the best possible way in this scenario. There isn't an alternative, except asking the aliens to help us do the job. Maybe they've got something we haven't. But this is the best, the only, way to do this job with the combined assets at our disposal, without developmental or experimental technology, and with any dispatch. NAMECorp engineers concur. In fact, they've been pressuring us to present this scenario as a finished and single option. If you want—" The general licked his lips. "If the Secretariat wants to look at additional technical options, you'll make fools of yourselves. But go ahead. Request a Plan B. There isn't one, but ask anyway. All you have to lose is your reputation."

"There's always a Plan B," Remson said flatly. "And if this simulation is as complete as it looks, there must be another set of options your people brought forward, in nearly the same state of readiness."

"There may be, but this is the single recommendation we're sending up to the SecGen, at his request," the general responded, "when you've seen the rest of it, and by then, I hope, with your concurrence. You can nonconcur, of course; that's your privilege. But we have a good consensus building for this plan, and it reveals no classified capabilities to the aliens."

So that was it. Remson sighed and said, "Sir, I really want to give Mickey the whole picture. You know as well as I that he hasn't the time to sit through this whole briefing."

"I wouldn't have taken the time to walk you through it myself, Mr. Remson, if I didn't know that. Now, can we get on with this?" The general's eyes flickered to the simulation in a holding mode, to the clock on the wall, and back to Remson. "I've got a number of people waiting to find out whether we're go or no-go on this. If the wheels are going to come off this thing, I'd rather have them come off now than later."

The challenge hung in the air between them: if Remson pushed his demands for Plan B, no cooperation was going to be forthcoming from ConSpaceCom Logistics Agency anytime soon, if that cooperation included delivering a Plan B that included revealing classified assets to the Unity aliens.

Remson put up his hands in a gesture of surrender. "Okay, General, let's go through the rest of this. Convince me that I can get the job done with your 'tried-and-true' hardware at hand, and I'll take this up to the SecGen myself."

A slight smile played at the corner of the general's mouth. His icy eyes grew warmer than Remson had thought possible. He touched a control on his notepad and the spacetime hologram began moving once again.

Sometimes you had to know when you were on trial, when to push, and when to give way. In the final analysis, the success or failure of the Threshold move rested squarely on this man's shoulders. Countless lives, and the future of the Stalk itself, lay in his stubby, pale hands. And the general was letting Remson know that with responsibility must come power, or ConSpaceCom was going to fight the Secretariat every step of the way.

Maybe there was a Plan B, but the price to the Secretariat for evaluating it was too high. Way too high.

Remson was going to let the general have his way, no matter what the rest of the operational scenario showed him. There wasn't another choice that wouldn't make him—and this enterprise—an enemy that the Secretariat just couldn't afford.

CHAPTER 17

▽

In-Laws

"Our kids have found Paradise without having to die first," Cummings said bluntly to the imam of the UNE's most powerful Muslim member.

The Mullah Beni Forat, religious leader of Medina and the planet's President for Life, scowled at Richard Cummings from behind his scraggly, waist-long beard. "Sacrilege," Forat replied just as bluntly, as the two men strolled alone along the grassy walking path that wound through the Blue Mid atrium, their retainers following behind at a respectful distance in long, black groundcars restricted to the central magnetic roadway. "Only an infidel of your hopeless sort could even mouth such sacrilege." Forat paced Cummings, head bowed, determinedly watching his slippers bend the grass underfoot as if motion, not discussion, were the order of the day. "Alive in Paradise, with an infidel husband, having broken so many of God's laws? It is impossible. Or if it is not impossible, it is evil, Satan's work. You have been tricked by devils, Mr. Cummings, either in your mind or incarnate. And so has my daughter."

Somewhere in the trees to either side of the grassy walking path which lined the magnetic roadway, a songbird sang, and a lonely peacock answered with a baby's cry. The atrium was a beltway of tubing around Blue Mid, built to celebrate Threshold's tricentennial. NAMECorp had been the prime contractor during the long project, which included bringing from Earth, under carefully controlled conservancy-policed conditions, representative flora and fauna from each of the UNE's three-hundred member states.

Cummings thought carefully as he framed his reply. Mustn't be condescending, patronizing, or overly bold. Forat must be allowed to change his mind without losing face, recanting faith, or falling from grace with his people. Cummings understood the problem, but he was not a diplomat, or a student of Muslim theology. The daunting task of constructing the atrium so that each UNE member state could have direct access from their Blue Mid administrative centers to a little piece of their ancestral homelands had been easier.

After a thoughtful silence, Cummings said, "Mullah Forat, love between human beings created everything we see here, and more: the societies that you and I represent, humankind in all its diversity, the power of the United Nations of Earth to keep Earth sacred and grow strong among the stars. None of it would exist if particular human beings had not, throughout the centuries, found their mates and dared even death itself to join together. Whatever we are as a culture, as a race, as a species, when taken as a whole, has been created by our instinctive need to reach across forbidden boundaries for love. To have children who in each succeeding generation surpass the accomplishments of the last, people must be allowed to marry for love. Love is nature's way of assuring genetic dispersion. Love is God's way of guiding humanity's destiny. Love is the movement of genetic traits across group and geographic boundaries—across societal and religious lines, if necessary—to promote diversity, a mixing of superlative traits, and to let genius come forth among us. Through a mechanism known only to God, specific human beings recognize in others the most desirable, irreproducible combination of genetic strengths for reproduction. Love produced Mohammed, as well as Bach, Copernicus, Einstein, and every accomplishment of man that allowed Medina to be settled and your great society to flourish. So how can we, parents but not seers, argue with the will of God as it is expressed in love—and in our children's determination to love one another even under threat of death?"

It had been a long speech; Cummings had no idea where it had come from. It was not the speech that Cummings had come prepared to give. Although he had articulated every word, it was as if someone else had spoken. He wasn't even sure he believed what he'd said. But he was responsible for the results. If his words were perceived by the Mullah Forat as pompous, immaterial, abstract, or manipulative, then all hope of cooperation between them was lost beyond repair. On the other hand, if the mullah had listened with both his head and his heart, then perhaps this new framework in which to view the behavior of their children might save the day. Ideas were more powerful than men, both Aristotle and Mohammed had known that. What Forat knew was an open question.

The mullah walked in silence with Cummings for a long time before he responded. "Love is man's way of finding God, perhaps this is so. But love is also passion, and foolishness, and ungovernable lust. We do not think of women as you do, Mr. Cummings, but we are not savages. We understand custom and ritual, and the benefit of discipline, the organizational power of religion—apart from any question of belief. Our society is organized to a different standard, and that standard is very old and very powerful. And yet," the mullah paused ruminatively before continuing, "I am the father of a daughter, and I have no sons."

Cummings glanced sidelong at Forat and kept silent, hoping that the mullah would continue. He could not guess where this was leading; he could only walk along and wait. He kept mirroring the mullah's body language, hoping to increase rapport by moving and breathing as the other man did. Heads down, arms clasped behind their backs, the two men walked on, their entourages following behind.

"When you say to me," the mullah sighed at last, "that my daughter has found Paradise whilst yet she lives, my heart quickens, then is filled with fear. If mine were the son and yours the daughter, this would be an easier matter to resolve."

Ball in Cummings court, but what was he to say to that? The Medinans were a last, great bastion of sexist ideology glorified as religious tradition. If the Muslims were still waiting for their long-prophesied savior, then so were the children of every other fundamentalist sect still thriving among the UNE's colonies. If that savior had to be a man to meet some ancient template, then this time the Medinans were shit out of luck.

"I don't know as much as I wish to about your religious

traditions, or the words of your Prophet. I do know that you and I have the great honor to be the fathers of children who will bring humanity peace in our lifetime, riches of the spirit and the flesh beyond measure, and open a door to a whole new chapter of human history. We should be proud of them. We should not persecute them. Of all people, we should recognize greatness among us, especially when it has sprung from our loins."

The mullah stopped. Cummings stopped, too. Above the grizzled beard, Beni Forat's face looked old and wan. In the simulated sunlight of an English countryside springtime, his eye sockets and cheeks resembled hard-used leather, deeply lined and much older than Forat's fifty-five years.

"All great prophets have been persecuted in their lifetimes," Forat said mildly. "If God has singled out our children for greatness, then we will not be able to interfere, no matter how we try."

"That's just what I'm trying to say," Cummings chattered clumsily, blundering in his excitement. He stopped. Forat's watery eyes still fixed him with a zealot's stare—or the calculating one of a consummate politician. Cummings pressed on. "We cannot continue persecuting our son and daughter, you in your way, me in mine. They are beyond our reach in ways I am only beginning to understand."

"No one is beyond the reach of God's justice," said the mullah.

"Precisely so. But man's idea of God's justice may be flawed, don't you agree?"

"Of course. Man is essentially flawed." The mullah put his head down and started forward again, as if disappointed in Cummings' ability to hold up his end of a theological debate.

"Man may be flawed, but humankind is on the verge of a great discovery, and our children have led the way. What use is it to call for their deaths? To commend them to impotent assassins? To put a price on young heads that the entire United Nations of Earth will soon be crowning with laurel? I wish a truce with you, in the name of my son, my daughter-in-law, and our joint future. We are both fathers-in-law of destiny." This time Cummings stopped and prayed that the mullah would join him, not continue on alone.

Beni Forat took one step more and turned to face Cummings. "You are more articulate that I had expected."

"And you are more reasonable," Cummings responded.

"You are saying, why give an order that cannot be obeyed? Why lose face when face can be gained? But you don't know my people."

"And you don't know what I've seen when I visited the children at their new home."

"You visited them? You saw them, touched them?" A sudden eagerness came over Forat. Pain, hunger, helplessness, and loneliness glittered in his eyes.

"I saw them. I touched them. They live in a true Paradise, I assure you. A world of wonders beyond measure. And they will not come back here so long as we represent a threat to their happiness. But we can go to them. They offer gifts beyond price. They have found a home among a community of beings whose knowledge and wisdom is far beyond our own."

"Beings?" Forat's forehead rumpled.

"It's another ... way to live. Maybe it's the only way we've ever lived—or the only way we were meant to live. Everything we've half forgotten, every truth that all religions have served to keep alive in our hearts, every intuition of godhead that all the races of man have independently experienced—all of that makes perfect sense where Rick and Dini live. I'm telling you, all your faith is true, and real, and your daughter has led the way. I can't help you come to terms with what's happening in any other words."

"Beings are not ... what our religion is about."

"I'm not saying that the ancient words of any religion will be proved true verbatim. I'm saying we must not persecute our children, who have found their way to what mankind has always been seeking but couldn't quantify."

"Blasphemer, hypocrite, fool," Forat told Cummings to his face. "Your sophomoric attempts to frame temporal events in spiritual terms disgust me." Yet the mullah did not look angry, only tired. "You wish a truce, for the sake of your son, your material greed, and your famous dynasty. If you will promise me not to characterize as spiritual what has happened—what you have seen, wherever you went, what you think you know about the race they have encountered, if not discovered—then I will find a way to lift the death sentence from their heads. But only if you keep silent with your maunderings and your infidel's dreams of Paradise in life. If you do not keep silent but spin your mercantilist's tales to all and sundry, hoping to capitalize on your son's discovery, and to use my daughter for your own greedy ends, then only evil will come of it, and we will mount a jihad against you and yours such as the universe has never seen. Do you agree to my terms?"

Terms? Threats and promises, more like. But Cummings said, "I agree to hold back from judgments as long as you do. I agree to stop futile efforts to break up the marriage of my son and your daughter. I agree to treat you as a member of my family, with respect and honor. And I agree to maintain this special relationship with you and with all your people until and unless we hear that you have begun once again to persecute your daughter." The mullah could change his mind tomorrow and declare a holy war, try the kids and declare them guilty of religious crimes, and levy another round of death sentences, threats, and rewards for their assassination. Forat had already proved that much to Cummings. But some agreement must be consummated. Now. Before the move to an orbit beyond Pluto's began. "So, since I have met your conditions, we have a truce. A treaty. And good reason to celebrate!" Cummings held out his hand to Forat.

Forat ignored the gesture. "We have a truce. You may tell my daughter that she and her husband have nothing to fear from Medina."

Before Cummings could offer hospitality, the imam brushed by him and strode away, back to his waiting car, idling at a respectful distance.

Cummings waited until the mullah was in his car and it had pulled away. Then he signaled his own waiting limo forward. He had accomplished something, if not all that he had hoped. If he'd been wrong to try to talk to the Medinan in terms of spiritual benefit, then he stood corrected. But the material benefit awaiting well-positioned humans through relations with the Unity aliens was clearly of interest to the mullah. Cummings should have realized. You didn't become a leader—whether of a secular corporate empire or a religious star-flung state, without bringing benefits to the people who followed you.

The next time Cummings met with Forat, he'd bring

spreadsheets. Now, he'd send Forat a few gifts and bide his time. He'd won the day for the kids, and for himself: he didn't want them to be afraid for their lives every time they entered UNE territory; if that was the case, he'd never see them again.

And he couldn't bear that.

As grueling as this meeting with Forat had been, he'd come away with what he wanted more than anything right now. He could tell the kids it was safe to come home—to come to his home, for a visit, for as long as they liked.

You couldn't build a trading empire if your key people were living in exile. NAMECorp had proprietary rights to Unity opportunities, as far as Cummings was concerned. He'd told Mickey Croft so in no uncertain terms.

Now he could tell Croft that he, Richard Cummings, had done what the Secretariat could not do: he'd negotiated a truce with Medina. As he slid into his limo, he was already reaching for the phone.

Mickey Croft might be preoccupied with sad-eyed, conical-crowned diplomats, but Cummings had his eye on the real plum: trade with a multiracial culture never before contacted by humanity. All those things he'd said to Forat about spiritual destiny. . . . Well, they might be true. He'd seen something during his visit to Rick and Dini's new home that stirred him deeply. He was businessman enough to know that if a hardened case such as he could be moved by the beauty and tranquility of a Unity world, then he could sell access to that world, and everything from it, to every soul in the UNE who could afford his price.

He'd bring Croft into line with less effort than it took to convince Old Man Forat, but then, Croft wasn't interested in killing children for reasons based in the need to maintain personal power. Croft just wanted to do the right thing for the UNE.

And Cummings, more than any other single individual, knew what the right thing for the UNE was. It was trade, multicultural stimulation, and expansion. Richard Cummings wouldn't give his son's life for it, but he'd have given almost anything else. He'd been ready to explain to the Mullah Forat how difficult life was going to be for the Medinan Empire without access to NAMECorp shipping, NAMECorp technical and spare parts support, and NAMECorp allies as trading partners.

He was glad he hadn't needed to threaten the aging cleric with an embargo. He'd done just right. He'd put it in terms the old man could understand. Damned if he knew where all that spiritual drivel had come from. Except for the moment when Forat wouldn't shake his hand, everything had gone just swimmingly. He could still see, in his mind's eye, his outthrust hand and Forat's unwillingness to clasp it. It bothered him more than it should, this unwillingness to touch flesh to flesh, to use an ancient Earth custom that surely wasn't foreign to the Medinan. He wished he could have touched the Mullah, physically communicated some of his newfound zeal for all things Unity.

But the lack of a handshake didn't mean anything, not between consenting adults. So why did he have this nagging sense that an opportunity had been lost?

No matter. Croft's office symbol came up on the videophone screen in Cummings' limo, followed in good time by Mickey Croft's big-eared, sunken-jawed face.

"Hello, Mickey. I've got good news. I've just come out of a meeting with Beni Forat. . . ."

That got Croft's full attention. Cummings enjoyed mightily the feeling of being unilaterally in control of information that the Secretariat would consider critical. So he would take his time telling Croft what had transpired with Forat, and put a spin on the story that would best suit NAME-Corp's needs.

After all, Croft worked for the people of the United Nations of Earth, and Cummings was one of those people for whom Croft sometimes needed to be reminded that he must work the hardest.

The project to tow Threshold to beyond Pluto's orbit was almost underway. The removal of resistance from Forat would help in the final days of decision making and implementation. By the time this conversation was over, Croft was going to know that, despite any lingering doubts or resistance on the Secretary General's part, Threshold was going to be moved to a new orbit. On time. According to plan. And with no obstructionism from the Secretariat. NAMECorp, prime contractor for the project, was going to see to it that every deadline, benchmark, and milestone was successfully met.

There was too much money and power at stake for Cummings to allow anything to stand in his way.

CHAPTER 18

▽

Message Delivered

Reice was sitting out near the Ball site in the *BLUE TICK* when the alien came to call. Imagine. There you are, sitting in your police cruiser, directing traffic, relaxed as you please, a jelly donut in one hand and a no-spill cup of half-cold coffee in the other, feet up on your console, listening to Traffic Control with one ear and your favorite late twentieth-century analog recording with the other, when all of a sudden your nice, cozy routine is disturbed so completely you just know nothing will ever be the same again—not your day, not your week, not your mission or your job or your life. Not ever.

Nothing external seemed to change when Reice's world turned upside down. The crowded traffic into and out of Spacedock Seven still moved at a snail's pace as towing rigs and tugs and destroyers and carriers and container ships with WARNING: EXPLOSIVES stenciled on their sides jockeyed for position in the MERGE lane bound for Threshold. None of the ConSpaceCom convoy vehicles with their military designators and security escorts noticed anything amiss when Reice's life turned from predictable to perilous. Nobody out there seemed to have an inkling that anything strange was going on aboard the ConSec cruiser *BLUE TICK*.

Reice should have been able to look forward to sitting out here every day for the foreseeable future, eating dozens of jelly donuts, listening to hundreds of good old tunes, and catching up on his paperwork. Because preparing to tow Threshold to a new orbit was such a huge undertaking,

Reice had every right to expect to be here a good long while, doing the usual. Breaking up arguments over priority access to the special convoy route. Taking names and kicking ass when the inevitable fender benders occurred. Stopping traffic altogether for the occasional hotshot with a diplomatic escort or a bunch of stars on the nose of his insystem cruiser. Today should have been, in short, a normal day, a day like any other.

But no. Today was the day the Unity aliens—or alien— invaded the *BLUE TICK*. It was a red-letter day in Reice's personal History of the Universe, and one which changed everything for him, nearly beyond his ability to endure.

Reice had to admit that it was probably the Ball site that was doing this to him—thrusting him in harm's way and into the center of events too damned big for guys like Reice to handle. You had to want to be rich and famous, like the old Scavenger, Keebler, who'd discovered the Ball and towed it to Threshold in the first place, to think alien contact with a Probably Superior Race was a good idea. You had to think your job description included Saving the Galaxy from Invaders to welcome a surprise visit from some cone-headed Unity alien on an urgent mission. You had to believe that your shift tasking included Carrying the Fate of The World on Your Shoulders to make such an alien welcome.

Reice was about as happy to get close up and personal with a Unity alien as he'd been when he'd been chasing two runaway rich kids out here and a perfectly good chunk of otherwise normal, unperturbed spacetime had opened up and swallowed them whole. So it came back to the Ball site again. The Ball site was always where trouble found Reice. He ought to stay away from it. The damned Ball had it in for him.

Once he got this alien off his ship, he was going to request leave, or rotation to other duties that were nowhere near the damned Unity Ball.

But thinking about what you should have done or were going to do didn't help you when you were face-to-face with one of those sorry looking Unity aliens with the black-in-black eyes and the decorated craniums that came up to a rounded point, as if the alien were wearing a crown or a wizard's hat or a dunce cap.

"How'd you get in here?" Reice asked it laconically, trying to exude power and calm and self-control. Maybe if it thought it wasn't scaring him it would go away.

The Unity alien replied, "Get in through doorway."

Bullshit, Reice thought. It wasn't like you left the door unlocked on your police cruiser. The alien was here, though, real as real could be. There was nothing halfway or semitransparent about it. It was a good two meters tall and its sneaky black eyes were busy cataloguing every inch of Reice's flight deck. He'd better say something, he thought, so it didn't decide he was hostile. He said, "I'm Reice, of ConSec. Now that you're here, what can I do for you?"

"Greetings, Reice, friend of valued friends. Pleasure to be nowtime in your company."

"That's right," Reice said through numb lips that could barely form words. He was actually having a conversation with one of these aliens, as if it was an everyday thing. And the alien was giving him a real clear hint that its presence here wasn't a random phenomenon. *Valued Friend* was the title that the Unity aliens had bestowed on the white-hole Scavenger who'd first brought the Ball to Threshold. "I'm a good friend of your Valued Friend, Micah Keebler, the guy who towed the Ball in here in the first place." Had to make the best of this. Reice's skin was crawling. The alien was less than four feet away from him, blocking the single corridor that led from the flight deck. There was no way out for Reice, nowhere to run. The alien blocked the only egress from the *TICK*'s two-place flight deck, unless Reice wanted to try punching out into vacuum by hitting his ejection seat control. "Now that you're here, why don't you sit down, take a load off?" Reice gestured to the copilotry station, at the same time letting his hand trail over the control panel long enough to disable the copilot's navigation and flight controls.

"Load brought here, is message. Load take back, is answer, soontime, friend Reice. Sitting is probable, thanks. Will attempt nowtime."

The alien moved toward him then, and Reice's whole body tried so hard to push itself into his seat, it creaked. Getting in here, the alien hadn't tripped a single alarm bell or intrusion warning of the *BLUE TICK*'s multicapability security suite. But then, Reice hadn't been expecting a boarding party. Now it slid or floated or wafted its way gracefully to the copilotry station that Reice had indicated with an ease that belied its mass. The thing was solid as a rock to the eye, but moved as if it weighed nothing—or as if the fifth-force generators on the *TICK* had given out.

The Unity alien stooped when it reached the copilotry couch, as if uncertain. As it was about to sit down, Reice urged expansively, "Go ahead. It's okay. We're all friends, here."

The alien climbed onto the couch, standing on top of it. Its conical head brushed the control suite above the station. It was facing aft, and it turned its head to meet Reice's eyes a whole lot further than any human could turn its head. "How do, sitting?"

It scrutinized Reice intently, and turned itself around, facing front, sort of: its eyes never left him, its head never moved, but its body nearly did a one-eighty.

"Um, bend your knees, sit on your butt, or cross your legs on the seat if it's easier." He demonstrated, forcing a wide and silly grin onto his face that he hoped proved that this was no trick and that he, Reice, was in no way threatening. He wished he was back home in his Blue Mid bed. He hoped it wasn't embarrassed. People could get real unfriendly when they'd been embarrassed publicly. But how was he to know that Unity aliens didn't know how to sit down? It wasn't like the Secretariat had passed out a contact manual for the Unity that said, *Under no circumstances, if a Unity alien invites itself aboard your spacecraft, should ConSec personnel ask an alien to be seated.* Maybe Unity aliens weren't built, physiologically, to bend in the right directions.

Miserably, Reice watched his visitor struggle to assume a posture similar to Reice's, and hoped he hadn't created some awful diplomatic incident or started some war because he didn't realize that Unity aliens couldn't bend their knees—if they had knees.

Just when Reice's face was beginning to ache so bad from smiling that he had to stop it, the alien seemed to turn into a viscous fluid and ooze over the surface of the copilotry couch. The gelatinous mass slid into the chair bonelessly, then reformed itself into a solid shape that mimicked his own posture precisely.

The joke was wearing thin. Reice had just seen that thing

pour itself as if it were plastic being poured into a mold of a chair, and then resume its former shape.

Before anything worse happened, Reice said, "Great. Now that we've solved that problem, can you tell me what the message is you've got? I'll give you your response and you can go back to wherever. I'm a busy guy, you know."

"Know Reice," said the alien gravely, as its conical head stretched on a flexible neck toward him. "Message bring from friend South, of UNE diplomat mission."

"Right, South. Should have known. How is old Southie?" Reice couldn't shrink back any farther. He didn't want that face any closer to his. Commander Joe South was a Relic, a pilot from the early days of space flight who'd popped up near Threshold one day nearly five centuries later than he'd left Earth, safe and sound of body if not mind, and then gotten himself adopted by the Secretariat because he was up to his neck in this alien thing from the beginning. You bet, Reice knew South. Reice had brought the Relic pilot into Threshold to begin with, and hadn't been able to shake the fool since. Wherever you had trouble, you had South. South was nearly as alien as these Unity boogies, five hundred years out of date and spreading bad luck everywhere he went. The Secretariat had figured that out, Reice was sure, and sent South on the contact party to Unity space to be rid of him.

"Southie fine, good, but not happy. Is wanting soontime ship, his *STARBIRD*, valued friend and machine, bringing to Ball site by friend Reice and other friend, Sling. Okay doing favor, please? Nowtime quickquick?"

Caution came up in Reice's throat like a badly digested meal. "I thought, that is, I heard that South was at the Embassy party that the Unity threw for Croft. Is that where you're from—the new Embassy?" Maybe South's spacecraft, *STARBIRD*, wasn't state of the art, but the Relic pilot had poured everything he'd earned since coming to Threshold into retrofits. Sling, the aftermarketeer who'd done those retrofits, was no slouch. And the Unity alien clearly knew all about South's ship, Sling and the retrofits, and the covert relationship between Sling, South, and Reice that had kept Sling's name out of more than one of Reice's reports. Who the hell was this guy—this thing—and how could Reice trust him—it?

"From? Where from?" The alien's face, on its elastic

neck, zoomed toward Reice until its harelipped mouth was inches from his. He could feel its warm breath, which smelled slightly of copper filings and jasmine, puffing against his cheek. "From Unity, alltime. From South, past-time. From Ball, nowtime. From Embassy, soontime. Spacetimer wish coordinates?"

Coordinates? To what? Or to when? In spacetime? Or in "alltime," whatever that was. Reice wanted the alien to get out of his face. He wanted it to get out of his ship. He wanted it to get out of his life. He wanted it so bad his whole person seemed physically or magnetically repelled by the alien head so close to his.

He had to say something that would end this interview, and do it soon. But he was afraid to promise what he might not be able to deliver. "Yeah, gimme coordinates for the delivery of the *STARBIRD*. I got to know where to park it. That's all I need. Then me and Sling'll get right on it. You can tell South that."

"Needing no problem. Having information, my pleasure, task and accomplishment." The alien arched its neck and stretched its lips over huge, white, pointed teeth in an imitation of Reice's smile. "Everything ready for ship, when-ever you keep promise. Telling South all things by self, if Reice friends want to see. Coordinates Ball site, your nomenclature, forty-two degrees east latitude, sixty-eight degrees north longitude, by one and one-fifth nautical mile." As it recited a formula clearly learned from South, or someone like him, by rote, the head of the Unity alien began to draw away from him, back toward the shoulders on its telescoping neck.

Reice found he'd been gripping the arms of his acceleration couch so hard that his fingers hurt when he uncurled them.

"Great," he said. "We'll see you out at the Ball site."

"Not me, seeings. For South, this favor is."

Sure. That made sense. South would have known that the only way he was going to get anybody to park that damned antique of his anywhere near the Ball was to come to Reice. Wouldn't you know it, here comes the damned Ball again, back into Reice's life like a bad penny or an old girlfriend. "You're sure of these coordinates, sure South doesn't want his ship towed out to Pluto with the rest of Threshold?" If the alien changed its mind, Reice would be off the hook. He wanted to fly South's antiquated experimental starship out to the Ball site and park it that close to the Ball—which opened up and swallowed things on occasion, things like spaceships and people in EVA suits—about as much as he wanted see any more aliens, soontime, nowtime, or anytime.

"Sure certainly," said the alien head, which had shrunk back almost onto its shoulders. "Towing longtime. Parking, shorttime. Unity Embassy thanking Officer Reice for fine cooperation, thistime. South person thanks Reice, and other Valued Friends, appreciating Reice, through this messenger."

"Right. Well, thank you for coming. Can I—"

Reice was about to ask the alien if there was anything else he could do for it *before it left,* but it started to ooze out of its chair.

The sight made Reice want to retch. The gelatinous goo of the alien rose up into the air like a snake, swirled around a little, and became its conical-headed self once again. Then that solid form bowed slightly and walked backward, right through the starboard bulkhead of the *BLUE TICK,* as if through a diaphanous curtain.

Reice sat for a long while, looking at the spot where it had gone through the heavily armored and insulated bulkhead. There were all sorts of sensitive fiber optics and electronics, cables and sensors, life support and fire control modules inside that bulkhead. Before he did anything else, he had to run systems checks.

He started the diagnostic programs running, still sitting where he was. He couldn't see anything wrong with the bulkhead. It had no scorch marks or bubbled paint, no alien-shaped discoloration, no fracture lines, and most definitely no textural changes or alien-sized custom-made space doors.

The area wasn't radioactive. The bulkhead had absorbed no energy transients which had altered its molecular structure. The place where the alien disappeared showed no sign of absorptive or radiant abnormalities, no traces of foreign substances. Every cable, fiber, and even the monocrystalline wireguides in the bulkhead wall were nominal.

Reice continued his system checks. Every fire control component, radar, tracking system, data fusion module, precision guidance component, and modular interface of his firepower suite was in working order. So was his life support, when he got around to checking that. But he'd known it would be.

The log of the *BLUE TICK*, when he reran the time frame in question, showed an absolute, not virtual, alien that had actually been on his flight deck. The real-time encounter that was stored in his cruiser's log matched his sense memory of how long the encounter had lasted. Every word and move of the alien, every nuance the intel boys would want to study, was recorded for posterity. The encounter had lasted twelve point three minutes, standard clock time.

The only anomaly Reice could turn up across the whole spectrum of possible anomalies was that two hours and twenty-eight minutes had passed for everybody outside the *BLUE TICK*,

You could go nuts, worrying about missing hours and minutes that don't jibe with your physical and internal clock reckoning. Maybe it was some kind of relativistic effect. Sure. That's all it was. The alien's presence had caused some discrepancy between the onboard ship time of the *BLUE TICK* and the external time of the rest of the local universe. Nothing to sweat.

Joe South had lost five hundred years, for God and country. Reice shouldn't be sweating two-hours-and-change worth of missing minutes. But he did sweat it. The lost time bothered the hell out of him.

Lost time was worse than molasses aliens and permeable bulkheads. Lost time was just downright spooky.

Eventually, Reice was going to have to tell somebody what had happened out here. Before that, he'd better find out where that lost time went, how to account for it, and why his virtual absence hadn't been noticed by anybody else. He didn't have a single unanswered query or undone task on his log for the entire "missing" interval. Great.

Reice got up from his couch and walked briskly over to the place where the alien had disappeared through the bulkhead. He touched the spot—something for which he'd done all the intervening work to avoid. It felt solid. It wasn't slippery, or sticky, or greasy, or yielding. It was just a bulkhead panel like any other.

Okay, then. There was no alien aboard his ship now, and he'd suffered no discernable harm. He'd made a promise he'd better see about keeping, though, before he turned in a report on this and got himself and the *BLUE TICK* so bound up in red tape that a bowel movement, let alone movement around Threshold or out to the Ball site, was impossible.

Sling was going to love this. All they had to do was get South's ship, fly it out to the Ball site using Reice's clout, park it and get the hell out of there.

South was behind this stunt, Reice had no doubt of that. The Unity alien that had come to Reice hadn't gone through regular channels, and almost certainly didn't have the savvy to realize how many chains of command and choke points were being cut by coming right to Reice with South's message.

When Reice got hold of Joe South, the Relic pilot was going to owe Reice one hell of a "favor" in return for what Reice was about to do.

Because he was going to do it. You didn't lie to something that could walk through your bulkhead anytime. You didn't break a promise to something that could mess with your clock time. You didn't ask for trouble, ever, in Reice's universe, and to his way of thinking, disappointing the Unity aliens after promising to do them a favor was more trouble than Reice—or maybe anybody in the UNE—could handle.

He glared out of his real-time monitors at the Ball as he made arrangements to go off-shift early, got a vector to Blue Mid, and set coordinates for home base.

Then he called Sling, using a couple ConSec priority channels to find the aftermarketeer through the All-Points Locator.

Sling's scared voice, patched to him through a ConSec ground cruiser, wanted to know, "What the hell do you think you're doing, asshole, sending your cop buddies out to roust me? Or have I committed a crime and just don't know it yet?"

"You're about to commit a service to your local law enforcement officials." The voice-only channel on which these communications were routed was redundantly secure. Reice began enjoying the moment of total power over the earring-wearing aftermarketeer as soon as he realized how frightened Sling was by Reice's estimable clout.

Maybe losing two hours and change was a small price to

pay for the fun Reice could have with keeping his promise to the Unity alien. "Sling, get whatever gear you need to deliver South's *STARBIRD* out to a spacedock parking orbit, and meet me in the ConSec Blue Mid docking bay in three hours."

"She ain't spaceworthy, Reice."

"You have three hours. Do whatever you have to."

"Screw you, Reice, you don't have the faintest idea what's involved. I can't—"

"You can, and you'd damn well better. I'll see you when I dock the *TICK*. Bring your tools, whatever you're going to need. Oh, and pack a lunch, Sport. You and me are going on a little joyride, ready or not."

CHAPTER 19

▽

Reunion

Joe South had been out of his native spacetime too long. Everything looked, sounded, and felt strange to him: his body; Riva Lowe, the woman next to him; and the Unity shuttle itself, once it entered the UNE cosmology, with its warped spacetimes and convoluted energy wells—or gravity wells, as the spacetimers thought of them.

As he should start thinking of them. This whole spacetime was filled with dangers he hadn't had to think about for a long time. They could kill him just as dead as they ever could, whether he acknowledged them or not. He was subject to all the laws of the local physics here. More than that, he was born in this special case spacetime, and everything about it had a real affinity for exerting power over his physiology. He had to remember what it was like to be here, before he made some stupid mistake.

"Riva, how do you feel?" he said with his mouth, moving his lips and tongue and manipulating the air coming out of his lungs to form the sounds he wanted. He turned in his cocoon enough to look at her.

She moved her head jerkily in hers, tilting it toward him so that he could see her face, distorted by the pull of gravity. "S-s-strange," she admitted, using her mouth as well. "Are we there yet?"

"Why, do you want to go to the bathroom?" He grinned weakly, trying out his face muscles and his old-style humor at the same time.

"Very funny." She sighed. "Damn, my throat is dry."

Neither of them had been to the bathroom, or drunk

liquid, or used these bodies for what seemed like years. Around them, the Unity shuttle shimmered and hummed softly to itself, its plasma walls undulating in gentle, even rhythms.

Around South, his cocoon started to vibrate slightly in rhythm with the innards of the plasma sphere as it made the corrections necessary to deposit them at their destination. The vibration would stimulate his body, his skin, his muscles, and through fibroid connections, the organs necessary for his survival. He could feel the tiny electrical impulses surging through him, reminding his heart how fast to beat, his brain how to process temporal stimuli, his nervous system how to answer his brain's command.

It was going to be all right. He believed it would because he'd programmed the cocoon and the plasma shuttle himself. He still trusted his ability to adjust to circumstances, even after so long a time of making circumstances adjust to him.

Underneath him, his cocoon started to shift, bringing the upper part of his body into a sitting position. Riva's cocoon was lagging a little behind his, which meant it wasn't getting the responses it needed from her physiology as fast.

"Riva, we've got to concentrate on syncing this reentry. You need to be helping the system a little more. Talk to me. Think about what you want to do when we get there. Who you want to see. What you want to say. What you want to wear—" His last remark was designed to get a rise out of her.

It did. She made a face at him, and her cocoon surged colors as it began to react to her realtime actions and contemplated activities. Soon enough, she would be thinking linearly and acting linearly all the nowtime.

Soon enough, they both would. South's cocoon was shifting into a control bolster under his arm. That meant he could resume manual control whenever he wanted.

He wasn't ready. His head ached. His eyes were pulsing. He could only see straight ahead and slightly through peripheral vision. He needed to remember what it was like to direct a physical self that was pointed forward, not only in time, but in space, and do so where those two concepts could be separated phenomenologically.

Riva Lowe groaned and sat up, her hands over her eyes. "I hate this." Her cocoon was pulsing red and gold, and her crooked elbows stuck out of it. "The sooner we get on the ground—into the spacetime manifold—the better. I can't bear feeling so ... rusty."

"Yeah, I know." South flexed his hand and watched the movement of ligaments under skin and across bone. The hand was pale, greenish, bluish, and flushed in places as he moved it. It was working fine. He balled a fist and extended one finger at a time from the fist. It hurt to straighten each finger out separately, in turn, but fine motor control was about to become a factor of his survival. "Have you thought out what you want to say to them?"

To the ones they'd left behind. To all their kind, through Mickey Croft, Remson, and the rest, when finally they had a chance to do so without Unity monitors present, without worrying about misunderstanding because of spacetime incongruities, or timeslip, or what might be misunderstood. When Croft and Remson had visited the Unity Embassy, the interaction had taken place in Unity spacetime. This meeting would be on the humans' home turf.

"I just want to see if I can stand up, okay, South? One goddamned thing at a time." Riva Lowe was elevating her cocoon and trying to step out of it. The physioshield plasma swathing her looked like cobwebs drenched in dew. She took one tottering step and stood on her own, her arms outstretched and waving wildly, the swathing hanging off her arms and torso like some fairy cape or gossamer wings. Suddenly, she moaned and fell back into the cocoon. "This sucks," she said. "I'm as weak as a baby."

"Take it slower, Madam Ambassador, and you'll get more for your calories." They hadn't worried about calories for a long time, either. South felt as if he'd been ejected from the Garden of Eden, but then, you could argue that people had felt that way for thousands of years.

A soft pinging sound reminded him of his linear place in sequential time. "We'll be actually inside the Ball very soontime—very *soon* now." He made the shift in terminology with an almost savage emphasis: they had to think the way their bodies moved, the way their brains worked, the way local physics demanded, or they would fail here. Perhaps die here. And he couldn't bear the thought of that.

"I'm not ready," wailed Riva Lowe softly.

"Sure you are. You were born for this—born to it, and chosen for this moment, out of how many possible others?

Come on, hotshot, show me what you're made of. Sit up, get dressed like a good ambassador should, and face the music.''

He was trying to arrange his own clothing requirements: space suit, underliner, power-driven helmet, gloves, the whole UNE package. The gossamer lining of his cocoon gave him the best reproduction it could manage, from his memory, the program he'd written, and the sample he'd encoded.

Still, the clothes felt restrictive, heavy, scratchy, and somehow stifling.

He turned the helmet in his hands, watching the plasma around his feet harden into spaceworthy boots with fifth-force soles. Coming here with the intention of leaving the Unity space of the embassy, of the Ball, and moving through his native spacetime was harder than he'd expected. But he'd volunteered for this when he'd agreed to go in the first place. Neither he, nor Riva Lowe, had realized how hard it would be to come back.

His lungs were fighting for air, burning, having trouble remembering what to do. Or else the air wasn't right. He had full instrumentation under his hand, now. He asked for a life-support reading and it was perfect.

He shouldn't have worried. The Unity plasma system wouldn't let him down. His physical body, however, was beyond Unity control. And only partly under his. Some things never changed.

When he looked at Riva again, she was sitting smugly in a good replica of an acceleration couch, smartly attired in the latest of fashionable spacegoing UNE gear, and her fingernails were drumming soundlessly on her helmet's faceplate.

She saw him looking at her. "Ready, Columbus?"

"Maybe you mean that," he frowned, "but don't think that way. I'm going to get my old ship, see a few friends, make an appearance, answer some questions. Period."

"Yes, yes. I know," she replied. "Give the spacetimers a reference point. Help them adjust." Her face crinkled, as if it might fall in upon itself. Then she took control and said in a husky voice full of suppressed emotion, "How long do you think this will take?"

"Notime. It's going to take notime. They promised us. We agreed to try this not because we had a choice, but because it's our job. We weren't invited to live alltime, forever, not like Keebler. We're the diplomatic contingent, such as it is. So we had no choice. Remember what you want to achieve. Why you came. Who you are. What you were." He shrugged and he felt the muscles of his mouth pull down in an expression that seemed so far in his past he was surprised he remembered it. But his body remembered. His body remembered everything. Muscle memory was going to be his salvation on this mission. He'd been through more displacement than any other human being. He'd flown the first mission to a Unity world, although he hadn't known it then. He'd felt this awful sense of loss before, and now he even understood why.

So he ought to be thankful for the favor the Unity had done him. He wasn't crazy. He wasn't mad from experimental flybys with developmental hardware that might have deleterious effects on the human brain. He'd learned everything he needed to trust his sanity and his heart.

Except that he'd lost everything he'd cared about. Again. First his century. His family. His culture. His career. His sense of self. He'd built it all up again, from scratch. Now this.

"You think we'll go back?" asked Riva Lowe, quavering like a child.

"I will. You've got to get your green card punched, your visa extended, and volunteer for another tour of duty out there."

"And you don't?"

"Immaterial," he snapped. "You care whether the UNE makes the right choice. I don't. I just care that I do."

Ambassador Lowe told him where to put his self-centered attitude, and he told her she'd better remember more about the mechanics of living in a past-to-future society, where some things just weren't physically possible.

Then he got real busy doing what he did: piloting. The plasma shuttle was extremely responsive, agreeable, and easy to manage. Its inboard intelligence was so far beyond the capabilities of South's beloved old ship, *STARBIRD,* that the two weren't in the same class. *STARBIRD* was an experimental vehicle of ancient parameters, with a primitive artificial intelligence shoehorned into her inert hull. The plasma shuttle was bred for speed, courage, resilience, and stamina. It aimed to please.

Still, bringing a plasma shuttle into a docking module inside the Ball, which resided in UNE space, was so tricky no Unity pilot had tried it successfully. The Unity had been forced to build the Ball to establish a beachhead close to the spacetimers. You lost less plasma shuttles that way.

South didn't want to lose this one. He concentrated on being in two continua at once, on obeying two sets of physical laws—his native ones and his adopted ones—and let the task roll over him.

All the way to the final docking coordinates inside the Ball, he never heard a thing Riva might have said, or even remembered that he was carrying a passenger. He existed in a plasma mode, a physical mode, and a sliding temporal mode that he couldn't allow to harden into a forward moving arrow of time until he'd put the shuttle in its berth.

When he heard the soft bump and felt the slight deformation that meant success, he was drenched in sweat and more tired than he'd ever been. But they'd made it.

Riva said, "It's okay, isn't it."

"Yep. Suit up. Debarkation in—" he turned to grin at her "—six minutes, Threshold Standard Time. Want to synchronize our watches?"

Minutes. Time. Here they were, for better or worse. Home where it all began. The shuttle under them thrummed softly, happy to be in a cocoon of its own, being carefully reconfigured from the outside in, before it was extruded in the local spacetime.

By the time the Ball opened up and sent them on their way through its portal with a soft kick in the collective pants, everything inside the plasma shuttle looked contemporary to the universe they were entering.

The surfaces around South were hard and unyielding, as they should be. Light was white and cast shadows, or colored and restricted to instrumentation. A monitor in front of him confirmed the exit of the shuttlecraft, past the portal, and South had just a glimpse of something his human eyes read as great lions rampant at the gate.

Then the shuttle was out in UNE space, the Ball was closing on all the radiance within, and South set a course for the agreed-upon coordinates.

Only then did he have time to check on Riva. "Lookin' good," he told her encouragingly.

"Feeling queasy," she shot back, but nodded: they were

both back in the rhythm of their bodies. If they could make the rest of this journey as flawlessly as they had negotiated the most dangerous part, then they'd be just fine.

The unremarkable looking shuttle headed smoothly for the two ships parked at the designated coordinates. To make certain that the trigger-happy Reice didn't panic and start shooting, South put out a standard hail and gave his call-signs.

Reice's voice came to them through the plasma surrogate of human-built communications gear with no deviation from the template. "I guess it's really you, South. Who made up those designators for your unlicensed vehicle, anyhow?"

South said, "Reice, don't get bureaucratic. Ambassador Lowe was with me, and she assigned the designator US-0001, for Unity Space Number One, with her authority. You want to argue with the ambassador, she's right here?"

"Naw," Reice's voice answered. "It's just that every time I see you, South, you're in some new unregistered space-craft or other."

"Speaking of spacecraft, how's my *STARBIRD*? And Birdy? Is Sling there?" Birdy was his ship's AI. He hadn't realized how much he wanted to be reunited with his ship and her artificial intelligence. They'd been through ten hells together.

"Right here, South. What's the damned hurry with this retrofit, anyhow?" Sling complained. "Reice is all over me about making that bucket of junk of yours spaceworthy."

"When I get there, okay?" Something seemed different about the two men. Something was slightly wrong with their banter and the tones of their voices. But that might have been due to the plasma shuttle's communications capability, or just an artifact of time having passed.

South asked for docking sync and then broke the transmission, using the shuttle's forward monitor to take a good look at the embassy near the Ball.

Coming along fine.

No need to worry.

Riva said, "South, are you okay? Is it—"

"Fine," he said aloud. "They're just tense. No problem." In this spacetime, she could just about read his mind. "Don't worry. Look at the embassy. No wonder these folks are sounding stressed. Next thing on their agenda is the ride out beyond Pluto."

Reice and Sling had every right to sound different, he reasoned. Joe South was a little different, himself.

CHAPTER 20

$\triangledown$

Up to Your Neck in Alligators

"The alien never touched me, I want to make that real clear before I start hearin' about contamination problems," Reice said to the effigy of Remson giving orders from the *BLUE TICK*'s central monitor. "I didn't have much time to decide and I figured a little initiative was in order." Reice was uncomfortably conscious of the fact that Sling was lounging just out of Remson's view at the copilot's station.

"That may be so, Mr. Reice, but your unilateral decision making in this case is worrisome." Remson didn't look worried. He looked like he was enjoying the privilege of rank to make life miserable for the lower classes. "Let me be equally clear. Since you're so certain that our prodigal ambassador and Commander South are reporting to you to collect South's ship before they report to us at the Secretariat, then you make sure they *do* report to the Secretariat. Immediately. Give them a police escort, personally. And don't take no for an answer. I want you to have South in an AIP/PDE evaluation chamber in Blue-Mid and Ambassador Lowe in the SecGen's Stalk office by thirteen hundred hours sharp, Mr. Reice. No sidetrips, no improvisation—and no excuses. Just do it."

Remson broke the comlink abruptly and Reice was left staring at a blank screen. South wasn't going to like being remanded into the custody of an AIP/PDE (Artificially Intelligent Preprogrammed/Pilotry Digital Evaluator), an AI shrink, any more than Riva Lowe was going to like being hustled off to the SecGen's office before she could set her own itinerary. Remson knew he was handing Reice a punitive assignment and it sucked. . . .

Sling cleared his throat in the awkward silence.

Reice turned on him. "Don't you say a word, Mr. Aftermarketeer. Not one word about this to anybody. Ever." It burned Reice's butt that Sling had been witness to Remson's tantrum. "This whole damned enterprise is classified, so far as you're concerned. You talk to anybody about the events surrounding this trip to the Ball site, I'm going to make policing you my personal business for the next twenty or thirty years. From now until I say different, you're on strip alert to support ConSec activities—you don't eat, sleep, or go to the can without reporting your movements first to my office. Got me?"

"Yah, boss." Sling was toying with the tip of his long braid. "See no evil, hear no evil, speak no evil—that's me. I just hope you're talking billable hours, here. I got a life to live, too. Or maybe you forgot, in all this camaraderie, that I'm not part of your governmental infrastructure. You issue me a gag order and a heads-up, it better be in relation to some sort of contract." Sling's single earring twinkled at Reice provocatively, punctuating the incipient smirk on the aftermarketeer's stubbled face.

"I'll keep your damned pilot's license in my hip pocket—as long as you're good. How's that for a contract?"

Sling looked away, at his copilotry sensor suite. Then he said, "Here comes the shuttle, right on time. I don't know why that fool thinks he can dock with *STARBIRD*. I'm a good retrofitter, but I ain't God. Nothing contemporary's going to dock with that antique without a whole lot of onboard help. You want I should tell him to park it here?"

"You bet your ass I do," Reice growled, and got busy trying to implement Remson's orders for South's psych evaluation before the pilot was breathing down his neck.

He shouldn't have worried. While Reice was still arranging for priority internal slippage to accommodate his personal convoy, plus vectors to cut through the ConSpaceCom traffic that was jammed up from here to Threshold, Sling let out a long, slow whistle and kicked back in his couch, arms dangling at his sides, eyes closed.

"So? Cut the theatrics, okay, Sling? We haven't got squat for time to waste." Reice brushed his comset off his head to encircle his neck. "What's the damned problem?"

"Don't know it's a problem. They say they're sending the shuttle back to the Ball and don't worry about docking procedures; they've already mated the locks. So we're invited aboard *STARBIRD*, soon as we're ready."

"Can they do that? Mate those locks?"

"Nope. Not in this universe, anyway. But there goes the shuttlecraft now." Sling swept a spread hand over the copilotry pad and the *TICK*'s monitors blossomed with four views of the Unity shuttlecraft headed back toward the Ball.

Reice said, "Nothing special looking about that shuttle. Nothin' special about remote controls, either."

"Yeah?" came Sling's voice. "From where? *STARBIRD*? The Ball? Internally controlled precision vectoring? Into the *Ball*? Past all that Spacedock Seven traffic? Without a comlink to Spacedock Traffic Control? For my part, I want to watch that shuttle make the Ball open up for it—shit!"

Reice didn't have to ask what Sling meant this time. The shuttlecraft was disintegrating before their eyes. The bits and pieces didn't come apart normally, either: they stayed together in a pattern or an orbit around an invisible gravity source, so that the view in Reice's monitor resembled a deep-water jellyfish or magnetic field lines on a subatomic particle. Then that too disappeared, and nothing Reice or Sling could do in any scanning mode, not even infrared, could track the erstwhile shuttle's mass any farther.

"Shit," Sling said again, almost prayerfully. "That can't be." But it was.

Reice got up fast. "Let's get over there, before we record any more phenomena we don't like."

The spacedock connecting Reice's *BLUE TICK* to *STARBIRD* was a flexible, pressurized tube about twenty meters long and lined with zero-gee webbing. Nevertheless, for safety's sake, they wore their helmets and gloves that made their suit life-support systems self-sufficient. Pulling himself along, toward *STARBIRD*'s antique front door, Reice found the going harder and harder. Probably the stomach-churning encounter with Remson had thrown his chemistries too far out of line for abrupt zero-gee to be tolerable. Bile kept coming up in his throat. His head was aching by the time he and Sling reached the lock and slapped the exterior cycle plate that Sling had installed there.

The lock opened and Sling, floating by the plate with one hand on the safety webbing, motioned Reice ahead of him, doing a weightless caricature of a courtier's bow.

Reice's feet hit the metal floor of the bulkhead, hard, as he entered the fifth-force field. Sling was right behind him, working the jury-rig manually to start the safety cycle. Red light flooded the tiny, closed compartment. Green light followed. Then the inner door opened before Sling could enable the controls.

And there was South, helmetless, with the lady ambassador right behind him, smiling brightly in the narrow corridor. Without helmets and integral comlinks, you couldn't even say hello or ask permission to come aboard.

Crazy fools, not to wear helmets during a lock cycle, especially between this ancient crate and a modern spacecraft.

Reice stepped smartly through and waited for Sling to follow before unsealing his gloves from his suit. "Here we go," Reice breathed.

Sling's voice in his com said, "So far, so good. At least the lock seals are tight. I can't figure out how they got over here from the shuttlecraft without disengaging my rig, but—"

"Do me a favor, Sling." Reice's breathing was too sharp. He ignored it. "Don't ask them, okay?" South was watching him, staring into his helmet as if following the conversation, as if the Relic pilot could hear every word being said.

"Okay, boss. No sweat."

You couldn't stand two abreast in *STARBIRD*'s narrow passageway. For the two newcomers to have room to take off their helmets, South and Ambassador Lowe had to move out of the way.

Piece of crap ship. Reice couldn't see what South thought was worth keeping. Any sane person would have off-loaded whatever special AI he wanted to keep onto new media and consigned the rest to the scraphead domain. But not South.

Reice had to crabwalk up the passageway, helmet in hand, once he'd gotten the damned thing off his head.

Sticky seal. He'd work on it later. Sling had moved forward, along the narrow passage. Reice's stomach was still feeding him fountains of hot, sour bile that hit the roof of his mouth disconcertingly.

Up ahead, he saw South hugging Sling like a long-lost friend and Riva Lowe pumping the aftermarketeer's hand as if they were of equal rank. He got goose bumps from the sight of the contact.

All of a sudden, he saw those black alien eyes inches from his, and he admitted that he was at least as jacked up about this mission as Remson. Maybe even agreed with Remson, that you didn't know what kind of hazard the Relic pilot and his ladyfriend ambassador might represent. Not after they'd been intimate with Unity aliens for so long.

So you were real careful. You took your time. You didn't make any false moves. When Reice straggled onto the cramped flight deck, South was sitting at his pilot's station, and Ambassador Lowe's pert butt was perched on the navigation console. There was barely room for Reice to crowd into the single-place cockpit with the other three. So he didn't. He leaned against the hatchway and stuck his head inside.

You had to be on your toes in here to avoid touching the two wanderers by accident. Contamination was a real consideration when you were dealing with the unknown.

Reice was determined to be as careful as possible. He finally admitted that he didn't want to be any closer than necessary to South or Lowe, and his stomach calmed down immediately.

Sling was saying, "—shuttlecraft broke up, far as I could see, without losing relative cohesion, and the bits stayed on vector. I can't figure it."

"Don't try," Joe South advised from his station. "We're just glad to be back, safe and sound. Aren't we, Riva?"

Riva Lowe was a beautiful woman, to Reice's way of thinking: compact, smart, sexy. But today he didn't want to go anywhere near her.

From less than four feet away, she said, "Absolutely. How have you been keeping, Reice? Ready for the big move out beyond Pluto?"

Reice had spent lots of energy, in the old days, trying to get into this woman's pants. He'd sensed something different about her and South over the ship-to-ship link, but that could have been his nerves. Now he was sure. He knew different when he saw it. He just couldn't put his finger on what that difference was. Well, that was what Remson's orders were meant to find out.

Looking her straight in the eye, he said, "We're gettin' there. Right now, you two better be ready for a command performance at the Secretariat. I got orders to escort you straight into a Blue-Mid slip, then up to the Secretariat for a couple meetings that Assistant Secretary Remson's got scheduled for you. Debrief, you know. Chop chop." He wasn't about to tell South right off the bat that South was getting an AI psych evaluation. "And we're on a tight time line. So we better get started. We're due at the Secretariat at thirteen hundred hours, sharp."

That was what Remson had said: sharp.

South said, "Sling, you want to ride with us? Go over these new retrofits with me?"

"If Sling goes with you, Joe," Riva Lowe said like they'd planned it between them, "then perhaps I'll ride in with Mr. Reice. Otherwise, it'll be too crowded."

How many times had Reice schemed to get Customs Director Riva Lowe alone on his cruiser? But Ambassador to the Unity Riva Lowe was a whole different piece of work. And yet there was nothing he could say against the plan that would make sense.

So he told Sling, "You remember, Sling, you're on my payroll and you better make all the hours you're billing for this worthwhile. South, you got any problems with Sling's work on this crate, you come to me and we'll fix it." Hearty. Friendly. And with a message for Sling that the aftermarketeer had better not forget.

"Some things never change." Sling sighed. There was no way that the four of them could pretend much longer that the awkwardness on the flight deck wasn't a real problem. So you got the hell off the flight deck. You prayed that Sling would play his part, keep his mouth shut. And you escorted the UNE ambassador to Unity space aboard your cruiser with as much aplomb as you could manage.

And without any physical contact whatsoever.

Maybe some things did change. Irreparably.

CHAPTER 21

▽

One More Time

Commander Joe South was back in the UNE and feeling like an outsider all over again. And the UNE wasn't helping. Here he was, in the damned inhuman clutches of an artificially intelligent shop vacuum cleaner with a voice module that thought it was going to map his psychological state and display it to Mickey Croft, Vince Remson, and other high-and-mighties with Need To Know.

The digital therapist said metallically, "Commander South, please describe your impressions of the Unity aliens' intentions toward the United Nations of Earth." Its goose-necked videocam arched back and stared at him with cyclopean patience.

This was the third time it had asked him nearly the same question in slightly different ways. Interrogation techniques didn't seem to have changed much over time. Maybe some of the delivery systems got more sophisticated, but this one was still as dumb as a post.

In the sterile evaluation chamber, he kept having the feeling that he was being watched from behind, as well as by the digital therapist. Fine. Let them watch. He resented the hell out of being chucked right into a psych evaluation, straight off the ship. He understood the reasoning, but the people doing that reasoning weren't having to endure the process.

So what if his psych profile of today did or did not match the one they'd taken from him when he'd first arrived in this century, dazed and fresh from an experimental spongespace jump that had taken him to X-3, a Unity world, and back to his own spacetime with a little wobble that had lost him five hundred years of UNE clock time, his own century, his friends and family, and everything he cared about.

If he'd known then what he knew now—including the fact that his experimental flyby of X-3 would have killed him if the Unity aliens hadn't leant him a helping hand— maybe he wouldn't have been so resentful when he'd ended up in twenty-fifth-century UNE space.

But maybe he would have acted just the same. The UNE had a way of ignoring your rights, your welfare, and your wishes when it suited UNE purposes. He couldn't help wanting to trash the crude, implacable robot torturing him, just like last time.

This time, he wasn't going to let it get his goat. This time, the UNE wasn't getting any information from him that he didn't want to give. And when he was ready to talk to them, they were going to meet his terms. Riva and he were agreed on a strategy. He just had to keep his head and not get flapped.

The machine asked again, "Commander South, what are your impressions of the motives of the Unity aliens toward the United Nations of Earth."

"Good. Positive. Curious. Cautious. They'd like a working relationship but on mutually acceptable terms." Same thing he'd said the last time he was asked. Same thing he'd say the thousandth time he was asked.

The AI therapist burbled to itself. Its videocam head arched back on its gooseneck and then curled in on itself. "This session is ended. Please await further instructions."

It turned itself off, apparently, and sat there inert. The white room around him was sterile and completely silent. South wasn't going to let them spook him. He was back. He had valuable data. He didn't blame Mickey Croft for wanting a definitive read on South's physical and mental condition and an evaluation from the AI shrink on whether his judgment could be trusted. But he minded like hell being ordered around as if he were just another piece of hardware they could turn on and off at will.

South had come back here to get Birdy. The AI therapist couldn't understand that. He wanted *STARBIRD* because the ship, and Birdy, its AI, had shared a mission with him that had nearly killed him, precipitated them forward in time into a world he didn't halfway like and wasn't truly fit to operate in, and every time somebody talked about junking *STARBIRD,* so far as he was concerned, they were talking about junking Joe South. He'd put all his UNE wages into acquiring and upgrading his ship because he couldn't really tell where he left off and *STARBIRD* began anymore.

These fools couldn't understand that when you were displaced, you anthropomorphized familiar things. And Birdy was a real intelligence, now—especially since Sling had been working on her. He'd have been content to stay in Unity space and never come back here, except that he wanted his ship back. He wanted to fly a normal spacecraft the hard way, using his hands and his heart and his reflexes and his brain.

In the Unity continuum, he'd flown other craft, other ways. He was now a more qualified test pilot than any hotdog ConSpaceCom pilot who'd lord rank and rating over him if he ventured into a pilot's bar. They didn't know that yet, and that was fine with him.

He was making a new life for himself, for him and Birdy and *STARBIRD*'s venerable hull. Despite, or maybe because of, what he'd learned in the Unity, he was more comfortable with the spacetime he'd grown up in than in the UNE. And since he couldn't get back there, even with Unity help, he had to make some choices. He wasn't a career diplomat with his own success all tied up with choices for the future of the human race. He was just a guy trying to adapt to a real bad run of luck, followed by a real abrupt change in circumstance.

You couldn't ask people to be more than they were. He'd been the top-rated test pilot of his generation, once. If he could just fly spacecraft again, in a spacetime topology that made sense to him, then he didn't care if he did it in nowtime or alltime.

He kept telling himself that. He had to keep telling himself that. Otherwise, the mission was going to suffer because South had never, really, made his peace with the UNE.

He was more comfortable in this spacetime, now that he was readjusted to it, than he'd expected to be when he transited back. If Mickey Croft would quit having surrogates poke and prod him, he could even enjoy it.

But Croft, or Remson, or whoever was in charge of the debrief, couldn't leave him be. He kept trying to understand it, excuse it, because even in his day and age, they pulled you right in after a mission and did their best to wring out your brain, impression by impression. They did it because memories, especially memories imprinted in stressful situations, fade and because serial memory in a crisis fades fastest of all. Every security type and intel jock knew the drill.

But UNE methods were too intrusive for South's tastes. When two human technicians came to get him for the "physical" part of his exam, he tried not to take out his exasperation on them. He just wanted to go back to his ship. That's what he'd come here for.

But they marched him down another white hall and into a virtual reality bay to do a bunch of reflex tests and physio tests. He cooperated the best he could by putting his hands in the gloves and his head in the helmet and reacting to the stimuli they presented.

The helmet started hissing in his ears, though, and the stimuli presented in the virtual reality helmet became pictures of people he knew—Riva Lowe, Mickey Croft, Remson, Reice, Sling. And then there were pictures of Unity aliens he knew: bad representations, poorly defined, of the Interstitial Interpreter and other representatives. Every time he saw a picture, he was supposed to choose a word defining it and pick from other columns of words the ones that he liked. The Ball came flying up to his face and spun there. He nearly laughed. The UNE didn't understand the Ball, yet. They had no idea what it was, or what it was for, or why it was still sitting out there at Spacedock Seven.

When he got his word list for the Ball, he picked out *rocket ship* and *home plate* and *vacation spot*. Those choices ought to give the UNE shrinks something to think about. He knew that the gloves on his hands were measuring his galvanic skin response, blood pressure, and muscle tension, so he was careful to tell the truth at all times.

Maybe the UNE could use this device to find out whether you were telling the truth, not just whether you were lying. There was a world of difference, South knew.

When they came to get him out of the virtual test bay, a gray-haired female technician whose placket read "Smith, E.E." told him, "The psychocorrection program can give you a number of insights into yourself, Commander South, if you'd care to view the results."

"I don't want my ass corrected, Doctor," he said bluntly. "I like me just the way I am." Had they been fiddling with his brain while he'd been in the helmet? When his heart stopped racing, he reminded himself that he would have known if they'd tried. He'd learned that much in Unity space: you kept your mind free, at all costs.

If he wanted to, he could screw up their program royally. Depending on what they thought they'd gotten from him during the session, maybe he should. He said, "Sure, let's go see what kind of snails and puppy dog tails I'm made of."

The woman glanced quizzically at him as she led him into an adjoining control room. Nursery rhymes had been lost to humanity somewhere along the way, then. Too bad. Lots of good images, lots of good advice, lots of good time-stabilizers in nursery rhymes. South had become real dependent on mantras of one kind or another in Unity space, and nursery rhymes were among the most culturally-specific.

The woman showed him his mind, mapped in three dimensions, as a bunch of colored blocks on axes. She rotated the axes for him, so he could see how his responses had clumped. There was a *good/bad* axis, longitudinally, and there was an *alien/doesn't matter* axis, latitudinally.

He'd given responses that clumped primarily in the *bad* and *alien* quadrant of the graph.

The technician said, "I've never seen anything like this before. You don't like much of anything, Mr. South—not your name, not your self, not any UNE person or capability—any better than you like the Unity experiences you've had."

"Remember, I'm an outsider here," he told her gravely, tense when he realized how much the test had revealed. "I'm an alien to this culture, as well as to the Unity culture."

The only name or noun that was anywhere near the *good* side of the graph was *STARBIRD*. It wasn't news to him, but it sure stirred up the technician. She called a bunch of other technical types in to view the data.

Then the group conferred, and Dr. Smith came back to South, still sitting before the graphic display. "I'm sorry to do this, Commander South, but we're going to void these results. There's obviously something wrong with the psychomapping program."

"I haven't got time to do this again," he said warningly, getting up and backing away from her to prove his point.

"We understand that, sir. And we respect your situation. We'll void the data and proceed without this test. We can't redo it anyway: you're too aware now of the test's purpose."

"Then I'm free to go?"

"Of course. I believe someone's waiting to take you to your next appointment."

The woman was flustered, disturbed. Maybe he'd done more than go along with the test. Maybe he'd screwed it up without really trying, instinctively fudged the results.

"I don't need another nowtime appointment. I need to be left alone."

"Excuse me?" she said, and he realized she had no idea what he was talking about. So he let go, just a little, of his determination to focus temporally on the rate of reality in this spacetime.

Timeslip didn't have to be a problem, if you knew what you wanted. And he wanted to slide by the guy waiting to take him to yet another evaluation, past the security guards at the elevator, and down into the Blue Mid slipbay without being questioned, bothered, harassed, obstructed, or accompanied.

It was so easy, a kid could have done it. He focused on his desired location and let his body find the way.

Not even the slipbay guard station alarms tripped to him. He moderated the vertigo of moving through a spacetime at an accelerated rate by choosing interim goals at which he would stop, walk a few steps, and recalibrate his attention on the next leg of his journey.

When he slipped past the checkpoint and stopped himself, *STARBIRD* was only a few feet away. Riva Lowe was sitting on the apron leading to his ship—and then she wasn't.

He blinked his eyes and walked every step between him and the ship, carefully, concentrating fully. He'd been playing fast and loose with the rules here, bending the local physics through his altered brain, and it served him right if he encountered some time-displaced phenomenology as a result.

Riva was clearly in trouble when he'd seen her. Her head had been down and her legs curled close to her body, encircled by both her arms. But when had he seen her there? Not nowtime, whenever he'd arrived here. He had to find out how much time he'd slipped and see if she was all right. Maybe there was something he could do.

He'd had so much trouble dealing with the UNE's assault on his person, physical and psychic, he'd forgotten all about Riva. They'd probably been gentle with him, compared to the way they'd treat one of their own who was accountable, as ambassador from the UNE to the Unity, for all actions undertaken and results attained in Unity space.

If he'd seen her in the alltime, then she was badly in need of help. If he'd seen her in the nowtime, maybe there was nothing he could do. But if he'd seen her soontime, he might be able to stop the problem, whatever it was, before it occurred.

He moved determinedly up the apron, touched *STARBIRD*'s access plate with his palm, and climbed aboard.

As soon as Birdy heard his voice, she started fussing over him, trying to evaluate his physical and mental state and normalize it. He'd forgotten about that. "Don't normalize me, Birdy, okay? Just help me patch a line through to the Secretariat—high as we can reach. Remson's office. Or Mickey Croft's, if we've got the clout."

If Birdy got him on his bunk and started playing with his physiology via his bunkside pharmakit, he'd be high as a kite in notime, and less capable of doing what needed to be done for Riva.

Whatever the hell that turned out to be. All he wanted to do was fly this ship out of here, feel like he'd salvaged something. He'd never signed up to salvage the whole human race in the process. But Riva Lowe had. And he couldn't let her down. They were as close to two of a kind as people could get.

With Birdy clucking and fussing over him like a mother hen, he began working his way up the Secretariat chain of command toward Croft's office. He didn't know where else to look for her.

When he found her, he was going to do some damned thing about what he'd seen. Nowtime. After all, he was

Commander South, expert on Unity space. They'd listen to him, whatever damnfool trajectory they were on that had upset Riva so.

They'd better listen. He had lots of options that the UNE couldn't counter, up to and including the ability to remove Ambassador Lowe from their custody, and their spacetime, by force.

CHAPTER 22

▽

A New Way of
Thinking

To Riva Lowe's senses, Mickey Croft's office in the Secretariat was a frontal assault. Beyond its sanctum's doors, harried staffers came and went, breathing streams of bile at one another, composing alphabet rubrics and incantations on electronic keypads that shouted lightspeed commands at full voice throughout the Stalk. Their scheming color-coded dreams of empires yet to be leaked in whispers through the walls of Croft's office to siphon all her energy and attention away.

The cacophony of the Stalk at work was nearly deafening, yet it had never bothered Lowe before. The soft blues and grays, creams and golds of Croft's office walls should have muted the sounds, blocked out the hubbub, baffled the hue and cry of government hounds on a dozen conflicting scents. Yet she was inundated.

No walls could keep so many intents at bay. No insulation could buffer her from all those minds set upon diverse duties, different goals, and multifarious ends. She might as well have been in a factory full of noise and steam, where some multicolored rug was being woven by a hundred hands, all tying knots and threading needles and loading spindles with colored threads that then fed into some huge machine that thumped and roared and whined and spun as it made myriad designs into one long, broad, field of view that as yet revealed no center and no theme.

She couldn't manage to sit still, yet moving about Croft's office made everything ripple and sway about her. Across from the Secretary General's desk was a video depiction of the Grand Canyon on mother Earth, with birds wheeling lazily on updrafts in a warm blue sky fleeced with clouds. Every time she got near the picture, she found herself on the wing, peering with sharp hawk's eyes into the canyon's depths, hunting dinner, warm flesh, anticipating a rush of air and stone and exhilaration.

So she stayed away from the canyon on the wall and from the stars in the Secretary's skylight window. She tried to concentrate on what Croft was saying, but he was a death's head with a mouth that moved. The desktop on which he leaned his sharp and awkward elbows was alive in the alltime with ancestral fish that schooled and darted in the pasttime through a sea that became stone and made them fossils in the nowtime.

How could Croft work in here? How could anybody think in here? Sort priorities in the dark? Make decisions blindfolded? Listen to reason with deaf ears? She was baffled, buffeted, bludgeoned with the uncontrolled force of randomicity hard at work.

And Croft wanted answers. He wanted answers to questions framed in ignorance, articulated with suspicion, couched in paranoia. He wanted her to remember everything that had happened to her since she left the UNE in terms of past, present, and future benefit or threat to humanity, and to evaluate her experiences in a context of opportunity or crisis.

Mickey said, "Are we correct in assuming that the Unity Embassy is actually and physically, not figuratively, Unity territory?" Under his elbows, ancient fishes swam in circles.

Riva Lowe replied, "Yes, certainly. When you and Remson were in the embassy meeting with us, you were existing in the heart of the Unity." Meeting the Secretary General there had been easier for Riva, freed from the din of so many spacetimers moving from their past to their future in lockstep, one heartbeat at a time. She took a seat in the chair before his desk, careful to cover all the intermittent distance, one step at a time.

The SecGen frowned and said, "You're confirming that the bulkheads or walls of the Unity Embassy contain a physically different spacetime from ours, in which natural laws obey a different set of rules—their rules? Unity rules?"

She shrugged, and the nowtime gesture rippled from her body through the air to his, the waves of its energy breaking against his frame, his face, and moving on. "The Unity Embassy is a physical construct with special boundary conditions, allowing passage across discontinuities from one spacetime to another, yes. But local universe rules can't be changed for ... all time. They can be bent, but not broken." What was he worried about? She didn't understand the point of these questions. The right answers were all around him in his own experiential reality.

Mickey continued implacably, "So when we enter there, into the Unity Embassy, we are actually *in* Unity space, with all its special properties and multidimensional characteristics?"

She said, "I don't understand what you're getting at, Mr. Secretary."

He said, "Don't you? Has the Unity created a permanent presence here, or not?"

"Permanent? Here? Nothing is permanent here."

"Something is sticking its multidimensional head into UNE space out there near the Ball site, and that's for sure."

"You gave permission for the Unity to build an embassy at those coordinates."

"Build, as in create a finite structure. Not a one-way door from their universe to ours."

"Oh," she said. "I see your problem." Croft was frightened, then—or at least overwhelmed. She hadn't just imagined it, or attributed her own distress to him.

"*My* problem? My dear Madam Ambassador, this is *our* problem. The UNE can't tolerate an invasion of its sovereign territory, even a seemingly passive one."

"You sent me out to Unity space as your representative. I didn't think you wanted me to spy on them. I thought we wanted to establish relations."

"I'm not asking you to spy. I'm asking you what you think their motives are, for taking such liberties with their embassy."

"I'm glad we have that point clear. As for what I think their motives are, they are simply proceeding to establish the physical base for diplomatic relations on a continuing basis. How else could they have interpreted your offer to build an embassy at the Ball site but to build one?"

"You're being purposely obtuse."

"I don't think so, Mr. Secretary." Riva Lowe's nails were digging into the palms of her hands. She spread her fingers and looked at them. Then she looked up at Croft and saw too many Crofts trying to fit into the same nowtime moment: a brave one, a tired one, a sad one, a frightened one, an old one, a wise one, and a foolish one who was afraid that he had opened a door he could not close, through which would come unknowable peril. "I'm only trying to answer your nowtime questions, which aren't wholly representative of your concerns." She nearly slipped and talked to his qualms directly, without a spoken predicate from him. She mustn't do that. He was already too close to rejecting everything she was saying, out of hand.

He said, "I'm concerned, yes. I'm concerned about contamination—yours, mine, even Mr. Remson's. Something happens to human beings when they're exposed to Unity aliens, even for a short time. You must have noticed certain, ah, changes in your perceptual and perhaps physical reality, Madam Ambassador. And in your mission staff. We're having a workup done of Commander South's psychometrics, as well as his physio stats. Since we have recent data on South from which to draw a comparison, perhaps analysis of that data will support my concerns, perhaps not." Croft paused and stood up. It seemed to her that his body was spewing emotional energy that was visible in the visual spectrum as harsh colored waves that bounced off the ceiling, the walls, her chest.

Was he dismissing her on that note? Did everything hang on Joe South's ability to be pronounced fit for duty? What if he was not capable of passing the Secretariat's tests? She wanted to curl up into a ball, close her eyes, and huddle there until the storm of Croft's emotional distress was past. She mustn't.

The Secretary General of the UNE walked over to his window on the stars, leaving a trail of Crofts behind him that stretched all the way back to his desk. She stood up, too, determined to join him, to explain to him, to convince him that his fears were unfounded.

Where was the man she'd known, the consummate bureaucrat she'd trusted, who'd sent her on this mission with such high hopes? Where was the diplomat par excellence, who'd inspired not only her but so many others to give more than they thought they had to give?

Riva Lowe took one uncertain step toward Croft, and then time slipped her grasp. Her body slid in one distended instant all the way to the Secretary General's side. Ignore the timeslip. Croft was having the same sorts of troubles, that much was obvious.

She said, "Don't base a decision this important on one man's physical state. Or yours. Or mine. We're reacting the way we must to survive—"

"That's what I'm afraid of." Staring out at the starscape that only the privileged of Threshold ever saw, Croft said, "I can't let contact with the Unity continue on an uncontrolled basis. We don't know what their intentions are. We can't evaluate the risks. We've got to slow down. We're going too fast."

"Human beings have been preparing for this moment for tens of thousands of years," she said numbly. "Please, don't do this, Mickey. We've been living the same way, thinking the same way, reaching for something more, but always trapped in a universe of confinement, for so long, we've stopped trying to free ourselves. We've forgotten how to grow. We want everything to be predictable and controllable. We're such good prisoners that we don't even remember that we once had an intuitive understanding that there was more to life than reproduction and death. And now, when the door of our prison is opening before us, and the key is in your hand, you want to turn back? Slow down? Board up the door again, maybe forever? We've got to learn to think a different way, that's all. Change isn't bad. Evolution isn't a threat. You can't institutionalize stasis."

"You're out of your mind if you think I can't, and won't, insist on caution, evaluate the potential risks and the opportunities, and make a reasoned decision *only when I am ready*. Time doesn't seem to mean one whole hell of a lot to the Unity, so what's the hurry?"

Croft turned to her then, and she was nearly staggered by the sudden hostility coming out of him.

She said, "The hurry is for us, not for them. They've gone to tremendous effort to offer us this chance. Rebuff them, and we may not have another. We don't have the science to reinstate contact if they break it off—"

"I'm willing to take that risk. I'm not willing to take the risk of moving Threshold out beyond Pluto's orbit until I see a reason to do so that outweighs the risk of two hundred and fifty thousand people who depend on Threshold life support. You've been out there in Unity space too long, Madam Ambassador. You've 'gone native.' Nothing you've said to me gives me a single overriding reason to take such a risk. What's out there in the Unity domain for the United Nations of Earth?"

"Everything you ever dreamed possible," she breathed, catching his eyes in hers and holding on for dear life in the maelstrom of conflict between them. "The Unity is made up of more than six hundred intelligent species, every one of them possessed of more sophisticated science and technology than our own. They have the keys to the kingdom, Mr. Secretary, and they're offering to let the human race in the door. Don't say no, I beg you."

"I can't base a recommendation on your subjective analysis, Riva. You should know that. What concerns me most is the way I've let myself be led into this. It should concern you, too. Now if you want to input my decision, then put together a reasoned assessment of the benefits available to the UNE from interaction with the Unity. And convince me, somehow, that the physical side effects both of us have experienced—are experiencing—aren't hazardous to humanity's collective health. Until then, nobody's moving anything out of orbit around here—unless it's the Unity Embassy and that damned Ball."

There was no use in arguing the matter further. If she told Croft what he wanted to know, nowtime, he would never permit Threshold to be moved. He was simply too hostile and frightened to be reasoned with. Riva herself was mentally exhausted and physically queasy from the strain of keeping this interview on a strictly four-dimensional level. "Yes, sir. I'll do that, sir," she said primly. "And thank you for the opportunity to submit an official opinion."

"That's why I made you ambassador to Unity space," Croft said, almost kindly, as he showed her the door.

CHAPTER 23

$\triangledown$

A New Home, A New Hope

South was nearly sick with worry when Riva Lowe showed up. By then he was all but barricaded in *STARBIRD*, curled up on his bunk with the life-support barrier down, letting Birdy take care of him so that the ship's AI could get used to the changes in her pilot and stop trying to retrofit South's body into an antiquated template of "normal."

If he was going to fly *STARBIRD* into another dimension, the ship and he were going to have to work off their rough edges and be a better team than ever before. Bringing *STARBIRD* into Unity space wasn't going to be a piece of cake, even then. But he'd come here to do just that, and he was trying to get the job done, despite all the problems he hadn't anticipated.

He had a firm promise from Croft's office that Riva Lowe would receive his message, and an escort to his slipbay, as soon as Mickey was done with her. So when Birdy told him that his visitor had arrived, he assumed she'd just come aboard when she was ready.

He retracted the bunk's life-support barrier, shook off Birdy's demands that he not move too fast or get too excited, and put on his boots. Touching them reminded him that they were plasma surrogates of UNE issue, and that wiped the last of the cobwebs from his brain.

Birdy had probably surreptitiously doped him when she

ran his pharmakit recalibration. He didn't blame the ship's AI for wanting a baseline and a template for somebody about half as jacked up as South was when he'd finished talking to Croft's Secretariat office.

Damned bureaucrats never took anything at face value. He clumped his way forward and nearly passed the lock before he realized it was open.

"Jesus, Birdy, don't we want some minimal security around here anymore?"

The ship's voice said, "Waiting for passenger Lowe to board, as instructed."

Then he looked out the lock and there she was, sitting on the apron, her back to him, head on her knees.

Just like in the alltime vision he'd had.

He didn't want to make things any worse. He said, "Leave the lock open, Birdy, and get me a flight window out of here, just a shake-out cruise around local area and back."

"Will do," said the ship's AI in Birdy's sweet, confident voice.

He wished he felt as confident, approaching Lowe on the apron. His boots thwacked loudly on the synthetic tarmac. She had to hear him coming. She didn't raise her head.

So he sat down beside her, assumed a similar position, and put one hand tentatively on her shoulder.

She was quivering, or shivering, or crying softly. Her flesh twitched when his touched it.

"Hey, Riva, what's the matter? Tough day?" Keep it light.

"Awful," came her muffled voice. Then she raised her head, but she didn't look at him. She looked straight ahead, staring at the nothing. "Croft is completely against the move out to Pluto's orbit."

"What? What the hell happened?" All the testing he'd gone through, all the pushing and prodding he'd endured, and now this. "They didn't like my psychometrics, or what?"

"I don't know," she said. "Mickey's so tired. You should see him. He looks terrible. He can't be thinking clearly. And he doesn't seem to have a good conceptual grasp of what's happening."

"Come on aboard," he said. "You need something to eat, maybe a drink. A little rest."

"Soontime. I just want to sit still and think. He wants a written report, detailing the benefits to the UNE from contact with the Unity—and the dangers, of course. Positive and negative. Problem and solution. Recommendations." She shook her head. "I'm in no shape to do that."

"Come on, we can handle it. I'll help you. Birdy will, too. We can do it all on board. I want to take *STARBIRD* for a little shake-out ride. It'll do you good to get out of here." It would do her good to get off the damned slipbay apron. Somebody was going to see them and then people would start wondering how come the UNE's ambassador was spending her time in a half-fetal position on the apron.

"Get up. That's it. Birdy did a good pharmacomp on me. I'm feeling a lot more ... compatible than I was before. You ought to try it." Say anything, just get her into the ship.

Riva leaned on him the whole way. She weighed a ton, more than she should, almost like dead weight. He got her into *STARBIRD* and slammed the lock's CLOSE mode hard, before Birdy could.

Birdy grumbled and started the pressurization cycle, getting ready for the flight he'd ordered. He felt a whole lot safer in his customized environment, with the lock cycle engaged. Nobody got in here now without asking permission.

In the red light of the cycling lock, he let go of her. She leaned back against the bulkhead and looked at him with all the hopelessness of a trapped animal. She didn't say a thing. When the red light turned green and the inner lock opened, he moved inside and told her, "Go lie down on my bunk. Let Birdy make you feel better. I'll get us something hot to drink and be back soontime."

He left her to find her way. You couldn't get lost on *STARBIRD*. The galley was just forward of his quarters. He moved to the right, and she squeezed past him without a word of argument.

Not a good sign.

He'd known something was wrong. Croft should have known better than to push her like that, though, after the strain of the trip back here.

But the Secretariat hadn't made it easy for either of them, and now their reasoning was beginning to make sense. So Croft wasn't in favor of moving the habitat, after all. Nice going, asshole. UNE policy was made in Mickey Croft's office. There was no higher authority to appeal to. There was just somebody in that UNE Secretariat driver's seat who wasn't up to it when a hard decision came along.

All the fury that had come over South when he'd seen the alltime vision of Riva sitting on that apron flooded over him, so that his hands were shaking as he made her some hot tea. "Birdy, give her a mood stabilizer and then take some baseline readings. We need Riva in top form."

When he went the few steps aft, tea in hand, her color was a little better. Birdy retracted the life-support barrier between them, and he sat down beside her on the bunk. As he did, the pharmakit strap on her upper arm came loose, signaling that Birdy was finished with her baseline evaluation.

She sipped the tea he gave her, and said, "I didn't realize how thirsty I was. I'm sorry for the scene out there. But I never expected Mickey Croft to have some secret agenda—"

"It's not a secret if he told you. He's just behaving like a typical, reactive bureaucrat. We need to feed the right information into the system, that's all. Then it'll come to the conclusion we want." He wished he were as sure as he sounded. He'd been so angry a few minutes previously, he'd have torn the Stalk and everyone on it apart to get to her. And the irony of that was, nowtime, he probably could. Things had changed for Joe South since the days when the UNE could squash him as if he were a bug and not even notice. Croft was right to be a little bit worried.

If you weren't a little bit worried, went the adage, you didn't understand what was happening to you. So South figured that Croft understood damned well what was happening—to himself, if not to anybody else. And the changes which human beings underwent subsequent to exposure to Unity entities weren't insignificant.

Maybe Croft had good reason, from his viewpoint, for putting on the brakes. South had never been convinced that the human race as a whole was ready for contact with any beings more significant than they. Sometimes he wasn't sure they were ready for contact with one another. A history of bloodshed attested to how humans dealt with culture clash.

"It's hardly your fault, whatever happens," he told her. You had to start somewhere. "You're not responsible for

Croft's ability to think his way through a complex situation."

"I'm responsible for our first official contact with the Unity. If it fails, then who else is responsible?"

"Come on, Riva, what did he do to you up there?"

"Nothing. He just froze me out. He's got his mind made up. He thinks the Unity Embassy and the Ball are an infringement on UNE sovereignty in the local spacetime. With that attitude, how can we make any progress?"

"There's one thing we can do—we can remove the Ball from play." He winked at the astonished eyes regarding him over her tea cup. "I was planning to take that sucker for a test drive sometime soon, anyhow."

"I'm not sure that's the answer," she said, but now her mind was engaging the problem.

"Not by itself. Let's do your report, and I'll help you deliver it. We'll tell Croft what's waiting at Pluto's orbit. He has a right to know. But we'll deliver it, hardcopy, so that what we say is on the record, retrievable, and not completely subject to interpretation by somebody who's overtired and maybe a bit paranoid. Okay? You up to it, soldier?"

She acted like a soldier half the time, in some sort of volunteer army of do-gooders. He wanted to show her that he was cooperating, doing his best to help her make her case. Then, when Croft did what any good bureaucrat would do and backburnered the whole issue of humanity's chance for an evolutionary upgrade for the next administration to deal with after he retired, *then* South would be able to convince Riva Lowe to stop trying to drag the whole UNE along with her on an adventure meant for two.

"Okay, South, you're right," she said after due consideration. "We'll put it all down and deliver it. If I can get another meeting. It's not so easy to get a meeting with the Secretary General, except when he wants to see you."

"He asked for the report, didn't he?"

She put down her tea and grimaced. "It's not that easy."

"Want to bet? Watch. Birdy," he said in a slightly louder voice, "get me an appointment with Croft in the Secretariat, for myself and Riva Lowe, urgent priority, anytime after sixteen hundred hours. Purpose is to deliver requested report, ASAP."

"South—"

"What, you think we can't write this up in notime? Come on, Madam Ambassador. You haven't seen what my flight deck has to offer in the way of transcription amenities."

"South, we're not ready to just bully our way back in there and deliver some off-the-cuff assessment. Maybe the SecGen's just having a bad day."

"If he is, he's not going to have any better days soontime. Come on. If we need to, we'll cheat a little, get some help from the Unity delegation." He knew how she'd hate to ask for help.

"I can do it. I'm just . . ."

"Ready. You're as ready as you'll ever be."

And she was ready enough. So was he. They had assets she wasn't counting on, but then, Riva played fair. South played to win.

In the best of human circumstances, with the best of human technology, it was going to take so long to tow Threshold to Pluto's orbit that Croft's hesitancy could harden into true intransigence if left to fester.

That was an easy case to make to the Unity, even though Riva was horrified that South would reveal what she considered to be "sensitive Secretariat intelligence" to the Unity monitors at the embassy site.

"Don't worry," he told her. "Nobody on Threshold will ever realize that any such conversation even took place." It wouldn't take place in UNE spacetime, so it couldn't be monitored by UNE devices.

South took a grim pleasure in end-running the Secretariat, especially for its own good.

STARBIRD's shake-out cruise was just going to have to wait.

He went aft to his bunk, put his head in his redundant command and control helmet, hooked himself up to life support, and ordered the barrier down so that Riva couldn't accidentally interfere with his body while he was moving it dimensionally, rather than linearly, and kill him in the process.

He dialed in the requisite coordinates using the command and control grid on his helmet's heads-up display and the life-support matrix around him, using *STARBIRD*'s sponge-jump capability to provide him with the necessary bolthole into another universe. If he understood what he'd been taught, he just had to cross two scalar beams at the apex of his physical and temporal coordinates, and pump enough A-potential energy into that spot to push himself through the resulting hole. His bioenergy would be ported to the new dimensional coordinates he'd dialed in, just the way a ship's hull would be.

As for his body, it would be occupying two spacetimes simultaneously—or spreading itself between them. He hoped.

He had one last spacetime-sequential thought that when he'd signed up for pilot training, years ago and centuries away, he'd never thought he'd be flying without a ship, let alone a safety net.

Then he was wrenched through a fine mesh by a cyclonic vacuum, strained to the texture of baby food, and semi-reconstituted in a soft warm topology full of nine-cornered objects projecting into eleven-dimensional spaces with vortices ending at a contact point inside the Unity Embassy construct. It hurt like hell.

The Unity monitors at the embassy contact point weren't happy about the energy expense involved. "Spacetimers laws apply, Friend South. Being careful with body human, please. Not stressing person to point of breakage."

He promised he wouldn't, said he knew his limits, but when he was done moving electromagnetic components of his "person" through a few more dimensions than was recommended by the manufacturer, without the benefit of a plasma cocoon, he was cold and weak and Riva was telling him mournfully that he was going to kill himself pulling stunts like that.

"You care?" he croaked, prone on his bunk, with Riva leaning over him and Birdy clucking disapprovingly in the background.

She held a glass of water for him, because he couldn't hold it himself without spilling it all over his lap, *STAR-BIRD*'s pilotry suite, and her, too.

"Of course I care," she flared.

"Nice to know," he managed. He drank slowly and it hurt his throat to swallow. "Let's go see the ogre in the castle."

"What?"

He sometimes forgot she was a twenty-fifth-century citizen, who'd grown up without fairy tales or nursery rhymes.

"Never mind." He groaned as he swung his legs over the bunk's edge.

"Promise me you'll never do that again," Riva said.

"No sweat," he replied. "If people had been meant to be in two places at once, we'd all have been born twins."

Now he was nearly as enervated as she was, but he had what he needed. The sorry pair of them made their way up to Croft's office by public transportation, a foolish choice that took even more of their depleted energies. He resolved to ask for a UNE car to take them back.

But when Croft greeted them, the Secretary General was curt and hurried, not in the mood for granting favors.

"This is urgent? Let's have it." Croft held out his hand impatiently and took the disk from South's hand without touching his flesh.

"And hello, how are you, how was your trip to you too, sir," South said. Croft's office was disheveled, filled with empty cups and plates and projectors and the other detritus of a long meeting.

"I'm sorry," said the SecGen stiffly, not sorry in the least. "What am I supposed to expect from this report of yours, Commander South, Ambassador Lowe?" Croft said as he went to sit behind his desk.

A tone sounded, and he held up a hand to take the call. Not a good sign. The caller was Remson, but that was all South could make out.

Croft put down the handset. "Summary?" he snapped.

Riva looked at South almost pleadingly, so he said, "The size and nature of the Unity itself requires a huge contingent of interacting species be present to greet human representatives if any real cooperative association is to begin. They can't do that inside somebody's solar system. Not only does convention and protocol preclude it, special conditions here are hazardous to the health of many of the species involved. So either you make yourselves available to meet a trade delegation from the rest of the civilized universe, or you don't. They ain't comin' here on your terms, that's for sure."

"You say 'you,' Commander South, as if you no longer consider yourself part of the human race."

"I'm no longer considering myself part of the scared part, that's true. I know old Richard the Second would like NAMECorp to have a swat at some of the trade opportunities the UNE could deliver, if it moves this habitat. But maybe you don't want relations with higher intelligence. Maybe humans just want to keep on exploiting and enslaving lower life-forms in a sliver of the galaxy with a fence around it that's posted: WARNING: VICIOUS HUMANS INSIDE. ENTER AT OWN RISK."

If that wasn't clear enough, South didn't know what was.

Riva Lowe said, "Mr. Croft, we've collected data on both the species of the Unity and the types of trade opportunities possible. We also have a verbal promise from the Unity to provide auxiliary power at the Pluto orbit, if you request it, and help in transit if you request that. There's no problem for the Unity in moving the habitat for the UNE, if the UNE wants massive aid or logistical support. Of course, there will be some coordination difficulties, and technology matching would be required to make sure that the Unity understands the special problems you have in moving Threshold."

"That's enough. I'll read your report, people. All of it."

Croft's face was masklike and very grave. He got up stiffly to herd them to the door.

"I hope you'll feel better when you've looked over the data," Riva added. "If there're any more questions we can answer, don't hesitate to ask."

"I won't, Madam Ambassador. After all, you're our expert on Unity aliens. Thank you for coming. And you too, Commander South. Good job."

Mickey Croft closed the door in their faces as if he couldn't get them away from him quick enough.

CHAPTER 24

▽

Hardwired
Reaction

Mickey Croft was scared to death by what Ambassador Lowe and Commander South had told him. So scared that, despite his loathing of space travel, he went out to Spacedock Seven to confer with the military in their redundantly secure crisis management stronghold.

He had good reason to be frightened. The Unity aliens could move Threshold *for* the UNE. Provide alternate power at the orbit beyond Pluto. What else could they do? Might they do? Would they do, if thwarted? What would happen if Croft simply said "Thanks but no thanks" to the whole thing, now? Broke off diplomatic relations, such as they were, entirely? Declared Unity representatives *personae non gratae*? Forgot the Unity, if the Unity would allow itself to be forgotten? Dropped South's "keys to the kingdom" down the nearest sewer grate and walked away?

Just how powerful were these aliens? From Joe South and Riva Lowe's report, the Unity was either omnipotent, in human terms, or damned close. Too close for comfort, in Mickey Croft's opinion. Way too close.

So he had to do something. Fast. Issue a policy statement to give the UNE government staff some guidance. Create a strategic plan that encompassed both his new knowledge and his crystallized fears. And do it before, through his own indecisiveness, Threshold began the long journey to

Pluto's orbit, found itself in trouble, and had to ask the Unity for help to survive.

Of all he'd learned from Ambassador Lowe and Commander South, the thing that chilled Croft's bones the most was the idea that the UNE might be forced to *request* Unity aid. The United Nations of Earth was not some backwater underdeveloped empire, some feudal state or charity case.

Yet the very fact that the Secretary General of the UNE had called a meeting of senior Secretariat, Consolidated Space Command, and Consolidated Security personnel belied a siege mentality at the highest levels. He felt as if he were some tinhorned dictator presiding over a military junta as he seated himself at the head of a long u-shaped table covered with the traditional green cloth.

The staff had been assembled long since, from the look of them. At each place were identical drinking glasses, notepad computers, and wan-faced men and women behind them. Bottled waters, tea and coffee, and biscuits were precisely aligned within easy reach, down the center strip. Copies of Lowe and South's report glowed from pocket datareaders by each place.

Mickey Croft entered from the rear of the room and took his place at the head of the table next to Remson without a word.

Vince Remson said, "Thank you, sirs and madams, for rearranging your busy schedules to join us here today. The purpose of this emergency session of the Joint Planning Staff is to evaluate new data brought back from Unity space by Ambassador Lowe's party and to formulate recommendations for a contingency action plan to be implemented in the event that United Nations of Earth forces are called upon to defend Threshold from Unity aggression en route to its new site beyond Pluto's orbit—or thereafter."

A buzz of voices began among the seated Joint Staff and rose in pitch as if someone had disturbed a swarm of bees to defend their hive.

Remson sat back, wry amusement playing at the corners of his mouth, waiting for the hubbub to subside. "You all have data readers in front of you that contain both abstracts and details of the first UNE mission to Unity space. We'll have time to go through the report, page by page, later in this session. Right now, the Honorable Michael Croft, Secretary General of the United Nations of Earth, will give us an overview of Secretariat policy guidance as it applies to the breaking situation. Secretary Croft. . . ."

Mickey let his gaze roam the room, making eye contact with General Granrud from ConSpaceCom Logistics, with Dr. E.E. Smith from Secretariat Intelligence, and others before he started to speak. "I'm going to keep this brief. After due deliberation, it has been determined that the policy of the United Nations of Earth toward the confederated species calling themselves the Unity must be one of caution and vigilance against any and all forms of aggression, overt or covert. We must be wary, but must continue to gather information about the capabilities of this powerful new force. In the twentieth century, nations of Earth were guided by the Churchillian doctrine of considering any state big enough to pose a potential threat as a real threat." Churchill's words didn't fit the situation, but his reasoning did. "We must do likewise. We are confronted with an alien cultural matrix possessed of science and technology that is arguably superior to our own. We are faced with a group of species with unknown goals and needs, and an inexplicable interest in humanity. We would be derelict in our duty to the United Nations of Earth not to prepare for possible conflict with these Unity species, even while we are evaluating opportunities for peaceful cooperation."

Mickey paused for dramatic effect, took a deep breath, scanned the table around which no one moved or even blinked, and continued. "Therefore, I am directing you today to develop and provide all possible means of defense of the United Nations of Earth against aggression from Unity forces. Starting today, Consolidated Space Command and Consolidated Security Command will prepare, with support from all necessary agencies, the strategic plan of attack which must be part of any prudent defensive capability."

They muttered among themselves. He held up his hand for silence, and continued. "Do the best you can. If there's any sign of aggression during the long trip to Pluto's orbit, or after, we must be ready to respond. And we must field a show of force to provide a psychological deterrent to any Unity interests who may, now or in future, contemplate aggression against UNE assets, habitats, or outposts henceforth. No one needs to be reminded that deterring aggression mounted by a superior force is not an easy task. We have already ruled out canceling the move to coordinates beyond Pluto's orbit: we must not show weakness. Therefore, we must demonstrate strength, steadfastness, and our territorial sovereignty in such a way that we are neither provocative nor an attractive target. At the sites of the alien constructions referred to as the Ball and the Unity Embassy, deep inside our sovereign territory, we will institute new security procedures which will provide an obvious deterrent and which promise a quick and deadly response to any sign of aggression on the part of the Unity."

He paused one final time and said into the silence made by thirty-two pairs of staring eyes, "In short, ladies and gentlemen, Consolidated Space Command and Consolidated Security must be ready, willing, and able at a moment's notice of foul play, to obliterate these Unity aliens on the spot." Mickey stood up and stepped away from the table.

People began to talk, to reach out to one another, to raise their hands. Remson said, "That's it, ladies and gentlemen, you've got your mission definition. Thank you, Mr. Secretary, for taking time to personally give us such clear direction."

Mickey was already headed for the door that would take him to his waiting flagship, and from there, under guard, back to his sanctum in the Stalk. In one more carefully staged and orchestrated act, he said over his shoulder, "It would be my pleasure, Mr. Remson, were the circumstances not so grave. By the way, I believe that General Granrud of Logistics already has a 'Plan B' in his back pocket. Perhaps you'd better start with him."

The doors before him slid back, revealing his personal bodyguards. He stepped through smartly, and the doors closed on the Joint Staff meeting in progress. Croft's part was now complete, for the nonce. History had just taken a new bearing. It was up to the Unity to convince all the three hundred colonies of the UNE that it posed no threat, now or in the future.

The high state of readiness that Mickey had just decreed would be implemented throughout the UNE worlds. A text of his speech was already being transmitted to every Secretariat mission, ConSpaceCom command headquarters, ConSec commissioner, and national government leader on the emergency communications network.

As he was hustled by two Secretariat bodyguards down a narrow security tunnel toward his waiting flagship, Mickey wondered how it had come to this, despite everyone's best intentions at the outset. He tried to conjure up just one comforting memory from his meetings with the Interstitial Interpreter and the honor guard. But he couldn't. The honor guard's smoking pots seemed in retrospect to be filled with narcotic gasses that had lulled him and made him complacent. The self-replicating, self-sustaining images that had corrupted and infected his psychometric modeler now seemed like a warning shot across his bow which he had failed to take to heart.

Too long had he been complacent in the face of unquantifiable risk. But not now. While he was making his way through this tunnel, technicians were cleansing the psychometric modeler—and every network component that could have been infected by the modeler—of all suspect data.

If necessary, they would shut down Threshold's life-support and central management control systems, one at a time, and scrub every one for incipient infection. Any latent or present virus must be eradicated before it spread through the artificial intelligence that controlled Threshold—before the trip to a new orbit began.

As with the modeler and the threat of infection by unseen Unity forces, so with the entire United Nations of Earth. Perhaps he was overreacting, creating metaphors of destruction and similes of disaster, but act he must, to preserve the life and liberty of the union under his care.

One of his bodyguards said, "Ready, sir? Right this way," and leaned forward to open a door responsive to his palmprint. Beyond it, a secure slipbay and his flagship, the GEORGE WASHINGTON, loomed from the shadows. Beyond that, the unknowable consequences of moving Threshold closer to the stars.

"Ready," Croft said. It was too late to turn back now.

CHAPTER 25

▽

Orders

When Reice got his destroy-on-warning orders, he was sitting on station in the *BLUE TICK,* playing solitaire on his fire control computer. He off-loaded the game guiltily and sat still, lemon donut half-eaten in one hand, staring out at the Unity embassy and the Ball nearby.

His donut was suddenly unappetizing. He threw it in the decomposition hopper by his knee. You had to have spit in your mouth to eat. He didn't even lick his fingers. He wiped the powdered sugar absently on his pressure suit's leg.

It didn't look any different out there. What the hell had happened?

You go from traffic cop to frontline soldier in a heartbeat, and everything·looks the same? It didn't figure. He imported every possible scan of the Unity Embassy that his sensors could upload in real time. No little green men in flying saucers could be seen. No monsters flapped their clawed wings in vacuum. The embassy looked just like it always looked: Like a shark's fin cutting the waterline, like a kid's toy that a truck had run over, like an incipient headache in eleven dimensions.

With a curse, Reice dumped his embassy scans and brought up the Ball. It was probably the Ball that had caused this red alert. It was always the Ball, wasn't it? The damned Ball was Reice's personal nemesis, his bad luck charm.

But there sat the Ball, silvery, spherical, and smug: no change there, either.

So maybe it was a change of heart, somewhere in the Threshold bureaucracy. Or a failure of nerve.

Whatever had happened, it wasn't up to Reice to question the wisdom of authority. He had real specific orders about what to do next.

He'd been ordered to arm the *BLUE TICK*'s formidable arsenal, run precision-targeting programs on both the Ball and the Unity embassy, light all the READY lights on his fire control grid until they blinked, and sit there with his finger on the buttons.

He had to go to the head, first. Being ordered to that state of readiness designated "Fire on Warning" had a way of curing even the most stubborn constipation. At least in the head, he wouldn't be watching the potential targets.

In the electronics-free environment of the tiny sanitary facility, he sat and stared at his boots, thinking hard. Why hadn't he heard rumors of this shake-up? He'd been on the right hand of the demigod Remson so long that he'd gotten accustomed to knowing what the Higher Orders had in mind.

But then South had come back, and Sling had gotten involved, and Reice's honeymoon with the Secretariat had abruptly ended. Not with a bang, but with radio silence. They didn't require him at their Spacedock Seven planning sessions anymore. Even though he'd basically put that team together out of nothing, done the lion's share of the work, provided the creative spark and operating engine of the Logistical Task Force, he was now out of the loop permanently.

These new orders proved that. Remson hadn't been at all happy with Reice the day that South and Ambassador Lowe had come cruising out of the Ball, with no apparent warning or prior notification to the Secretariat. Not that Reice was at fault. But he'd shown some initiative, involved Sling, a civilian, and generally been present and accounted for at the wrong time.

It didn't take much to get yourself sidelined, not with the Secretariat. Any sign of not being thoroughly controllable, any hint of trouble, any question of loyalty or dependability, or even inadvertent involvement in some action or reaction that wasn't squeaky clean and by the book, and the folks on top simply lost your number.

They didn't call you. They didn't include you. They

didn't inform you. And you ended up eating too many jelly donuts. The thing that burned Reice's butt the worst was that somebody else was obviously getting credit for all the work that Reice had done, putting together the Logistical Task Force Report and the infrastructure that was now handling follow-on actions.

He'd always known that fat lab rat was after his slot. As he pulled up his pants and consigned his waste products to vacuum with a roar of plumbing, he remembered how welcome and integral to the team he'd felt the day on Y Ring when General Granrud had congratulated him for work well done.

File it in the mental scrapbook, son. He should have realized before now that he was back on the *BLUE TICK* for good. "So what?" he muttered aloud, but his feelings were hurt.

They had no business issuing "destroy on warning" orders to every beat cop in a ConSec uniform. Not with the number of hotdogs out here. Not with the traffic back and forth to the Stalk still so thick. Not when you weren't even sure you could *destroy* either the Ball or the Unity Embassy, no matter what kind of firepower you engaged.

There was a world of difference between the command to his ship's artificial intelligence to "Fire on Warning," like the enabled button said, and the cocksure directive "destroy on warning."

What was going to happen if the Ball, or the Unity Embassy, decided to fight back? Nobody knew what the Ball was made of, yet, let alone the proper way to destroy an alien construct that only poked a small part of itself into your universe.

Back at his pilotry station, Reice slumped into position and looked at his fire control indicators. Dear oh dear, this was going to get sticky, if somebody actually implemented those orders and started shooting.

Reice suddenly realized he ought to be real sure he wasn't in the way of any line-of-sight beams or missiles that were fired at the Ball or at the Unity Embassy, or of any backspill or transient radiation effects that might ricochet off at an angle and fry him and *BLUE TICK* through some unintended fratricide.

Who'd thought up this stunt, anyway? Reice asked for

and received a head count of the weapons-carrying UNE vessels within shooting distance of the Ball or the embassy.

One hundred and twenty-three.

One hundred and twenty-three chances to get accidentally killed by your own side if fighting broke out. One hundred and twenty-three sources of friendly fire.

He asked the *BLUE TICK* to show him a breakdown, ship class by ship class, of what kind of firepower was out here, plus how many and what kind of weapons were on each ship. Order of battle data came up in long streams of disturbing complexity.

If anybody started shooting out here, the chances of destroying one another and/or Spacedocks One through Seven were at least as good, if not better, than those of destroying either the Ball or the Unity Embassy.

Reice said, "*TICK,* find us a set of coordinates where we're least likely to be hit by friendly fire and yet are still obeying our mission parameters." There was always an edge to be had, a safety precaution you could take, a hedge on your bets, if you were smart enough to look for it and determined enough to find it.

That computation would take a while. As he waited for the numbers to come up, he composed a notification of change of station for a better field of fire. When that was done, and the *TICK* was still working the problem of finding a safe place to hunker down if and when all hell broke loose out here, all he could do in the interim was worry.

Maybe the Unity Embassy was showing some signs of aggressive activity. Reice looked at the eye-teasing form, all curves, dapples and dimples in the errant starlight. Nope. Looked just the same. Maybe the original configuration of the embassy construct had been revealed as a threat in and of itself.

The thought raised his hackles. He'd wanted to blast the Ball out of existence numerous times since it had first arrived. He could attest to its inexplicable capabilities. But today it wasn't doing anything different, or special. It wasn't opening up. It wasn't gobbling up the heavy freighter traffic and military convoys tirelessly circuiting from Threshold to Spacedock Seven and back.

The Ball was just being the Ball, as usual. If Reice was forced to choose a target, the Ball would be his first pick. But his orders had deployed his firepower evenly between the two constructions, and he couldn't change those orders. He could only modulate his responses for the greatest personal survivability.

Having taken a second long look at the problem, he liked his situation even less. He waited for the *TICK* to give him the most survivable coordinates with his heart pounding, expecting to be ordered to shoot up the Ball, or the Unity Embassy, at any second.

He was so tense he jumped in his seat when the *TICK* put up new coordinates for him. He looked at them a long time before he sent his repositioning data to Traffic Control.

The *BLUE TICK* wanted to sit right "under" the Ball, at what Reice had come to think of as the Ball's south pole. The good news was that the new coordinates gave him an entire alien Ball's worth of protection from the sphere of conflict. Another advantage was that, in any line-of-sight engagement, the Unity Embassy was "between" him and Spacedock Seven, from which the heavy firepower and reinforcements must come in any real shooting war.

The bad news was that to take advantage of all the natural cover provided by two large alien masses, he'd be nearly up under the Ball's skirts. If the Ball decided to open up and suck him inside, or spit some death ray, Reice wouldn't have a prayer of outrunning its lethal reach. Not from so close by.

But you had to place your bets. And Reice knew enough about the Ball, if not the embassy construct, to know that the Unity aliens' superior technology ought to mean superior survivability—and a better place to hide from ricochets and strays.

What was the Secretariat thinking? he wondered once more as he laid in his new coordinates. Any fool soldier or cop knew that blindly attacking an indubitably superior force when you were armed with demonstrably inferior weapons was a bad idea.

You hunkered down behind some handy cover and sent for reinforcements. But that was cop thinking, or maybe military thinking. Not diplomat thinking, or bureaucrat thinking.

He just hoped the diplomats and the bureaucrats *were* thinking. It would be a shame to die out here over some miscommunication or because somebody'd had a bad night's sleep.

He got his okay from Traffic Control and began making his way as unobtrusively as possible to his new coordinates. Not that those coordinates were unobtrusive. Only when he'd been out here to meet South and Ambassador Lowe had he been so close to the Ball for any length of time.

He just hoped it didn't misconstrue his approach as some sort of suicide attack or kamikaze move. So he sidled up to his new station nice and slow, real careful, and without any of his weapons armed during the flight.

He knew that the Ball could sense him. He wasn't fooling himself that proximity had any effect on its efficiency. If it could tell he had live weapons trained on it from close at hand, it knew he'd drawn a bead on it from his earlier post.

The Ball didn't reach out and grab him, suck him into a hole in spacetime, spit colored fire, or do anything much when he finally arrived on station.

It blinked at him, that was all. Or winked. It pulsed a small whorl of colors right in his face. Just one time. And then it went back to being its inscrutable Ball self.

He didn't know whether to report the anomaly of the blink or not. In the end, he didn't. Too many hair triggers around to chance it.

Reice wasn't a praying man, but he was praying now that no jokers from the Secretariat or ConSpaceCom lost their heads and started something that humanity couldn't finish.

CHAPTER 26

▽

Start-Up

In the command and control center fitted to the apex of the Stalk like a witch's hat or a missile warhead or a radar mast, Richard Cummings watched the final systems check with an inexplicable optimism that bordered on elation.

All around him in the circular C&C module walled with multifunction displays, anticipation was high and discussion animated. White-jacketed NAMECorp structural engineers huddled with LabCom propulsion mavens in rumpled leisure clothes, whispering incantations over topological spacetime maps. ConSpaceCom astrogators in orange coveralls dappled with mission patches stalked from station to station, datapads in hand and comm beads gleaming in their ears. Astrophysicists and geochronometrists conferred with Threshold traffic control experts, leaning over desktop lidar, microwave radar, and infrared scanners showing the latest turbulence and space hazard tracking reports. Gesticulating Secretariat staffers in pin-striped flannel suits guided pampered Threshold media personalities through the astronic wonderland in search of vidcam opportunities and talking heads. Logistics Agency brass, their uniformed chests resplendent with multicolored field decorations, signed manifests and gave orders with equal flourish. ConSec security personnel in weapons-belted khakis kept an unobtrusive record of who came and went through the doorways they guarded.

Richard Cummings sat alone, in the eye of the storm, waiting patiently for the moment when everyone would take their places, braced and ready for ignition, and Threshold would begin to move. Cummings was proud of the work that NAMECorp had done on this project—as proud as he'd ever been of any work his people had produced, here at the Stalk, or out beyond the nearer stars.

General Granrud came by, intent on managing the effort by walking around where he could be available to anyone who needed him, trailing three aides and a bird colonel behind him like a tail.

"Everything meet your expectations so far, Mr. Cummings?" the pear-faced general asked.

"Everything's smooth as silk, General. Quite an accomplishment, so far," Cummings replied, careful to add the salt needed when one old professional spoke to another of a project just getting under way.

The general's casual mood evaporated. "We'd like to burn in with a test run—or a hot wash, if we need it."

"What did you have in mind, General?" A test run was clearly feasible; a "hot wash," during which everyone came back in from a failed test or trouble-plagued exercise to determine what went wrong, and how to fix it, was the military's typical response to less than perfect field-test results.

"We figure we can move Threshold a half-naut or so without wasting too much time, fuel, energy, or trouble. We want to make sure these plasma thrusters are going to give us the sort of fine attitude correction we want from them. Then if we've got a problem we haven't solved or anticipated, we can fix it here, while our spacedocks are still available."

"Fine idea, General, if we've got the time and the fuel to burn." Richard was accustomed to last minute cover-our-ass thinking from the military. Sometimes he thought that the planning staffs and the action staffs really didn't communicate at all. Now that Granrud was commanding an action staff, he was thinking like an action officer. An action officer wanted to do some damned thing and see what happened, because he knew you couldn't simulate real time, no matter how much computational power you engaged. Of course, action officers didn't care what things cost—they were trained to get the job done in real time, with as few disasters as possible, but including any and all screwups, and bring their people through to the objective with the least possible deformation of mission parameters.

Winning came first. Casualties came second. Equipment loss or damage came third. "I assume you've got consensus from my people and the science types that we're not adding unnecessary stresses on the superstructure with an unscheduled reorbiting test like this?"

Granrud wanted to put the mobilized Threshold through her paces: start-up, short flight, attitude corrections, precision astrogation drill, and new orbit acquisition, all without losing access to Spacedocks One through Seven and the technical capabilities there.

The ConSpaceCom general replied, "The consensus is that we don't want a problem we can't handle cropping up at a good fraction of the speed of light. Maybe we'll stress the superstructure some, but I'd rather find out now, when I can do something about it, than later, when I can't."

When they left orbit for real, they'd lose contact with the Spacedock necklace for the duration of the journey: each Spacedock would be recreated at the new orbital site. Mankind wasn't moving out of the home system, not on this or any other day. Mickey Croft's grand plan included having NAMECorp begin constructing another, more modest but more modern, habitat at the old Threshold site. Cummings had gracefully concurred, not simply because it meant another huge project for his corporate empire, but because Earth, the mother world, must be constantly monitored and protected from do-gooders and exploiters alike.

Cummings said, "Let's go do it, General. Your way. You're the operational authority ... shall we throw those newsies out of here or let them stay so we can look good on the eighteen-hundred news?"

Granrud winced theatrically. "I forgot to bring my public affairs officer over here. Didn't think I'd need him. Can you field their questions from NAMECorp's point of view? I just want to run my mission, and I'd be happier if I didn't have to look my best."

"I understand," Cummings said gravely. "We'd be delighted to handle the press, using your guidelines. I'm sure the Secretariat has lots of statements it wants to make, as well. Good luck, General."

"To all of us. Test flight begins in seventy minutes. Real start up at nineteen hundred hours, and we don't want anybody broadcasting live from in here."

"You have my word on it." As the general turned away,

Cummings left his quiet spot at the mission integration console and ambled over to the Secretariat chief of staff, who was finessing the press delegation.

"Vince, congratulations on your new appointment."

"Thank you, Mr. Cummings." They shook hands and a dozen cyclopean-eyed vidcams glared their way.

"Don't thank me, it was well deserved. Can I see you a moment in private?"

Remson shook off the media with professional grace. "Sir?" Blond, athletic and Teutonic, Remson was looking especially photogenic today. His energetic air and commanding, perfectly groomed presence seemed to exude competence and the assurance that the Secretariat had everything well under control. Remson was fooling the newsies, anyway. He might have fooled Cummings, if not for Richard's deep familiarity with the way the Croft Secretariat worked.

"How's Mickey?" Cummings asked casually. Mickey Croft's absence, and Remson's promotion, spoke volumes to the initiated.

"Getting some well-deserved rest," Remson said stonily. "It's been a trying interval for all of us."

"You and Forat didn't help much."

"I'm so sorry, but real differences of opinion take time and effort to settle. Tell the Secretary for me that I hope he's well enough to make an appearance soon." Cummings was fishing, but he knew damn well there was a big fat trout in the pool.

"He'll make a statement once there's something to say. We're not getting ahead of our technical and military agencies on this. You shouldn't, either. If something goes wrong at this early stage, so far you're the only one who'll have egg on his face."

"Speaking of something going wrong, get these media succubi out of here within the hour. We're going to run a field test. If you want to risk them going live from a mini-disaster, it's up to you. But after that, the C&C center is off-limits to nonessential personnel. If egg on faces is your paramount concern, I'd recommend moving them out now, before the test. Then you'll have time to spin the results your way."

Remson's tongue darted out to wet his lips. "We'll be talking to you later, of course—at the press conference."

"Wouldn't miss it."

As Remson stalked away without another word, Cummings wondered if Mickey Croft's new Chief of Staff had ever seen a real egg, let alone understood the reference. Cummings had promised himself that he'd spend some time at his Montana ranch when this was over—and take along his son and new daughter-in-law as a belated wedding gift, a conciliatory gesture. Montana summer might remind Ricky that Earth was his homeworld, and that the first Garden of Eden was still the best. He'd even offered to arrange for the Mullah Forat, Dini, Rick, and himself to visit Jerusalem. You had to know what the other man wanted and be ready to give it to him, to really cement a change in relationship or shore up a strategic weak point.

Remson's sudden promotion was designed to cover for Mickey Croft's absence. If he'd had more time, Cummings would have been assiduously rooting out the truth of Croft's condition. Now, it didn't seem to matter a hell of a lot.

The test reorbit was going to answer many more pressing questions. It would also cost the Secretariat a bundle, but that was to Cummings' benefit. He busied himself circling the room, making sure all of his people knew that NAME-Corp was heartily in favor of supporting General Granrud's idea of a short burn-in.

By the time Cummings was done, Remson had removed every last media personality and couture-clad staffer, and the C&C center was beginning to look like an operational facility at last.

Countdown numbers started. "Zero minus sixty minutes."

The next time Cummings truly noticed the simulated human voice announcing the countdown, there were only twenty-three minutes left until start-up of the complex matrix of astrogational and propulsion modules, outboard tows and tugs.

"—and holding." The countdown, once stopped, was a silence resounding louder than one could imagine. One of Richard's senior space scientists came over to him. "Sir," said the big-headed youngster determinedly. "We ran these stresses again, in light of a recently detected magnetic front." Behind the NAMECorp scientist was a light colonel with hands thrust in coverall pockets and a sour look on his pockmarked face.

"Go on," Cummings said.

The scientist eyed the astrogator. The astrogator added, "You see, sir, it's the space debris problem we're going to have, combined with the magnetic storm—it's makin' the original flight window downright unviable."

The scientist picked up where the astrogator left off. "We think it's crazy not to use this so-called test window to take advantage of a clear shot out past the vector of the incoming disturbance. If we don't go now, we might be socked in for days. Everybody'll lose their edge. . . ."

Anxiously, the astrogator in orange said, "ConSpaceCom Astrogation thinks either we abort the test and use the test window to mount the mission, or we'll be lickin' our chops for the next seventy-two hours."

"And," the young scientist began before the astrogator had finished, "we can't be sure that the incoming magnetics aren't going to give us all sorts of corollary problems—stress the systems more than a test would, if we have to sit it out. We're real exposed where some of these sensing systems are concerned. They aren't going to like a magnetic bath one bit. We can outrun the bath this system is going to take if we hurry, but if we sit here . . . Well, I wouldn't want to warrant NAMECorp equipment after its been through the dual stresses of an outbound magnetic storm and this test run."

"It's sort of like sunspots, sir: can't live with them, can't stop 'em."

"I get the picture, Colonel. All right, you two. Let's see the supporting data. I suppose you've decided I'm the guy to tell your boss?" General Granrud had wanted that test. The Secretariat had been counting it as a bonus, a chance to hold a press conference, put their spin on events, make sure everybody on Threshold was prepared for what was to come, but not worried.

Back to the original plan. You didn't always have to like reality in order to adapt to it.

Cummings found Granrud and handed him the data without a word. The general knew what was up; his squat, muscular body was hunched over a com console. He scrolled through the supporting documentation with his chin on his fist and said, without looking up, "Well, Mr. Cummings, it's your ass, too. Want to go for it? Outrun our bad luck from a cold start? You built this equipment."

"To your specifications," Cummings reminded him, then added: "In consultation. Yeah. I'd go for it, if it were my call."

"Good." Granrud straightened up, rubbing the small of his back. "Then, let's go do it." He grinned as he motioned his staff, waiting at a polite distance, to come close.

The count resumed shortly thereafter. Cummings took his station at the command and control integration center and inserted comm beads in his ears, so he could hear some of the message traffic as well as the count and the room.

Everywhere but at the astrogators' console, people were strapping into acceleration couches, checking life-support and auxiliary power supplies, and making sure they had space helmets and escape vehicle assignments in case the worst happened and Threshold broke apart, disintegrated as soon as the propulsion modules ignited.

You couldn't evacuate everybody on the habitat. You could evacuate the C&C staff—very quietly, just like you evacuated the Secretariat staff.

As the clock talked down, Cummings admitted that he was glad that Rick and Dini were safe somewhere else. Sometimes you needed to know you weren't risking everything you cared about.

He looked at his console, pressed a toggle, and his main integration module lit up, giving him a good idea how the system was coming on-line. Each time a component somewhere on the Stalk or on the outriding spacecraft or the add-on modules was tested and brought on-line, it lit up on his graphic.

It was comforting to watch Threshold come alive. She'd never been meant to be mobile, but she was built to last. It was like lighting a huge Christmas tree one tier of decorations at a time, or turning on the power to a new generator or office tower. He'd done it all before. He cupped the comm bead in his left ear and attenuated the one in his right, but only joined the operation in progress when there was confusion about priority access or section reporting.

The next time he noticed the countdown, they were real close. But he knew that. Only the suite of massive scalar drive units remained to be brought on-line. If even one of them failed by overloading and exploding catastrophically, they could lose part of Blue South or even Blue Mid. If one or all of them failed to produce ignition power levels, Threshold wasn't going anywhere.

The countdown in his right ear was synchronized with the voices coming from far "below" him, on the three integrated scalar power modules.

Cummings couldn't help those engineers now. All that remained in his universe was the slow count to ignition. Seven. Six. Five.

Number One came on-line. Four. Three. Number Two roared to life. But Number Three was hesitant, vapor-locked, or frozen up. Silence interspersed by curses filled the room.

The countdown clock announced the hold.

You couldn't hold long, with Scalar Drive One and Two at full power.

A tiny voice in Cummings left ear said, "Okay. Let's try it again."

The count resumed at "One Minute to Zero."

Scalar Drive Three kicked in. The countdown announced "Zero," and "Ignition."

A roar rode up the Stalk from her south pole. Vibration came up Richard's legs from his feet. Not good. Too much vibration, and—

An integration emergency light lit, from one of the Con-SpaceCom tugs. He took it himself, talking a nervous outrider through a resynchronization of his astronics to the main system. "Just a little glitch somewhere," a distant voice told him. "Artifact of the interrupted countdown," he agreed.

Then he sat back and realized that the vibration running up his legs from the decking was gone. They were moving. And Threshold was holding together.

His integration console didn't show a single emergency light. His palms were wet. He wiped them on his thighs, his eyes never leaving the integration schematic.

Maybe this mission was going to work after all. Outrun their bad luck at the beginning, the general from Con-SpaceCom had said. Maybe they could do that.

They were out of Threshold's old orbit, he saw when he sneaked a glance at the topological locator on the wall. And gaining speed.

Threshold hadn't come apart from the start-up. The scalars hadn't blown at ignition. If he'd dared leave his station, Cummings would have found General Granrud and bought the man a drink. The steady pace of acceleration wasn't fazing the tugs, or towing vehicles, or the Threshold system, badly enough to show on the sensor net.

So they were all right, for the time being. The next really dangerous moment was a long way off, when they tried to synchronize a jump out of the local spacetime. If they couldn't manage it, the ride to Pluto over every inch of the intervening spacetime topology was going to take far and away too many years of Richard Cummings' life.

If they tried and failed to make a cleanly synced jump, some or all of the outboard or modular parts of Threshold were going to be scraped off as they bored their way into a custom-drilled hole from this spacetime to the energy sea beneath. If that happened, it was hard to tell which components of this jury-rigged bucket of wishes and prayers were most likely to survive.

CHAPTER 27

$\triangledown$

Joyride

Sitting in *STARBIRD*, alone with Birdy and his thoughts, Joe South watched Threshold pull out of orbit with all the detachment he could muster. Why was he worried about the habitat's survival? Nobody on it, pasttime, nowtime, or soontime, worried much about his. Maybe he should have cast his lot with the Secretariat crowd in their custom-retrofitted Flying Dutchman, but he didn't think so.

As far as South was concerned, the home system looked a lot better without Threshold squatting in your path like some medieval castle, complete with a moat of spacedocks around her. If Spacedocks One through Seven had trundled off in Threshold's wake, then the way to Earth would have been clear.

South hadn't believed a thing he'd heard since he got back, so he hadn't really believed that the spacedocks were going to stay on station between Mars and Jupiter. But they did, a working component of Mickey Croft's Grand Plan to claim More of the Universe for Humankind.

Humanity's fate wasn't linked to one space habitat full of bureaucrats and luckless service personnel: Mickey Croft was wrong about at least that much. South had gotten real tired of listening to all the highflown talk and overblown expectations of the Threshold media, the propagandists from the Secretariat, and the newly philosophical Ph.D.'s who popped up on every vid show telling the Threshold audience what a great honor was in store for the habitat's population and how they were the Chosen People of the Human Race.

By the time Threshold started to move out toward the edge of the home solar system, the political bullshit was flying so thick and fast that once the habitat reached Pluto's orbit, you'd be able to tell your designated coordinates by the smell.

Joe South vowed once and for all to give up on the politics of Threshold: you had to be a native of the UNE culture to play the game or even handicap the players.

Was Mickey Croft serious, when the Secretary General went on all-station vid and proclaimed the beginning of a New Epoch of interstellar peace, prosperity, and exploration for the United Nations of Earth and its new ally, the Unity Confederacy? The vid speech not only preempted every alternate entertainment or news source, it was beamed at exorbitant cost across the priority A-potential comm network to every UNE outpost, habitat, and monitoring station in the galaxy.

Since Joe South's psychometric revaluation, he wasn't exactly in the SecGen's confidence. Or much of anybody else's. Any camel-lipped Epsilonian in the Loader Zone of Threshold could make as good a guess as South about the depth of the Secretariat's commitment to the new plan.

The habitat was on the move, so somebody was committed to at least looking committed. South had been around these political chameleons too long to dream of taking anything they said—most especially anything they blatantly proclaimed—at face value.

And then there were the rumors. Sling had told him, confidentially, that NAMECorp was building a brand-new Stalk, out at Spacedock Seven, for emplacement right where the old one had been. When South asked the after-marketeer how come, Sling said, "Can't leave the home system unguarded, fella. Too many cone-headed beings around, y'know. Or would y' believe the Loader Zone version, which is that all the Loader Zone types, all the subhumans and the bioengineered species, are going to be rounded up during the flight and dispatched back here, surreptitiously, and stashed in the new habitat, cause the Secretariat wants to put humanity's best foot forward, and that don't include the dock workers and the nonproductives—like you and me."

It sounded farfetched to South, but what did he know—really know—about Threshold society? Maybe every word was true and modules were going to start peeling off the moving habitat, destined for reorbit right back at the original coordinates, under the watchful eye of ConSec and ConSpaceCom, the only real authority left at the Spacedock necklace. If it was true, the home system was about to become a social refugee camp under martial law.

Or was the scuttlebutt around the Stalk more truthful? Had the Secretariat decided to close the door to Earth on the way out, and let ConSec and ConSpaceCom turn out the lights? Had the Secretariat really ordered an all-points alert, upped the readiness status of all ConSec and ConSpaceCom craft to Defensive Condition Three: "destroy on warning"? Drawn a bead on the Unity Embassy and the Ball?

Could they be that stupid?

South wasn't waiting around on Threshold to find out. *STARBIRD* was his first priority—the real reason he'd come back here. Forget the fact that *here* had decided to move to *there,* taking him with it. Anyway, no pilot with a rudimentary understanding of space physics wanted to be sitting around helpless in the marginally spaceworthy Threshold as it picked up speed, heading for a spongespace jump it might or might not be able to execute intact.

Jumping Threshold, its diaphanous web of aftermarket interconnects, and its outriding escort vessels into a custom-punched hole in the universal fabric, was about as safe as South's first experimental flight in *STARBIRD* had been. Only this time, Joe South wasn't the pilot. South had always been a terrible passenger. You didn't become a test pilot if you wanted to trust your life to somebody else's reflexes and intelligence.

Threshold looked like a tree infested with gypsy moths when South got *STARBIRD* clear of the slipbay and brought the habitat up on his monitors to take a look. *Bye-bye, folks. Have a nice trip. Don't forget to write.*

He'd miss Riva, certainly. And Sling, sort of. As for the rest ... Well, they were on their way to meet their destiny, with bells on.

South had met his, longtime past, on an experimental flyby of a planet then designated X-3, a place of lavender skies and sad-eyed aliens, and every lost dream he'd ever had. Sure, maybe the home system wasn't the safest place to be, if shooting broke out or martial law was really about to be declared, but South wasn't planning to make permanent camp at Threshold's old orbit. He had his ship back now, and she was in fine shape, thanks to Sling. In fact, *STARBIRD* was more competent than he'd ever dreamed a ship could be when he'd first reentered this spacetime, trying to get home to Earth.

He could try and make it to Earth now, past what was soon going to be a skeleton policing capability here between the orbits of Mars and Jupiter. Once upon a time, making it home to Earth had been the only goal that mattered to South. But Earth was still a restricted area, a preserve of the rich and powerful, a shrine to man's beginnings.

And Joe South had found out that what he really wanted wasn't on Earth at all. Not anymore. And not even the Unity aliens could help him roll back the clock, even if he thought he could reenter his past and live there, after all he'd learned.

South crossed his ankles ruminatively on his console bumper. Sling's retrofitted flat screens and AI-synchronized scalar drives gave *STARBIRD* all the capability somebody like South should have been able to imagine. Zero-point energy, which was the inexhaustible by-product of the A-potential field's effect, gave *STARBIRD* infinite range and competence limited only by the amount of electromagnetic force available to the scalar drives to open and maintain a tap into Dirac's energy sea—and the human body's ability to function at high fractions of the speed of light or in notime. The electromagnetic generators on *STARBIRD,* which powered her new fifth-force field, life support, upgraded astronics and scalar drive units, pumped out eight gigawatts and could pulse up to twice that, as long as her plasma fuel cells held out.

So he hadn't really been lying when he'd told Riva Lowe he'd catch up with Threshold—when he was done doing what he had to do. She'd known something was fishy, when he'd told her he was off on his long-delayed shake-out cruise. You couldn't lie to someone who'd been where she'd been and learned what she'd learned. Or, at least, he couldn't. The human race was going to have to learn some new tricks if it wanted to keep up its bad old ways once it started intermingling with the Unity.

He'd gone to see Riva Lowe in her Blue Mid office, but

she wasn't there. He found her in a fancy ambassador's suite up in Blue North, in the Secretariat Executive complex. She seemed distant and preoccupied, when he'd said he wasn't going with the habitat.

She'd looked around her new office, as if to check for eavesdroppers. And then she'd said, "South, whatever it is you're doing, don't get killed, okay?"

"Okay," he'd replied, because he didn't understand her anymore—not since they'd come back here. She hadn't wanted to come back here at all, into these constrained physical venues with their severe limits and limiting vistas.

Now he couldn't drag her away. Had she forgotten everything that had happened to them in the Unity? Had it become a dream for her, half-remembered, half-discounted? He'd forgotten more than he remembered, the first time he'd encountered the Unity. He'd been alone, unready, and all he'd wanted was to go back and resume his old life.

But Riva and he had performed a difficult task, learned too many lessons, and come back to give a full report. So she couldn't have forgotten. The Unity hadn't wanted her to forget all she'd learned, all she'd become. Maybe she had metabolized the memories—found a way to fit them into a four-dimensional framework once she returned. But how could she have forgotten the plasma shuttle, the pain of readjustment? And how could she bear to simply go back to living among these dangerous, deaf and dumb sleepwalkers at the Secretariat?

He couldn't say any of that. He just watched her as if he were mourning her loss. Maybe he was. He couldn't find her in the storm of their unsynchronized intentions. She was as lost to him as she would be once the habitat went its way, and he went his.

They'd done so much together. He couldn't just leave her. They'd shared the alltime, they'd shared a mission, they'd found a new way to live. But none of it seemed to matter to her then.

He knew she'd made a decision to go with the habitat, and he couldn't change her mind. He didn't try. But he didn't want her changing his mind for him, either. He had his own agenda.

She could feel the nervousness and determination emanating from him, the uncertainty, the doubt. He couldn't hide his feelings. His emotions splashed around her office in the Secretariat like hydrobath waves in an agitated tub. She was a creature of the Secretariat—he'd forgotten that until the Threshold move stopped being theoretical and started being operational.

Maybe she'd forgotten, too. Or maybe she was as torn as he. But when the Secretary General and his Chief of Staff needed her expertise on the Unity aliens, she responded like an old fire horse.

Maybe it was better this way. No room in *STARBIRD* for two. Never had been. Not really. You could shoehorn another person in here, shorttime. But not comfortably. And not longtime. Still, leaving her on that erector set covered with cobwebs and pulled and pushed by space tugs and destroyers, to find her fate with the masses of sleepy folk who didn't understand what was happening to them. . . . He felt like he'd deserted her.

There was no guarantee that human science was going to get that aftermarketed habitat safely through to its new orbit. He'd said that to her.

"I know," she'd sighed. "If there's trouble, I should be here." Her face was stonily set: she had her orders.

He knew better than to argue with her. He had his own orders, after a fashion. There was something he'd been wanting to do for a very long time. And this might be his last—his only—chance to do it.

So he'd left her in the Secretariat and made his way to the Blue Mid slipbay where it had all started—where he'd first met her. He was lots more savvy now about Threshold ways. He was a high-ranking Customs officer, seconded to the Secretariat, and First Secretary to the Ambassador to Unity space. He had clout to spare, in Threshold terms.

He used it getting a priority slot for departure from Threshold, just as the habitat was attaining cruising speed.

Out *STARBIRD* popped into a spacetime only slightly more perturbed than usual. It wasn't any harder than it had to be, leaving Riva and Sling behind.

He didn't belong to Threshold. They did. End of story.

The habitat's course had taken it only a bit past the Spacedock necklace.

He'd come this route once before, long ago in pasttime. On that occasion, he'd left a lot more behind than Threshold. He'd left his century, his culture, his life, and most of his sanity.

This time, he at least had his equilibrium and all of his soontime promises to keep.

"Birdy," he said to his AI copilot, "set course for the Unity Embassy."

This could get tricky if there really were a large number of weapons trained on the embassy and on the Ball. He uncrossed his legs, sat up, leaned forward, and talked to Traffic Control himself.

"What do you mean, prohibited? How can a vector to Spacedock Seven be a restricted area?" he asked the flat-voiced controller.

"Commander South, you'll have to talk to my supervisor about that. I'm just following orders."

So then he had to figure out what strings to pull. Technically, as a Customs official seconded to the Secretariat, he could call Threshold for clearance to pass. Or he could call Reice.

"Yo, Reice! What's the magic word to get over there to see you at the Ball site? I got to talk to you in person. Some things are unfit for open channels." It always worked before. Tell some official you've got information that's too sensitive to be discussed on an open line, and you don't have your secure unit with you.

Reice said, "South, old man. I was just thinking about you. How do you propose to get here?"

"*STARBIRD*." Reice had been the first human of Threshold he'd ever encountered. Now maybe Reice would be the last. It had a certain symmetry that the Unity Council would have approved.

"Will that can of outmoded technology get you here—this time—under its own power?"

Reice remembered that first encounter with a pilot from his distant past, a Relic called Joe South. And Reice was in rare form today. South wished he had a vid connection, but for some reason *BLUE TICK* was accepting voice transmission only.

"Look, I can still reach Threshold for a priority vector, if you don't have the juice, Reice." That should be about all the prodding necessary.

"Shit, don't do that. You want to come back in here, join the party? Give me your ETA, current coordinates, and five minutes to grease the wheels."

Worked like a charm.

STARBIRD hummed to attention under him, full of power and speed. Birdy muttered contentedly, executing all of the pass-through checks and vector hand-overs in this overcontrolled traffic lane. They sure didn't want anything getting loose out here, or any uncontrolled excitement.

The traffic check-points you had to pass by to get into the Spacedock necklace, South soon realized, were artifacts of the UNE's paranoia concerning Unity constructs. Then it hit him like a slap between the eyes: the firepower out here was enormous. ConSec and ConSpaceCom really *were* on a destroy-on-warning alert.

Idiots.

The only thing these hotdogs would destroy would be themselves, if they showed the poor judgement to open fire on Unity constructs.

He should have realized that something more than simple distraction had been wrong with Riva Lowe. Maybe he'd been wrong: maybe you could still lie to someone who'd passed through the alltime, touched the notime, and poked their physiologies into eleven-space and lived not to tell about it. He'd known it was too easy, getting away from Riva without the usual spate of prying questions. It was so easy because she didn't want to answer any questions from him.

Where were her loyalties, anyhow? He was still wearing his plasma-formed boots. She'd been through all that— flown a plasma shuttle, met the Unity Interstitial Council, and she still put humanity first.

He wasn't sure he did. Not anymore. If the sleeping race called humanity could awake to its potential, it wouldn't be without a few buckets of cold water in its collective face. The bristling armaments deployed around the Unity Embassy and the Ball proved that beyond a doubt.

"What does the UNE think it's going to do, Reice?" he demanded, as soon as he got *STARBIRD* parked in a matching orbit next to *BLUE TICK* and Reice let him on board. "Blast the embassy out of existence? Because it doesn't exist here in the way of ordinary matter. Neither does the Ball. You ought to know that."

Reice was parked right under the Ball, hanging under her anus in a Ball-stationary orbit.

"Yeah, I know that, South. Could you just wait until I institute a couple basic security precautions?"

Reice was a paranoid crazy who'd finally found a situation that suited his preconceptions. He was smiling slightly as his fingers rippled over a SECURE keypad, and *BLUE TICK* put up so many cancellation waveforms that South's inner ears buzzed from the harmonic resonances.

To get Reice to let him come aboard, South had had to goddamned spacewalk. Reice wouldn't even attempt a dock with *STARBIRD*. Something about being ready, willing, and able to engage the enemy not including a nonstandard mating of locks.

South tapped the helmet under his arm and the sound of his gloved fingers on his faceplate was swallowed up by the damping modes Reice had engaged for privacy. *BLUE TICK* was virtually an anechoic chamber with exterior microwave baffling for good measure.

"Finished?" South said. He barely heard, let alone recognized, his own voice. It was muffled and soft, as if he were wearing earplugs.

Reice said, "Yep. Shoot. What are you doing back here, anyway? Don't you want to go to the party?"

"Immaterial. I need to ask you to cover my behind while I go check something at the embassy site. Secretariat business."

"Christ, why didn't you guys think of this before you set up a no-pass zone?"

"We didn't set it up for us." Reice couldn't tell he was lying. And Reice wouldn't call Threshold for confirmation—not when he was hiding down here in case some shooting did start. "We set it up for them—the Unity. I don't look like a Unity vehicle to you, do I?"

Reice was chewing gum manically. His jaw worked. He said, "South, I know it's above my paygrade, but I'd really like the skinny on what's going on here. How come you're stayin' behind?"

"Going to take the Ball on a little joyride. Want to come?"

Somehow, he had to get to the embassy without getting *STARBIRD* shot at. And into the Ball without starting a shooting war. Reice was the best chance he had.

"You want to *what*?"

"Come on, Reice, you a pilot or what? You want to ask questions, or get some answers?"

"You can do that? Get the Ball to open up?"

"You know I can. You've always known."

That worked. Reice's eyes got real wide. "Yeah, I guess I did. So this means I'm invited to the party, too?"

"Guest of honor. Just handle this unexpected bunch of trigger-happy naval officers, and we're sportin'.''

"Ah—yeah. Well, let's see." Reice chewed faster. Every muscle in his jaw seemed involved in the process. His face rippled as if he were about to molt. "How about I put *BLUE TICK* on autopilot, and we go in your ship?"

"Thought you had doubts about my spacecraft." South was beginning to enjoy himself.

"Just talk, friend. Just talk."

So in the end, they did that. Reice EVA'd over to *STARBIRD* with South and manned the horn to Spacedock Seven traffic control from South's bunk, while South prayed that he'd done the right thing.

If Reice couldn't pave the way across this minefield, South was going to be a realtime target. So was *STARBIRD*. But then, so was Reice.

The astronics that Sling had retrofitted into *STARBIRD* included a surely illicit threat detection module that knew when hostile targeting systems were locking on. There was one hell of a lot of threat out there. But nobody shot at him, so he supposed that Reice was doing a good job.

Parking *STARBIRD* at the embassy site was a piece of cake, if you didn't worry that any minute the combined forces of ConSpaceCom and ConSec were going to open fire, either because they'd contacted Threshold for verification that this mission was authorized, or because they didn't care and were happy to have a pretext to start shooting.

Reice came forward when South was suiting up—you couldn't exactly slip off *STARBIRD* without anybody knowing you'd gone. "What's this?" Reice said, between manic chomps of his jaws.

"Told you, I thought." South spoke through a retracted visor, as he checked his glove seals and self-tested the Manned Maneuvering Unit on his back. "I gotta check something out at the embassy."

"Won't they send a shuttle for you, or something?"

"Sort of. Don't worry. I'll be back, soontime—in a few minutes."

"And if you don't come back?" Reice put his hands on his hips.

"Get *STARBIRD* out of the way before you let your buddies start shooting," South advised, and slapped his helmet down as he backed into the open lock.

The door closed on Reice, still chewing his cud.

For one instant, South wasn't sure he was doing the right thing. But then the lock cycled, and the outer hatch opened. The plasma shuttle was already nosing around the airlock, glittering pulses of welcome rolling over its surface. He stepped toward it, and it enveloped him. His boots, his spacesuit, his life-support system, and his heart all merged with the craft as it bore him happily toward the embassy portal, swooping with joy.

An Interpreter was waiting in the access tube, all color and light. South wasn't sure if he should be here, if he was intruding. But he'd come this far.

The plasma shuttle had no such doubts. It bumped its way into the tube and extended itself. All around the Interstitial Interpreter, the plasma shuttle flowed caressingly.

The Interpreter never would have come aboard if South was out of line. South said, "I'm afraid for them. For all of this activity. They don't have the wisdom to know when they're trying to do too much. I need to do something to help. Or you do."

The words were difficult to enunciate. They filled his helmet. He retracted his faceplate, and the Interpreter touched his face.

A soft touch. A swift, retreating touch. All of his answers were in his mind, now. He knew what he needed to know.

"Sorry to bring you such a long way, but it's time to take the Ball out of play," he muttered, but the face of the Interpreter, its head glittering with a crown of stars, twinkled at him as it slowly disappeared from nowtime.

The eyes were the last to leave. They were curiously concerned and full of mild warnings.

He understood, or hoped he did. This meeting of eleven-space and four-space bodies was difficult at best. No wonder Croft had gotten confused. No wonder South had been frightened, when first he'd had such an encounter.

The shuttle nuzzled him, rubbed against him, and reminded him to put down his faceplate once the Interpreter had gone away.

The trip back to *STARBIRD* was full of South's questions and the shuttlecraft's quiet confidence. He was glad the craft was well, and that it remembered him. He'd see it again, his stroking hand told it, once this mission was done.

The shuttlecraft wanted to take him wherever he needed to go, but he was committed to his decision. The plasma shuttle slipped along *STARBIRD*'s hull and let him stick his gloved hand out to push the exterior lockplate that Sling had installed. Then it squeezed its way inside to give him a gentle entry.

He watched it go before he let the lock cycle, suddenly afraid that the fools from ConSpaceCom would see it and shoot it, without knowing what they were shooting at.

But he needn't have worried. It wafted back to the embassy portal without emitting a signature that human equipment could read, except a winking colored farewell to South just before it disappeared.

He slapped the lockplate, stepped resolutely into *STARBIRD* and blustered, "Reice, let's get a move on. We're go."

Reice scrambled into the secondary astrogation couch at South's bunk.

South moved forward, telling Birdy, "Let's go. You've got your Ball coordinates. Execute," before he'd strapped in or taken off his helmet.

This was one of those missions when you leave your helmet on—just in case.

The Ball had tortured him, lured him, fooled him, and obsessed him. This time, he was going to have his turn.

"Reice, you want to watch, ask for full scans back there," he called out. The Ball was going to put on quite a display this time, now that South knew what he was doing.

He watched it split apart in his own forward scanners. The silver sphere coruscated, rippled, and began to iris open. Silver turned to sunrise, and a leading edge of shockwave ran from west to east as the Ball manifested completely in nowtime for him.

He saw the lions at the portal, and he heard Reice whoop aloud. He saw the dragons in their splendor, weaving spacetime, one atop the other, throughout eternity.

And then they were in. *STARBIRD* was inside the Ball. He slapped the rear viewscreens manually, afraid he'd see ConSpaceCom open fire before the Ball closed.

But no torpedoes followed him. No missiles were locked on his tail. He said, "Nice job running interference, Reice."

Reice just grunted.

"You okay, Reice?"

Silence. Then, from South's bunk. "You did that? You saw that? You understand this?"

Reice must still be looking forward. "Dump your forward scans. Pull up an aft scan. Don't look forward again. You want to look at time that's formed, not forming. Got me?"

A sick-sounding voice said, "Yup. Roger."

STARBIRD glided flawlessly into the Ball's slip bay, beside the resting plasma shuttles. South kept looking out his aft scanners, until the whorls and vistas calmed, and the great eleven-space ship around him began to settle down.

Then he said, "Okay, Reice, want to fly this sucker with me?"

"This thing's a spacecraft? You're shittin' me."

"Nope. Spacetime craft. Interdimensional craft. Call it what you want. You'll get the ride of a lifetime, either way. You can stay here and monitor what's going down, or you can come along and play copilot."

"I think . . ." Reice's voice was very small. "I'll just stay where I am, right here in *STARBIRD*. But you'd better not leave me here too long."

"Not a problem," South said, slipping out of *STARBIRD*'s cockpit. "You'll be able to see me the whole time."

He was finally going to do it. Fly the Ball! South stepped out of *STARBIRD*'s open lock into the control room of the great multidimensional craft, where plasma navigators waited impatiently for their pilot, and a skein of starways could take him, and *STARBIRD,* anywhere they pleased.

CHAPTER 28

$$\triangledown$$

Nowtime

Mickey Croft was trying to get some long-delayed sleep when Remson phoned to tell him that the Ball was gone.

"What do you mean, Vince, by 'gone'?" Had the destroy-on-warning orders that Mickey had left behind with ConSpaceCom been executed? If so, why? What aggression had precipitated the shoot? Was it successful? Had the Unity returned fire?

Unasked questions tumbled through Croft's brain as he levered himself up on one elbow in his bed, rubbing sleep from his eyes and blinking at the vidphone image of Remson on his nightstand.

"By 'gone,' I mean disappeared without a trace, and without any warning," Remson said carefully in that clipped, precise diction of his which signaled that Croft's Chief of Staff was at pains to make sure he was not misunderstood.

"Oh, I see," Croft said, not sure whether he was relieved or disappointed. So it hadn't been a shoot. No warning issued from ConSpaceCom had precipitated a volley of ConSec fire. "And the Unity Embassy? Any word from them on this phenomenon?" Croft's mouth was so dry his lips were sticking together and his tongue clicked when he spoke. He reached for the cut-crystal decanter by his bedside, filled a tumbler of water, and sipped it. "Surely we've requested an explanation?"

"Ah, well—that's what I'm calling about. The Unity hasn't made a peep about this. They're closed up tight in their embassy and it's the middle of the night there. Con-

SpaceCom cedes responsibility for any official enquiry to the Secretariat. They're not prepared—or chartered—to initiate contact on the diplomatic front."

Croft swung his striped pajama legs over the edge of the bed. He felt better with his feet on the floor, even if the floor was moving through space at an ungodly speed. "It's the middle of the night here, too, Vince," Croft said sourly. He dug his toes into his bedside Aubusson rug. The tactile pleasure of skin against soft, carved wool was somehow calming. He had to think. But events were moving too fast. Worse, *he* was moving too fast, headed toward a jump into n-space, a custom-built rift in spacetime that felt no less threatening because the old pros called it spongespace, an allegorical reference to the actual shape of the universe as early theoreticians had envisioned it. "Can't those generals and admirals keep their pants on until morning?"

"Ah ... look, Mickey, when we upped the alert status, we put everybody back there on tenterhooks. We left them without a diplomatic attache and with minimum guidance. Now something has happened, but not what the Con-SpaceCom and ConSec brass expected. I think they basically want to know if the Secretariat considers the disappearance of the Ball a sufficient provocation to fire on the Unity Embassy."

"What?" Croft slapped on the lights and leaned forward until his long nose nearly touched the miniature Remson on his bedside vidscreen. "Of course it's not a reason to start shooting," he snapped. "The Ball is theirs, isn't it? If the Unity wants to recall it, that's their business. I'm not sure it's our job to wake *them* up in the middle of the night to ask why they removed an object that's clearly their property." Well, almost clearly their property. The Ball had been towed to Threshold by a white-hole scavenger named Keebler, and the old reprobate had claimed it as his personal property. But Keebler was now a "Valued Friend" of the Unity, off somewhere in Unity space. For all Croft knew, the Unity had reclaimed the Ball for Keebler's personal uses—whatever those might be.

"Mickey, look here. It's me, Vince, not some hostile player. I didn't say anything when you issued those destruct-on-warning orders, but I was worried then that something like this might happen. You can't leave a bunch of military officers in unilateral control of the home system, with their civilian control mechanism increasingly far away and difficult to contact."

"The famous Remson hindsight?" Croft accused bitterly.

"Mickey, this is our last chance to give those soldiers, sailors, and cops back there some policy guidance before we're too far away for a quick response. They can't contact us during the jump. After the jump, we've got a limited scalar communications capability until we're established at the new orbit. Conventional communications lag-time is significant over billions of miles."

"Don't you think I know that, Vince? Just what, exactly, are you trying to get me to suggest that we do?"

"Talk to the Unity Embassy. Now."

Croft reached for his water tumbler and took one sip, then a second. He was afraid of that. He didn't want to talk to the Unity aliens about their missing Ball. To be truthful, he wasn't sure that he wanted to talk to them again, ever. His glass began to quaver in his hand. The surface of the water sloshed against the crystal. A fine fix he'd gotten himself into: here he was, on the way out to a new orbit, having uprooted the entire Threshold community just so that his Secretariat could interact with the Unity, and he didn't *want* to interact with the Unity. Not anymore. Not ever.

He was experiencing a failure of nerve, and he might as well face it. Remson knew. Vince had probably known since the moment Mickey had issued the destroy-on-warning order. If the damned ConSpaceCom and ConSec brass hadn't been so infernally competent and disciplined, Mickey's troubles would all now be over: they would have fired on the Unity constructs, before Threshold made the leap into another continuum. End of budding relationship with a superior confederacy of races. End of Mickey's doubts and fears. End of threat.

But, no. ConSpaceCom had to behave perfectly. ConSec had to prove itself to be more than a bunch of trigger-happy cops. And now Remson was calling Croft on the deliberate oversight of failing to leave a diplomatic liaison at the Spacedock necklace.

"Very well, Vince. Let's do something about this situation until, that is, *before* it degenerates into a real problem." Mickey sighed. "Since you're so damned prescient where UNE/Unity relations are concerned, why don't you take a fast cruiser and go on back to the Spacedock necklace? Set up a meeting with the Unity representatives, and sort out this bit of confusion personally. After all, *I* can't leave Threshold now, and you're the next most experienced Secretariat staffer where direct contact with the Unity Council is concerned." His voice betrayed him: he'd been hoping to sound professional and dispassionate. Instead, he sounded spiteful and mean.

The tiny Remson face regarded him critically from his vidphone monitor. "Sir, I'd be glad to do that if I didn't think you needed all the support you can get right now. Of course, if you order me, I'll go. But my recommendation is that neither of us go. That we simply contact the Unity while we're enroute."

"What makes you think we can do that?"

"Ambassador Lowe makes me think we can do that, sir. I've debriefed her thoroughly, and I'm convinced we can do what she suggests. Meanwhile, I'm sending up the text of a message designed to give ConSpaceCom and ConSec some comfort. I'd like you to consider ordering them to stand down for a while, from the destroy-on-warning order, at any rate. Just until we sort things out enough to appoint a military attache from among the personnel at the Spacedock necklace. I have a short list of candidates that both services have put forward for your approval. I'll send that up, too. If you'll choose the appointees, we can suggest to the Unity when we contact them that they give us a point of contact of parallel rank. Then we've got a safety valve in place."

Remson was going too fast for Croft. He vaguely realized that Vince must have been planning this mediation of Croft's hardline stance for some time. Not even Vince Remson could pull a stop-gap mediation plan out of his ass on a moment's notice.

"You son of a bitch," Mickey said nearly inaudibly, shaking his head back and forth at the image bedeviling him.

"What's that, sir?"

"I said, don't send your recommendations up here. Bring them up, personally. And bring Riva Lowe with you." Croft slapped at the vid to end the conversation, and sent the unit tumbling to the floor.

He wasn't going to accuse Remson of staging a quiet coup d'état, but only because Remson wasn't expendable, not because Remson wasn't trying to grab the reins. Vince was just one hair short of insubordination, of unilateral actions taken with insupportable hubris, of posting a guard outside Croft's door.

Thinking the unthinkable, that real treachery was upon him, Croft padded across his bedroom, then through his bed sitting room, through the library beyond, and down the darkened reception hall to the front door to his suite.

Croft touched the lockplate gingerly. What if the door wouldn't open? When if Remson really had decided to claim that Mickey was temporarily indisposed or taking a short but well-needed rest? As Chief of Staff, Remson could then administrate Threshold in Mickey's stead, without precipitating a Secretariat Security Council meeting, an interim appointment of one of the Secretariat deputies, or any other changes in personnel.

The door to his suite obediently drew back in response to his touch. Croft stuck his head and shoulders out into the penthouse hall. He looked to the right, and then the left. No burly guardsmen stood there, ready to restrict his movements. No white-coated strangers lurked with dripping syringes to tranquilize him. In fact, everything seemed normal, peaceful, and even friendly.

Feeling flushed, Croft slunk back to his bedchamber and through it. A shower was what he needed. A hot shower, followed by ice-cold water. Then coffee and something to eat. He wasn't going to let Remson spook him.

The water in his shower ran fierce and steamy, softening the image of the tired, haggard man in the mirror before him. Had he lost sight of the UNE's best interests? Was he reacting from personal biases? Was he irrational?

Stepping into the hot spray, he was sure he could handle Remson. Vince would come to heel once Mickey demonstrated firm resolve and a clear agenda. But Croft must not let Remson see that there was distrust on his side, that he was afraid of Remson, or even of the Unity aliens. Because he mustn't be afraid.

And yet, when Croft closed his eyes in the shower, he saw the black-in-black, sad eyes of the Unity's Interstitial Interpreter regarding him with pity and disdain. Or was it apprehension?

Even the coldest of pummeling sprays from his shower massage couldn't wipe away that image. It haunted him as surely as the self-replicating images of the Interpreter and his honor guard had haunted his psychometric modeler.

Why wasn't Remson concerned? Remson had seen the Unity aliens close at hand. Remson had been inside the Unity Embassy, which was nowhere near the physical coordinates it occupied in Earth's solar system. Remson had been touched by the Unity aliens, and even had touched Riva Lowe and her cohort when Croft's human ambassador had stretched out a hand to him across a gulf of continua.

Didn't Remson have the sense to realize that the Unity was a superior culture, scientifically, technically, and therefore militarily? But of course Remson did. Vince's agenda included asking for a Unity point of contact of equal rank to a military attache that Croft must now appoint.

So if Remson understood, then perhaps Vince wasn't trying to maneuver events to suit some shadowy purpose. Unless, of course, the Unity aliens had gotten to Remson during Remson's visit to the embassy. When Croft had arrived there, Remson was standing straight and tall with the Unity diplomatic contingent, watching Mickey through wise, pale eyes. . . .

When the door chimed, Croft was nearly ready for visitors.

He gave his tie one final tug and strode purposefully to greet them at his door. Exude power, calm, compassion, and control. Don't let them see your doubts.

But when the door retreated, there was Riva Lowe on Remson's arm. The two of them seemed to Croft to be equally changed, creatures of Unity machination, simulacra, pod people, objects of demonic possession, or worse. He stared at them wordlessly, horrorstruck.

"Mickey? We're sorry to disturb you so late, but we've brought all the documentation you asked for," Vince said smoothly, covering for Croft's lapse of courtesy.

"Of course. Come in, come in. Good to see you, Madam Ambassador."

Riva Lowe's face seemed pinched, her movements jerky and ill-timed as she paced him into the reception room. She took a seat when he did, watching him too closely.

Remson came over and handed him a notepad to scan. He waved Vince away with a flick of his fingers and pretended to read.

Whatever was written on the notepad's screen would

have to do. He scrolled through it, saying judiciously, "Yes, yes," and finally, "Splendid. We'll just send these orders out immediately." He pushed his thumb in the signature block and laid the notepad aside on the table.

Remson came to take the documents and whispered, "Mickey, you've got to appoint the military attaché, remember? The short list?" To minimize the awkwardness, Remson found the relevant list and proffered the notepad once again.

There were only three names that Croft recognized: Granrud, J., Major General (UNECSC/A); Reice, T.D., Lt. Col (UNECS); Smith, E.E., Dr. (UNESI). He appointed them all to serve as points of contact and consular attachés for their respective services and handed the accursed notepad computer back to Remson, saying, "Don't stick that thing in my face again, Vince. Use a little initiative, for heaven's sake."

Then he returned to Riva Lowe, perched uncomfortably on the edge of a chair. "Ambassador, Vince tells me you believe we can contact the Unity directly, from here, and forestall any confusion or unfortunate suppositions that might otherwise arise from the abrupt leavetaking of the object we call the Unity Ball."

"Yes, sir," she said. "I'm ready to do that, if you're ready to authorize it."

"Why wouldn't I be?" Mickey said expansively, as if Ambassador Lowe had just given him the best of all gifts. "Proceed immediately, and let me know of your results as soon as you're done."

"Immediately?"

"Immediately," Croft confirmed. Out of one corner of his eye, Mickey saw Remson's brow furrow and his Chief of Staff give a hand signal advising caution.

Lowe was reaching into her briefcase, pulling out a handphone.

The unit was so quotidian, so low-powered, and so innocuous that Croft didn't understand what was happening until Lowe put the handset to her lips and said, "Patch me to my Preset Three coordinates."

Before Mickey could move to stop her, the reception room behind her disappeared. The walls fell away. The floor melted in on itself. A howling vortex spun behind her head in midair. Spiral arms came out of it, spreading a miasma of color and light. Then, from the center of the vortex, a spark flew with a snap and a jolt that raised Croft's every hair.

For an instant he was flash-blind, as if a photographer had gotten him right in the face. White balls of light centered his vision. Around them, at the edges of his sight, bits of his reception room could still be seen. He clutched his chair desperately, refusing to move, refusing to react visibly. He blinked, and blinked, and blinked again.

As the balls of light obscuring the center of his sight faded, an alien vista loomed in their place. It was as if a tunnel had been dug from his reception room into the Unity Embassy. The vista of recurved purple plains and impossible angles jolted his nerves. A thousand strands of light glowed in a serpentine flux that appeared and disappeared above the head of the Interstitial Interpreter, who had his hands in his sleeves and was looking compassionately at Croft.

Behind the Interpreter, smoking pots swung from invisible arms.

Sometimes Mickey wondered if the Interpreter he encountered each time was the same being. But not this time. He could already smell the cloying incense of the smoking pots, leaking out of the hole punched in his quarters, straight into the Unity Embassy. On one side of the hole, calm as could be, sat Riva Lowe, as if posing for some Victorian photo. On the other side, Remson stood, facing the Interpreter.

Mickey wondered what would happen if he got up and pushed Remson into the hole? Would Vince take one step and find himself in Unity space?

But Croft did nothing of the kind. He was the Secretary General of the United Nations of Earth and he must maintain decorum at all times. He would, unless the Interpreter, uninvited, took one step into Mickey's parlor. If that happened, he would not warrant what he might do.

The Interpreter cocked its conical head at him. Its harelip worked. Its mouth opened and smoke came out. The smokey breath of the Interstitial Interpreter said, "We offer assistance in the matter of acquiring a safe passage nowtime through the notime. In the alltime, everything is prepared for your safe arrival. Fears unfounded, but Unity provides safe passage, nowtime, as well as notime, as it is written in the alltime. Accepting is required."

Accepting is required? Croft's head ached, a sudden, blazing pulse that sent zigzags of light across his peripheral vision, as if a migraine might be coming on.

"I'm sure that any help from the Unity in safely acquiring our new orbit will be gratefully accepted by our engineers and astrogators," Croft said dully. "Meanwhile, we must discuss the matter of the disappearance of your Ball from our space."

"Ball in good human hands, we, Unity, agree. Our pleasure serving human spacetimers growing up nowtime. Mickeycroft, Ball not gone from space, just spacetime locus. Sorry for distressing thoughts. Not destroyed, never, notime. Pasttime locus no good, now. To make talking in notime, spacetimers need persons in the alltime. Reice human say, 'ready, willing, and able,' nowtime, anytime. Ball will be with Threshold, soontime, guiding. Okay Mickeycroft? Fears all go bye-bye now?" The Interpreter bared its teeth in a human indication that it was pleased with both its speech and the speech's context.

The smell was getting to Croft. The smoke was curling into his nostrils, trying to choke him. He coughed softly, cleared his throat, and said, "I beg to differ. I don't believe we had anything to do with your Ball's disappearance. But we're pleased to learn that we have no problem."

The Interpreter took a step back, into the smoke. It seemed as though it conferred with the honor guard. It then stepped forward again, just as Remson caught Mickey's attention with a cautionary wave.

So Remson wasn't as cocksure of the Unity aliens' intentions as he'd pretended. Good. Every time Croft encountered a Unity alien, he was more and more certain that these short conversations had greater meaning to the Interpreter and his staff than to Croft and his.

The Interstitial Interpreter seemed to sway back and forth, saying, "Mickeycroft, problems with wanting-to-destroy humans not possible. Unity not allow destroying. Unity wanting Mickeycroft find peace in the alltime, courage soontime. Future assured okay. No problems, only notime transit to soontime accomplish. Mistakes, possible. Spacetimers come grow up with us, nowtime, soontime, sometime. We see this in the alltime. You want come Unity nowtime, rejoin habitation later, avoid danger? Interpreter bring you by self, so safe and sound forever, through the alltime."

And the Interstitial Interpreter held out his hand, with its wrongly-numbered digits, as if Croft could take that hand, step into Unity spacetime on the arm of the Interstitial Interpreter, and from there go wherever he pleased.

Didn't these Unity beings credit anything but direct contact? Couldn't Lowe have arranged a simple vidphone call, an electromagnetically transmitted message? Did half of his reception suite need to be dematerialized, and the rest physically mated to another spacetime?

Croft pushed back in his chair, keeping his distance from the outstretched hand, which wanted to translate him into another dimension. "I think I should be here, with my people, especially if there's any chance of a 'mistake' in the voyage. You just go back where you came from. Feel free to aid us however you wish. Tell your Ball pilots or any other astrogators, we'll be glad to cooperate." *But get your intrusive presence out of my goddam personal spacetime.*

The Interstitial Interpreter dropped the outstretched hand as if it heard thoughts as well as words. It took one step back into the swirling colors of its embassy—or its homeworld. Croft saw the mist part, and clouds of gold and fuschia in a lavender sky. Then the sky disappeared, to be replaced by a spiral-armed pinwheel of stars that spun the mist and the smoke and the Interpreter and his honor guard in on themselves, until all that was left amiss in Mickey's reception room was a vortex of crackle and light, spinning in midair.

Then that, too, disappeared, as if it had never been.

"Well," said Remson into the silence in which Mickey was composing something scathing to say to Ambassador Lowe. "I think we must assume that we've solved at least the most pressing of our problems, and that we've now got help during the jump, if we need it. I must admit I personally feel better, knowing that the Unity is going to be right there with us, smoothing the way for this historic journey."

"I'm glad you're reassured, Vince," said Croft dryly. "And I must congratulate Ambassador Lowe on her quick action in this regard. I'm sure we all are agreed that a 'mistake' during this crossing is something that none of us can afford. Now, if you two don't mind, it's still the middle of the night, and your Secretary General would like to get some sleep."

Remson and the ambassador both got hastily to their feet, apologizing. Vince tried, as Mickey saw them to the door, to explore Croft's feelings about Unity aid during the spongespace jump.

Mickey Croft refused to be questioned. The Unity had declared that nothing was going to be allowed to stop mankind's voyage to destiny. So be it. Whether on Mickey's watch, or someone else's, contact with a race whose invitation could hardly be refused was about to commence.

When Riva Lowe and Remson were safely beyond Mickey's closed door, he slumped against it, exhausted and not sure what to hope for. Mistakes were still possible, it seemed. Even the Interstitial Interpreter was not infallible.

If Threshold, as the Unity believed was possible, had trouble during the jump, and was destroyed, would the result be better for humankind as a whole? Would a disaster put off this contact for enough years to matter?

The Interstitial Interpreter didn't seem to think so.

For Croft's part, he was content now to throw in his lot with the other spacetimers of Threshold who were about to grow up, Unity style. For better or for worse.

CHAPTER 29

$\bigtriangledown$

Flying the Ball

Reice was willing to bet that he'd seen things today that nobody of his pay grade had ever seen before. It was one thing to see the Ball open up, its spherical mass rippling like the disturbed surface of a pool; to see a purple wave run across it like the edge of night over a planetary surface, or an atmospheric shock wave seen from orbit. It was something else again to see those colors trying to tear themselves apart, a whirlpool of calm opening in their center to swallow your spacecraft whole. . . .

A few other guys had seen the Ball do its stuff from outside and lived to tell about it. There'd been some reports. Reice knew that for certain because he'd made one, when the Cummings kids disappeared, stolen freighter and all, sucked by the Ball into a gravity well or worse.

You knew South had seen the Ball do its stuff before. Maybe the SecGen had, as well. Up among the Secretariat's privileged elite, they had access to lots more information than Reice did. Than he used to have, he corrected himself, pacing back and forth along *STARBIRD*'s antique flight deck.

Three paces to the left. Stop before you hit the bulkhead wall. Turn. Three paces to the right. Stop before you exited the cramped flight deck entirely. Turn. Don't look out the real-time viewscreen, at the interior of the Ball beyond. Not yet.

Had anybody but South and Reice ever been inside the Ball? Reice was willing to bet nobody had. Had anybody even seen inside the Ball? He could make a fortune going on vid shows once this was over, telling about his experiences. If the Secretariat and ConSec would let him talk about it. If anybody'd believe him when he tried describing what he was seeing.

Reice was running a log of everything that happened out there, because otherwise nobody was ever going to believe him. Now Reice understood how Keebler, the white-hole scavenger who'd found the Ball in the first place, had felt.

The Ball was more than an alien artifact. It was more than a construct of an alien civilization possessed of advanced science. It was a portal. A gate. An arch of lions with gaping jaws. A curve of dragons whose spread talons kneaded the threads of spacetime into a universal order.

And it *was* a ship. South hadn't been kidding. South was a Relic of humanity's past, the pilot from the dawn of time, and Reice had learned not to take the twenty-first-century man too seriously. But the Ball into which South had steered them was really an alien craft, just like South said.

Now *STARBIRD* was parked in the slipbay of a huge, circular ship with command stations and view stations into ... everywhere, it seemed. And Reice was huddled inside *STARBIRD,* waiting like some maiden aunt for South to return from a dangerous voyage.

Reice wasn't trained to sit around and wait for somebody else to do his job for him. But it was spooky out there. Somebody had to bear witness to what was happening. Somebody had to stay alive to make a goddamned cogent report about what it was like out there.

The last thing Reice wanted to do was set foot outside this nice, antique but functional, human-made vessel. There were alien *things* out there, and not the run-of-the-mill lower life-forms of your typical colonized planet, either.

Beside *STARBIRD*'s ancient hull were breathing, phosphorescent hulks that South called "plasma shuttles," as if Reice should have known. As if all this was familiar territory.

"In your dreams, Relic," Reice muttered aloud. The sound of his own voice startled him. He'd better get hold of himself. But how did you do that, considering what was happening here? Considering what was happening out there?

He stopped in mid-stride, turned and resolutely faced the

real-time viewscreen, quadranted to give him 360 degrees of exterior coverage.

Beyond *STARBIRD*'s bulkheads, beyond the plasma shuttles snoring softly in their slipbay berths, was a huge and busily humming ship full of lights with streaming tails and unfathomable machines happily at work generating colored pulses and prismatic waves he could feel coming up through his boots.

If you watched the colored waveforms too long, your eyes began playing tricks on you. You began seeing salmon clouds and white temples on green hills. You saw lavender skies alive with disembodied alien eyes. You saw planetary rings gleaming like cotton candy in the ruddy sunlight. You saw plasma shapes cavorting among crystalline mists in impossible aerobatics.

You saw places, faces, spaces familiar and yet completely strange. You saw the boundaries of your own perceptions and beyond. You saw gates to everywhere, and nowhere, all displayed in eleven-space matrices as if access was as easy as taking a step, throwing a stone, making a choice.

Reice didn't want any part of a universe in which two dimensions of time and nine of space made up the local rulebook. His eyes ached and began streaming tears from trying to make sense out of what he saw in *STARBIRD*'s viewscreens.

But here he was, ready or not, swallowed like Jonah by an alien craft that none of the Secretariat's intelligence personnel, ConSpaceCom's rocket scientists, or the Stalk's astronics wizards had understood well enough to even recognize as a craft.

So he focused on South, a nice, comprehensible, three-dimensional object in a sea of optical illusions, surrounded by shapes that flickered and pulsed into and out of focus, as if South were standing on the bottom of some planetary sea and curious deep-water jellyfish were drifting over to take a look at the invader, rub up against him, dart away, and glide close on invisible currents.

Sometimes the creatures pulsed lights in a Morse code or alien ballet, and then you couldn't see much of South—maybe an arm, maybe a foot. Or just his helmet. South still had his helmet on his head.

Reice wiped his eyes with the heel of one hand. The liquid coming from his eyes was sticky, not like the salty tears of good old human emotion, more like some protective fluid generated to ward off eyestrain. Or blindness.

He depressed the ship's allcom toggle and closed his burning eyes. "South, do you read me? It's Reice." That was stupid. Who else could it have been, calling from *STARBIRD*?

"Yeah, Reice," came South's voice through *STARBIRD*'s speaker grilles. "Ready to come out? You're missing all the fun."

Reice didn't need to open his eyes to see the strange shapes moving around South at the "command station," as South called the place where he stood. The alien shapes, or beings, were all over him. Nuzzling him. Caressing him. Or trying to find a way inside his spacesuit.

Reice's skin crawled. Damn, why had Reice called the Relic pilot, anyhow? He could have sat this mission out, safe and sound. All he'd wanted was a little reassurance that South was okay. Now, South was challenging him. . . .

"Don't look like fun from here, Commander. I was never much for the zoo. But if you need help out there, I'll be glad to lend a hand." Was South actually trying to signal Reice that he needed help? Reice's hand dropped to his A-potential side arm. He was armed and dangerous in anybody's spacetime. If South was in some kind of trouble, Reice was duty-bound to go out there and do what he could to help.

"A helping hand wouldn't be a bad idea," came South's response, all banter and bravado. "We're going to be underway in a soontime minute. You really ought to come on out."

Reice was on his way. Helmet. Gloves. Systems check. Exterior life-support module over his shoulders. He checked the EVA-pack in *STARBIRD*'s lock corridor twice, before he'd trust it to feed him oxygen and monitor his physiological well-being through the old-style pharmakit. Sling may have retrofitted this bucket of bolts, but he'd kept to the spirit of the period.

As Reice stepped through into the lock, he patted his side arm and loosened it in its holster. Just in case. He pulled down his faceplate and breathed the canned air of the EVA pack. He pulled up a quadranted multi-spectral visor-display with a center-punched hole for real-time imagery, so he could see where the hell he was going. He toggled through his com-selects until he had an open feed to Birdy, *STARBIRD*'s AI.

He told the AI, "If we have a problem out there, we're going to need to get out, quick. Leave the outer lock open, with a priority emergency cycle so we can move out before you've dumped the local air. Set an exact retrace of your course in here and be ready to execute without human guidance if need be. If we're in the lock, you go. Copy?"

Birdy made the weird processing noises that South had never programmed out of her, because he was a solo pilot on a long mission and he needed the company.

The AI said: "Clarification, please. Go where?"

Dumb piece of outmoded technology. The light around Reice was green. Now that he was going out there, he wanted to haul ass, not lounge around talking go-to-shit plans with an artificial semi-intelligent astrogation module.

"Clarification follows," Reice told it, trying to be precise and neutral. No use wasting exasperation on an AI. They just got confused. "If both of us people reenter this lock, close the outer lock immediately. Don't wait for human guidance. Blow the local air. Set course to retrace exactly the course that got us here. Navigate out of the Ball and back to the *BLUE TICK*'s orbit without additional orders. If the Ball won't open to let you out, ram your way out. Clarification understood?"

Birdy burbled.

Reice hit the plate to open the outer lock and the local atmosphere, wispy and misty, poured inside.

Reice could barely see his lower body through his real-time punch window. That was okay. Infrared gave him a good idea where the step-down ramp was.

When Birdy's voice in his helmet said, "Confirmed: Clarification understood," Reice nearly jumped out of his skin.

"Terrific," he muttered, toggling to include South in his comlink.

"What's that?" South whispered in his ear, sounding distracted.

"Ready or not, Southie baby, here I come, soon as I can find my way through this steambath."

"I'll send somebody for you—"

Some*body*? "No, that's okay. I can see you. It looks flat enough on my infrared. So if I come straight—"

"Christ, Reice, there's no such thing as 'straight,' not the way you mean. Just stay put. A steward will come to get you."

"Gee, thanks. I can't wait." A steward? Reice almost turned around, climbed the step-ramp he knew was behind him, and barricaded himself in *STARBIRD* for the duration. But then South would know he was a coward.

And Reice couldn't stand that. South already knew exactly why Reice had parked *BLUE TICK* under the Ball's anus. So he figured his reputation was at stake.

He just hadn't realized how big those plasma shuttle things were, or how close he'd be to one of their heaving sides. Was it really breathing?

He reached out a gloved hand to touch the nearest one, but as he got close to what he thought was its skin, a bunch of lights started to snake off his fingers, as if he was discharging electrical energy. He pulled his hand back and cradled it, moving one finger at a time. Felt okay.

When he looked up, something was hovering in the mist before his face. It looked like a giant gelatinous tektite with eyes and a mouth, and it was glowing slightly in different places along its surface, as if it were becoming more solid here and there as he watched.

It extended a part of its substance, and the protuberance reshaped itself into an uncanny mock-up of a human hand, which beckoned. Reice was really sorry he'd decided to come out here.

He sidestepped to avoid contact with it. "Lead on, my man," he said fliply, toggling his exterior speaker so it could hear him.

It was already moving forward. Or spiraling upward. Its head, or its eyes, anyway, never left him, no matter what its body did. As for Reice, he found that if he looked at his infrared quadrant, he seemed to be stepping on thin air. So he didn't look at it. He kept his eyes on the eyes of the steward and walked up some spiral ramp that didn't read on any of his signature viewers.

Neat trick.

Eventually, they meandered over—or up—to South, who seemed to be standing on a level platform.

South's helmet inclined slightly. "Good to have you on board."

Where the hell had Reice been before? Wasn't *STAR-BIRD* "on board" this thing? "What's the trouble?" Reice asked bluntly, taking a quick peek over his shoulder, back the way he'd come. The jellyfish steward still hovered in the mist. Now it was streaming phosphorescent tentacles that sparkled and swayed. Behind it, he could see *STAR-BIRD,* nestled in the slipbay between two oval-shaped jelly giants that seemed to be snoozing, the way their hulls rose and fell.

"No trouble. I want you to pick a destination. Anyplace you want. This will be the first time a human has ever flown a Unity eleven-space vessel. Most test flights have some preflight parameters. If you specify them, it'll be easier to quantify the results."

Crazy bastard. "I thought you did this all the time, twice before breakfast."

"Uh-unh," said South distantly, touching something in front of him that looked like a box of living ribbon candy. "Nobody—no spacetimer—has ever flown one of these babies. I can handle a shuttlecraft okay in certain modes, but those modes didn't include maintaining a four-dimensional set of criteria."

"You mean this could get dangerous?"

"Nah, if I screw up, one of the plasma astrogators will take over. We just need to find out if it can be done this way, or whether we'll violate some local laws too violently by trying to take this craft into notime—into spongespace, if you like—while maintaining both a forward moving arrow and an alltime link."

"Speak English, South. What if we can't do this whatcha-macallit jump? What happens then?"

South's helmet dipped his way. The voice in Reice's ears didn't sound crazy, but the words didn't make astrogational sense to Reice.

South said, "Reice, this is an interdimensional craft. It can manifest in any spacetime you say, no problem. It can move through interstitial or collapsed dimensions, if it wants to. The question is, can we? If we're going to fly it real-time, find the Threshold flotilla, and steady the Stalk's jump into the energy sea and out again, then we've got to be sure that we don't generate any unintended discontinuities."

"Unintended discontinuities," Reice said numbly. Creating discontinuities by putting matter where it didn't belong meant huge discharges of energy, especially when nonstandard matter crossed boundary conditions meant to separate different spacetimes following different sets of laws. When you collected antimatter molecules, one at a time, the only thing that kept them stable in your universe was the electromagnetic storage vessel you put them in, which had an equal charge pushing the antimatter molecules together and keeping a pure vacuum between the antimatter and the matter of the containment vessel. "The universe I grew up in, South, doesn't like unintended discontinuities one bit," Reice said.

"The universe we all grew up in was created—is created—from discontinuities, Reice. That's one thing I've learned. Don't sweat it. We'll take one interdimensional short hop for fun and to establish a baseline. Then we'll see if we can get to the Stalk through spacetime, notime, or however."

Finally, the real import of what South had been saying penetrated Reice's overstimulated brain. "You're telling me that the Threshold jump is in trouble? That's the problem?"

"I'm telling you we've got permission to go see if we can assist the Threshold spacetimers en route, yeah. The Unity can't do it directly: you need biologically-synced spacetimers—us—to find Threshold and its outriders in the notime and help them navigate through it without losing outriding craft—or clocktime."

"Nobody's going to find anybody in spongespace who doesn't go in together," Reice said with finality, trying to keep the horror out of his voice. What was this fool saying?

South's fingers were stroking the incomprehensible colored ribbons of the control station. His helmeted head turned away from Reice, then back, as if he were looking inside Reice's helmet.

"Wanna bet? That's why we brought *STARBIRD*—and you—to establish a baseline for clocktime, or real-time. Me, I just want to fly this sucker. If you've lost your nerve, go back and sit in *STARBIRD* and let Birdy take care of you. She can put you out for the duration of the n-space jump. You don't need to validate the short interdimensional hop. I've been doing fine learning this stuff without help from spacetimers, so far."

"And what are you, buddy, if not a 'spacetimer' just like

me?" Reice put his hands on his hips and his right knuckles bumped the side arm in its tie-down holster.

"Easy, Reice. No offense. I'm kind of in transition. It's hard to talk about places you haven't been yet and experiences you haven't had. Watch the third monitor on your left, second tier."

"South!"

But it was too late. Reice's whole body knew it for certain, even thought he felt no vibration or jerk of ignition or g-force or any other sign that the Ball was moving.

The area where South had directed his attention was full of speeding images, colored lights, octagonal grids whirling over embedding diagrams of spacetimes that weren't quite right. And then a place came up in the second tier monitors.

A real place. Reice saw an approach vector and beyond it a planetary horizon half-obscuring a sun's corona. A moon spun by him, receding at an impossible speed. A half-dark planet loomed so that he stuck out his hands to grab something. Handholds were under his fingers. He held on hard as they drove straight into atmosphere at a rate that couldn't be possible, then leveled out and skipped along a stratospheric surface.

"Where the hell are we?" Reice breathed.

"Earth," South said. "You didn't give me a destination. I had to have something incontrovertible. You didn't even feel the translation, right?"

What the hell was Reice holding on to? His hands were gripping something resilient, almost like flesh with bone under it. He used all four signature scans to try to identify the material. All he could figure was that it was alive.

He let go fast and wiped his gloved hands on his hips.

"Reice, you okay? You see the Earth, right?"

"Right. I see it. We've just broken half a dozen laws and we're about to get shot out of the sky to boot." Reice kept waiting for ConSpaceCom to come roaring after them, demanding surrender.

"No chance," South chuckled. "We didn't trip any alarms getting here: we came intradimensionally. Only the atmosphere-skipping is phenomenally real for spacetimers."

"Oh. Well, that's okay then, right? Can we go someplace else, since this worked and we aren't dead?"

"Name it."

"I don't goddamned know what to specify. Let's get out of here before we get hurt. Go save Threshold or something."

South sighed in Reice's comlink. "I always wanted to come home. Now I'm here and there's a chance to look around. Okay, we'll test the notime sync in a minute. First, I want to show you X-3."

X-3 was the planet out to hell and gone from everywhere that South and *STARBIRD* had found on their experimental sponge-jump in the early days of interstellar spaceflight. When South hadn't returned, the whole mission had been written off—for five hundred years.

"South," Reice said, "I'm not ready—"

But then he was ready. His whole body coruscated as if he were bathing in light. His indrawn breath came out of his lungs in a glowing stream of energy. He leaned back and something supported him, as if the universe itself was cradling him in its arms. Before his eyes, every speeding vista of creation unfurled, endlessly. And stopped.

The second tier monitors showed green fields carpeted with flowers, a soft cloud-banked sky, a city that looked more as if it had been grown than built, and a sea that lapped from the foreground of the viewscreen to a gentle amber shore.

"Want to get out here, verify that we're somewhere new?" South's voice said in Reice's ear. "We've been here nearly an hour on UNE clocktime. Another one won't matter where we're going."

"No. No, I don't." An hour? He couldn't remember the time passing. Then he did, dimly, recall some dreams he might have had, with sweet grass in them, and soft singing crystalline spires around him, and a choir of plasma angels, singing.

What had happened to him? Had he left the ship? Was he back from somewhere? His sequential memory was shot to hell. It was a nice dream, if it had been a dream, of a picnic on a shore with cherubs and plasma dogs fetching living sticks.

He could feel a soft salt spray on his face. But that was impossible. He still had on his helmet. Didn't he?

Reice's whole body felt wrong. His skeleton felt as if it had been dismantled, reconstituted, and was now slightly different than before. His muscles tingled strangely. He could feel the blood coursing in the soles of his feet, his pulse throbbing in his ears, and he imagined he could feel the neural firings of his brain and of his muscles as he rubbed his arms. "We can joyride some more later. Let's finish these tests. Threshold's in trouble, remember?"

"Might be," said South, and when Reice looked over at the pilot, Joe South was wrapped in a pulsing, amber cloak of flesh with veins and spiderwork tracery glowing from it.

"South!" Reice croaked.

The thing that dipped its round head toward him was a foot taller than South, a pod shaped from ambergris and filled with milkweed, with South's spacesuit inside it as if the pilot had been embalmed.

Reice grabbed for his side arm without thinking, but his hand couldn't find it. His body, his hand and arms, all of him was cocooned in the same awful manner as South. He started screaming.

The South-thing took a step forward, and Reice tried to run. He couldn't move. He was rooted to the spot. He lunged back and forth in his prison. He couldn't break free.

Gasping for breath, he finally realized South was shouting at him through the allcom. "Don't panic, damn it. You're just inside a different kind of protective suit, for this kind of travel. Stop thrashing, before you hurt yourself!"

Reice couldn't quite stop sobbing. Gasps of breath roared into his lungs and out again. If he could get his A-potential handgun, he could blast this disgusting, sticky stuff off of himself and . . .

And then what? Blast South's covering away, as well? Without hurting either of them? Or would he kill South in the process and be marooned here, wherever this was, forever?

He slumped back against the fleshy encasement and it supported him, hugging him close. It was warm in here. At first he thought his suit was trying to cool him, then he realized that the cocoon had grown into his suit, and that tiny tendrils were all over him, against his skin, moist and sticky.

"Christ, South," he said hoarsely, "why didn't you warn me?"

"How was I going to explain it? You're now a veteran of interdimensional travel. It gets better."

"I bet."

"Just wait. When we come back out into spacetime, you'll have a chance to customize your gear by just thinking about the optimum suit system."

"I just want to be able to get at my weapon, that's all," Reice muttered.

The thing in the cocoon next to him said, "Reice, you don't need a weapon. But you do need to be careful what you wish for. These custom-bred astronic systems, and the life support, are real accommodating. Don't build any bogeymen for us, okay? I wouldn't have brought you along if I didn't think you were up to it. Riva Lowe's been this far and she didn't wet her pants."

"Okay, South, okay. So I overreacted. If you'd have told me what to expect, I woulda done better. There's always next time."

"Coming right up," said South's amused voice in Reice's helmet comlink, which didn't seem to be negatively affected by having a crop of tendrils or scilla growing out of it.

Reice promised himself silently that, when this was over, if he lived through it and wasn't some sort of monster afterward, he was going to find a good woman, settle down on a colony world, and raise a bunch of unremarkable children.

But he didn't believe he could keep his vow: everything was different, from now on. He'd had plenty of warning. He'd ignored all the evidence. Croft, South, Riva Lowe, none of them had managed to get through this alien encounter business unchanged. The whole UNE was on its way to irrevocable change.

Somehow, this time, when he looked at the second tier monitors, the twists and turns of so many multidimensional images didn't make his stomach queasy. He even thought he could make sense of the instrumentation around him. You just had to realize that these systems were grown, not computer designed and manufactured.

Then all the screens dumped, and everything was dead black.

"South!" he yelled, struggling in his cocoon again. "What's happening?"

"Notime translation," came the test pilot's voice, "in progress." Except all the words spilled into Reice's helmet at once. He had to get out of this place. Get back to *STARBIRD*. Implement his emergency escape plan.

But the universal foot of gravity was on his chest and he couldn't move. Notime. . . .

Dark.

Empty.

Full.

Light.

South's voice: "That's it. We get an A for effort. We've got coordinates for the Stalk."

All the sights and sounds of the alien vessel rushed in on Reice in a cascade of stimuli. He tried once more to move his gun hand, and this time, part of the cocoon gave way. He raised his hand and stared at it, a horrid thing covered with orange gelatin and coconut, or with sprouts, or with milkweed floating on a gentle breeze. . . .

"South, how do you keep your concentration? Your focus?"

"Practice," South's voice said. "Like learning to walk. Complicated but worth the effort. Imagine your spacesuit in perfect shape, with whatever new capability you want, but make sure it's compatible with *STARBIRD*'s systems."

"How do I do that?" Reice was staring around at the monitor tiers. Plasma tektites and jellyfish were floating around caressing control panels with their Portuguese man-of-war tentacles. Music was tinkling in his ears. The monitors showed clouds with sparks inside them, graphs with past/future axes, north to south, and spatial event baselines intersecting them, east to west.

Reice had been a pilot for a lot of years. He could almost make sense of the simpler graphs. The more complicated ones, with dual time axes at a forty-five degree angle to the north/south grid, gave him the willies.

There was one representation he didn't need Joe South to interpret: the poles of its horizontal axis were labeled in English: Bad—Good. Its vertical axis read: Alien—Doesn't Matter. And clumped to the left of center on the horizontal were lots of four-dimensional colored blocks.

Just as Reice was going to ask South what South's psychometric profile was doing on a Unity craft display, the whole clumped block of psychometric data shifted until it was centered on the intersection of the vertical and horizontal lines. "What's that psych graph for, South?"

"Just doing some mental housekeeping while I have the time," said the voice in his ear. All the words came out sequentially this time—or else Reice was getting used to operating in a milieu where seconds ran together and your pulse was one giant throb in your ears.

"We've got our fix on the Stalk. Thanks, Reice."

"What for? I didn't do nothin' but be real scared and hope like hell we'd get through this."

"Look at your hand," South's voice suggested.

Reice's hand was safe in its space glove, and the glove was mated to a perfectly normal suit sleeve. He tried to turn his head and nothing limited his movement. South was standing at the control station, one hip cocked, playing with his ribbon-candy controls, looking just the way Commander South ought to look, dressed for spaceflight, not Halloween.

Reice realized he was still leaning back into—something. He stood up straight and turned around. A nice spacegoing acceleration couch, ratcheted up nearly vertical, was behind him. He wished it wasn't that ambergris color, and it turned blue.

"You okay now, Reice? Fit to fly?"

"Yeah. You bet." He was getting the hang of it. He stepped up to a control station on South's left hand and stared at the unknowable configuration until it began to resemble something like a conventional astrogator's station.

"Ready to go to the party?" South wanted to know.

"What party?" Reice wasn't taking South's banter for granted anymore. Not ever.

"We've still got to get Threshold and her outriders through to their new orbit in one piece. Just coast along and give them a little hand when they need it."

"You're sure they're going to need it?"

"I'm sure that if they do," said the pilot, turning his helmeted head, visor down, to Reice, "we can be a whole lot of help to them."

All Reice could see in the reflective curve of South's helmet was his own image, less distorted than the impossible angles and chaotic colors of the multidimensional craft in which they were riding to Threshold's rescue.

Hopefully. And only, of course, in the event that Threshold needed help with the jump out of and into spacetime.

The reflection in South's helmet seemed to contain the whole of the interior of the Ball, all its expanse coming to a center behind his head. He saw *STARBIRD* there, nestled between two plasma shuttles, waiting.

He could haul out his A-potential pistol now and shoot up the place, but what was the point? Reice didn't want to go guns blazing into a future that was going to be whatever you made of it, for better or worse.

South had adapted to this environment. South was thriving, in fact. And South wasn't afraid.

Maybe there wasn't so much to be afraid of, just the unknown.

After an interval of systems recalibration that was beginning to make sense to Reice, South said, "Ready for a real honest-to-God, seat-of-the pants test flight, Reice? Find the Threshold needle in the notime haystack, sync clocktimes, and lend a hand without scaring them to death?"

Reice knew just what to say. "Let's go do it, hotshot. It's going to be just like old times, keeping your butt out of hot water."

And they did.

CHAPTER 30

▽

Parking Orbit

"Riva, explain to me about these time terminologies that you and Mickey keep using," Remson said to her as the two of them watched the stars fall back, streaming colored Doppler tails behind them. "I've heard the Interstitial Interpreter talk that way—nowtime, notime, soontime, pasttime, alltime—but I'm damned if I know what any of it means. Am I missing something?"

Remson's words rode the wobbling growl of mock-banding engines hard at work below. The noise was reverberating from the spiral stairway that connected the observation lounge atop the new NAMECorp-built command and control center to Threshold's Blue North tubeway. She'd come up here with Remson to wait for the jump where they wouldn't be in anyone's way. So close to a critical phase of their journey, the observation lounge was otherwise deserted.

Still gazing out at the mesmerizing starscape, she replied, "You're not missing anything the rest of us didn't, until we had to face facts." They were alone together with their doubts, their fears, and their hopes. But not as alone as Mickey Croft was, barricaded in his quarters with an electronic DO NOT DISTURB sign on his door.

"And those facts are?" Vince Remson was determined to have an answer to his question.

Ever since the incident in Mickey's residence, Remson had been on her like glue. As if it were her fault that Mickey took the Interpreter's visit so badly. What had Croft expected the Interstitial Interpreter to do, send him a fixed and immutable statement, handwritten on scented paper, when to the Unity, any communication about the future had to take place in the mutable present, or be construed as hostile, or, worse, as history? The Secretary General had demanded immediate communication with the Unity and he got his wish, in all eleven dimensions. Mickey should know by now that when you dealt with the Unity you had to be careful what you wished for.

"Riva?" Croft's Chief of Staff prompted. "I want an answer."

Riva Lowe sighed. What should she say? Her permanent appointment as ambassador to Unity space probably depended on her response. But that appointment wouldn't mean a thing if the jump through spongespace failed. If the Stalk lost its outriders or split apart from the stresses of the punch into n-space, Vince might have eternity to answer his own questions about alternate experiences of time. If all of Threshold broke into small enough pieces during the jump into or out of the energy sea, none of them would have to worry about answering trick questions. Ever.

But she had to say something, in case the Stalk made it to its new orbit intact and the Threshold bureaucracy reestablished itself on the far side of Pluto. The Unity was sending help, which meant that it saw not only a serious problem, but a viable solution.

For Riva Lowe's career, it might have been better if the Unity had left humanity completely on its own, sole architect of its fate, without devising a way to render aid and comfort in four-dimensional terms. It was the Interstitial Interpreter's offer of help in the jump phase that had pushed Mickey Croft over the edge and given substance to all of the Stalk bureaucracy's fears of being manipulated by an omnipotent force.

"Vince, I understand you need answers, but it's both too early and too late to be asking these questions. We weren't asking Commander South any questions when he showed up fresh from his experimental flight to X-3 and began to reopen the X-3 question. Oh, no. We classified the whole matter and shelved it—out of sight, out of mind. We weren't any more receptive when Keebler first towed in the Ball, full of questions of his own. We sure as hell weren't asking—or answering—any questions when the Cummings boy and the Forat girl disappeared before our very eyes—

or when Reice and South logged the event for the record. Only when their parents raised a stink did we set up the permanently manned science station at the Ball site, and that was pro forma. Why did you think that the Unity established a physical presence out at Spacedock Seven? built and staffed the embassy, a stable, multidimensional construct and a truly Herculean feat and gave the UNE constant access to Unity Interpreters, on demand? provided the Secretary General with the psychometric modeler data that gave him a real-time link to Unity officials?"

"I think that's what I'm asking you," Remson said levelly, never taking his eyes away from the cosmos speeding past, as the clock ticked away to jump time and Riva squirmed.

"Why? Because the Unity functions diplomatically only in the *present tense*," Riva nearly shouted in his face, then got control of her frustrations. Was there no way to explain the critical difference between the UNE and the Unity, which was causing so much unnecessary strain in an already crucial and possibly degenerating situation? "The Unity doesn't make unilateral decrees about real-time events and consign them as faits accomplis, decisions taken, to the *past*, the way the UNE does, so it won't take static one-way communications from the Secretariat seriously. If we send the Unity a message other than a request for a real-time conference, it considers the information contained in that message to be an artifact of humankind's propensity for creating a nonrepresentative, artificial historical record and not pertinent to current events. The Unity doesn't understand how we can make decisions about the future from a reasoning base they consider to be a figment of our imagination—the dead and unreachable past."

Remson turned to look at her then, his brow furrowed. "So where does that leave us? How do we create a bilateral agreement, a permanent framework for treaties, technology transfer, and trade relations, if the Unity is culturally incapable of working on a document setting out both parties' responsibilities?"

"It leaves us on our honor," Riva said softly.

"On our *honor*?" Remson repeated, staring at her in disbelief. Behind Remson's head, the Doppler tails of the stars were lengthening into pastel streamers. Very soon it might not matter whether or not the United Nations of

Earth could create An Historic Document memorializing its relationship with the Unity worlds. Overcoming cultural incompatibilities wouldn't matter if everyone opposed in the Stalk bureaucracy was dead. Maybe the death of a space habitat full of bureaucrats was worth the sacrifice of her own life. Maybe the Unity would fare better with humanity when the race was more mature—in a few thousand years.

"On our honor. We do have some. Or at least we did, the last time I checked. Perhaps we'll have to dust it off and polish it up, remember how to use it without wearing our collective heart on our sleeve, but it's there. The Unity has waited for humankind a long time. They believe the time is right." She was trying to convince herself as much as Remson. She hoped it didn't show.

A chime sounded, cutting through the mock-banding. "Ten minutes to jump. Five minutes to roll call. To your stations, all personnel." The computer-simulated female voice was cheery, calling the command and control center staff to attention and the Stalk to its destiny with enviable aplomb. The same call was being heard in every add-on power module, data-fusion pod, and outriding vessel.

Remson took a step back from the stars. "I think I'm beginning to understand—at least, the part about living in the present. We've just got time for you to explain about the terminology, the way I first asked you. I wouldn't want to go into this crisis still wondering about the difference between notime and nowtime."

Riva didn't care anymore what Remson—or the Secretary General—did or did not understand. She wanted to spiral down the stairway, into the command and control center, where she had wangled a slot at the integration console. She needed to be where she could mitigate or at least interpret any surprises that might be in store for the operations staff.

She said hurriedly, "Nowtime is what you're currently experiencing—a present that's elastic, containing the immediate past and present, where you can mediate actions. Notime is where we're going: the energy sea, where nothing sequential occurs, no duration is possible, and no phenomenal time passes. Pasttime is what's in the historical record and can't be altered. Soontime is the bridge from the nowtime to longtime, what we call the future, along which the forward moving arrow of human time flows, and where duration exists as a malleable force shaping events and pulling them into soontime. Longtime is the temporal baseline, necessary to have forward-moving, sequential durational intervals. Okay? You got it? There'll be a quiz after the jump." She turned to go.

Remson grabbed her arm. "Not so fast. What about the alltime?"

He wasn't as thick-headed as he was pretending, then. "The alltime is a nondurational, infinite interval, an undifferentiated instant in which everything exists that ever was, is, or will be. And that's where the Unity Council is most comfortable. That's where they're *from*, or at least, it's their natural state of being."

Remson's hand dropped from her arm. His eyes narrowed. He craned back his neck as if to get a better look at her. "You're saying they're gods? *Gods*? Eternal? Omniscient? Omnipotent?"

"I didn't say anything of the kind," she replied carefully. "I was just trying to answer your questions as you asked them. All of these terms are English equivalents for experiences we aren't intellectually capable of validating. Why don't you wait and see? Make your decision on the far side of the jump."

Then she did turn and run, away from Remson and his dogged pursuit of linguistic revelation, down the spiral stairs and into the tense nowtime of the command and control center below.

As she took her place at the integration console, Richard Cummings II nodded hello, one hand cupped around a com bead in his ear, the other caressing the control panel before him. Cummings radiated excitement, challenge, confidence, and anticipation.

Riva wished the Secretariat were reacting so well.

She wished Mickey would come out and show himself, make an appearance, take part in the moment, be with his people as a commander-in-chief should.

But Mickey didn't appear as the clock shaved seconds with a deadbeat count. Remson came, squeezed her shoulder, and took the seat next to hers. She was feeling superfluous, regretting her conversation with Remson, regretting her own inability to translate her experiences in the Unity into words that would comfort her human compatriots, who were facing the unknown with less information than she.

But what did you do? You listened to the count. You watched muscles tic in Remson's jaw as he reacted to words you couldn't hear through his Secretariat-only comm channel. You watched the military officers slide their chairs back and forth along the channeled decking. You took a moment to relax enough that the courage and determination of the astrogators made you feel better about your part in creating this moment.

Riva took a deep breath, sat back in her own wheeled chair, and slipped a com bead into her right ear so that she could hear the jump coordinator talking to the outriding spacecraft.

She wasn't here to do anything, unless called upon to give an opinion. Or unless the Unity really did send someone.

Send help.

Send the Ball.

Send spacetimers. . . . She sat up straight as she realized what the Interstitial Interpreter's words to Mickey Croft could mean.

"Four minutes, twenty seconds," tolled the jump coordinator in her ear. Damn South for leaving her to deal with this on her own, for escaping in *STARBIRD* the way he'd always wanted. Or had he? The Unity couldn't have seriously considered what she now suspected. Could they?

A disturbance behind her leaked into her reverie through her free ear. She swiveled in her chair and there was Michael Croft, spidery and wasted, all elbow, jaw, and ears, with those limpid, bloodshot eyes darting from person to person, as if uncertain of where he should sit.

Remson sprang to his feet and went to assist the UNE Secretary General. Mickey seemed as old as creation. Or as drunk as a lord. Riva nearly got up to move when she realized Remson was guiding Mickey to the vacant seat next to her.

Uncertain, she hesitated, trying to catch Vince's attention.

Croft was saying, "So glad you all could be here today for this awesome occasion. Mankind's future is in our hands, my friends. Let's handle her gently. Easy as she goes." He waved his free hand about, casting spells of patronage with his long, spidery fingers.

Mickey must be drunk. Had to be. Riva got up, removing the com bead from her ear, to make a place for Vince to sit while he babysat his boss.

The count, coming through the speaker grilles now was "Two minutes, forty-three seconds."

One of the astrogators said, "Ambassador Lowe, can you come over here a sec?"

She was so relieved to be asked to move somewhere, to attend to something, she didn't give the astrogator's purpose a second thought.

"What is it, Colonel?" she asked the orange-coveralled ConSpaceCom officer, bending down over his station. He had hair cut barely two millimeters from his skull. He was so scrubbed his skin shined. His clear blue eyes met hers as he held up a wire headset. "Call for you, ma'am. Secure Comm Three—that's your Unity preset, isn't it?" His voice was so low she found herself nearly head to head with him to hear.

She took the headset, with its throatpad mike, without straightening up. Cupping the beadmike, she said, "Lowe here."

Static spit in her ear, as if the transmission were coming from very far away. "Say again?" she whispered.

The colonel tapped her wrist. "Magnetic storms," he mouthed. "May I?"

He wanted to listen in, tune the transmission.

She nodded. He hooked a com bead in his ear, palmed it, and played with his equipment.

Static spat again, and then she heard, "Riva? Riva Lowe? This is NAMECorp XIA, Rick Cummings commanding. Do you read? We are about to make visual contact with your outboard escort. The Unity wants you to sync to our powerplant for the jump. South will take a handoff from us once the jump is under way. Do you copy? You've got a full-time escort, spacetimers plus. Inform your astrogators. We need to feed them some new data. Do you copy, Ambassador Lowe?"

"I hear—yes, I copy. I understand." Eyes closed to hear better, she was whispering into the bead she held to her lips with perspiring fingertips. "Let me give you to someone more qualified."

She opened her eyes and met the cool gaze of the Con-SpaceCom astrogator, who had one eyebrow questioningly raised.

"Please, Colonel. Do what he says. It's the Unity help we've been expecting. I'll inform the Secretariat staff."

"Yes, ma'am," said the squeaky-clean colonel with a quick jab of a thumb in her direction, before he forgot her completely, hunched down over his console.

She laid the colonel's second headset gently on the console and made for the integration station dazedly. She told Richard Cummings first, "Your son is out there, in a Unity vehicle, providing assistance for the jump."

Cummings cursed, "Damned fool kid." But he was smiling slightly as he started dialing in a monitoring frequency.

Remson was next. Vince already had his hands full. Mickey was sitting stretched out, ankles crossed, sprawled expansively at Remson's station. All the SecGen needed was a drink in one hand and a cigar in the other to seem like some ancient politician posing for a candid portrait.

The clock intoned, "One minute, three seconds."

Rick Cummings to the rescue? In a Unity vehicle he was designating as a NAMECorp X-class craft? Joe South taking a handoff? When? How?

She didn't want to think about it. "Vince, the Unity support we were promised is on-line," she said softly enough, she hoped, that Remson would hear but Croft would not.

Remson flicked a miserable glance her way. "Thanks. Let's hope it's enough."

Meanwhile, the Secretary General was dispensing campaign rhetoric full of all-purpose cliches and didn't notice her. Drunk he was, from the smell of him.

She wouldn't have had Vince Remson's job for anything in the world. But right now she had no job. There was no place for her to sit. She didn't want to disturb anyone with work to do, and she had none. She found herself a quiet corner and leaned there.

The clock counted, "Forty-eight seconds," and continued to talk its way to zero as she watched the nearly motionless room.

They were all in this together, she told herself, as the time to jump decreased to single digits.

She closed her eyes, trying to find South, if he was really out there, with her inner sight. What could possibly be gained by risking everyone? Young Cummings? The pilot from humanity's past?

Perhaps the Unity was not as benign as she'd believed. A shiver ran over her.

"Ma'am?" said a young lady in a white coat. "The colonel over there sent this comm unit over for you. He said you'd want to be in the loop." Anxious young fingers helped her potentiate the unit. "I've got to go. Five seconds and counting," the girl breathed, and fled back to her station.

Riva pressed the com bead to her ear with inexpressible relief. The chatter in it was at first difficult to separate. Then she could make out what was happening as six or seven men furiously made last-minute recalibrations.

Five voices spoke nearly simultaneously:

"Correction, entered. This damn well better work, Control."

"Outboard Three confirming Go on sync mode, over."

"Outboard Six, all stations reporting ready, over."

"Engineering, full up and RWA, over."

"Task Force leader, you good to go? Control, over."

And then, one more: "On your mark, Control."

Only then did Riva realize that Control was the colonel who had given her the headset.

"X-Craft, with me. Five ... Four,"

Then the voice of Ricky Cummings joined the colonel's, and two voices said together: "Three ... Two ... One ... MARK."

The wall behind Riva's back bucked, seemed nearly to buckle, and pushed her violently forward. Unprepared, she went to her knees. The deck shuddered under her.

Then everything stopped.

She couldn't hear a thing. Nothing moved. Total silence reigned. Not even the com bead in her ear was producing static.

She couldn't move. She couldn't budge. She was frozen in place. Her mind wouldn't function. She couldn't think. She didn't feel anything but one unending instant of panic, a sensation of falling endlessly.

It seemed to her that the universe was holding its breath.

Then she saw something, not in the control station, but in her mind's eye. She saw the Ball. The bright, spinning, glorious, multicolored, silver-hulled Ball was right in front of her, inhaling her, enveloping her and everything around her.

Silence broke like a soapbubble. Engines roared around her. Men scrambled, shouting, from station to station. In her ear, she heard a distant voice saying, "That's a wrap, Control, X-Craft. Handover complete. You're relieved, Ricky. Have a nice flight. Next stop, Pluto orbital zone."

"This is Threshold C&C Control. What the hell's happening? Commander South, that you? You got sync and helm contact with us, or what? Request confirmation. Control, over."

"No sweat, C&C Station. We got clocktime commencing on my mark, as promised: seventeen thirty hours, fourteen minutes, fifty-three seconds and counting: Two . . . One . . . *Mark*. All your outriders are on my scope, safe and sound—"

Riva Lowe took the com bead out of her ear and got to her feet, brushing off her knees. She hadn't known what she'd expected, but not this. Not an instant suspended between worlds with overlaid omniscience. She put her hand to her forehead. You shouldn't be able to remember anything from notime. You shouldn't remember anything at all.

So maybe superior Unity science is magic to the savage spacetimer, she told herself. But South was a spacetimer, and so was Ricky Cummings.

The astrogators were laughing nervously and congratulating each other. Monitor scans were coming up of all the outboard craft, who were in turn sending real-time images of Threshold, undamaged, her spiderweb veil of critical external hardware unrent, gleaming in the pale light of a far-distant sun and the nearer glow of external, manmade arc lights. And beyond the Stalk, off the starboard bow of an outriding destroyer, hung the Ball. The imported scan of Threshold, seen through the sensor net that had made the Stalk into a simulacrum of a single spacegoing vehicle, made the Ball look like a Christmas ornament covered with angel hair.

"Spaceworthiness check, all stations, sound off," chortled somebody, and Riva cast a look backward long enough to ascertain that it was the colonel in the control position who had spoken.

She went over to the integration console and sat on its

edge. "So we made it," she said generally, dully, remembering the one instant that she had no right to remember, when Threshold came apart, when the bulkhead behind her back buckled, when all had been lost in the notime.

She scanned faces. Nobody at the integration console—not Remson, trying to make the best of a bad situation; not Mickey Croft, more sober now and shamefaced; not Richard Cummings, trying to cover his exultation at his son's performance, and NAMECorp's—not any of them gave her any reason to suspect that they'd experienced what she'd experienced.

Had they really lived through this, all systems go?

Or had they failed, broken apart, died and been reborn in the notime, reconstituted without a glitch on the other side of oblivion? Without a glitch, except that she remembered.

The bucking, crumpling, bulkhead, the floor hitting her knees, and then—nothing.

Nothing until Commander Joe South, resurrected pilot from humanity's ancient past, announced a handover complete. Handover from where? From beyond death itself?

She shivered, walking aimlessly among the busy staff. When she was called upon to do so, she murmured congratulations to the triumphant, relieved command staff who all had irrepressible smiles. You wandered around, approving, nodding, glancing at meters proclaiming perfect performance and scanners displaying one hundred percent systems integrity.

The United Nations of Earth, ConSpaceCom, and ConSec had a lot to celebrate. Maybe they had more than they realized. Or maybe she was just dazed, overtired, and a foolish woman who hadn't had a place to sit when the jump jolt had hit.

Remson found her, after he'd gotten Mickey off to bed. He said, "So, it'll be an hour or so before we're finished with our after-action reports and fine-tuning. Another day or two to reach the designated coordinates. What are you going to do now?"

"I don't know," she said dully. "Breathe. Sleep. Try to be ready if and when you need me."

"South's coming aboard."

"Is he?" she said icily.

"And he has Reice with him."

"Does he?"

"He does. Let's go finish our chat before they get here, shall we?"

"Is that an order, Mr. Remson?" Did Remson remember something? suspect something? Or was she simply unsettled by the sponge-jump? Jumping through the underlying fabric of creation had a habit of playing tricks on puny human minds.

"It's a suggestion," Remson said.

She went with him, back up to the observation lounge. When she first topped the spiral stairs, she thought she saw a great crack in the Stalk's new glassed-in dome. Shards of glass on the rug and bodies everywhere, bloodied and bent. Mangled. Sucked against the glass. Floating.

Then she blinked and everything was fine. The observation lounge was being readied for a late meal for the C&C crew: a table was set with a stack of plates and drinks on a gay paper runner. Chafing dishes were warming food whose smell filled the room. Somewhere behind the far door, cooks and waiters talked in low voices.

"What is it you want to chat about?" she said. "I need to go lie down, now that we're safe."

"Mickey wasn't drunk. Just overreacting."

"Absolutely right. I never thought differently." She nodded reassuringly.

"We've done a wonderful thing, today. The UNE and the Unity."

"Performed a miracle, more likely," she muttered, watching him closely for any sign of doubt or distress.

"Your appointment as ambassador will become permanent, of course."

"That's nice to hear." So she'd imagined it. The jump had been flawless, or at least within survivable limits. There had been no momentary destruction on the Stalk, no intermittent loss of Threshold in the interstitial realm between dimensions, no course correction by Unity Interpreters—no death in the notime.

Of course there hadn't. Instead, there'd been Joe South, cocky and wild as ever, dragging the Cummings boy into his mad stunt to grandstand his way back into the limelight. "We probably didn't need any help from the Unity. From what I saw, the command and control system worked just fine."

"Probably did," Remson said gravely, looking out at the heavens. "You were telling me about the Unity's perceptions of time, and I want to finish that conversation before I encounter any more Unity Council members."

She thought she could see just the edge of the damnable Ball, over Remson's shoulder, through the observation window.

Music was coming from somewhere, softly playing a Bach piece she thought was "Jesu, Joy of Man's Desiring." She said to Remson, "You never give up, do you?"

"Nope. We've got a lot to learn in a very short time. The sooner we get started, the better."

She still couldn't be sure that Remson didn't remember some of what she remembered. Maybe it didn't matter. Maybe nothing mattered but success. "All right. Consider this: the Unity thinks about time differently. Their brains, their biology, are adapted to multidimensional experience. They exist in an eleven-space manifold—that should have told us something, but we didn't come to terms with the implications. Not at the beginning, anyway." She was coming to terms with those implications now. "Their reality wraps around ours, not just in space, but in time as well. Their phenomenological past is a living part of their present. Their present is multiplex, not just because they recognize more than one dimension of time intellectually, but because they live in a physically different reality that obeys different laws. Their future is intimately connected with both their past and their present through their experience of a second dimension of time, in which everything is happening at once—in one undifferentiated instant of 'now.' So, we should keep in mind," she finished, very carefully, "that they can control a lot more of what happens—of what we think of as reality—because they have access to what they call the alltime, where every moment is equally available."

"They're omniscient, like gods," said Remson levelly, and then she was sure he did know, or at least suspected that in one reality, all of them—herself, himself, Cummings, the Secretary General, and the whole of Threshold—had been destroyed in their attempt to cross n-space.

But not in this reality. *Hold onto what you got, Vince. Grab the reins and pull real hard. We've got a real opportunity here. Don't panic. Life is the big prize, and we've won it.* "Not in the way that you mean," she replied aloud. When you can access the alltime, you'll be just as omniscient, if that's the word, as they are. The Unity doesn't think about themselves that way. They're accustomed to living multitemporally. They've been looking in on us, evidently, over the millennia."

"I figured that out."

"We were at far greater risk before we became technologically competent. If they wished us harm, they had all of our evolutionary life to play with us or destroy us or whatever. Now we count for something. We're grown up enough to be interesting. All we have to do is take things as they come."

"That's all?"

"That's all."

From behind her, another voice said, "Attagirl, Riva, give him all four barrels."

She spun on her heel. "South, where did you come from?"

The Relic pilot smirked. "Ain't that just like a woman, Remson? You bust your butt to come riding to the rescue on a silver steed and all she can do is demand a full afteraction report. I came from the Ball, honey. Sort of like coming down the chimney once a year. You wouldn't like it. Get your pretty self all dirty."

"I think I'll leave you two to it," Remson said.

"No, Vince—" she objected.

On his way out, Remson slapped South on the shoulder. "Nice job, Commander. You have the Secretariat's gratitude for actions above and beyond. We'll make if official as soon as things calm down." And Croft's chief of staff strode away.

She glared at South. "What did you think you were doing?"

"Saving your pert ass."

"Involving the Cummings boy? And, for all I know, the Forat girl? They could have been killed!"

"They wanted to be here to greet their parents." South shrugged. "Nobody got killed. Everybody's safe and sound. No harm done. Let it go, Riva."

"I—I'm sorry. I was frightened. I saw things during the jump—"

"Everybody sees disturbing stuff in spongespace jumps.

Don't let it bother you, okay?" he said quietly. His face was in shadow; only his eyes showed, sparkling in some errant beam of light.

"Okay," she said. "Truce. You must be very proud of yourself. You flew the Ball. You wanted to do that from the very beginning, didn't you? Fly the Ball? From the first time you saw it. You had to prove you were right about—everything."

"Yep," he said. "About everything. From the very beginning."

CHAPTER 31

▽

The Party

Threshold sat smugly at her designated coordinates half a million miles beyond Pluto's aphelion, glimmering in starlight and the soft glow of the Unity Embassy in its matching orbit nearby. Beside the embassy, and almost as large, a huge, teardrop-shaped Unity mothership was parked, radiating multispectral pulses and colored lights that chased each other along its length like the lights of a theater marquee on a gala opening night.

The carnival of color and starshine reflected from the tracery of antennae and wire that still wrapped the Stalk like a lace mantilla and gleamed from the ConSpaceCom hulls of the outriding flotilla of freighters, tugs, and destroyers of Threshold's honor guard.

Mankind had come dressed to the nines to meet its destiny at the edge of the home solar system. Not until the Stalk had taken its place at this interstellar bargaining table did the Unity Embassy make its appearance, poking its brain-teasing mass slowly through the firmament with its gigantic escort vessel close behind.

All the protocols were being painstakingly established for this first of many meetings. All the niceties of place and space were punctiliously attended to by Unity Interstitial Interpreters. All the decorous formalities attendant on so momentous an occasion were duly observed by the Unity Council. All the introductions of Unity world representatives who were just beginning to arrive by the shipload would be slowly and conscientiously made, to make sure that humankind understood its role as host, its place and part as Valued Friends in a venerable society. And, most importantly, to make certain humanity didn't become afraid or doubt its territorial supremacy, its security, its primacy over all things human.

Joe South had made sure of that as soon as he docked the Ball inside the Unity mothership. You had to go very carefully when so many new experiences were pushing people to their limits. You had to be sensitive to crowding folks. Human beings reacted aggressively when they felt cornered. Through no fault of the Unity's, human assumptions were crumbling to dust in the face of the unalterable changes at work.

So he warned the Interstitial Interpreter who met him and Reice outside the Ball in the mothership slipbay to be very cautious in getting this festival of introduction and welcome under way. "They don't know what to expect. You've got to give them plenty of notice. Don't spring things on them, nowtime, without prior consultation." Prior consultation wasn't a Unity strong suit.

The Interpreter dipped its head toward him agreeably. "Talking nowtime with Mickeycroft." Behind and around the Interpreter, the mothership loomed with portals and gates into eleven continua. South could see dragons hard at work, ancestral skies, huge generators streaming power grids, deep-sea thermionic converters bubbling atmosphere, and worlds no man had ever seen before. The Interpreter floated before them on a circular screen of light that shifted under its feet slightly when it moved. "Soontime party okay with Honored Friends and Hosts, similarly okay with Honored Friends and Guests from Unity worlds coming," the Interstitial Interpreter assured South.

Reice elbowed South and blurted, "Yeah, but you should have warned the UNE. Before a bunch of other ships start showing up from all over town, you better make sure the Secretariat understands you're throwing a surprise party for Threshold."

"Reice," South said warningly. "They'll handle it." No use critiquing pasttime. The Unity and the UNE still had lots of rough edges to file off their relationship. And South still had to give back the "keys" to the Ball.

He held out his hand, palm up, and offered the small black septagon to the Unity Interpreter. "Here's your Ball back. Thanks for the chance to fly it. I really learned a lot."

The screen on which the Interstitial Interpreter was standing rocked like a surfboard. "Joesouth keeping Ball, thank-him gift from all us Unity Council. Ball not okay? Joesouth want different gift? Must indicate preference. Ball special-fixed for growing-up spacetimers, not standard for our using. Ball good Joesouth vessel, having inside place for spacetimer's craft. Place for being home, wherever being going. Good for visiting, all journeys, any spacetime places. Good for traveling throughout Unity. What Joesouth not like, Unity maybe fixes? Make better?"

"No shit?" Reice said wonderingly.

"Shut up, Reice." South wasn't really angry at Reice. Without Reice there as his witness, South might not have been able to believe his ears. "Your Excellency—I don't . . . have any problem with the Ball's performance. I gratefully accept this Unity gift. Thank you." You had to be careful how you expressed yourself, just like you had to be careful what you wished for. Had he wished for the Ball? Could be. Flying it had been like nothing he'd ever experienced, but he never would have asked. "Thank you and all the others." South closed his fist around the key to his Ball and put it in his pocket.

"Thanking this entity not necessary," said the Interstitial Interpreter, whose conical crown was throwing sparks. "Thanking all others, you have nowtime opportunity, Joesouth."

The Interstitial Interpreter began to spin on his platform. Reice grabbed South as the surface under them began to spin as well. South said through gritted teeth, "Just hold on, Reice. It'll stop. It's like a lift, or an escalator, where spaces aren't linear."

They spun past the Ball in its berth. They spun up a wall, past a half-dozen open portals. And when they stopped spinning, they were facing a throng of celebrants, none of whom were human, but all of whom were clearly having one hell of a good time.

Reice staggered off the platform and pulled South with him.

"What do you make of this?" Reice whispered intently. "You think they're all Unity aliens?"

"You bet," South said, looking over the heads of the

throng, hoping to find something he recognized as an exit. "Just like our test flight, see?" He pointed to one crystalline shape that moved in a personal mist, and another that floated through the air, colorful tentacles caressing whatever it passed.

"I don't remember much about that test flight," Reice admitted as South urged him through the throng and Reice slunk along, wide-eyed and staring.

"Don't worry about it," South counseled. "The memories will come back to you eventually. They did for me, anyway. It's partly the Unity way of making sure we don't overstimulate new neural pathways while they're still forming. Your brain is being asked to do different things—things it was meant to do eventually but hasn't done until now. There's a lot of unused potential in these craniums of ours. If you have trouble remembering, we can get the Unity to help you. They helped me." With Unity help, South had regained all his lost memories of his X-3 flyby and his first visit to a Unity world.

"I don't want nobody messin' with my mind," Reice said, shying away from contact with an ambergris-like mass as they passed it, then rubbing his own skull ruminatively.

"I know just what you mean, but don't be scared." South wasn't about to tell Reice that it had been South's flyby of X-3, and what followed, that had convinced the Unity aliens it was time to make contact with humanity. He wasn't sure he'd ever tell anybody that. "I was scared to death, myself, when I first saw things I couldn't catalogue and had experiences I could store but couldn't retrieve except allegorically. You didn't see your dead relatives. You didn't see angels, exactly. You saw the alltime."

"I did?" Reice said, awe in his voice. "You know, then, I mean, what I saw."

"Sort of. Just hold on to the images and let your brain metabolize the stimuli at its own rate." A six-armed something wearing some kind of life-support module over its gills ambled by on more legs than South could count. South made way for that one, right along with Reice.

But it stopped, swung its torso around, twisting on its mop-like legs, and came their way so fast that both men retreated into the crowd and bumped against other beings.

Suddenly, they were the center of attention. The six-armed thing wanted to hug South, and he couldn't dissuade it. It smelled vaguely of seaweed. Other creatures touched him, tickled his face, tugged on his clothes.

When he got out of the animated mop's six-armed hug, Reice was leaning over, talking to a plasma steward as if he'd been doing it all his life.

"It says it can guide us to the other humans."

"Great, let's go." South could use some human company. He was never much for parties. They followed the plasma steward through the throng, onto another lift, and from the lift into a bubblecraft. "You don't need to put on your helmet," South advised Reice, but Reice didn't believe him once the bubble oozed down the access tube into visible vacuum and started heading for Threshold's docking tubes.

"Oh, man, oh man," Reice kept saying, or maybe praying, until the bubble made it safe and sound to the Blue Mid slipbay.

Then they were in the real party zone, where they knew the players and where the action was. By the time they found a tubeway and ordered a ConSec levitation car, they were already three blue beers apiece the worse for wear. When the car came, Reice couldn't wait to call Sling and invite the aftermarketeer up to Blue North, on Reice's authority, to have a look at the command and control center.

You couldn't get to the center itself, there were so many people crowding around the Secretariat party floor. South lost Reice somewhere around the time that Reice saw Ricky Cummings and the Forat-Cummings girl, both being hugged by Richard the Second, holding forth at a refreshments table with a big NAMECorp insignia behind it.

Some things would never change. South hadn't had blue beer for a long time, and he never could hold the stuff without getting drunk. He found the spiral stairway to the observation deck and got halfway up it before he had to sit down.

Below him, humans and Unity Council members, Interstitial Interpreters and plasma beings, and even subhuman UNE races were mingling with seeming success. South tried to take a head count, but some of the Unity races didn't have discernable heads.

He could make out Remson and Mickey Croft, though, surrounded with Interstitial Interpreters whose crowns were especially ornate. Croft was being handed one of Dini

Forat-Cummings' racoonlike pet Brows, and the empathic animal was curling up in Croft's arms like a baby.

Whatever was going to happen, you had to give mankind credit for walking into the unknown, eyes open. It hadn't seemed to the Unity aliens that they were asking too much of humanity to move a little space habitat a few billion miles for a little elbow room, but it had been one close call.

South was prayerfully glad he hadn't had any more to drink. His ability to control timeslip when in contact with other humans was badly degraded by the blue beer he'd drunk. He felt like holding onto the railway of the spiral staircase to keep from falling, or sliding away into some other spacetime.

He had *STARBIRD,* and Birdy, too, safe in the Ball. He had the Ball, a gift from the gods. Nearly literally. Every person in this room had been so close to Dead on Arrival that South couldn't bear to think about it: you had to be careful what you wished for.

His mind still shied away from the jump mission. When you do the impossible, you want to forget about it as soon as you can. Maybe he could get the Unity to help him forget. But he knew he wouldn't.

Every person down there had a life to live, thanks to Unity technology and their own guts, no thanks to him. He was just in the right place with the right piece of equipment.

He heard footsteps on the stairway above him, but he was so accustomed to Unity constructs that he didn't move aside or even think to stand up.

"South," somebody said. "Joe South, you crazy old Relic of a coot! Git up 'n let m' lookit ya."

South craned his neck and looked up. "Hiya, Keebler. How's the scavenging business in Unity space?"

The greasy, white-haired, green-toothed old goat hunkered down and held out a gnarly hand. "Fan-tas-tik! C'mon up, and I'll tell ya all about it. You and me c'n do some business, Mr. Test Pilot."

"I bet we can," he said, and levered himself to a standing position.

The stairs spiraled up forever. He focused on Keebler's hand, and when their flesh touched, he was up on the floor of the observation lounge in a heartbeat.

Riva Lowe was up there, too, looking proud and ambassadorial in some fancy dress made out of tiny stars. She was talking to the woman who'd run South's psychometric evaluation. He didn't want to go over there.

Keebler still had him by the hand. "C'mere, Southie. Lookit them ships. All them ships. Lookit the *kinds* o' ships! D'ya realize what this means?"

"I guess," South said. "We've got a future, in human terms."

The white-hole scavenger who'd become Valued Friend of the Unity grabbed him by the shoulders and squeezed, his rheumy eyes very bright. "Better than that, Commander South. We *make* the future. We got the alltime, we got the notime, we got the whole of the Unity worlds open fer human exploration—"

"Exploitation, he means," said Riva Lowe from behind Keebler's back. "Don't let him snow you, Joe. Our friend Keebler's not content with being rich and famous; now he wants to cut a deal with the Secretariat to guide us to technology transfer opportunities in the Unity worlds."

Keebler let go of South and turned to her. "You need the help, Lady Ambassador, from a Valued Friend o' the Unity like me."

"Maybe we do, Mr. Keebler. Would you excuse us?"

She motioned South away from the man who'd brought the Ball to Threshold, pasttime. "South, say something nice to Mickey. Remson's not having much luck calming his fears."

South was looking out the observation window. "Did you see all this," he murmured. "Keebler's right. I never expected so many. . . ."

Outside the observation window, spacecraft and dimensional craft such as no human had ever dreamed were still arriving, one after another, to wish humanity well and welcome them into intergalactic society.

"The Unity explained about the . . . extraordinary number of visitors to Mickey, but I wish they'd done it earlier. He's still nonplussed, to say the least." Riva Lowe came up beside him. The gown she wore seemed to be nothing but tiny specks of light woven together over bare skin.

What could he say to the Secretariat ambassador? "The Unity is working hard to anticipate our flash points. Tell the Secretary General that for me." She was as beautiful in that gown as any of the wondrous craft arriving at humanity's front door. ConSec must be going nuts, trying to park all those vessels.

"You tell him." She flashed him a look like iron and he couldn't refuse her. Together, so close, they must have lost their grip on clocktime. Colliding wills can do that. The next thing he knew, he was shaking hands with Remson and the Secretary General and telling Mickey Croft that the Unity wanted South to "express their pleasure at being able to throw this little surprise party for us, sir. I was over on the Unity ship and there's lots of ambassadorial types from various Unity races waiting to meet you."

"I imagine there are, my boy." Croft looked exhausted, sepulchral, worn to a razor's edge. "I suppose you ought to take me over there to meet them." Croft sighed deeply, grimacing at the traffic outside the observation lounge. "We seem to be the only A-list party in the universe tonight. But first, I think Mr. Remson has something for you—a token of our esteem, a small recognition of your service to your Secretariat."

So that was why Riva had kept trying to get him to talk to Croft. He put his hands in his pockets, and his knuckles brushed the keys to the Ball there. *His Secretariat*, Croft had said.

Remson cleared his throat. "Commander South, under the circumstances, we don't wish a public ceremony, but we nevertheless are pleased to present you with this official recognition of your distinguished service." Remson held out a small box containing a tiny, striped bar pin. "And to give you this Secretariat visa for a month on the home planet, Earth, to be taken in part or at one time, at your discretion and our expense."

Riva Lowe reached up from his side and kissed him, just a peck on the cheek. But her eyes were shining.

"Thank you, Mr. Remson, Secretary Croft." He took the data disk that would get him past the ConSpaceCom guard around the world where he was born. He could go home now, anytime, with full privileges.

The next thing he knew, he was up close to the observation window, his nose nearly pressed to it and Riva Lowe beside him. He vaguely remembered telling Croft that he'd be glad to take the Secretary General and his party across to the Unity ship whenever they wanted to go. Time must have slipped his hold again.

It didn't matter. He said, "Thanks for the all-expenses paid trip to Earth."

She said, "It was the only thing I could think of that we had to give you."

"I got everything I want. Except . . ."

"What?" she said.

"A little friendly companionship. Somebody who understands. We're not exactly like anybody else, anymore."

"What are you saying?" she wanted to know.

"Want to take a ride with me, nowtime? They won't miss us. We'll be back soontime. They won't even know we slipped away."

"Where?" Her eyes were pinwheeling, but he didn't mind.

"Earth," he said. "In the Ball."

"In the Ball? What about *STARBIRD*? Surely you haven't given up *STARBIRD*, your first love."

"We'll take *STARBIRD* with us. Birdy, too."

"Well, that's okay, then," she said, and the observation lounge began to slip away under them as her fingers found his.

ROC

(0451)

ISAAC ASIMOV BRINGS THE UNIVERSE TO YOU

☐ **THE BEST SCIENCE FICTION OF ISAAC ASIMOV by Isaac Asimov.** Here is a collection of 28 "best ever personal favorites" from the short works of the master of science fiction, featuring brief introductions to each story by the author. "Illustrates the amazing versatility and endless originality of Isaac Asimov."—*Booklist* (450698—$3.99)

☐ **ROBOT VISIONS by Isaac Asimov.** From the Grandmaster of science fiction, 36 magnificent stories and essays about his most beloved creations—the robots. And these "robot visions" are skillfully captured in illustrations by Academy Award-winner Ralph McQuarrie, production designer of *Star Wars*. (450647—$5.99)

Prices slightly higher in Canada.

If you and/or a friend would like to receive the *ROC Advance*, a bimonthly newsletter featuring all the newest and hottest ROC books and authors, on a complimentary basis, please fill out this form and return it to:

ROC Books/Penguin USA
375 Hudson Street
New York, NY 10014

Your Address
Name _____
Street _____ Apt. # _____
City _____ State _____ Zip _____

Friend's Address
Name _____
Street _____ Apt. # _____
City _____ State _____ Zip _____